# SAY NOTHING

T0380303

# SAY NOTHING

*Philip Warner*

iUniverse, Inc.
New York   Bloomington

iUniverse books may be ordered through booksellers or by contacting:

iUniverse
1663 Liberty Drive
Bloomington, IN 47403
www.iuniverse.com
1-800-Authors (1-800-288-4677)

ISBN: 978-1-4401-8189-4 (sc)
ISBN: 978-1-4401-8200-6 (ebook)

Printed in the United States of America

iUniverse rev. date: 10/27/2009

# ACKNOWLEDGEMENTS

I owe a deep debt of gratitude to my good friend, Carol Larkin. I've known Carol for many years but I know I'll surely be in her bad books if I call her an 'old' friend rather than a long-term one!

Carol has involved herself fully with my writing and has helped me a great deal . Not only is she an excellent proof-reader but she has offered me lots of excellent advice. She'll see from the final draft I've not only listened carefully to her suggestions but I've acted on them. I'm equally certain this novel is better for her thoughtful input.

I'm also extremely grateful to my long-suffering partner, soon, I'm proud to say, to be my wife. Betty has borne the long sessions I spend at my computer with enormous patience. I dedicate this, my second novel, to her with all my love and with the hope she thinks all the time and effort has been worth it.

# Prologue

THE IDEA JUST POPPED into his mind. It was a shocking idea. Later he tried to convince himself someone else was responsible for planting it there. A voice in his head then attempted to persuade him there was nothing wrong with the idea. Another part of him said no, it was evil, thoroughly evil, and he should have nothing to do with it.

Sometimes he could go for days without thinking about the idea but then the different voices would start talking to him and arguing among themselves, pulling him one way and then the other. For a month or so it got that he felt pretty confused.

It was then he made himself sit down and examine the idea. He considered it deeply for a while. And it came to him quickly enough how wrong it was to have such a wicked thought lurking in his brain. Of course it was. Whatever had he been thinking of? He knew deep down he should be totally ashamed of himself. And for a couple of days he was.

It was such a relief when he stopped thinking about the idea and the guilt all but disappeared. Then, suddenly and without warning, a new thought, much more terrible than the first, flashed into his mind. The original idea had been diabolical enough but this new one plumbed the depths of fiendishness and depravity. He recognised at once it was completely and utterly wicked. It was so dreadful that merely thinking about it sucked the breath from his body and made him tremble from head to toe. Especially when the voice suggested he must put the idea into action and make it happen.

But he couldn't possibly consider the idea, let alone make it reality. Certainly not. The consequences would be far too shocking. And yet the idea filled his mind, insidiously at first and then extensively. He tried desperately to fight it, to expel it and quieten the voices inside his head.

When that failed he attempted to convince himself it was acceptable to harbour the idea so long as he abandoned any notion of putting it into action. And he was never actually going to do anything about it, was he. Was he?

One point was abundantly clear. It was absolutely imperative he keep the idea secret. Keep it buried deep inside at all costs. Give no inkling of it to anyone, ever. Act always as if it didn't exist, had never existed. *Say nothing.*

# 1

BYRON FULLARD KNEW HE was going to score. There was no defender within yards of him when the ball arrived at his feet. Time seemed to stand still as he calmly teed up the shot and side-footed the ball past the goalkeeper's despairing dive. Old Trafford exploded into pandemonium as seventy eight thousand voices roared their approval. Byron joyfully raised both arms high into the late afternoon sky before being mobbed by his Manchester United team-mates. Underneath the congratulating ruckus, he could hear the crowd yelling his name: "FULL-ARD, FULL-ARD."

When he was able to come up for air, he gazed at the huge electric scoreboard. It made great reading for the home fans: 'Manchester United 3; Aston Villa 0.' It was early May and the last league match of the season. United were not going to be champions but they had clinched the runners-up spot, which meant automatic selection into next season's European Cup. And Byron was proud of his part in the campaign. He'd fought his way back into the first team after a number of crippling injuries had ruled him out of playing any football for two and a half long seasons. For over thirty months he'd struggled to get fit, often fearful his career was already over in his mid-twenties.

Byron took a moment to look round and savour the scene: Old Trafford, home to the Red Devils, perhaps the most famous football team in the world. And graced over the decades by truly great players: Best, Charlton, Cantona, Giggs, Rooney, Ronaldo, an endless list. The stadium was nicknamed 'The Theatre of Dreams'. It was well named. The heavy lunch-time storm had moved northwards and the floodlights, on because of the leaden skies, washed the whole scene with a dazzling array of colour. And the commotion from the excited crowd never wavered. Old Trafford rocked!

Byron glanced towards the stand where his parents were seated alongside Johnny Hampson, his best mate. He raised his arms again in their direction, certain they were feeling as ecstatic as he was. The 2010 World Cup was due to kick off in South Africa in less than six weeks' time. Ten of the Manchester United team had been selected to take part but Byron was not one of them. It would have been marvellous to play for England in the world's second greatest sporting tournament but it was only three months since he'd recovered from his latest knee injury and he was more than happy at the moment to concentrate solely on playing for United. In truth, he was longing for the summer break. It would mean returning home to Cartmel and living quietly with his parents again for a spell. With their support, he was determined to get himself in great shape ready for the next season. And then he could score more goals and share more success with United. Of course, he would miss spending the summer months with his girlfriend, Tyler, in his luxury Manchester flat, but she'd just been promoted and had nursing courses to attend so he'd not have been seeing much of her anyway.

As he contemplated his immediate future, Byron couldn't help looking forward to a lengthy period of tranquillity and rehabilitation in Cartmel. After all, hadn't the village in south Cumbria been a peaceful haven ever since the twelfth century? But he was soon to learn that a quiet life was definitely not in his stars.

# 2

NICKY REED WAS IN no hurry. She strolled along the country lane near her Cartmel home, not heeding Lee's requests to hurry. Her attention was drawn to the flourishing hedgerows and the beautiful Cumbrian countryside beyond and by other pressing matters on her mind. She'd willingly agreed to go with Lee Bennett, her interest roused by the story he'd told. Now she was having second thoughts. He was only a casual acquaintance and she'd seen the way he glanced at her. She'd noticed that look often enough from other males. It was obvious he fancied her. But she was confident she could cope easily enough with that. After all, he was only recently out of his teens so he was half a dozen years younger than she was. Anyway she already had a boyfriend. But it was the tale he'd told her she was beginning to doubt. He claimed to have an exciting secret no-one else 'in the whole world' knew anything about. And he'd stressed he wanted to share it with her before he left England for a new life abroad. Was she being very gullible believing his story and going along with him?

"Come on, Nicky, get a move on. It's not far now and I promise you'll really like what I've got to show you."

Nicky stopped in the middle of the lane and concentrated on Lee. He was a short lad, a bit overweight with curly, auburn hair and lots of freckles. But, whatever else, he was not lacking in self-confidence. "Where exactly are you taking me?" she demanded.

"I thought you'd have guessed by now. To Mill House, the place your stepfather bought from my father. It's just round the corner." Without further pause, Lee carried on walking and soon disappeared from sight.

Nicky didn't stop for long. She recalled her mother telling her that her latest stepfather, Ray Templeton, had purchased Mill House, a seventeenth century property on the edge of Cartmel village. She was intrigued. It was a large, rambling house that had undergone serious modernisation during Nicky's lifetime. She'd walked past it many times but had never been inside. She had no plans to live there because she fully intended to stay in her present home with Martin, her first stepfather, but it would be fascinating to see something of the solitary house she'd often dreamed of exploring. And what was this special secret Lee wanted to show her? She was certainly still fascinated by what that could be.

A sudden clap of thunder compelled Nicky forward. The storm that had raged over Manchester earlier in the day was fast approaching Cartmel. She quickly caught up with Lee by the front door of Mill House, some twenty yards from the road. At present the house was empty but Nicky was in no doubt her mother would soon be filling it with costly furniture and furnishings, which was most definitely one of her talents.

But Lee was on the move again. "Let's go round the back," he said, leading Nicky towards the side gate and pointing skywards towards some ominous slate-coloured clouds. "We need to get inside before the rain starts."

The back garden, unlike the house, was small and neglected. It merged into sweeping woodland and, immediately behind the house and only yards from it, were huge slabs of natural rock. They lent the house a great deal of privacy but, Nicky guessed, would tend to make the back rooms rather gloomy.

"You'd better stand over there while I get the key," suggested Lee, pointing to a pair of massive oak doors. He then ran to a line of rocks at the edge of a tiny lawn and held up a large key from under the smallest of them. As he made his way back to her, waving the key and grinning, rain began to fall. At first there were only a few drops but they were large and very wet. By the time he got the doors open, they were both getting a soaking.

They fell laughing into the space behind the doors, which Lee made sure he re-locked. The room was an L-shaped library, surprisingly complete with shelving and books. "Dad sold it just as it is," Lee explained. "He's never been one for reading so I don't think he ever used the library. He just had the books for show."

Nicky studied some of the leather-bound volumes, noting they were old and covered in dust. She turned her attention to a single door opposite the pair of oak doors.

"That leads into the kitchen and the rest of the house," said Lee. "Its always locked but there's a key if you should need it." And he casually pointed out a Yale key hanging on a nearby nail. A serious look suddenly appeared on his face. "What I want to show you, Nicky, is special. I happen to think it's *very* special but it'll be up to you what you do with it." He took a deep breath and rushed on: "Two years ago, on my eighteenth birthday, the man who sold Mill House to my dad said he had an extraordinary present for me. He was a really frail, old man. He swore he was going to show me something that was a total secret. I don't know why he wanted to show it to me but he did. Just in time, as it happens, because he died a couple of weeks later. Why am I telling you all this? Well, I think you know I'm off to South Africa with my dad tomorrow. I can't wait. We've already been there for long holidays the last six years or so but this time we're going for keeps. I have family out there and, ever since my mum died, there's nothing to keep us here. So I've got absolutely no need of my secret any more, which is one of the reasons I'm showing it to you. The other is that I really like you a lot." He looked at her shyly and grinned.

Nicky smiled encouragingly. Still intensely curious and not sensing any danger, she allowed herself to be ushered to the very end of the room. This part of the library was round the corner and out of sight of the doors and window. She was still totally mystified about what was happening here so she watched Lee with great interest. Moving confidently to one of the upper corner shelves, he pushed aside a bulky encyclopaedia. This action revealed a light, cross-grained wooden panel marked by a large, dark knot. He pushed hard on the knot with his index finger. There was a sudden low noise behind her, like air being quickly displaced. Nicky swung round and stared in total amazement. A whole section of the library shelving had slid to one side revealing an open doorway. It looked forbiddingly dark and uninviting and she took an instinctive step backwards. But Lee bounded forward into the black opening, beckoning her to follow. "Come on, Nicky. There's something I want to show you."

# 3

BYRON FULLARD FANCIED A drink. First he had to deal with the hordes of fans flooding the lower levels of the Old Trafford stadium. They were present after all games but they seemed particularly numerous after this last match of the season. Some players couldn't be bothered with the fans but Byron liked to mix with them whenever he could. He spent a quarter of an hour chatting and signing autographs before making his excuses and heading for the nearest stairs.

A Chinese teenager making his way downstairs saw a tall, wide-shouldered, narrow-hipped young man with short, blonde hair, a full-lipped mouth and ice-blue eyes striding his way. He recognised him instantly and called out, "Hi, Byron, great goal!"

Byron was reminded just how multi-cultured United's fan base had become. He also thought for about the millionth time about his Christian name. Byron! It had been his mother's idea. She'd studied poetry for her English Literature exam and she'd been captivated by the story of Lord Byron's life and his death in Greece, aged thirty six. But she wasn't the one who had to endure all the taunts at junior school. The name-calling hadn't lasted long. There are legions of kids who can be bullied and a few who can't. Even the older lads had soon learnt it wasn't a good idea to mess with Byron Fullard. Mind you, it could have been worse, he supposed. His mum might have been charmed instead by the likes of Wordsworth or Shakespeare.

Byron made his way to one of the upper hospitality suites at the stadium. These are executive rooms, usually hired at great expense by local businessmen to entertain their customers. They have stunning views of the pitch and are the last word in luxury. If your ambition is to watch football in lavish style then this is definitely the way to achieve your aim. This particular suite was currently being leased by friends of his Cartmel neighbours, the Reeds. There were about a dozen adults present, most of them congregating near the bar, but the room certainly didn't seem crowded. They all saw him enter and acknowledged his presence with nods or waves but none of them rushed over to his side, a fact he appreciated. They appeared to understand his need to wind down after the match and have some space. He observed his parents were in animated conversation with another couple and that his pal, Johnny, was on his own, hugging a pint of beer. Byron smiled. It was always good to see his best mate. Johnny Hampson was as tall as he was but much broader, weighing in at over eighteen stone. For the last four years he'd been the All Weights World Champion at Cumberland and Westmorland Wrestling. But he was a gentle giant with wavy, blonde hair, limpid blue eyes and a fair, open countenance. He lived with his dad, a detective in the Cumbrian police force, next door to the Fullards and Reeds in a small enclave of Cartmel properties. Byron had known him since the first day of junior school and had once joked he got on so well with Johnny that if he'd been a girl he'd have married him.

Johnny looked across and caught his eye. "How about a soda water with ice?" he asked.

"I'd rather have what you're drinking, if you don't mind. I've still got a week's training to complete but the season's virtually over and I really fancy a beer."

Johnny raised his eyebrows but his only comment was: "Good goal. You played much better in the second half but you should have been booked for that tackle on their right back."

Byron laughed. "Rubbish! The little turd had at least two hacks at my bad knee. A bloke's got to look after himself and I hardly touched him."

They talked more about football and wrestling then, a little later, as Johnny started his third pint and Byron still nursed his first, Byron asked, "And how's your love life, then?" It was a leading question. Johnny had been dating Nicky Reed, his neighbour and his boss' step-daughter for about three months. Nicky was Byron's neighbour, too and, like Johnny, they'd known each other most of their lives.

Johnny stretched his long legs and managed a lop-sided grin. "Straight to the point as usual, By. You always liked poking sticks into wasps' nests, didn't you? Actually it's much the same as it was the last time I mentioned it. To be honest, it might even be worse."

Both of them knew this was not a reference to how Johnny was getting on with Nicky but rather to Nicky's relationship with her half-brother,

Simon. Just to confuse matters, Nicky had two half-brothers, the twins, Simon and Adam, but it was Simon she doted on. She was fond of Adam but she totally adored Simon, or 'Spud,' as she sometimes called him, and had done so for every one of the twenty two years since his birth. Put simply, Nicky and Simon were soul-mates who trusted each other implicitly and who shared all their secrets. It was sibling love but it was very, very deep. And that was the root of the current problem. Simon had gone off to Salford University to study engineering but apparently he was hating it and becoming more and more depressed. Nicky, four years older, had always felt responsible for Simon and was growing increasingly anxious for his well-being.

Johnny wrestled with his pint. "You know Nicky. She's a great lass and we've been getting on fine. I'm, well, I guess I have to admit I've grown very fond of her these last few months. But she can't help getting involved in Simon's life," he said, trying to clarify the situation as much for his own sake as Byron's. "It would never occur to her to let him sort out his own life. I'm not indifferent to Simon's problems. It's just that they always manage to have such an effect on her. But my main concern has to be for Nicky."

Byron sipped his beer thoughtfully. "She won't ever change, you can be sure of that, and in a way you should be pleased. I'd be very happy to find a girl who has the capacity to bother about me like Nicky cares for Simon."

"I'm not jealous or I don't think I am. But if it's not one headache with Simon, it's another. I suppose it cheeses me off that she always has him on her mind. Always, or it seems like that since we've been going out. I blame his parents for the mess he's in. It would be an absolute wonder if Simon wasn't totally mixed up after the way they've treated him. And don't forget Adam isn't without his troubles, too. I work with him, remember. When he can be bothered to turn up, that is."

Byron said, "You obviously see more of them than I do, but if I was pointing the finger of blame at the parents it would be at Jane, not Martin. If Simon's screwed up, it's surely Jane's fault. Everyone knows Adam is her favourite and that she constantly undermines Simon. She's never been the best mother in the world but many would say her treatment of the twins, Simon in particular, is unforgivable. Martin, I reckon, has done his best to balance things up but he's no miracle worker."

"You're probably right but where's it all going to end?"

Byron sought to lighten the mood. He lent forward and nudged Johnny playfully in the chest. "Of course I'm right. It's a well-known fact I know a lot more about human nature than you'll ever know."

Snorting with disbelief, Johnny responded, "In your dreams! You've come out before with that load of garbage. I think you live in cloud cuckoo land!"

"Not me. You're a good lad, Johnny, but a babe in arms when it comes to understanding basic human nature."

"We'll see about that. Sooner or later I'll make you eat your words for all this rubbish you spout. You really have no idea how naïve you are, and I'll be the one proving it to you."

Byron laughed and shook his head but, as Johnny took his empty glass to the bar, he couldn't help feeling a bit anxious about his friend. Normally Johnny could take good care of himself but he was vulnerable where Nicky was concerned. It wasn't merely because he was in love with her. It was because she was so close to her Spud. And what about Nicky? Byron cared for her and felt uneasy about her, too, but she could no sooner extricate herself from Simon's problems than she could cut off her own head.

Byron had his own vivid memories of the twins growing up. Right from their birth, Jane had gone out of her way to dress them exactly the same. As they were identical, even those who knew them well had great trouble telling them apart. Jane seemed to get a real kick out of that. But when the twins went to the local comprehensive school, aged eleven, they started to revolt and do their own thing. Byron, five years their senior, was just leaving the school and consequently saw them less frequently but he recalled how they started to go their different ways. Simon, for instance, grew his hair longer and was invariably neat and well-scrubbed, whereas Adam had his hair cropped and always appeared scruffy in old jeans and torn T shirts. These differences magnified as they got older. By their mid teens they'd developed their own group of friends and interests, so much so they spent less and less time together. Just a few years later, Simon did well in his exams and eventually went off to university while Adam, now shaven-headed and wearing studs in his ears, showed no interest in books and learning and chose to stay at home to work as a labourer for the family business.

What Byron could never forget was how Jane and Martin fell out over the twins' upbringing. He saw how Martin encouraged both his sons to do well at school, which meant having a go at them now and again. This is what parents do and, perhaps, *should* do. Jane could never see it. She became convinced Martin was picking on Adam and she rushed to his defence. At first, Martin had reacted patiently but when Jane began to belittle Simon while praising Adam, they took up diametrically opposite positions and argued openly. The constant rowing seemed to be the catalyst for the break-up of their marriage. And then, while Martin poured his energy into the family business, Jane turned to other men.

Johnny plonked his fourth pint on the table. "I'll accept you're probably right about Jane," he conceded. "Her behaviour's been inexcusable and I've come to feel sorry for Martin. When he first came on the scene, her dad's business was in meltdown and her marriage in ruins. After her dad died, Martin took over as managing director of McAdams and performed marvels with the business. He's really turned it round. I should know because I help Nicky with the books. He turned Jane's life round as well when he married her and accepted her children as his own. I happen to know both Nicky and her brother, Jack, think the world of him. And how does Jane repay him? By ruining the twins and having a series of affairs right under Martin's nose. They call her 'the Cartmel Open' in The King's Arms."

Byron threw up his hands in mock horror. "This could be your future mother-in-law you're discussing! Let's hope she settles down with this new husband of hers." He downed the last of his bitter before adding, "These problems have a way of resolving themselves. I'll be home in a week or so and I expect everything will have blown over by then." He tried to feel confident for Johnny's sake but the thought crossed his mind that maybe, just maybe, his optimism sounded a bit hollow.

# 4

NICKY STEPPED HESITANTLY OUT of the library and into the darkness. She was in time to see Lee reach for a torch from a shelf just inside the doorway. Moments later a beam of light probed the blackness ahead and she was able to observe they were in a narrow passage that stretched into the distance. The floor was uneven, beaten earth but it looked very dry. There was sufficient headroom for her and Lee but someone tall, like her boy-friend, Johnny Hampson, would probably need to stoop.

Lee grabbed her hand. "Come on, Nicky," he said, leading her away from the light in the library, "it's not far now."

She allowed him to pull her into the pitch-blackness. The wavering torch-light cast such lurid shadows she was actually grateful to hold onto his hand. They covered about a dozen paces before the passageway turned abruptly to the right. The next few strides took them to stairs, which also appeared to be of beaten earth. With Lee still clutching her hand, she climbed the steps. She counted ten of them. There was then another sharp turn which took them into an altogether bigger space. As Lee directed the torch beam from side to side, she saw they were in a narrow chamber measuring roughly six metres by two. Unlike the passageway, it provided good height. The area looked empty except that in the far corner she spotted an old office desk with a much more modern swivel chair next to it.

As she studied the chamber more closely, Nicky became aware that Lee was still holding onto her hand. She sought to extricate it but, for the moment at least, he was determined to hang on. Suddenly the torch snapped off and in the pitch-darkness she felt him moving closer. He muttered something huskily into her ear but she didn't catch the gist of it.

But there was no mistaking his next move. He drew her to him and kissed her on the lips. She went with it for a couple of heartbeats before pulling away.

She said calmly, "Let's have some light, Lee. This total darkness doesn't do a lot for me."

Almost immediately the torch clicked back on, illuminating the corner of the chamber where the furniture was situated. As if nothing untoward had happened, Lee walked over to the desk. He announced in level tones, "I've removed all my possessions. You can put your stuff here now. Even the mice don't know about this place so all this will be yours, and yours alone." He flashed the torch from wall to wall to show her the extent of what he was passing onto her.

Nicky looked all round, somewhat disappointed. Was this it? Was this all that Lee had brought her to see? It was very interesting, fascinating even, but what on earth was she meant to do with it? As if reading her thoughts, Lee spoke out: "There's just one more secret to show you and then it'll be time for me to be on my way." He moved away from the desk and shone the torch onto one of the side walls. The flickering light showed what Nicky hadn't spotted before: a small, dark panel, at head height, in the middle of the wall. Then, as she watched, Lee reached forward and, in one fluid movement, grasped the side of the panel and pulled. It opened noiselessly, revealing a small glass window or mirror about a foot square through which Nicky could clearly see light.

Curiosity urged her forward and she found herself staring intently through the glass into another room. It was about six metres square, containing a large divan bed and, right underneath where she was observing, a small wash basin. There was no other visible furniture. The light she had seen came from two uncurtained windows on adjoining walls, which seemed to suggest the bedroom was on one of the corners of the Mill House property. One final study of the small glass window, through which she was peering, confirmed it was a two-way mirror. She recalled Lee telling her she'd really approve of what he had to show her. But she wasn't at all sure at the moment whether she liked it or not. Who, for instance, had installed the two-way mirror and for what purpose? And what on earth was she meant to do with it?

She turned to question Lee but he was no longer in the chamber. Her heart beat faster and she suddenly felt alarmed. Had he lured her to this secret chamber with some dark plan in mind? She relaxed somewhat when she spotted the torch by her feet. It appeared he'd done what he'd set out to do before making his escape. But had he left the door from the library into the passageway open? Nicky knew it was time for her to leave and prayed silently she'd be able to do so.

Remembering to secure the wall panel over the two-way mirror, she used the torch to retrace her steps down the stairs. Her racing heartbeat slowed when she saw light at the end of the passage. Thankfully, the doorway into the library was still wide open. She left the torch on the shelf where she'd found it and stepped back into the library. It was empty and very quiet. Wondering how to close the sliding door, she sought the wooden panelling containing the dark knot that Lee had pressed to gain entrance. She found it quickly enough and pressed the knot once again. There was the same satisfying hiss of air as the section of shelving slid back into place. One quick glance was sufficient to assure her the room now looked like a library once again and she headed for the double doors. Lee had left them closed but the key was still there.

Moments later, Nicky was outside in the rain, locking the doors and replacing the key under the rock at the edge of the lawn. It was time to return home but, as she set off towards the side gate, it came to her she had no idea when she would revisit her secret chamber and the room beyond the two-way mirror.

# 5

THE CUMBRIAN VILLAGE OF Cartmel, situated between Morecambe Bay and the renowned Lake District, attracts numerous visitors all year round. A great many of them visit the world-famous Racecourse, situated just behind the olde worlde buildings of the Market Square. Many believe the square is the heart of the village but others consider the focal point of the community is the beautiful Priory Church of St. Mary and St. Michael, established in the twelfth century and barely a hundred metres from the square. Yet more tourists are attracted by the delightful assortment of inns, shops and private dwellings, while some remember the village only for its celebrated sticky toffee puddings, made and sold in the local post office.

Cartmel provides something for everyone, villagers and visitors alike, as they wend their way past well-stocked shops, inns and cafes, over cobbled pavements, across humpbacked bridges and along streamside walks. The visitors are a mixed blessing where the locals are concerned, loved by some and resented by others. Byron Fullard and his parents and near neighbours, the Hampsons and Reeds, tolerated them for most of the year but definitely not on spring and summer Bank Holiday weekends when the horse racing meetings were held. At these times the village filled to capacity and they made themselves scarce. Many professional footballers love to gamble but Byron was not one of them. Anyway, unless you truly enjoy the sport of horse racing, it's wise to avoid Cartmel on race weekends as the local roads get well and truly clogged. Go at any other time and the racehorse park provides plenty of parking, with an 'honesty' collection box to remind twenty-first century drivers of earlier and, perhaps, more relaxed times.

Barely a stone's throw from the back of the Priory is a secluded walled area, formerly a field, called Orchard Park. It contains four large, detached houses. Each of these properties is a small estate complete with ample parking spaces, a very genuine luxury in a village like Cartmel, with its narrow streets and dense housing. The Fullards, Hampsons and Reeds owned three of these properties and had done so since they were built, some twenty or so years earlier.

Martin Reed was on the phone at his home in Orchard Park. He was clearly not enjoying the call. His partner, Beth Alderton, had lived with him for nearly six months and knew the signs well. It wasn't so much what Martin was saying or even how he was saying it. It was the way he kept gazing up at the ceiling and rubbing the back of his neck. It was a dead give-away!

Beth liked studying people and working out what they were really thinking. She particularly enjoyed watching Martin but that was probably because he was easy on the eye and she loved him. Aged fifty, he was tall and of medium build. Although he couldn't be described as very handsome, he certainly looked extremely distinguished with his upright stature and curling, grey hair. It was his crinkly, hazel eyes and wide, generous mouth that had first attracted Beth. But what marked him out from other men, she had to admit, was that he possessed loads of charisma and charm. Women, particularly, thought so. Had he been so inclined, he'd have made a most successful womaniser but that was definitely not his style.

Martin was speaking to his son, Simon, though it was Simon who was doing most of the talking. The longer the one-sided conversation went on, the more Martin stared upwards and massaged his neck. Beth groaned. This was Simon's third call in less than a fortnight. From the first two they'd gleaned he'd become desperately unhappy with college life and wanted to return home. This third call merely confirmed it. As far as Martin was concerned, it was really bad news. It was he who'd persuaded Simon to go to Salford in the first place and he was most unwilling to contemplate his son abandoning university before he'd completed the full course of study.

When Beth had moved in with Martin she was already familiar with the Reed family problems. She'd helped him through a messy divorce and heard a detailed account of all that had gone wrong. Martin blamed most of the difficulties on his ex-wife and had the support of both Jack and Nicky, his step-children, in this view. But, when Beth had finally met Jane, they'd got on very well together. Instead of this annoying Martin, he'd actually been amused, especially as he understood it didn't mean his new partner was sympathetic to his ex-wife's cause. He'd merely said, "It just goes to show how thoroughly beguiling Jane can be when she chooses. And I should know!"

Martin finally plonked the phone down and threw himself into an armchair. He was silent for a full ten seconds before remarking, "I'll have to ask Nicky to pick him up from the station. That'll solve one problem. I've got a hectic work schedule the next few days."

"Simon?"

Martin scratched the back of his neck vigorously. "Yes. He's invited himself home for a couple of days. But from what I've just heard we'll have a tough time getting him to go back. And here's me hoping he'd sail through his degree and take a load off my shoulders."

"We ought to get to the bottom of why he's so dead-set against university," said Beth thoughtfully. "Any ideas?"

"Well, it's not because he misses Adam, or me or his mother, but it could be because he misses Nicky. You know how close they are. I'm coming to think he can't function without her. Anyway, it's a waste of time me trying to persuade him to stay on and finish his course. He's already made up his mind to leave and we both know there's only one person who can talk him out if it at present. I'm thinking of asking her to have a word with him."

Beth looked concerned. "That might be a bit unfair on Nicky. Don't you think she feels enough responsibility for him already?"

But Martin waved that aside. "I can't help that. I've got one under-achieving son as it is and I'm not ready to accept another, not without a good fight. Nicky's always been on Simon's wavelength and we have to make use of that, whether we like it or not."

Beth knew when it was best to keep her views to herself. She merely said, "We'll have to hope some good comes of his visit. It might well do if his mother doesn't put her spoke in."

"Not much chance of that. Jack mentioned this morning that she's in London entertaining some of Ray Templeton's business contacts. Jane might have come rushing home to see Adam but not to see Simon. Definitely not. Anyway, I'm glad she's out of the way for a while. She still insists on sticking her nose into the business, though it's got nothing to do with her any longer. When it suits her, she likes to forget I'm in charge now. I could, perhaps, understand if the business was still in the doldrums but it's doing better than ever. Even Jane admits that going over to paving driveways and building conservatories saved the company."

Beth said, "You work too hard. You should have some time off for a change. Here's another weekend when I'm not going to see much of you."

"We both work too hard. You're always marking or doing something extra at that school of yours, you know you are. And someone has to put in the hours. If our workers were all like our Adam, hardly anything would get finished and then where would we be?"

"I thought you told me Adam was doing a lot better."

Martin smiled wryly and shook his head. "That was last month. I thought we'd got through to him at last but he still lets himself down. I've had to send Jack to finish two of his jobs recently. You can't leave customers for days on end with their drives only half finished. Well, Adam obviously can but I can't."

"He's still only young, Martin, Give him a chance."

"Give him a chance! When I was his age, I.....but never mind that. Do you know where Nicky is? I need to talk to her."

"She went off this afternoon with Lee Bennett. You know, that lad whose father sold Mill House to Ray Templeton."

Martin gazed across the room abstractedly and then shivered as if he'd seen a thoroughly nasty ghost. He suddenly stood up and began pacing the lounge floor. "Families!" he exclaimed. "Who'd have them?" When Beth offered no comment, he sat back in his armchair and added, "One good piece of news, at any rate: Byron scored this afternoon and United beat Villa 3-0."

# 6

BYRON COULDN'T HELP THINKING about Cartmel and his home in Orchard Park. He liked Manchester well enough and reckoned he made the most of his life in the city but he'd grown up in south Cumbria and he was happy there. His end-of-season training was nearly over and he was looking forward to spending time with his parents and friends. It didn't help that his girl-friend, Tyler Seddon, was away and his Manchester flat seemed empty without her.

He looked round his massive city-centre apartment. Like a lot of men, he'd let his partner take charge of the furnishing. Tyler certainly liked that sort of responsibility. She'd gone for the minimalist style, with Italian furniture and a large, matching abstract painting on the wall opposite the windows entitled 'Natureza,' which was a harmony of blues and greens and made Byron seasick if he stared at it for too long. But she had encouraged him to include a few personal touches. Pride of place on his Zanotta aluminium coffee table was a group of three photographs. In the one on the left, he had his arm round a grinning Wayne Rooney, his highly-talented team-mate. The photo on the right showed him signing for Manchester United with a delighted-looking Sir Alex Ferguson, the team manager, looking on. It was a favourite of his. But the photo that meant the most to him was the one in the middle. It was taken by a pool in Scottsdale, Arizona, and showed him in a clinch with Tyler. She liked it, too, though she had been heard more than once to make disparaging remarks about the skimpy bikini she was wearing, or "nearly wearing," as he'd put it.

Byron gazed out of the window at the wonderful view of central Manchester below. It was such a contrast to the rural outlook from his

Cartmel bedroom. Here he was on the twelfth floor looking right along Deansgate towards the Arndale Centre and the Printworks beyond. The lights were already on and the city centre was ablaze with a multitude of static and moving lights. In the near distance, he could just make out ant-like creatures entering and exiting the large Marks and Spencer store. Then, even through the thick, double-glazed glass, he heard the distant wail of an emergency vehicle. Half turning he searched for and found the source of the noise. From its size, he deduced it was an ambulance. He watched the flashing lights casually as they sped along Deansgate beneath him.

Abandoning the view, Byron threw himself into his leather armchair and took up a well-thumbed cookbook and turned his attention to the meal he was about to prepare himself. Tyler might well be in charge of furnishing but he'd taken control of the cooking. And not merely because Tyler's idea of a perfect evening was to be taken to her favourite Italian restaurant, the Palmiro, followed by a trip to the casino. Byron actually enjoyed cooking. He found the chicken section and was contemplating a number of tempting options when the phone rang. It was Johnny Hampson.

"You're earlier than usual," said Byron, consulting his watch. "Are you taking pity on a poor, lonely soul, or what?"

"Well, I knew you'd be missing Tyler but it's not that."

"What, then? I'm about to prepare a late dinner and I'm drooling at the thought."

"You and your food!" said Johnny. "But I'll not keep you long. It's Nicky again. She's called off our date tonight and I just thought I'd get your angle on it. Seeing as you claim to be the great expert on human nature."

"Let's have more respect for your betters and less sarcasm, please. What reason has she given for calling off your date?"

"Simon. He's up here for a couple of days."

"Ah! Am I right in thinking Nicky wants to spend time with him while he's at home?" asked Byron.

"Yeah. That's exactly what she claims."

"Right, so what did you say to her, Johnny? Did you put your foot down, give her your blessing, or what?"

"That's just it. I told her to go ahead and see her Spud and that I'd meet her later in the week. But was that right, do you think, or is she simply taking advantage of my good nature?"

Byron sat back in his armchair. "Seems to me you've no option. I know Nicky well enough to realise she makes up her own mind. And you should know that, too, especially where Simon's concerned. If you put your foot down you'll lose her. Anyway, if you were to make her choose between you and Simon, who do you honestly think she'd choose?"

"Not me and that's for sure."

Byron grinned. "Ten out of ten for perception. That was straightforward enough, wasn't it? You're actually learning about the fairer sex. But the point is, can you accept her decision? I mean really accept it, even though it cheeses you off?"

Johnny was silent for a while. "That's the trouble. I guess I don't have any choice," he said, hesitantly. "I love her so she's got me by the short and curlies. I suppose I've got to go along with her, even though it's definitely not easy."

Byron remarked light-heartedly, "Don't ever expect love to be straightforward. And I should know. I wanted Tyler to spend the next few nights here with me because they'll probably be my last in Manchester for quite a while. I mean, she could have gone on the same course next week, if she'd wanted, but she chose to go this week. In fact, she made it absolutely clear she'll put her job first when it suits her. So there you are: you're not the only one with girl problems."

"Well, thanks a lot for your input, By. I knew I could count on you to cheer me up. Why don't you give up footballing and become a full-time relationship counsellor?"

"Sod off, you cheeky bugger! If you weren't such a hot-shot wrestler, I'd sort you out. You ought to be showing a lot more deference to a person of superior personality, like my good self."

Johnny guffawed. "You superior? That's a laugh! Have you forgotten I grew up with you and know you too well. By the way, when are you coming home?"

"My last training session is the day after tomorrow and it'll finish mid afternoon. I've nothing to keep me in Manchester so I'll be driving straight home when I've finished at Carrington. How about if we catch up at the King's Arms later? I'll let you buy me a pint."

"Sounds good to me. Give me a ring when you get home."

Byron gazed into space for a couple of minutes then put his cookbook to one side and stood so he could stretch his long legs. He wasn't sure why but the thought of cooking dinner had suddenly lost its appeal. He decided to wander down to the Printworks instead and buy himself a Chinese and maybe catch a late film. It came to him he couldn't wait to get back to Cartmel.

# 7

SIMON 'SPUD' REED HAD returned to Salford after his brief stay in Cartmel. Nicky, who'd done much to persuade him to go back and resume his studies, was now having serious doubts about whether she'd acted in his best interests.

Nicky wandered round her bedroom listlessly. Martin had given her time off work to spend with Simon. She didn't question why but suspected it was part of Martin's plan to persuade Spud to finish his university course. Being given some free time was an unusual occurrence but she didn't know whether it was a good idea or not because it gave her plenty of time to think. Perhaps too much. As she tried to make up her mind what to wear, her common sense told her it really would be in Simon's best interests to stay on at university and get his degree, but now he was back in Salford her heart was telling her something very different. Gazing at her full-length wardrobe mirror, she was critical for once of the reflection she saw and decided she could do with some fresh air. Normally a ride on her horse would be the order of the day but Casper would have to wait till later. Instead, Nicky decided a walk would be preferable so, after quickly brushing her long, blonde hair, she donned dark jeans and a thin cotton jumper. They accentuated her willowy slimness but she couldn't help that. A pair of well-used but comfortable trainers completed her outfit.

Ten minutes of brisk walking, which did wonders for her complexion, brought her to Mill House. She hadn't consciously set out to visit her secret room but she needed time to mull over Simon's problems and she could think of nowhere more private. The house still looked deserted as she made her way round to the back garden. In no time at all, she'd fetched the key and let herself into the library. All was quiet. Moving to the back of the room, she found the dark knot and pressed it before confidently walking through the opening into the passage beyond as if she was already a regular visitor.

Using the torch to light her way up the stairs to the secret chamber, she moved over to the swivel chair and sat down. She'd already established it was as comfortable as it looked. She then stretched her legs out before turning the torch off. On her first visit to the chamber, she'd led Lee Bennett to believe she didn't like the dark but, just at this moment, she found it very comfortable. In the intense blackness, she let her mind wander over the last two days.

It came to her that Simon had been excessively jumpy and out of sorts throughout much of his recent stay. From the moment she'd collected him from the station, she'd spent every wakeful hour with him, even when he'd spent a morning with his twin brother, Adam. But she'd never known him so restless and tense, not even during his late teens when his mother's criticism and disapproval had been at its worst. He'd been tight-lipped about the reasons for the tension, which was most unusual because he was normally so open with her. She had at least been able to establish one possible reason for his stress: girl trouble. He told her he'd fallen for one of his fellow students but the course of true love, it seemed, was not running smoothly. This was not the first time Simon's love life had encountered difficulties and Nicky admitted surprise. Her half-brother, she'd found, was very easy to get on with. Although he could occasionally come over as a rather intense, brooding individual, he was also intelligent, handsome and had a good sense of humour. She therefore fondly imagined other girls would see him in the same light. Unfortunately for Simon this didn't appear to be the case. His latest student girlfriend was playing hard to get and, according to Simon, was favouring a lad she knew back home in Wales.

Nicky felt it important to reflect on Simon's visit and consider carefully all that had happened while he'd been at home. Apart from his girlfriend trouble, he was clearly unhappy and she felt an urgent need to discover what else was bothering him. There was such a deep bond between them so she couldn't possibly stand idly by if there was anything she could do to help him. Her thoughts went back to Cark Station where she'd gone to meet him. Were there any clues in how he'd looked? Certainly not in his general appearance. He'd been smartly dressed in navy trousers, bright red sweater and a well-used anorak and, as ever, looked tidy and cared for. His clean-shaven face was scrubbed as usual and his fair, wavy hair was well-brushed. The hair, perhaps, was a little longer than usual but that might only suggest he was short of haircut money, a consideration not unknown to the average student. If there *was* a clue in how he looked, it was, perhaps, in his expression. It came to Nicky there was a subtle difference from the Simon she knew so well but, for the life of her, she couldn't determine what it was, let alone work out whether it was significant or not.

She let that ride and turned to the time Simon had spent with his father. It had been very brief. Martin was up to his ears with work and, initially, they'd met only over a hurried breakfast. As Martin had chewed on a slice of toast, gulped a cup of coffee and sorted through the contents of his briefcase, he'd merely stated, "Nicky knows exactly how I feel about your course at Salford, my boy. Please listen to her carefully and mark what she has to tell you. I'll catch up with you later." And with that, he'd fled the house claiming he was already late for his first appointment of the day.

Simon had been eager to argue with his dad but had to be content with making his views plain to Nicky: "I know he wants what's best for me. I do know that and I'm very grateful. But he doesn't realise what it's like for me at Salford." He'd then added mysteriously, "Nobody understands."

What concerned Nicky was that her half-brother wouldn't clarify what was troubling him. When she attempted to prise more information from him he would only mumble generalities before blatantly changing the subject. It troubled her even more that Martin had left her with explicit instructions what she was to say to Simon on his behalf. Her stepfather was not one to compromise and neither was he prepared to countenance any 'back-sliding,' as he called it. As far as he was concerned, Simon must finish his university course and that was that.

It put Nicky in a most unenviable position. She was extremely fond of her stepfather and had the utmost respect for him, but Simon was going through a particularly vulnerable stage and depended on her. Beth had done her best. She'd intervened, voicing her concerns and trying to soften her partner's approach, but Martin could be stubborn and he was unwilling even to discuss his son's aversion to Salford. In the end, Nicky had ended up doing what she thought was best: she had persuaded Simon to resume his studies. But it certainly hadn't been easy and the experience had left her with very mixed feelings, especially as she had absolutely no idea how matters would resolve themselves.

There had been at least one positive outcome from Simon's visit and that was his reunion with Adam. The twin brothers had had little to do with each other for a number of years and had increasingly gone their separate ways. Now, suddenly, they were behaving as if they truly cared for one another. Nicky, who witnessed their meeting, felt it was Simon who was chiefly responsible for this welcome transformation. He had insisted on strolling round to Adam's small flat in Market Square and making himself thoroughly agreeable. Adam might have been a little slow to respond but he'd soon thawed and showed Simon round every nook of his apartment, the two of them laughing spontaneously as if they really were old friends. Nicky couldn't help smiling when she recalled how engrossed Simon had been in all aspects of Adam's life. He'd asked numerous questions about his brother's job and hobbies, all of which Adam had answered fully and good-humouredly. They'd even compared their love lives. While Simon admitted his was positively floundering, Adam declared he'd just dumped his girl-friend and was enjoying a lads only existence for a while.

It had done Nicky the power of good to observe this warmth but she had to admit it was becoming increasingly difficult to appreciate the pair were actually identical twins. They looked so different! Adam flaunted a shaven head with at least three sets of ear studs. His pride and joy was an old but much-loved Harley Davidson and he enjoyed dressing in elaborately-decorated black leather like the keen biker he'd become. Observing the twins side by side was like seeing chalk and cheese rather than two peas in a pod. But at least they had taken notice of one of their father's pleas as neither sported tattoos. The only downside of the reunion Nicky detected was that Adam had once again absented himself from work in order to accommodate his brother's visit. But that was nothing new.

On reflection, what had pleased Nicky even more about Simon's short stay was that their own relationship had stood firm. It had definitely been a testing couple of days but, despite all the difficulties, she and Simon still appeared to be very close. Maybe her half-brother hadn't been as transparent and open as usual but, for her part, Nicky certainly had been. It had become a habit with her to share all her thoughts with Simon and she continued to do so now, including telling him she'd been dating Johnny for a while. Simon had actually laughed out loud at this news, commenting she'd made a good choice but joking she should definitely avoid being hugged by a world champion wrestler.

As she sat in the dark, Nicky could come up with no other reasons for Simon's unhappiness, other than his stated antipathy for university life. Even his return to Salford had passed smoothly and uneventfully. And yet she was aware there was something about her half-brother's demeanour that left unanswered questions at the back of her mind. She tried to reassure herself she'd made the best of a difficult situation and that Simon was back where he should be and working towards the engineering degree his father was determined he should obtain. But it only partly worked.

Deciding she could do no more at present, Nicky snapped on her torch and prepared to leave the chamber. Curiosity urged her to open the wooden panel so she could peer through the two-way mirror into the secret room beyond. A shock awaited her. The quilt covering the bed had been thrown to one side and the bedroom door stood wide open. The room had clearly received a visitor. As Nicky speculated who the unexpected caller might be, she was thoroughly astonished when her mother entered the room carrying a bottle of wine and two glasses. Jane Templeton was supposed to be with her new husband in London so why had she told none of her family she was back in Cartmel?

Jane was in her late forties but looked younger. Of medium height and weight, with thick, auburn hair and beautiful, hazel eyes, she had a lively, engaging face that complemented a forceful personality. But the expensive, fashionable clothes she was wearing looked far more in keeping with London society than life in rural Cumbria. Nicky was reminded that her mother was undoubtedly attractive to men and, perhaps more significantly, knew how to exploit them. As she wondered what to make of this totally unexpected appearance, she was shocked again when her mother reached into her shoulder bag, pulled out a packet of cigarettes and a lighter and lit up. It was the first time Nicky had ever seen her mother smoke but far more telling bombshells were in the offing. No sooner had Jane checked her watch than she was joined by a man. The newcomer was a stranger to Nicky but clearly not to her mother. Nicky judged him to be in his late thirties, noting he had tanned good looks and that he, too, was impeccably attired as if he'd just stepped out of the Austin Reed store on Regent Street. While Nicky looked on, Jane spoke to him at some length while he skilfully opened and poured the wine. But it was like watching a silent film because no hint of the conversation permeated the two-way mirror.

As the pair sat side by side on the bed sipping their wine and chatting soundlessly, Nicky was extremely curious to discover the purpose of their visit. She didn't have long to wait. In unison, the couple put their wineglasses to one side, stood and began to undress, carelessly dropping each costly item of clothing onto the floor. This action thoroughly unnerved Nicky because it seemed so premeditated and casual. After all, this was her mother, a newly-married woman, undressing in front of a man who was not her husband. Dozens of questions and disordered ideas rushed through Nicky's head. But the disturbing thought uppermost in her mind was that her mother looked extremely comfortable in this situation and swiftly deduced she'd almost certainly had many similar assignations.

Nicky found herself studying her mother's nude body analytically. She couldn't help admiring all she observed. Jane was well-toned and slim in the right places, despite the four children she'd borne. As she raised her arms to release two side combs, her long hair fell onto her shoulders like a dark veil. Her breasts, her daughter noted, were more voluptuous than her own but, like her thighs and bottom, they were quite firm for her age. All in all, Nicky couldn't help appreciating her mother was definitely not short of sex appeal, so much so it would be easy to see men lusting after her.

Nicky wanted to look away from the scene in front of her but found she was unable to avert her gaze. She watched fascinated as, in almost slow motion and totally silently, the naked pair lay together on the bed and made intense, urgent love. Voyeurism had never been her scene but there was something about her mother's performance in bed with this younger man that she found truly mesmerizing. Perhaps it was the enthusiasm and obvious enjoyment. Whatever it was, Nicky attempted to drag her eyes away but they were drawn irresistibly to the intertwined bodies as they slowly writhed beneath her. Completely overwhelmed, she felt something snap deep inside her. She continued to watch until her mother climaxed and only then, emotionally drained, did she fall back into her swivel chair and stare sightlessly towards the far wall.

# 8

TRUE TO HER NATURE, Nicky wasted no time in phoning Simon the following morning. There were important matters she was bursting to discuss. Most of all she wanted to tell him about their mother and the secret room. He was the only person she could ever share this news with and she was keen to hear what he made of it. She spoke to him, without interruption, for two whole minutes but he brusquely brushed the matter aside: "Can't say I'm shocked but I haven't the time to be bothered with our mother and her lovers right now," he said, dismissively. "Truth is I couldn't care less about her. Anyway, I've trouble enough with my own love life. It's make or break time for me. But I can't go into that now." He then swiftly broke the connection.

Nicky was hurt. It hadn't been easy to be frank about such a delicate matter and Simon had shown no interest whatsoever. It really upset her he'd been so offhand about the secret room and what had happened there. All things considered, it was no great surprise because she understood his lack of concern. But, when all was said and done, he'd still slammed the phone down on her. In all the years she'd known him, he'd never treated her so badly and she felt his indifference keenly.

Nicky's distress ran deep. The more she recalled her mother's uninhibited behaviour the more churned up and confused she became. She felt totally destabilised by what she'd witnessed. For perhaps the first time in her life she didn't know what to think or how to proceed. She'd been relying on Simon to help her through her maze of emotions. Now she was going to have to sort out her feelings without his support.

But she quickly realised she had an even more vital problem to worry about. Something was obviously wrong with Simon. For a while now she'd been aware he'd been acting strangely. She realized his odd behaviour was so out of character it needed some urgent investigation. Their recent phone call was a case in point. Exactly what had he meant by 'it's make or break time for me'? The more she thought about it the more enigmatic and sinister it sounded. As she sipped her mid-morning coffee, Nicky realised she could no longer overlook her growing disquiet. There and then she made up her mind to put her own problems to one side and ring her half-brother again. There were pressing matters she needed to discuss with him.

She rang his mobile and left a brief message when he didn't answer: "Spud, phone me. It's urgent." By the end of her lunch break she'd made three further attempts to get in touch with him. As he still hadn't called back by mid-afternoon, she changed tack and called the number in Salford where he lodged. Nicky knew from previous conversations with his landlady that she was a renowned chatterbox who had a soft spot for Simon. But on this occasion the landlady was in no mood for talking. In fact, Nicky formed the impression she was being deliberately evasive. It was as if overnight she'd become a mother hen guarding a favourite but vulnerable chick. Hard as Nicky tried, she was unable to get the landlady to drop any helpful information. She therefore abandoned the call, coming to the conclusion it was time to act much more decisively. Deserting her office and the accounts she was engaged on, she drove home to Orchard Park and went straight up to Simon's bedroom. It was in an untidy state, just as he'd left it after his brief stay. That, too, said much about his disturbed state of mind because he was habitually very tidy. Normally she would never have dreamed of searching through his private belongings but right now she felt she had compelling reasons.

It took her only a few moments to discover a notebook in the middle drawer of his desk containing a list of telephone numbers. Closer inspection revealed one of the entries to be Simon's college friend, Jamie Benson. Nicky remembered meeting Jamie when he'd stayed overnight in this very room a year or so earlier. She smiled at the recollection. Jamie had spent the whole evening staring shyly at her, like he'd never spent time in the company of an attractive girl before. Impulsively she rang the number.

A hesitant voice said "Hello" and then went on to sound even more faltering, if that was possible, when Nicky explained who she was. But as soon as she made it plain it was essential she got in touch with Simon, Jamie responded more positively: "I think he's chased off after his girl-friend," he revealed. "He's really upset about her. Last night he told me he'd be missing a few lectures and to tell anyone who asked that he wasn't feeling too well."

"Why do you think he's gone after this girl?" Nicky asked, "And who is she, by the way?"

Some of Jamie's hesitancy returned: "Her name's Charlotte Owen and she's studying modern languages. Simon's been distracted by her for ages. She's been going out with him, dropping him and then agreeing to see him again. When he was at home with you all last weekend, she sent a text telling him he was dumped. But he told me they went to the pictures together and it was all back on. Last night he discovered she'd driven off to see another boy-friend who lives near her home in north Wales. I'm just guessing Simon's gone after her because he rushed off to hire a car first thing this morning and there's no sign of him here."

Nicky attempted to assimilate this information before trying another approach: "How's he been lately? I mean, has he seemed different at all?"

There was a pause before Jamie answered. "He's depressed," he said shortly, "and not just because of Charlotte."

When no other information was forthcoming, Nicky said gently, "I've noticed he's not been himself for a while. I'm really worried about him, Jamie, and I'd like to help him."

"I thought it was only me. Worried about him, I mean. You must know he's fed up with his course. He doesn't want to be an engineer any more. And he can't stand Salford, or so he says. Claims he can't stand *any* city any longer, even Manchester, which you must know he used to love. He appears to have lost interest in everything and everyone. Everyone except Charlotte Owen and she's just dumped him!"

It was worse than Nicky had imagined. She suddenly felt she'd let Simon down and her uneasiness mushroomed. "He's not answering his phone," she said grimly. "Any ideas how I can hold of him quickly?"

Jamie's answer was not particularly helpful: "Nope. Apart from driving round north Wales looking for his hire car. Or getting the cops involved."

Nicky didn't consider either option for long. She was far from convinced it was a practical solution to rush off to north Wales searching for Simon. Anyway, there was no actual proof he was hard on the track of this girl, Charlotte Owen. And as for getting the police involved, that, also, didn't appear a very wise move just at the present.

But although doing nothing might well seem the sensible way forward, it was certainly no easy option. What *was* indisputable was the intense concern she felt for her half-brother. And, as the day wore on and nothing was heard from him, that anxiety continued to grow apace and gnaw away inside her.

# 9

BYRON LAY FULL-LENGTH ON the sofa in his Manchester apartment, mobile to his ear. It was late evening and Johnny was in full flow.

Byron knew when not to interrupt his friend. Johnny was clearly worried about something but he'd only get round to talking about it when he was good and ready. He'd already chatted inconsequentially about his latest exploits in the wrestling ring, gone over some local gossip he'd heard the night before in the Kings Arms pub and had progressed to filling Byron in on the current drug scene in south Cumbria. This was information he'd acquired from his father, a Detective Inspector in the Cumbrian force, whose patch included the Furness peninsular towns of Barrow and Ulverston.

"You know my dad," said Johnny, warming to his narrative. "He'd never reveal any confidences where his job's concerned and all I'm telling you is in the public domain. But it just goes to show how widespread the drug problem is. I sometimes wonder if any of the blokes I meet in the ring are on drugs. Do you remember the bout I had last year with that chap Sebastian Brennan from Workington. There were more than a few rumours flying round about him being on steroids. He was a real powerhouse and I had a right old ding-dong with him, I'm telling you. But where did all his muscle come from?"

Byron let his best friend prattle on. Johnny was not normally so voluble so whatever he wished to get off his chest must be important. He finally ran out of steam and took the opportunity to catch his breath before remarking carelessly, "You've probably already guessed by now I've got something on my mind. It's Nicky again. Hardly surprise of the night."

But Byron *was* surprised and said so: "Johnny, I know you wouldn't try to make a mountain of a molehill but I know Nicky pretty well, too. I've always thought of her as a very level-headed, down-to-earth sort of girl; really nice and sensible with it. You two might have had a few problems recently but I didn't think it was much to bother about. I happen to think you're really suited to each other. So what is it with the pair of you? You'd better spill the beans."

"She's changed, Byron. I can't put my finger on it but she's changed."

Byron frowned. "Changed? You'll have to explain what you mean."

"She's different. These last couple of days she's been very distant, like she's pushing me away. But I don't know why and she won't tell me. It's not so much that she's cancelled our last two dates but the offhand way she's gone about it. She's just very different." Johnny's fluency had ebbed away and he suddenly sounded subdued and uncertain.

"I'm trying to understand what's happening here," responded Byron, "but it's not easy. Help me out. What do you think has caused this change?"

"Not what but who. It has to be Simon. He's got to be at the bottom of it. I've told you before that Nicky always puts him first. Not only first but second and third as well, all the time."

"I don't get it. You've been telling me for a while that Simon's not happy and that Nicky's worried about him. Are you now telling me he's the reason why she's pushing you away?"

"Yeah, that's exactly it, short and sweet!" confirmed Johnny. "Nicky's always affected by Simon. She's always ready to jump through hoops for him. She can't help it. And I'm sure there's nothing else wrong with her."

"Well, you might be sure but I'm not," countered Byron. "Definitely not. I think you're wrong; in fact, I'm certain of it. It's only a gut feeling but there **has** to be more to it than you think. Someone kind and caring, like Nicky, wouldn't dream of pushing you away just because her half-brother is going through a rough patch. Take my Tyler, for instance. When her mum had that heart attack last year she didn't shove me away. She needed me; she wanted me to be there for her. That's what happens in times of stress. You depend on your loved ones for support. Ordinarily, Nicky would need your help with Simon. The very last thing she'd want to do is push you away. There must be something else that's upsetting her and making her act like this, something you don't know about."

"Like what?"

"Don't ask me," said Byron. "I've no idea. Check it out with Nicky. She's the one you should be talking to. But it must be pretty serious and I reckon you'd better find out what it is and quickly."

Johnny was unconvinced: "I honestly don't see it. I'm positive there's nothing else. If there was I'm sure I'd know about it. I see Nicky every day, remember. You really do cheer a person up, don't you!" he grumbled. "And I do try to talk to her. I only know I'd have more joy at the moment chatting to a brick wall. As it happens, she's even more frantic about Simon than ever. I've never known her so down."

"And why's that?"

"He appears to have gone missing. Apparently he's having girl trouble. Nicky thinks he hired a car this morning and rushed off to north Wales after this student he's keen on. She keeps trying to phone him but he won't answer. She's been so desperate she's even tried calling Adam a few times. Apparently he's in Manchester attending the Doctor Who Convention but he never bothers to turn his phone on; it seems he's well-known for it. She's absolutely beside herself with worry. I even asked dad if the cops could get involved but they can't because Simon's not officially missing yet. Anyway, I'm really glad you'll be home this time tomorrow. You'll be able to meet Nicky and see for yourself I'm right about her."

Byron decided it was time to sound more cheerful and supportive. "I know you're doing your best, Johnny. Just hang in there, even though it's difficult. From all you tell me, Nicky's going to need the support of all her friends, including you. Especially you. And for my part, I can't wait to get home and see you both."

Byron put his phone to one side and considered Johnny's call but deduced there was nothing further he could do while he remained in Manchester. He therefore returned to surfing the net. His searching of the Amazon site had unearthed the latest thousand-page tome on the Plantagenets, who ruled England from 1216 to 1485, and he was determined to order the book and have it delivered to his Cartmel address. After all, it was one of his interests and he confidently expected he'd have plenty of time to read it while he was home.

# 10

I T WAS WELL AFTER midnight on a deserted mountain road somewhere in north Wales. A lone car came into view. Low cloud and driving rain made for poor visibility and the car's headlights cut only a narrow swathe through the murky blackness.

The car was being driven slowly as it descended the steep gradient. Had there been any casual observers in this remote spot, they would not have been too fearful for any occupants of the vehicle when it sluggishly veered off the narrow roadway onto the adjacent wide strip of rough grass. This was because there was plenty of leeway to correct the error and manoeuvre the car back onto the carriageway. But the car didn't deviate off its new course. Maintaining its leisurely pace, it headed towards a wooden fence some thirty metres away. Even then the car, and whoever was inside it, would have been in little danger had the fence been of a sturdy construction. Unfortunately, this was most definitely not the case; the wooden barrier was, in fact, much-repaired and, at best, a flimsy affair.

The car collided at an angle with the insubstantial structure and continued its forward momentum with barely a pause. A dozen yards further on the land fell away precipitously into a deep gorge. The vehicle appeared to hesitate momentarily on the edge of this abyss before plunging out of sight into the ravine below.

Long seconds later a great flash of light shot up from the depths of the chasm as the car's fuel tank exploded, followed at once by a reverberating blast that shook the immediate vicinity.

# 11

AT FIRST GLANCE, CARTMEL appeared to be sleeping in brilliant late May sunshine. There was a scarcity of visitors in Market Square and at the Priory, perhaps because it was market day in the nearby town of Ulverston. But closer observation revealed that plenty of locals were immersed in their everyday work.

At a few minutes after noon, Martin was in his office on the edge of the village meeting two of McAdams' largest suppliers. He'd become owner of the firm as part of some very complex arrangements in his divorce from Jane. Although he was not currently inundated with jobs, he was still working to a hectic schedule. As managing director, he liked to keep his finger on the company pulse and was generally reluctant to delegate duties. He was a strong believer in excellent customer service and his catch phrase, regularly quoted to every one of the eleven staff at McAdams, was 'the client is king.' All new customers could expect to receive a home visit, almost always from Martin in person, and if an estimate was required then Johnny would also be called in with his book of plans, tape measure and calculator. This was a task equally well performed by Jack Reed, but he'd moved onto being in charge of construction and now spent all his working hours on site. It was an open secret at McAdams that Jack was being groomed as the next managing director. But Martin still had plenty of schemes he wished to put into practice and was often so involved in his responsibilities he lost track of the time. It was not unknown for him to work right through to mid afternoon before his protesting stomach urged him to consult his watch and grab a snack. More often than not he was the last to leave the office and he usually took a briefcase of papers home to work on. Beth made sure he had a hot dinner waiting for him so he could be certain of at least one good meal a day.

Beth herself had a healthier respect for meal-times. At five minutes past midday she'd already found a corner seat in the Cartmel School staffroom and had begun to unwrap the pack of sandwiches she'd prepared earlier. As a teacher of German, which includes plenty of oral work, she also drank copious amounts of water to keep her vocal chords well lubricated. As she participated fully in after-school activities, her free time was limited. Any moments left over tended to be taken up with lesson preparation and marking her pupils' work. But, once home, it wasn't only her partner for whom she felt some responsibility. Martin had told her frequently enough he'd come to rely on her intuition where his children were involved. Beth was more than happy to accommodate him in this respect, and watching over four young adults was normally much less stressful than having charge of thirty or so teenagers. Having said that, two of Martin's children were currently causing Beth a great deal of worry and were the cause of her missing a night's sleep.

Jack was not one of the sources of Beth's concern. At midday he was fully engaged on the construction of a large conservatory at the Royal Oak, another of the Cartmel inns. He'd not be thinking about his lunch for another hour. Aged twenty-eight, Jack had certainly had his share of problems. His teenage years had been littered with school exclusions and bouts of drunkenness, during which he'd sometimes behaved very aggressively. One Christmas he'd been intoxicated for three whole days and during a two-hour period of mayhem had repeatedly bullied his twin brothers, pushed his stepfather down a flight of stairs, causing him to break an arm, and had actually flattened Johnny, which was definitely no mean feat. Further havoc had only been avoided when Byron faced him down. Jack continued to get into unseemly scrapes well into his twenties but his life was transformed when he met a young couple recently arrived from the south. They were committed Christians who were intent on setting up a new church in Grange-over-Sands, a seaside resort virtually next door to Cartmel. To begin with, Jack had scoffed at this couple's religious views but they'd eventually persuaded him to attend the fledgling church, after which he couldn't keep away. Almost overnight the wild glint disappeared from his eyes and he changed from a drunken, belligerent bully into a sober, gentle follower of Christ. Perhaps more important, at least where the family business was concerned, people tended to like and trust him.

Beth was not particularly anxious about Adam either, though she was mindful he'd missed yet another morning's work. But Adam's absence had been anticipated. He'd spent the previous two nights in Manchester at the

Doctor Who convention and it had been expected he'd return home very late. All those who got to know Adam quickly learned there was nothing that would induce him to miss any opportunity of pursuing his obsession with Doctor Who, even though none of his Cartmel mates shared his enthusiasm. Adam was well-known for taking advantage of his dad. He would put in an appearance at work when it suited him, no matter how much his father might huff and puff. At five minutes past noon he was enjoying a long shower with no thought of work or lunch hampering his brain.

Beth definitely felt uneasy about both Nicky and Simon and with good reason. Nicky had spent all the previous evening and most of the night in a distressed state. Simon had not returned any of her calls and she was convinced he was in serious trouble. The night hours had been long and difficult ones, during which Nicky had clung to Beth as if her life, and maybe Simon's, depended on it, continually staring at the phone and willing it to ring with news of her beloved Spud. She was reluctant to discuss her fears but her torment compelled her to chatter non-stop about unrelated matters. Beth merely sought to listen patiently and interpose helpful, calming comments. During the dark hours, both women had consumed large amounts of coffee and sought their beds only when the first hint of dawn smeared the sky.

Nicky didn't arrive at her office desk till nearly eleven. She then drank another large mug of coffee before telling Johnny, whose desk was adjacent to her own, some more details about Simon's disappearance and his subsequent silence. But when Johnny offered his support, she waved it away, grumbling in a low voice, "I'm very sorry but I really can't deal with this right now. I've got problems you don't understand." She was unwilling to go into any detail and her relief was clearly visible when he drove off to an appointment with a client, leaving her alone in the office. There was plenty of work to be tackled but she couldn't get beyond staring at her blank computer screen and waiting for the phone to ring. In the following hour there were two calls but her optimism was swiftly replaced by apathy when neither of them produced any information about her missing half-brother. For once she was totally unaware of the superb views across fields towards the Priory and, as the clock ticked past midday, she was just as unresponsive to the thought of lunch, feeling she'd be unable to swallow the smallest morsel until she discovered what had happened to Simon.

For his part, Johnny was delighted to escape the frosty atmosphere and get out into the fresh air. While he was more than willing to help Nicky through her difficulties, she was sometimes impossible to please. He understood her present fears and felt plenty of sympathy for her, but she seemed determined to block him out completely and that was doing nothing to further their relationship. And what of these other problems she referred to? He was at a loss to know what to do for the best, other than to continue to offer the love and support she didn't appear to require. And he was still totally convinced Byron had got it all wrong and that normal service with Nicky would be resumed once Simon was found safe and well. Shrugging his huge shoulders, Johnny decided a pub lunch, washed down with a pint of beer, would work wonders, at least for his morale, and turned his company van towards Market Square. A male voice on the radio interrupted a rendition of Shania Twain's 'You're Still the One,' which wasn't exactly in keeping with his mood, to boom out a time check: it was 12.05.

At exactly five minutes past twelve, Detective Inspector Ed Hampson, Johnny's dad, was finishing a hasty lunch in a back room of the Barrow police station, some eighteen miles away. Ed was an older version of his son, his hair a little thinner and his broad shoulders more bowed. He was no wrestler, though, preferring a regular round of golf with his friends in the police force. He'd been on duty since eight a.m. and had spent an extremely frustrating morning following up leads that had quickly petered out and pursuing suspects, none of whom were at home. Anticipating a bout of indigestion, a common occurrence whenever he rushed his food, he reached in his jacket pocket for a supply of Rennie's. Breaking off two of the pills, he popped them in his mouth and began to chew them slowly, contemplating how he could best proceed with an enquiry into a serious bout of shoplifting in Barrow's town centre shops.

Ed's deliberations were interrupted by a telephone call, which was officially recorded as being received at six minutes past twelve. He stood to take the call. The first few words had him straightening his back and widening his eyes. He listened attentively for three minutes before quietly asking a series of questions and listening to detailed answers. After replacing the receiver, he flopped back into his chair, closed his eyes and concentrated hard. He sat motionless for a further five minutes while he considered carefully all he'd heard. Then, having settled on a suitable course of action, he got back to his feet and made two rapid telephone calls, both to Cartmel numbers. Detective Inspector Ed Hampson's bad day had just got a whole lot worse.

Forty minutes later Ed parked his unmarked police car in the main McAdams car park and made his way to the reception area. The site had first been developed in the early nineteen hundreds as a brick-making plant and had been much added to since. The reception area was part of the original building but had been tastefully modernised since Jane's father, Joe McAdams, had acquired the business a quarter of a century or so earlier. Martin, Joe McAdams' successor, was waiting in the foyer. He was very anxious to know why Ed had driven out from Barrow to see him and his mind was whirling with endless possibilities, most of them thoroughly unpleasant. He and Ed had developed much mutual respect since they'd become close neighbours and he greeted the detective warmly before ushering him a few yards down the corridor and into his office. Ignoring the upright chairs at the desk, Martin led the way towards more comfortable armchairs next to the window overlooking the car park. Once seated, there was an expectant pause.

Ed knew he could delay no longer. Overall he loved his job but there were aspects of it he really hated. This was one such time and the only way to make it bearable was to do it to the best of his ability and try to be meticulously professional. He took a deep breath and launched right into it: "I'm sorry to say I have some very bad news for you, Martin. But there's one point I must stress right at the outset: I'm unable at the moment to confirm any of the details I'm about to tell you. I can only promise to share further information with you as soon as it becomes available."

Martin swallowed hard and nodded perceptibly. Ed continued: "There's no easy way to tell you this. At about eight o' clock this morning a North Wales police patrol discovered a car at the bottom of a ravine in the Gwydyr Forest not far from Betwys-y-Coed. They estimate the car had been there only a matter of hours. They called in the emergency services who found a badly-burnt body in the wreckage, believed to be male. They checked the vehicle and identified it as a Hertz hire car. According to the Salford police, it was rented out yesterday morning by your son, Simon."

Martin was visibly shocked but remained silent so Ed went on, "The Salford police have visited Simon's digs. They found his mobile phone there. Initial checks show he sent a number of texts early yesterday morning to a girl named Charlotte Owen. I'm advised the texts reveal he was desperate to meet up with this girl. His in-box contains a number of messages from your daughter, Nicky, all of them urging Simon to get in touch with her as soon as possible.

Martin finally stirred and raised a pallid face. "I know about Nicky's calls," he almost whispered, "and she told me something about this Charlotte Owen."

Ed nodded, feeling a great surge of sympathy for his neighbour. He said, "Unfortunately, there's more. When the North Wales police visited Miss Owen's home near Denbigh later this morning, a neighbour told them about a noisy caller who woke her just after midnight last night. It seems the Owen family are away on holiday so the caller was unable to gain access to the property and eventually drove off. From the description the neighbour was able to provide, we believe the visitor was your son in his hire car. At this stage, we can only speculate what happened next, but our provisional timescale fits in well with the theory that the car involved in the fracas at the Owen household was the same vehicle that ended up in the ravine in Gwydyr Forest."

Ed paused, waiting for Martin to digest this awful information and question any of the details. When no comments or queries were forthcoming, he asked gently, "Do you have any reason to believe, any whatsoever, that your son, Simon, might *not* be the occupant of this crashed hire car?"

It was quickly evident that Martin, though utterly devastated by the turn of events, had no cause to doubt, not a single one. On the contrary, it was abundantly clear he was convinced and that his thoughts had already leapt forward. "What am I going to say to Nicky?" he almost pleaded. "How can I possibly tell her Simon is dead? And how on earth do I tell Adam and Jack?" He rocked back and forth in his armchair, his head in his hands, as he attempted to come to terms with the enormity of what he'd been told and how he was going to deal with it.

Ed slowly shook his head. He had no idea how to answer these questions and could offer no advice. "At this stage," he said, "our priority must be to establish the identity of the occupant of the car. With that in mind, do you think you or Adam could provide us with a DNA sample?"

Martin seemed not to hear because he continued his rocking awhile. Finally he roused himself, climbed to his feet and paced back and forth in front of his desk. "I'll get Beth to take care of Nicky. Yes, that's what I'll do. She'll know how best to handle her. I'll go and tell Adam and Jack. That'll be hard enough." He then fell back into his chair and stared up at Ed, his face totally distraught. "I'll ask Adam to give you a DNA sample. After all, he is Simon's identical twin."

Martin turned away and stared helplessly out of the window, adding so quietly that Ed had to strain to hear, "Heaven help me! Simon is dead!"

# 12

"**S**IMON IS DEAD!" NICKY whispered the words aloud as if it might make them easier to bear. It didn't. As she paced her bedroom, she found herself wondering desperately whether anything ever would.

It was already two hours since she'd heard about the car accident but what did time matter now? Although she'd been expecting to hear bad news after Simon's long silence, nothing could have prepared her for the awful information about the badly-burnt body in the ravine. Beth had been extremely kind and gentle but her words had still overwhelmed.

Nicky felt so guilty. She couldn't help it. Why hadn't she done more to find Simon before the accident happened? After all, she'd known for hours that he'd gone chasing off after the Welsh girl. Why on earth hadn't she…? But it was far too late now. Simon had driven to Wales without any check or hindrance and now he was dead. She threw herself onto her bed, needing release from some of the deep-seated pain she felt. That didn't help either and she rocked herself back and forth in total despair.

She'd sought the solace of her bedroom because she couldn't bear to witness the naked grief of her family at close quarters. It had simply been too much to bear. Adam had sat totally still on a dining room chair, looking absolutely devastated and incredibly pale. Jack had stood rigidly by the window, his lips continually moving as if he was reciting a never-ending prayer. And Martin, normally so strong and contained, had broken down uncontrollably in front of everybody. Nicky couldn't cope with the raw agony of it all and had fled to her bedroom. But the comfort she'd hoped to find there hadn't materialised. While it was impossible to stay with her loved ones, she couldn't bear to be on her own either.

There was just one tiny shred of hope to which Nicky clung tenaciously:

that the badly-burnt body found in the car at the bottom of the ravine was not her beloved Simon. While her whole being shrieked that Simon was dead, she nursed this hope and even found herself praying aloud the body belonged to someone else and that Spud was still alive and well. It was the first time she could remember praying and it actually brought her some fleeting peace of mind. But such relief might only be temporary. Adam had already provided the police with DNA swabs so, if all went according to plan, they'd soon know for certain whether the accident victim was Simon or not. Nicky shuddered helplessly at the thought.

# 13

BYRON HAD FINALLY COMPLETED his end-of-season training sessions at Carrington, the superb Manchester United training ground, and was hurtling up the M6 towards Cartmel and home. He now faced six whole weeks without having to kick a ball. Much as he loved competitive football, this was a luxury he had every intention of revelling in.

Fancying a short break, he pulled his BMW into the Charnock Richard service station near Preston. He ordered a Costa coffee, took it to a quiet corner table and opened his latest copy of 'History Today,' a magazine he received every month on subscription. Within seconds he was fully relaxed and immersed in an article on Edward IV, one of the Plantagenet kings, written by an old college friend of his. Not many people, including some of his Manchester United team-mates, were aware that Byron was enthusiastic about medieval history and was an avid reader of any works, fiction or non-fiction, connected to his hero, Edward IV. A few of his acquaintances, had they known, would no doubt have tried to mock him for this passion but Byron simply didn't care what they thought. He guessed he had an obsession with the fifteenth century English king but it was one he was proud of.

Normally when he was out and about he liked to wear a baseball hat to help disguise his identity but he'd forgotten to pack one. It didn't take long for a group of older teenagers to recognise him and make their way over to his table. Byron didn't mind and put his magazine aside. He'd come to understand you were bound to be constantly in the public eye when you played for a team like United. The half dozen teenagers were amiable enough so chatting to them and signing autographs was no bother.

As the lads moved away, an elderly lady seated with her husband at a neighbouring table, lent across and asked, "Do I take it you're famous, young man?"

Byron was enjoying himself. And why not? He was on holiday for six weeks and all was well with the world. Life felt good! Taking note of the lady's strong American accent and the twinkle in her eye, Byron grinned and said, "I'm a professional footballer for a well-known team a few miles down the road from here. But we Brits use a round ball for our football, not an oval one. You Americans know the game as soccer."

The lady smiled back. "Like that handsome David Beckham when he played in Los Angeles?"

"Exactly, though I don't get paid as much as him!"

As he picked up his magazine and prepared to return to the car park, his phone rang out. He took the call as he headed for the door. It was Johnny and the tone of his voice stopped Byron in his tracks: "There's all hell to pay here. Prepare for some bad news, the very worst. Simon is dead!"

"What?"

Johnny said grimly, "His hire car, the one I told you about, has been found at the bottom of a deep gorge in north Wales with Simon inside. At least, the police are pretty certain it's Simon. The body's badly burnt."

Byron, a supremely fit athlete accustomed to a racing heart, had to take two deep breaths before his heart slowed sufficiently to enable him to respond. All well-being abruptly abandoned, he could only mutter, "This is awful! Poor Simon! And what about Nicky and the rest of the family?" He shook his head in absolute disbelief then took another long breath and let it out slowly. "I'll head home at once, drop my things off and come straight round to your place. Give me an hour or so, OK?"

Still clutching his phone to his ear, he fell into the nearest empty seat but, as he tried to put his muddled thoughts in some sort of order, Johnny almost sobbed down the line, "That's not all. When I went round and tried to console Nicky, she told me we're through. She says she wants us to stay friends but she made it abundantly clear she won't be going out with me again. I've been well and truly dumped!"

Five minutes later and still attempting to come to terms with all he'd just learnt, Byron drove his car back onto the M6 and headed north. Normally he loved to play a music CD and sing along to it loudly and out of key, but he was so affected by Johnny's news he stayed silent, his brain racing with a multitude of thoughts and emotions. He'd had some limited experience of death but it had never seemed so close to home as now. His last pair of surviving grandparents had died when he was a toddler and he could recall only vague memories of them. Then a talented eighteen year-old Manchester United footballer he'd played alongside had died in a rock climbing accident. The tragedy had been totally unexpected but the club had provided wonderful support and he'd got over it. Other than that, the death causing the greatest effect had been Johnny's mum, who'd died of a massive heart attack when Johnny was only ten. That had been seventeen years ago but he could still recall the raw shock of it and Johnny's desperate grief. Now Simon had died in a dreadful car accident and Nicky had dumped his best mate. Byron, who'd been really looking forward to getting home, suddenly wasn't so sure any more. But the moment of doubt swiftly passed. He would be needed in Cartmel and the Reeds especially would be relying on all the help and support they could get.

And so would his mate, Johnny! He'd sounded so forlorn on the phone but it was hardly surprising in the circumstances. Just for a moment, Byron felt angry with Nicky. Why on earth had she ditched Johnny? And why now? It didn't make any sense but then neither did his own anger so he let it go, deciding he wanted to hear both sides of the story before passing judgement.

With his brain dominated by random morbid thoughts, Byron set the car to cruise control, mentally ticking off landmarks as he spotted them. It was only when he passed the large Cumbria sign that he sensed he was nearing home. The Lake District mountains loomed up on the horizon, helping to soothe his troubled mind, and then it was time to turn off the motorway and head towards Kendal and Barrow. As the side road was still dual-carriageway, he maintained good speed until he reached the outskirts of Grange-over-Sands, where the road narrowed as it meandered alongside Morecambe Bay towards the resort's town centre. Grange required his full attention. The streets were full of tourists and elderly people, some of whom were not the most careful pedestrians or drivers. As he climbed the hill past the main shops, he wondered, and not for the first time, why so many senior citizens chose to retire to an area not exactly noted for its level walks. Near the top of the winding hill, he had to brake hard to avoid an elderly man who'd strayed onto the roadway. Realising he was travelling too fast, he made himself slow down and concentrate on his driving, which meant banning all thoughts of Simon from his mind until he reached home.

Past the last housing estate was a level area dominated by a golf course. Byron recalled spending many happy hours playing there after he left school. It was then only a quick downhill run into Cartmel but it was certainly not easy on his already-raw emotions. The nearer he got to home, the harder he gripped the steering wheel. What had until very recently seemed a straightforward, relaxing trip had now taken on a much more complex significance. But he made himself drive slowly and absorb his surroundings so that his eyes worked overtime as they drank in familiar sights. Byron had been fortunate to have travelled extensively, particularly throughout Europe and the United States but, unlike many Brits, he had no desire to live abroad. If it was up to him, he'd settle in north western England when his playing career was finally over, and preferably not a million miles from this very area.

At the bottom of the hill he approached Cartmel School, the local comprehensive, set in a large expanse of playing fields on the edge of the village. He couldn't help staring at the buildings where he'd spent so many of his formative years and where Beth was still teaching. The school appeared virtually unchanged, which he found oddly comforting.

The attractive medieval village of Cartmel is situated in a long, narrow valley, surrounded by gently undulating hills. It looked tranquil and slumbering in the late afternoon sunshine but it would have inspired Byron no matter what. Swallowing hard to suppress all the emotion that suddenly threatened to swamp him, he headed for the centre of the village and the priory which, now only a few hundred yards away, dominated the skyline. But he couldn't help noticing the number of cars abandoned haphazardly along the verges and recalled his father's warning that the glut of tourists and their vehicles would sooner or later ruin the village. He'd ignored the prophesy at the time but perhaps his dad had a point after all. Heavy traffic was already blighting large parts of the Lake District and Byron definitely wasn't keen for Cartmel to be similarly affected.

Driving slowly past the lovely priory church, he spied a group of villagers he knew well and waved in their direction. They acknowledged the gesture but in a subdued manner, suggesting the news of Simon's death had already spread. Byron suddenly realised he was gripping his steering wheel even tighter and tried hard to relax. Two hundred yards further on, he turned into Orchard Park and the end of his journey. It was a gated community. There were no private guards on duty but it did have CCTV and other electronic aids. The whole development was also surrounded by high walls so it really was a secure area. Byron keyed in the password necessary for all vehicles and drove towards the four large, detached houses that comprised the estate. All were surrounded by mature trees and shrubs and large, unfenced lawns. Passing the first two properties, owned by the Reeds and Hampsons, he headed another fifty yards to the house on the left of the remaining pair.

Just as he was thinking how good it was to be home, despite the current doom and gloom, and was retrieving his bags from the boot, his parents came out of the side door. This was absolutely typical of them. Although Byron was nearly twenty-seven years old, they still treated him as if he was in need of regular supervision while he was living under their roof. They'd probably been watching out for him most of the afternoon. He found this attitude both endearing and infuriating but had learned to accept it because he knew they'd never change.

It was always great to see them and he studied them keenly as they made their way across the tarmac to welcome him. Both were fully retired from the hotel business that had been their livelihood but they'd taken up active hobbies and still led busy, purposeful lives. Now in their early sixties, they claimed to be fit and well. At first sight this contention appeared well-founded. Dennis Fullard, tall and slim, still carried himself erect but walked with a slight limp, the result of breaking his leg while skiing some years before. Since leaving the hotel trade, he'd made a point of dressing very casually and boasted he'd thrown away all the long-sleeved shirts, suits and ties he'd once been required to wear. Jilly Fullard, also tall and casually dressed, walked more slowly but only because she was scrutinizing her son all the while. A warm smile enlivened her face. She, too, was slender and upright but, as she got nearer, Byron spotted a few grey hairs and wrinkles he'd not seen before and his heart lurched as he realised his parents were beginning to show their age.

Without further ado, Byron dropped his bag, strode forward and shook his dad's hand before giving him a swift hug. But there was nothing quick about the hug he gave his mum. As he stepped back, he said gravely, "Wonderful to see you both, as usual, but I'm going to have to ask you to excuse me for a while. I have to visit our friends." And he pointed meaningfully back towards the two houses he'd just driven past.

Both parents nodded but it was his dad who spoke: "Of course. We've already been round. It was….but you'll find out for yourself soon enough. Take as long as you need."

"Yes," his mum agreed. "Please don't feel you need to rush. Matters couldn't be more difficult over there. But I'll have a meal ready here when you need it."

Byron smiled his thanks. His homecoming was certainly not turning out how he'd hoped but it couldn't be helped.

He carried his gear up all the stairs to his bedroom under the eaves, dropped it onto the bed and had a swift look round. The sloping walls were covered with a mixture of beer mats and posters, not all of them connected with football, by any means. The largest picture, in pride of place over his bed, was a wonderful photo of Lewis Hamilton in his McLaren F1 racing car leading the British Grand Prix. Byron had met the driver a couple of times and was a real fan. The bedroom had been his for nearly twenty years and was exactly as he remembered it. Once again he felt strangely pleased, perhaps because so much of his life as a professional footballer was in a constant state of flux that it was gratifying to find some important aspects unchanged.

Ten minutes and a quick change later he approached the Hampson house, determined to be the friend Johnny needed but, when the front door opened, he was in for a genuine shock. It wasn't Johnny who stood on the threshold waiting to greet him; it was Nicky.

# 14

BYRON WAS MORE THAN a little surprised to find Nicky at the Hampson's place but he recovered rapidly and stepped forward to give her a hug. Words were sometimes superfluous and this was such a time.

Nicky was undoubtedly slender but she was also supple and strong. Byron, used to well-toned bodies, recognised one now but it was hardly unexpected when one considered the regular use she made of local gyms. It also crossed his mind that in order to control her horse of seventeen hands she needed to be fit and sinewy. Even so, her body was full of tension, like a thick, fully-wound elastic band.

As Nicky stepped back into the hall, she gave Byron the opportunity to study her. A superficial glance might have suggested she was coping with the dreadful news she'd recently received, but a more searching scrutiny revealed the severe strain she was clearly under. Her mouth was unusually tight and there were dark rings under her eyes. Byron felt a sudden rush of compassion for this girl he'd known so long and impulsively gave her taut body another hug. She responded by throwing her arms round his neck and sobbing convulsively into his shoulder. She then attempted to recover, dabbing her eyes with an already-damp bunch of tissues. Having regained some composure, she looked steadily at Byron and said, "I'm going to need all my friends right now so it's great to see you. And dare I say you look even fitter than you do on television."

Byron grinned. "You can dare all you like, but please count on my support, Nicky. Always, I promise. And you look pretty good yourself, considering all that's...."

"How's Tyler?" she asked quickly. "Have you brought her with you this time?"

"She's fine and, no, I haven't. I expect to see her soon but we've made no firm plans yet." Then, determined to seize the opportunity she'd just fed him, he asked: "And how's Johnny?"

She seemed taken aback by the question and replied defensively, "I had a special reason for coming over to see Johnny. He's OK, but you'll see for yourself soon enough," and she nodded towards the kitchen, from which direction sounds of music clearly emanated. She then seemed to make a snap decision and said more spiritedly, "We've split up, but I'm sure you already know that. Johnny tells you everything."

"Not quite everything, Nicky, I promise you. But I must admit he told me you're no longer an item. He actually told me you'd dumped him."

When she pursed her lips and half turned away, he couldn't help asking, "Why, Nicky? You've just admitted you need all your friends right now. This is not like you at all." And he watched her searchingly because he couldn't for the life of him understand her motives and he really wanted to, if only for Johnny's sake.

She shrugged and turned back to face him. "It's for the best, I promise you," she said, suddenly looking excessively sad.

Byron waited for more but, when it was clear no further clarification was forthcoming, he declared passionately, "I just don't get it. I really thought you and Johnny were made for each other, so how about spelling out for me what went wrong."

Nicky shrugged and more tears rolled down her cheeks, which she hastily wiped with her sleeve. "I like Johnny a lot, more than you'll ever know actually, but some things aren't meant to be. And us two living together happily ever after is one of them."

Byron shook his head. "Nicky," he said, "as an explanation, that's as clear as dirty dishwater. Play it straight and tell me what you really mean."

Nicky was suddenly hesitant. She then seemed to shake herself and come to a decision. Looking Byron straight in the eye, she said softly, "There's something you should know. I'm certain in my own mind it **was** Simon who died in the car crash. Nothing else makes any sense. All the family have reached the same conclusion so I came round here to talk to Johnny. I didn't know what else to do."

Byron found himself hugging Nicky for the third time in as many minutes as sobs shook her whole body. He made no move to force more answers or push her away.

A few minutes later he let himself into the Hampson house, which never failed to amaze him. Built to exactly the same design as the Fullard family home, it contrived to be so different. Whereas the Fullard house was light and airy with pale timber throughout, here the woodwork and furnishings were dark and sombre-looking. Byron was reminded that Johnny's mum had chosen the colour scheme and Ed had clearly not wanted to alter it. Anyway, Ed didn't earn enough money as a detective-inspector to make expensive changes. It had been his wife's money that had provided for the initial purchase of the Orchard Park property, and it was the money Ed had inherited from her that enabled him to stay in the house and afford the not-inconsiderable running costs.

Byron carried on into the kitchen. It was a large country-style room with a multitude of dark oak units, thick granite worktops and grey flagstones. The electric lights were on and the French doors at the far end were wide open, letting in shafts of early evening sunshine. Johnny stood by the central island unit preparing food. There was a lot of mess on the nearby worktops, Byron observed, and the music, a Radiohead track entitled 'Paranoid Android,' was pulsating very loudly from two small, black loudspeakers hung opposite each other on the kitchen walls.

Johnny, wearing knee-length shorts and a singlet liberally daubed with flour, turned the music down to a low throb when he spotted Byron, who wasted no time in saying, "Nicky talked to me about Simon before she left."

Johnny chose not to hear. "Tell me something about Edward IV," he ordered, rather too loudly in the sudden hush.

This was part of a game they sometimes played but Byron was swift to observe Johnny's eyes were unusually bright and he realised there were some other serious thoughts currently dominating his friend's mind. He still went along with it: "The Battle of Towton that Edward and the Yorkists won in 1461was the most bloodthirsty battle ever fought on British soil."

Johnny considered this information. "Your Edward IV was a fighter, then, like me."

"Yeah, he was a fighter, that's for sure."

"Did he do a lot of fighting?"

Byron nodded. "He fought in about ten battles and skirmishes."

"And how did he do?"

"He won every single one. He was never beaten."

Johnny was impressed but then he sighed heavily. "That's *not* like me, then," he said. "I've just lost a big battle. I've lost Nicky."

"You've lost a battle, not the war," countered Byron, continuing the conflict theme. "She's going through a rough time, I'll concede, but don't give up on her now. Maybe it's time for you to fight back."

Johnny was unconvinced. "We've been through all this. Anyway, you weren't there when she told me we're finished. And you didn't hear the *way* she told me. I happen to believe she meant every word of it." He paused and then changed the subject, as if he was already fed up with talking about Nicky: "How about doing something useful now you're here? Help me clear up this mess. Dad's on his way home so I need the place looking decent."

Byron couldn't help shaking his head in disbelief. His best mate was so predictable. Johnny's way of solving problems was to pretend they didn't exist. Then, when he'd discovered that option didn't work, he liked to magnify them out of all proportion. Byron fervently hoped his friend's natural resilience would shine through this current setback. Nicky had clearly hurt him but it remained to be seen how deeply. As it was, he still managed, unsuccessfully, to try to boss Byron as they set about cleaning up the kitchen and washing the dirty dishes. By the time Ed got home, he was a bit more like his normal happy-go-lucky self.

Byron was pleased to see Ed again, which had much to do with the fact that Johnny's dad was not your typical policeman. He was a thoroughly reliable, conscientious cop but one who attempted to forget all about his duties once he got home. Many policemen aren't able to achieve that distinction but Ed tried hard to keep his home and work lives separate. Mind you, it was easier for him because there was not much crime in his home village and what did occur tended to be trivial, low-grade dishonesty. True there were the usual petty offences but the more serious scoundrels tended to give Cartmel a miss. Even when the village was inundated with visitors for the bank holiday races, the local constabulary managed to contain lawlessness to a minimum. The worst crime Ed could recall was a spate of about a dozen burglaries, which was one of the reasons why Orchard Park had become something of a fortress. But the villain involved had soon found Cartmel too hot for him and had been 'encouraged' to return to Liverpool.

Ed was not unwilling to comment on his investigations but he always took pains to be discreet. And so it was now. When he heard about Nicky's visit, he said, "It's just as well the family can accept his death and start coming to terms with it. But we'll know for sure whether it's Simon or not when the DNA samples are compared, and that should only take a couple more days."

"Wow! That's quick," said Byron, obviously impressed.

"When matters go smoothly, that's all it takes."

Johnny then asked the question that Byron had been keen to voice: "Was Simon's death an accident, do you think?"

Ed shrugged. "It's early days so at this stage we still don't know. We're calling it an accident but the investigation is ongoing and who knows what we might discover."

Byron pondered this statement as he strolled over to the Reed's house. It had crossed his mind Simon might have felt depressed enough to take his own life. He had plenty of hearsay evidence to support this view but he still couldn't help feeling guilty for thinking it. Putting the idea aside, his thoughts turned instead to food, especially as he'd left Johnny and Ed to have their evening meal. Food was a subject close to his heart but, before he could consider his own needs, he must first offer his condolences to the Reeds, a task he regarded as far more challenging than, say, facing the likes of Chelsea or Liverpool in the Premier League.

It was Beth who invited him in. Once again he couldn't help noting the marked differences in house layout. While the Reed house shared a similar basic design with the other Orchard Park properties, here the downstairs living area seemed so much larger and more open than either the Fullard or Hampson properties. Byron decided it was a matter of the same external plans with very distinct internal modifications and he couldn't help finding it absolutely fascinating observing such variations.

Beth was wearing no makeup and looked decidedly tired and strained. Unusually, her dark, shoulder-length hair was hanging loose, rather than in the French pleat she normally favoured, especially for school. As she summoned up a smile, her long fingers played nervously with her gold ring, betraying inner turmoil. But she still managed to give him a warm welcome: "It's lovely to see you, Byron. We've all been following your footballing career with such interest. I'm so pleased you came round. Come through and see everyone."

Byron had a soft spot for Beth. She may have lacked Jane Templeton's slim good looks and sophistication but she was a kind, caring person who, unlike Jane, had the ability to make people feel comfortable and welcome. It was a top skill in Byron's opinion and he admired her greatly because of it. He followed her into the lounge, wondering what on earth he could possibly say to the Reed family that might alleviate their misery.

They were all there. Martin and Jack were seated behind an open laptop and mounds of paperwork at the long, rectangular dining room table, while Adam had an arm round a still-tearful Nicky on the huge, coffee-coloured leather sofa. None of them made the effort to rise from their seats but they all called out a greeting, Martin beckoning him to sit at the table beside Jack. Before he did so, he went to them all, beginning with Nicky, and gave them each a few words of comfort. Nicky responded with a kiss and the men with hand shakes and Byron realised that, although he'd been absent from Cartmel for many months, he was, to all intents and purposes, still accepted as a very close friend of the family. It was both incredibly sad and a wonderful privilege to sit among them for a while. Although shocked, stunned and tearful, they still sought to support each other and come to terms with their desolation.

Later, after Byron had eaten his belated meal and the evening of sorrow had passed, when his parents had finally said all they wanted to tell him and had retired to their room, he lay on his bed, closed his eyes and tried hard to sort out his many memories of Simon Reed.

# 15

MARTIN HAD TAKEN THE day off and had excused Adam and Nicky from work. This left Jack and Johnny to run the business, a very unusual occurrence considering Martin's aversion to delegating his authority. But he certainly wasn't contemplating a lazy day. There was a great deal to be done, including a funeral to start organising.

For once, he didn't have to rush his breakfast but he was so consumed with anguish his toast and marmalade lay untouched and his freshly-brewed coffee barely sipped. As he sat on his own at the kitchen table trying to work out a simple plan of action for the day, he kept jumping to one single thought: Simon, his son, was dead and life would never be the same again.

Martin's thoughts doubled back to the events of the previous day but they remained a muddled blur. He recalled his ex-wife had phoned at least three times from London demanding to speak to her three remaining children. Jane still had the power to make him angry. Despite promising himself he'd not lose his cool when she came on the line, a few words from her left him fuming. It happened every time! She had the right, of course, to speak to her children; it was just....but what was the point of raking up all the misery of their divorce once more? She was now married to Ray while he was living with Beth. Live and let live, he counselled himself, but it was never going to be that simple.

Jane had duly spoken to her children, concentrating on the younger two, Nicky and Adam. That was fair enough, in Martin's opinion, as it was this pair who were most affected by Simon's death and who needed counselling. But he couldn't help noticing Jane had spent much more time talking with Adam than with Nicky, while Jack only merited a very brief conversation. He definitely didn't agree with that sort of inequality. He was reminded Jane had always made it obvious Adam was her preferred one and that her favouritism had eventually got way out of order, causing huge family rifts. Yesterday's unequal telephone calls were typical of her, but how dare she favour one child more than the others. It was not only unfair it was totally unacceptable.

Martin took time off to consider the effects of his ex-wife's one-sidedness on the twins. He tried not to feel bitter. Adam was never allowed to be criticised in any way; Simon, on the other hand, was constantly belittled. This uneven treatment had an impact on the whole family and so many problems could be traced right back to Jane's biased treatment. What had been so frustrating was that Martin had been unable to trace the origin of his ex-wife's unfair behaviour. But then Jane had always been a law unto herself. He could count himself very fortunate that Jack and Nicky had readily accepted him as their stepfather, and he'd been equally delighted when these two welcomed the twins' birth. Nicky, particularly had loved the twins from the beginning, especially Simon, with whom she established an extremely close relationship. Jack, too, had an easy relationship with both the boys but that was to change radically for a while when he took up drinking and became a bully. Over a period of months, he persecuted both twins but the greater impact had been on Simon. While Adam overcame a bout of bed-wetting and got on with his life, seemingly none the worse for the experience, Simon reacted really badly to the tormenting. On one occasion he actually attacked Jack with a hammer, and Martin had had to intervene before any serious harm could be done. What made the situation worse was that Jane had done nothing to discourage Jack's bullying behaviour and had seemed secretly pleased by Simon's distress.

Staring straight down the long room towards large picture windows and the garden beyond, Martin recalled other situations where his ex-wife had behaved less than even-handedly. He was so absorbed by melancholy thoughts he didn't hear the postman delivering the mail. It was only when Jess, the family Labrador, barked and made a sudden dash for the front door that Martin became aware there were letters on the mat. Glad of the opportunity to put his gloomy thoughts aside for a while, he strolled over to the pile of post and returned with it to the table. There was the usual abundance of business letters and junk mail but one envelope grabbed his attention and made his heart leap up painfully in his chest. He recognised the handwriting instantly. It was Simon's!

Pushing his plate away, he placed the envelope carefully on the mat in front of him and sat staring at it for at least twenty seconds, his heart refusing to resume its normal beat. The handwriting was so neat and precise, so like Simon, that Martin thought his chest would burst. He observed the letter had a first class stamp and had been posted in Salford two days previously. Unable to bear further delay, he snatched up the envelope with wildly trembling fingers and, surprisingly carefully in the circumstances, tore it open to reveal its contents. Inside was a single sheet of paper. Martin removed the folded sheet, opened it out and read and re-read the message. It didn't take long. Hanging on grimly to the sheet, he closed his eyes but the action couldn't stop tears sliding down his cheeks and falling unchecked onto his white cotton shirt.

A few minutes later he took out his mobile and, with fingers still shaking uncontrollably, dialled the contact number Ed Hampson had given him only the day before. He attempted to wait patiently for someone to answer his call.

# 16

D I ED HAMPSON LIKED nothing better than to start his morning shift at Barrow's central police station by scanning the main news items in his Daily Mail, preferably with a large mug of steaming coffee close at hand. But a couple of important matters had turned up. He therefore reluctantly abandoned his paper and turned to the two items, both relating to the Cartmel case.

The first was a fax he'd received from his north Welsh colleagues in Betwys-y-Coed.

This was an initial report into the car accident in the Gwydyr Forest, which the detective inspector fell to studying. It was a detailed account but an entirely factual one. It came to no assumptions and made no recommendations. That would be solely for the coroner's inquest to decide which, more than likely, wouldn't be convened for many months.

Ed considered the report's main findings before jotting down some notes:

(1) Accident in remote, uninhabited area.
(2) No witnesses.
(3) Crash took place on dark, wet night.
(4) Lack of light/bad weather not thought to be contributory factors.
(5) No sign of skid marks on or off carriageway.
(6) Hire car's brakes not used throughout incident.
(7) No evidence any other vehicle or person involved.
(8) Recovered body thought to be that of Simon Reed.

Ed placed his newspaper, the report and his jottings into a battered briefcase and turned to the second matter. It was the result of the DNA tests, which was a straight comparison between samples taken from the body in the crashed car and the swabs provided by Adam. He read the report and its findings carefully and went immediately into thinking mode, reluctant to come to any hasty conclusions regarding Simon's death. When he'd first become a detective he'd made ill-considered decisions in a number of cases, but experience had taught him it was better to withhold judgment until much fuller evidence was available, or till such a time as proof was overwhelming. It was still early days regarding this particular car crash, as he'd pointed out to Johnny and Byron, and the data gathered to date, though not exactly insubstantial, was certainly not full and watertight either.

He didn't get far with his thinking and was spared further brain-searching when his phone rang out. It was Martin, in a very distressed state, informing him that a letter from Simon, containing significant information, had just been delivered in the post. Ed immediately found himself relaxing. He had much admiration and respect for his near neighbours but sudden family deaths often throw up the possibility of conflict and the last thing he wanted was his friendship with the Reeds compromised. A letter from the deceased suggested the evidence was starting to pile up. Matters, it appeared, were proceeding very satisfactorily.

And so it was that Ed made a speedy return trip to Orchard Park. Driving straight to his neighbour's home, he was met by a very distracted Martin Reed, who informed him that Nicky and Jack had already been shown Simon's letter and that Adam had been summoned from his nearby flat in Market Square so that he, too, could be made acquainted with its contents.

A further five minutes passed before Ed, clutching anther mug of coffee, moved through to the Reed's lounge. Like Byron, he was enthralled by the variety of styles in the Orchard Park properties. Secretly he couldn't help preferring the lighter, more open Reed design, which he felt was more elegant and tasteful than the scheme in his own home. His wife had always favoured darker colours and he'd gone along with her choice. Now he had neither the will nor the finances to make radical changes.

Turning his observation to the four members of the Reed family sitting side by side opposite him, he couldn't help noting the atmosphere was extremely tense. It was to be expected, yet it was equally obvious the quartet were supporting each other fully. This sense of togetherness pleased Ed as it would undoubtedly assist him in carrying out his own demanding duties.

He put his coffee to one side when he was handed Simon's letter then, having carefully scrutinised it, he read it aloud, at Martin's request:

> *Dad,*
>
> *I know I'm about to let you down very badly, and everyone else, too, but I can't go on, I just can't. So much has gone wrong with my life and I can't fix it any more. I've tried very hard to work things out in Salford but nothing seems to help. In fact, all I do seems to make it worse.*
>
> *I really thought that going home for a few days and seeing you all might make a difference. And it did seem to be okay for a while, then I ended up back here in Salford and I HATE it so much. Charlotte walking out on me is the last straw.*
>
> *I know you'll all miss me terribly, especially my dearest Nicky, and I know you'll feel very guilty, dad, for sending me to Salford. But you mustn't. You always did your best for me, which is more than I can say about my mum. She never cared for me.*
>
> *Tell Adam it was good to have a laugh with him recently and that I actually felt jealous of him and his lifestyle. He'll think that's a right hoot!*
>
> *Please don't hate me too much for what I'm about to do. I'm sorry but I can't see any other way.*
>
> *Simon*

Ed avoided looking across at the Reeds, concentrating instead on folding the letter and replacing it in the envelope. Only then did he turn to Martin and say gently, "I'm going to need this letter."

Martin took a deep breath. "It's what I anticipated so I've already scanned it and made my own copy."

"That's fine. Can you confirm the handwriting is your son, Simon's?"

"Yes, it's Simon's. I'd know it anywhere." Martin was not the only Reed to nod.

"I will require a further specimen of Simon's handwriting, just for our records, you understand," the DI announced gently.

"Of course. That's not a problem."

Then, while Ed reached down to put the letter in his briefcase, Adam spoke up, his voice crackling with emotion: "I wish he hadn't said that bit about not hating him; I wish he hadn't said that. As if we could *ever* hate him, whatever he did."

Nicky, her face looking like it had been dusted with flour, nodded vigorously and put an arm round Adam before starting to weep. Suddenly she rose from the sofa and called out, "Simon should have blamed me, not dad. I sent him back to Salford. I sent him to his death. He killed himself because of me." She stared round defiantly, daring anyone to contradict her.

Ed had witnessed similar outbursts during his career. Seeking to keep the proceedings on an even keel, he asked, in a deliberately hushed voice, "Do I take it, then, that you're convinced Simon took his own life?"

Wiping away her tears, it was Nicky who answered. In a similarly subdued tone, she said: "I'm sure. And I can speak for all of us."

Ed Hampson was pleased to receive such a positive reply. Turning to Martin, he said, "I promised I'd keep you updated whenever possible. This morning I received two reports relating to Simon's death. Would you like me to tell you their main findings?"

"Yes, that would be useful, but please tell us all. We have no secrets here."

Ed nodded and retrieved the information from his briefcase. "The first is the DNA result," he stated. Looking at no-one in particular, he went on, "I can confirm the body discovered in the car that crashed in the Gwydyr Forest has definitely been confirmed as Simon's. I should add that DNA testing has become such an exact science that the chances of a false result are many millions to one."

There was a noticeable intake of breath. Nobody spoke but Nicky sobbed and was comforted by Adam.

Ed allowed the news to be absorbed before continuing: "The second report is from my Welsh colleagues concerning the car accident in the Gwydyr Forest." He found his jottings and virtually read out his brief notes, without comment.

There was another shocked silence before Nicky said shakily, "He chose that isolated spot deliberately, I know he did. *And he didn't use his brakes*. But what on earth was he thinking when he went over that cliff edge? I can't bear to imagine."

It was all too clear her father and brothers couldn't bear to think about it either.

As Ed put his papers away, he remembered something and turned again to Martin. "By the way," he said, delving into his briefcase, "did you know your photograph is in today's Daily Mail?"

Martin paled. "I had no idea. You'd better show me," he said, ominously quietly.

Ed produced his copy of the newspaper and turned to an inside page. "Your photo accompanies an account of Simon's car crash. Take a look. It's a very good likeness."

Martin almost snatched the paper and examined the picture and report. Bristling with sudden anger, he bellowed, "This is a copy of a photo from our local paper when I was president of the Barrow Rotary Club last year. How dare they print it in a national newspaper without my permission. I've a good mind to....but the damage is already done. Damn and blast them anyway!" He threw the paper down as if it was tainted, sat back down and shook his head as if he couldn't believe his dreadful luck.

Ed was not the only one present who was totally shocked by Martin's outrage. In all the years he'd known Martin, he'd never once seen him shout and lose his cool like this. But he reasoned that grief can display itself in strange ways and decided to change the subject: "I fully expect the authorities to release Simon's body shortly," he declared. "I can therefore see no reason why you shouldn't go ahead with the funeral arrangements."

Martin inclined his head but said nothing. It was glaringly evident he was still incandescent with rage. Ed had been delighted how well the meeting with the Reeds had proceeded and how totally natural the family's response to Simon's death had been. But there was nothing normal about Martin's reaction to seeing his photograph in the Daily Mail, nothing normal at all.

# 17

BYRON CHECKED HIS CRASH helmet for the umpteenth time before Johnny powered the Kawasaki 1400GTR into life. He then clung onto his friend for dear life as the fearsome Japanese motor cycle roared out of Cartmel, heading for Ulverston and the coast road to Barrow.

Byron was used to speed; his BMW 535d was an amazing car, capable of speeds in excess of 150 miles per hour and widely acknowledged as one of the best vehicles on the road. But Johnny's Kawasaki was an altogether different beast! And Johnny was a changed personality once he bestrode his beloved bike; it was as if he and machine became one. While he treasured his wrestling career and was exceedingly proud of the four world championships he'd collected, he had a genuine passion for riding the Kawasaki. He'd purchased the bike, courtesy of a legacy from his mum, against his dad's advice. Ed reckoned he'd attended the scene of too many fatal motor cycle accidents and didn't want his only son adding to the statistics. He also didn't fancy living in a large four-bedroom house on his own. But he had to admit Johnny never took unnecessary risks and never misused his bike's awesome horsepower. And so it was now. As Johnny drove the narrow, winding lanes, the only danger Byron experienced was to his dignity, as the wind tried its best to whip his shirt off his back.

It was the weekend and they were both glad to escape Cartmel for a few hours. It was a week since Simon's death and the doom and gloom in the village had been unrelenting. Family arguments had quickly surfaced. After consultation with Simon's three siblings, Martin had decided a funeral service in Cartmel Priory, followed by a simple burial in the nearby graveyard, would be the best option. But Jane was having none of it. She seemed deaf to the views of the others and insisted the service should be at the crematorium in the nearby town of Barrow and that Simon's remains should be cremated. There was a huge row, made worse by the fact that Jane remained in London and conducted her cremation crusade on the telephone. The majority will finally prevailed but it left simmering resentment all round.

Byron and Johnny couldn't avoid being caught up in all the misery. Orchard Park had been constructed with security in mind but the barriers seemed to enfold and contain the tension, and there was plenty of it, so the Park now seemed heavily claustrophobic. Byron was free to escape at will and took to running the numerous lanes round Cartmel, which he enjoyed and which helped keep him fit. He had quickly adapted to being home again, helped in no small measure by parents who, clearly doting on him, set out to pamper him whenever possible. Byron knew from past experience it was best to let them get on with it and do his best to stay sane and unspoilt in the process. Poor Johnny had no such freedom. It was made even worse for him because he'd been given extra work responsibilities in these troubled times. Hard as he'd tried, he'd been unable to escape the sombre atmosphere at McAdams. It was wonderful, therefore, to flee for the afternoon from an area infected with gloom and despair.

As they crawled through Ulverston's traffic lights then blasted down the coast road, Byron wondered how it was you could always feel cool on a motor bike even on the hottest days. At Bardsea, where the road ran alongside the sea, he spotted an ice cream van and tugged at Johnny to stop. Minutes later, having shed their outer layers, they were wandering along the beach clutching large cones and enjoying superb views across Morecambe Bay to Fleetwood and beyond.

Johnny slurped his soft ice cream like a toddler and kicked out at a nearby pebble. "I feel I've been let out on parole," he said, grinning, "and, boy, is it good! It's great to wander round doing nothing. I tell you what, By, let's not go back. Let's be totally irresponsible for once in our lives. We can camp over there under those trees and go home when the funeral's over." He took a sidelong look at Byron before adding, "Oh, don't worry, I've not lost my senses. It's just…well, what's happened with Nicky has really thrown me. You know I managed to win the All Weights wrestling at the Langholm Show last Saturday. But only just. My mind was all over the place and this young farmer from Grasmere almost beat me. I tell you, a girl could have given me a good fight. In fact, there was a Ladies Open Wrestling class this year which attracted quite a few entries. I should have encouraged Nicky to take part. In her present mood, I'd have rated her chances! But, in all fairness, she's been really nice this week. I know she hasn't been sleeping much since the accident and she looks like death, but all that frostiness I told you about has disappeared. She's actually been pleasant to me."

"That's because she's a great lass. We all have our off days."

"Of course we do. But I can't pretend I begin to understand her. I know her life's been totally blighted by what happened to Simon but that moodiness I told you about has disappeared. You'd have thought Simon's death would have made her more touchy, not less. Shows what I know about women. It's not all good news, though. I've really missed her company so I plucked up the courage and asked her out. I offered to take her for a ride on the Kawasaki and she turned me down flat, which is a bit mean because I know she gets a thrill from riding with Adam on his Harley Davidson. It looks like she'll never give me another chance. But guess who's been nosing round her again?"

"No idea," said Byron. "Tell me."

"That creep, Gaz Morris."

Byron recalled a lanky individual with spiky hair and a constant scowl. "No kidding! Didn't he go out with her before you?"

"Yeah, but not for long," confirmed Johnny. "She quickly found out he was a real waste of space. He was a labourer at McAdams but he had more days off than Adam, and that's saying a lot. He was absolutely bone idle. Martin eventually fired him, not before time, and got a lot of foul-mouthed threats for his pains. But I'm certain it was Gaz on the phone yesterday. Nicky was very coy about it but it *was* Gaz. I only spoke to him a few times but I'd know his voice anywhere."

"Did Nicky mention anything about it?"

"No, she zipped her lips and said nothing, and I didn't ask her directly because it's none of my business. But I checked later with Jack, who usually knows what's going on, and he confirmed Gaz Morris is back in Cartmel. It seems his mum kicked him out ages ago and he legged it down south but Jack reckons she's taken him in again, though he still doesn't have a job so he can't have much money. And there's something else that's common knowledge in the village: he's boasting to all and sundry he's going to get Martin back for sacking him."

Johnny finished his ice cream, kicked out moodily at another stone and stared across the Bay towards Blackpool, which was just a distant blur in the shimmering sunlight. He seemed to come to a decision and moved closer to his friend, adding quietly: "And I'll tell you something else I found out two nights ago that might interest you: Nicky's been seeing Ben Nicholson. Please keep that to yourself for now. She's tried to keep it secret but I know she's had at least two dates with him. Dad told me about one meeting because he saw them hand-in-hand on the road near Mill House. It's no wonder, is it, she's kicked me into touch."

Byron snorted in amazement. "Ben Nicholson? That lady-killer! I wouldn't have thought he was Nicky's type."

Johnny shrugged. "Neither would I, but then what do I know about women? Ben works on Jack's team so he comes in our office now and again. He's not the sharpest pencil in the case but he's a real Jack The Lad and has a way with the girls, or likes to think he has. His technique is to date them, bed them, drop them, and then boast about his exploits to his mates. Nice sort of bloke, wouldn't you say! He's sniffed around Nicky before but she always totally ignored him. Until now."

"Very strange indeed," said Byron, observing his best friend was much more upset with this development than he was letting on. "Nicky's definitely not wasting her time, is she? Perhaps there's something after all in what you told me about Simon's death changing her."

Johnny forced a smile and gave Byron a playful prod in the ribs. "Don't tell me the world's greatest expert on human nature might have got it wrong. Wow, that truly would be an admission. And before you rush to your own defence and remind me how truly knowledgeable and worldly-wise you are, just let me tell you *we're doing it again*."

"Doing what again?"

"Talking about Nicky. It's a bad habit and I'm going to have to put a stop to it."

And for the rest of the afternoon he was true to his word. The nearest he came to referring to his ex was when he commented pensively that he was looking forward to getting Simon's funeral over and done with so that "we can all get on with our lives." It was a sentiment Byron fully understood but he had a sudden premonition it wasn't going to be nearly as straightforward as Johnny imagined.

The rest of the afternoon passed quickly. If it was to be judged on how far Johnny had chilled out, then the few hours on Bardsea beach had been most successful. But Byron was well aware his friend would only settle completely when he'd sorted out his relationship with Nicky. And with all the talk of Gaz Morris and Ben Nicholson, it was clear that wasn't going to happen any time soon. One way or the other, Byron reckoned, the funeral would surely sort matters out. But which way? That was the rub.

Later that evening Byron enjoyed a long phone call with Tyler, his girl friend. He'd missed her company and couldn't wait to see her again. Now the date of the funeral was known, Tyler had promised to attend. Satisfied with progress in one direction at least, Byron let his mind wander over recent events and had a sudden, startling revelation. He recalled what Nicky had told him soon after he'd got back home. She'd maintained that Johnny had no secrets and always told him everything. But that wasn't entirely true. Johnny was usually very open on all matters but, concerning the personal side of his relationship with Nicky, he'd told Byron virtually nothing.

# 18

I T WAS THE DAY of Simon's funeral. Byron lay in bed watching Tyler Seddon brush her long, chestnut hair, one of her regular morning rituals.

Tyler had grown up on a large estate in south Manchester and had long passed the point where she was bothered by being stared at. At a fraction under six feet tall, with big-bones and a captivating face, she was certainly an eyeful. Byron had met her in the A & E Department of the Manchester Royal Infirmary following one of his footballing injuries and had fallen for her charms immediately. The attraction, fortunately, had been mutual. Johnny had once remarked Tyler could have made a lucrative career in wrestling, had she been so inclined, but the only aggressive tendencies she ever exhibited were on behalf of the underdogs of this world. She hated deprivation of any kind and was committed to caring for the people of Manchester. She'd made it her number one priority, as Byron had ruefully discovered to his cost on a number of occasions.

"So who am I going to meet at this funeral?" Tyler asked, gazing at Byron's reflection in her mirror.

"The usual crowd. All our neighbours and most of the villagers will be there. Simon was popular with the locals and the Reeds are well-respected round here. There will be one new face. You won't have met Jane's new husband, Ray Templeton, but then neither have I."

"Jane collects husbands like I collect hairbrushes," commented Tyler, wielding her own brush skilfully. "What do we know about this fellow?"

"He's very rich. His business is based in London but he's bought a large house on the edge of the village for occasional visits. Jane has just started to furnish it. Apparently she's using one of her interior designer friends from London."

"All right if you can get it," said Tyler, without the slightest hint of envy. "Sounds like he'll suit Jane down to the ground. Has this latest marriage calmed her down, then, or is she still as feisty as ever?"

Byron grinned. "Jane hasn't changed one iota in all the years I've known her. She's the most opinionated, bossy, aggravating woman I've ever met. I wonder if Templeton knows what he's let himself in for."

"Probably not, poor fellow!" said Tyler, with feeling. "But tell me something I picked up on last night over dinner. Why did Nicky call Simon 'Spud'?"

"He was the older twin and was christened Simon Tatum Reed. Tatum was his grandmother's maiden name and 'Spud' became a bit of a family joke. But don't mention it to Jane because she never thought it was even vaguely amusing."

"She wouldn't," said Tyler sourly. "So is there anything else I should know about today?" And she watched her boyfriend as he sat up in bed and hugged his knees, noting there was not an ounce of fat on his superlatively-fit body.

"There is actually." And Byron explained about Nicky breaking up with Johnny and Johnny's view that Nicky had changed a lot in the past fortnight or so. He added, "Johnny is positive the change is all to do with Simon and his accident. But I think there's a lot more to it than that. I won't bore you with my reasons but I'd appreciate your opinion. You've come to know Nicky pretty well so check her out today and tell me what you think."

Tyler was non-committal but Byron knew she'd keep her eyes open. He'd stirred her curiosity and he knew he could trust her intuition in such matters. One way or another, it looked like being an interesting day.

Just down the road in the Reed household, matters weren't proceeding nearly so calmly. Nicky, for one, was finding it hard to cope. Unable to sleep, she'd risen at the crack of dawn and sought comfort in the company of her horse, Casper. She'd enjoyed a long, relaxing ride but, soon after returning home, she'd broken down in tears and had retreated to the solitude of her bedroom in an effort to compose herself. The funeral was bound to be an ordeal and she knew she'd never get through it without a great deal of support. But she wouldn't be looking to her mother to sustain her. Jane was not your typical caring parent. The first sign of emotion would see her backing away with disapproval. Nicky realised she'd do better turning to Beth or Martin.

By eleven o'clock, Martin was dressed and ready for his son's funeral. He was attempting to keep his cool but the younger members of the family were trying his patience and it wasn't easy. Nicky had already broken down in tears for the third time that morning and Beth had taken her back to her room to offer comfort. Adam had been ordered to return to his flat and change into something more appropriate for his twin brother's funeral than his favourite motor cycling gear. Even Jack was testing his stepfather's composure. He'd found an unopened bottle of Martin's best malt whisky and was already on his third double.

Martin decided to swoop before any more damage could be done to Jack or to his beloved whisky. "Do me a favour, Jack," he said, seizing the bottle and putting it back in the drinks cabinet. "Try to keep your mother off my back today. She's never at her best at family get-togethers, and I know from experience that funerals bring out the worst in her. If she mentions cremations just one more time, I won't be responsible for my actions."

Jack managed a half-hearted smile. "You can ask all you like but it won't do any good. I've never had any influence over my mother's behaviour. None whatsoever. Anyway, she's Ray's responsibility now. You'd better have a word with him."

Martin muttered under his breath before nervously straightening his tie and checking his appearance in the large mirror over the fireplace. He said, "I met your new stepfather at a cocktail party your mother organised. As far as I'm concerned, Templeton's a chinless nonentity. Bland doesn't begin to describe him. He might be a successful businessman making pots of money but what on earth does your mother see in him?" He shook his head in disbelief. When Jack shrugged and made no reply, Martin paced across to the window and added, "I *hate* funerals. I absolutely hate them. I've never been to one yet that didn't end in disaster. I've had nightmares all week that Simon's will be the biggest catastrophe of all time. And I wish someone would tell me where I went wrong with the twins. I still can't understand why Simon's life was so awful he had to end it all. And what about our Adam? He genuinely thought it would be all right to attend his brother's funeral in his motor cycle kit! I mean to say...." He shook his head again incredulously, checked his watch and strode over to the drinks cabinet. "I need a stiff drink," he announced, reclaiming the newly-opened bottle, "and then it'll be time for the funeral. Let's get the show on the road and pray things go smoothly just for once."

Ray Templeton was already bored with country life. He was a city man through and through and, after a single night in Mill House, he'd exhausted any interest he might have had in Cartmel. He'd travelled up with his wife for the funeral but he couldn't wait to get back to London. He considered the few local people he'd met to be very provincial and their pastimes totally worthless. He felt unable to raise the slightest curiosity in horse riding, fox hunting or other rural pursuits. And, while keeping in touch with his business interests by laptop and phone was all very well for a few hours, it soon palled. That was because Ray was a man who liked to keep on top of matters, especially where large sums of his own money were concerned. With his mind back in London, he surveyed the scene out of the master bedroom at Mill House with lacklustre eyes. There was plenty of blue sky overhead but towards the west a large, black cloud hovered ominously. Ray simply didn't notice. He'd just had a huge row with his wife over her choice of furnishings for their new Cumbrian home. While he'd done his best to pacify Jane and was still in a conciliatory mood, she remained incensed that he'd actually dared to criticise her choices. Add to that, she'd discovered a stain on the outfit she'd been hoping to wear to her son's funeral. As she had less than an hour to find an alternative, she was in a really foul mood.

Ray shrugged. He was beginning to understand why his wife caused such consternation among all the men in her life. She could certainly be very difficult, often obnoxious, but he tried to remember she did have some talents. Being very attractive was certainly one of them and he smiled to himself as he felt his loins stir. Taking up one of his latest invoices, he sat on the edge of the bed intending to study it, but he couldn't help noting how his wife flounced off to the bathroom, clearly still in a dreadful temper. Shaking his head wryly, he abandoned the invoice and thought of the approaching funeral. He'd met all of Jane's children but the experience had only confirmed his wish to have as little to do with them as possible. He couldn't be bothered with children in any shape or form and was delighted he had none of his own. They invariably caused problems and he could do without the hassle. He even treated his only nephew with indifference though he had assented to the lad's request to obtain Byron Fullard's autograph, so long as it could be achieved with a minimum of fuss.

Johnny sighed loudly as he walked away from his home. He felt most uncomfortable in his smart, new suit but it was the tie that caused him most discomfort. His huge neck fretted at the constraint. He recalled his last day in the sixth form when, aged eighteen, he'd gleefully cast his hated school tie into the river, promising himself he'd never wear another. But here he was doing so out of respect for his dead neighbour. He patted its unfamiliar shape hoping it would bring some measure of reassurance. It didn't. Only a couple of weeks ago he'd have been looking forward to sitting next to Nicky and holding her hand at this most difficult time in her life, but now he'd have to be content sitting by his dad some rows away. As he walked on his own towards the Priory, Johnny couldn't wait for the funeral to be over.

In the centre of Cartmel the eight hundred year-old Priory looked stunningly beautiful in the late morning sunshine. It was already attracting a crowd of onlookers who had gathered in small groups on the grass near the main door. Most were interested locals who'd come to pay their final homage to Simon Reed, but a few were the usual funeral ghouls. Fortunately the day was warm and dry but the forecasters had warned of the possibility of thunderstorms moving in later from the west.

There was a buzz of excitement when Dennis and Jilly, accompanied by Byron and Tyler, walked into the churchyard. While his parents chatted to some of their friends, Byron signed a few autographs and talked with a group of senior villagers he knew well. One of the old-timers introduced his ten year-old grandson but the lad turned red in the face and could only regard the Manchester United player with complete awe. Byron did his best to put the lad at his ease before gathering up Tyler and moving on. He'd spotted Johnny approaching and wanted a word with him.

"You are to a suit what an elephant is to ballet dancing," he whispered in his friend's ear, then stepped smartly out of the way as Johnny aimed a feeble slap at him.

"It's all right for you," grumbled Johnny. "You look elegant whatever you wear. I feel a right prat in this penguin suit. And as for this tie...." He touched the offending article as if he'd like to hack it into tiny pieces.

Byron grinned. "Come and join Tyler and me. We've important matters to discuss." He shepherded his friends to a clear space on the grass.

Johnny looked interested. "What's going on, then? And by the way, Tyler, you look as lovely as ever but it still beats me what you see in this footballer of yours."

Tyler smiled. "I sometimes wonder myself. But he has persuaded me, against my better judgement, to keep an eye on Nicky, for your benefit, or so he claims. He reckons she's changed a lot recently." All at once she became more serious. "But don't expect too much from me today, Johnny, nor you, Byron. My priority will be to comfort Nicky, not check her out."

Byron waved that aside and winked at Johnny. With a poker face, he said, "I'm still prepared to bet on it. Six pints of beer says you're wrong about Nicky and I'm right."

Johnny patted his tie self-consciously, feeling more uncomfortable than ever. "Six pints? You must be pretty sure of yourself, that's all I can say. But I still figure you don't know the first thing about Nicky so I'll enjoy downing your six pints later in The King's Arms, thanks very much."

All eyes turned to the churchyard gate as Jane made her entrance, leaving her husband to trail in her wake. She appeared not to hurry but Ray had almost to run to keep up with her. Wearing a simple black mini dress with a light blue Pashmina shawl of finest cashmere and matching black, high-heel shoes, she swept past Byron and his group, pausing only long enough to snap, "Byron, Johnny, good day to you. Tyler, you look larger every time I see you. My husband, Ray." She jerked a thumb over her shoulder to indicate her unfortunate husband before they both disappeared into the building.

"Hallo to you, too," said Byron loudly and cheerfully to the empty doorway. "And it was good to meet you, Mr Templeton."

Tyler's face broke into a broad smile. "What a wonderful lady," she remarked. "What charm! And there was me thinking marriage might have softened the old witch!"

Two minutes later, at exactly midday, Martin led his family contingent into the churchyard behind the cortege. With his grey hair contrasting with his black suit, he looked particularly distinguished and Beth, stylish herself in a mulberry suit, gazed at him proudly. The five family members linked arms in solidarity, Jack in the centre with Nicky and Adam either side of him. Adam had followed his father's bidding. Although he didn't own a suit, he'd found a dark jacket and flannels and borrowed one of his father's more sober ties. He happened, also, to be in white trainers, which Martin had chosen to overlook, but he strode towards the Priory with his head held high, unlike his half-sister who appeared to be studiously studying the ground. Nicky was wearing a well-cut Chanel suit over a white blouse and, when she eventually raised her head, it was evident she was taking advantage of a pair of dark glasses, excellent camouflage for her tear-swollen eyes.

Martin halted briefly to speak with the Fullard family group, which also included Ed and Howard Tyson, a retired barrister, who owned the fourth property in Orchard Park. All of them had waited outside to greet the procession and Martin, who'd been concerned how he was going to get through the day unscathed, was relieved to have the support of neighbours he could count on. Still feeling very uneasy about Nicky and her state of mind, he was particularly pleased to see Johnny with the Fullard group. He had a great deal of respect for the young man and maintained hopes he and Nicky would eventually patch up their differences. While Beth shared her partner's concern, she felt as much anxiety about Adam, who had been unusually reticent since the accident. Adam had always been the quieter twin but he'd become even more tight-lipped following his brother's death.

But there was no time for further talk as the funeral procession, with Simon's coffin at its fore, led the way into the Priory. Martin, proud his son was being remembered in this wonderful building, founded late in the twelfth century by William Marshall, Earl of Pembroke and Earl Marshall of England, held his head high. His eyes quickly adjusted to the gloomy interior but his well-being evaporated when he spotted his ex-wife pacing back and forth in the sanctuary. Earlier pessimistic thoughts returned and he was left hoping this was one occasion when Jane would be on her best behaviour. As the procession made slow progress towards her, it was clear from the expression on her face that these hopes were to be well and truly dashed. Jane was clearly in a disagreeable mood and spoiling for a fight.

As the coffin reached the head of the sanctuary, she picked out the most vulnerable person in her sight. Ignoring the setting and the occasion and, in a voice that carried to every person in the Priory, she hissed, "For goodness sake remove those stupid sunglasses, Nicola. You look like a cheap tart!"

No-one moved, not even Martin, who might, perhaps, have done more to forestall any trouble. But it was too late; the damage was done. After an audible intake of breaths, there was a sudden, intense silence. It didn't last long. As a strong shaft of sunlight from the magnificent west window illuminated the whole Reed family, Jane pounced again. Swooping like a black bird of prey, she grabbed a stunned Adam by his jacket and almost shouted in his face, "Look at this. Look at this blood on your shirt collar. Didn't you notice your ear is bleeding? How dare you come to your brother's funeral in such a mess! You're a disgrace!"

But if Adam was stunned by this treatment, it was nothing to how all the others reacted. Jane had actually *criticised* her favourite son. It had never, ever happened before. She'd frequently berated Simon but never Adam. Never. Family and friends alike were completely dumbfounded, so much so that the astonishment following her outburst was absolutely total.

It was at this very moment the Reverend Canon Evan Hopkins, vicar of the Priory Church of St Mary and St Michael, stepped forward out of the shadows to begin the funeral service for Simon Tatum Reed.

# 19

THE FUNERAL SERVICE HAD ended and they were all outside on the grass. But there was only one topic they were still discussing: Jane had publicly criticised Adam.

Shielding his eyes from fierce sunlight, Byron said, "I can't get over it. Even by Jane's standards that was absolutely dire. Did you see the look on Adam's face when she grabbed him? Talk about flabbergasted. The poor lad couldn't move."

"Whatever possessed her?" asked Tyler, shaking her head in disbelief. "Her own children!"

"Par for the course, if you ask me," Johnny said. "It's Jane's way. That's how she is. But it's Nicky I feel sorry for. "

"It was rough on Adam, Nicky *and* Simon," agreed Byron. "Martin's eulogy hardly registered after that performance." He thought to lighten the mood. Gazing all round dramatically as if expecting a sudden onslaught, he reached in his pocket for his dark glasses. "Do you think I'm safe in these?" he asked.

Tyler gave him a push. "Behave yourself and remember where you are. I think Jane must have had a row with that new husband of hers. They weren't exactly close, were they? That might begin to account for her behaviour." But the sad shake of her head suggested even she didn't believe this explanation.

A dozen yards away, Martin was still livid. His ex-wife had caught him out yet again. Had caught them all out, if the truth be told, and made a mockery of their son's funeral. But when he looked towards Jane he could see she was completely unconcerned by what had taken place. She was actually smiling and chatting with acquaintances as if nothing untoward had occurred, as if her recent outbursts were entirely acceptable. How pleased he was he'd divorced her. She was totally unpredictable, so what might she do next? It didn't bear thinking about, but just let her attempt to ruin Simon's burial! He put protective arms round Nicky and Adam before exchanging comforting glances with Beth and Jack.

For his part, Ray was shell-shocked. Was this what he'd travelled all the way from London for? Was this a foretaste of how his marriage to Jane was going to develop? He shuddered and wished fervently he was back in the city getting on with his life. Business there was certainly cutthroat but none of his competitors had ever behaved as deplorably as his wife had just done. And in a church during her own son's funeral! Ray had never regarded himself as religious but there had to be some standards, after all. As a consequence, he'd ignored Jane throughout the service. In his opinion, she'd thoroughly disgraced herself and he'd felt the need for some distance. Instead he'd stared at Adam's bleeding ear, wondering why any sane individual could possibly want three studs in each ear. Yet again it came to him he was out of his depth in the country and in the company of young people and he determined to get away from Cartmel as soon as he possibly could. In future, he'd definitely be giving the place a wide berth.

The crowd of well-wishers had thinned but there was still a score or more hanging on to see Simon's coffin make its final journey to the graveyard nearby. Byron, used to people staring at him, noted a couple, perhaps in their late twenties, looking in his direction. When he gazed back, the girl immediately averted her eyes but the man continued to scrutinise him coolly for a few more seconds before he, too, looked away. Byron noted how slim they both were, particularly the girl. At a time when obesity was commonplace, it was rare to see someone so elflike. She was not only very slender, she was extremely attractive. Beside him, Tyler commented, "Wow, she could easily be a model or a film star. She's a beauty!"

"Isn't she just, but I've never seen her before."

Nor, it transpired, had Johnny but he was more interested in keeping an eye on Nicky, who was heading towards one of the funeral cars that had drawn up by the gate. Seeing an opportunity to get back in her good books, he leapt forward to open the car door for her. Inexplicably, Nicky ignored his offer and scrambled into the vehicle unaided. Johnny immediately backed away, his broad shoulders slumped. He turned to face Byron, his flaming cheeks betraying his agitation. "Tell me something about Edward IV," he commanded.

Byron didn't hesitate. "Edward was only forty when he died. He'd grown very fat from overeating and he died very suddenly."

Johnny tried to concentrate on this information and keep a level voice. "Only forty, eh? He was lucky, then. That's five years longer than my mum managed."

Byron didn't answer. He was busy watching the funeral cars drive off and was in time to catch a distraught Nicky mouth a very clear 'sorry' in his direction as she swept by. He sighed. Nicky's behaviour was getting stranger and stranger but was this all down to Simon's death? He though not but matters were getting so complicated he was becoming less sure by the minute. He shrugged and turned to his friends. "Come on. A brisk walk will do us all good."

The first large spots of rain began to fall as they entered the graveyard. Blue sky had been replaced by dark grey but the inclement weather had been foreseen because one of the funeral directors was available to hand out large umbrellas. In suddenly heavy, driving rain, not uncommon in these parts, Byron led the way between two yew trees and over grass to the open grave. Here family members were hastily getting under the cover of their own umbrellas. There were two distinct groups at the graveside as the burial service got underway. The two Templetons stood to one side entirely on their own, as if ostracised by Martin's family and its much larger group, which included Byron's parents, the Reverend Canon Evan Hopkins and two of the Priory vergers. The latter held huge umbrellas over the vicar, who was already encased in a long mackintosh as if he was all too aware of the power of Lakeland storms.

Despite the adverse weather, this was a wonderful site for a burial ground. Set amid fields and only a stone's throw from the grandstand of the world-famous Racecourse, it exuded peace and tranquillity. Cartmel Races are very unusual. At most other racecourses the spectators assemble outside the track and watch as the races unfold in front of them. But at Cartmel it's so much more intimate. The spectators gather inside the course and see the races take place all round them. Even so, there can be few courses anywhere in the world with a burial ground so close by. But the Reverend Canon Evan Hopkins seemed oblivious of his surroundings as he endeavoured to hurry through the burial service before the storm washed them all away.

Byron shielded Tyler from the driving rain as much as he could but Johnny didn't seem to care how wet he got. He was more intent on tearing his tie off and shaking his neck free of its confinement. It was when the first flash of lightning illuminated the scene that Byron realised the thin couple he'd spotted outside the Priory were standing behind them some twenty yards away. They appeared to be there to observe the proceedings but, as neither of them wore coats or carried umbrellas, they were getting a thorough soaking. Byron immediately hurried over to them, holding his brolly out. He had to shout to make himself heard above the storm: "Please take this."

But the thin man stepped forward in front of the girl, shook his head at the proffered umbrella and yelled back, "We'll manage. We…" But the rest of his reply was lost as a clap of thunder reverberated round the valley.

It was certainly no time for niceties but Byron was most curious about this couple and was reluctant to leave until he knew who they were and, perhaps, why they'd made the effort to attend Simon's funeral. Holding his brolly firmly against the wind and rain, he tried again: "My name is…" he began.

But the slim man interrupted him: "We know who you are. You're Byron Fullard, the Manchester United player. I'm Rob Bailey and I'm here with Kim, my girlfriend. We support Arsenal." He spoke the last sentence dismissively before abruptly turning on his heel and ushering the girl between the yew trees and back towards the gate.

Byron stared at their backs. He'd learned next to nothing about the couple, other than the man was brusque to the point of rudeness and the girl, though very dishevelled, was extremely pleasing on the eye. But who were they and what were they doing at Simon's funeral? Knowing he could discover no more at present, he returned to his place at the burial service and cosied up to Tyler. It was difficult concentrating in such a downpour, especially as the rain did its best to seep everywhere. All the others, he noted, were standing motionless and scrutinising the sodden grass as if their lives depended on it, all that is except Jane, who was searching the heavens as if she half expected to spot her dead son in the storm-filled skies.

Byron's attention turned to a nearby gravestone. At one time impressive but now decidedly shabby, it was dedicated to someone called Claude Quilter Fitzsimmons, who'd died in 1856, aged eighty-two. The date, Byron recalled, was the year when horse racing first began at Cartmel. He then wondered vaguely who Claude was and what his story might be. He wasn't the only one to find his mind wandering. Martin, relieved his funeral ordeal was nearly over, was reassuring himself that family matters were bound to settle back on an even keel in a day or so; Ray was already regretting the purchase of Mill House and was persuading himself he'd never return to Cartmel, whatever the circumstances; Jane was thinking about Adam, convinced his confidence would increase by leaps and bounds now he was no longer in Simon's shadow; Johnny, more worried than ever about Nicky, was afraid she was about to sink into even deeper depression; while Tyler had concluded there was nothing more seriously wrong with Nicky than a severe case of grieving, realising this opinion would please Johnny but not Byron.

Only time would tell if these convictions were accurate or not, but one thing was for sure: Nicky's day was not about to end on a high note. A mixture of rain and tears had already played havoc with her make-up and, when it was time at last for her to speak about her beloved Simon, her words were all but lost in the storm. Byron managed to catch only 'accident' and 'Spud' before Nicky collapsed haplessly into Martin's arms in a paroxysm of tears. Moments later, the service was over.

While Reed family members stayed on to pay their final respects, Byron led his parents and friends out of the graveyard, hoping there'd be room in one of the funeral cars for a ride back to Orchard Park. Able now to look forward to a hot shower and a change of clothes, he glanced over at Johnny, realising all too clearly his best friend needed much more than a luxury or two to transform his black mood.

# 20

TYLER SHOOK HER HEAD in amused exasperation. "It's very simple," she said. "I bet they were college friends Simon knew in Salford. Why do you feel the need to dramatise everything, Byron? You've gone on about that thin couple for long enough. And on top of your theories about Nicky, I'm at a loss to understand you."

"It's because he's a bad loser," said Johnny, enjoying the moment. "He can't bear to concede he's wrong about Nicky. And I'm ready for the first of my six pints, thank you very much."

Byron ruffled Johnny's hair good-naturedly. "I'm not dramatising. I'm telling you there was something odd about those two. That Rob Bailey was shifty. I can't say much about Kim, his girlfriend, because she never opened her mouth. But, Johnny, if you think I'm caving in over Nicky, you're living in a fantasy land. I'm more than ready to buy your beer but only because I think it might cheer you up a bit. You've had that scowl long enough."

It was the evening of the funeral and they were sitting in the saloon bar of The King's Arms in the centre of Cartmel. The jukebox was playing the Beatles' 'The long and winding road.' Someone had turned the volume down and everyone was talking in unusually subdued tones, which seemed to capture the mood of the day. Even the landlord's dog, normally a lively mongrel ready to perform outrageous tricks for the merest morsel of food, was lying indolently under one of the tables.

Next door in the public bar, Jack and Adam were taking advantage of a drink and a chat together. This was an uncommon occurrence, not because they didn't get on but because they had very different friends and pastimes. While Jack's Christian friends participated in a wide range of mostly sober activities, Adam's pals tended to be beer-swilling Harley Davidson enthusiasts, rather noisy and fun-loving. At present, though, Adam was definitely not full of high spirits, nor was he seeking the company of his mates. Instead he stared down moodily at his trainers, leaving Jack to wonder how on earth he could help his half-brother recapture his zest for life.

Half a mile away, on the edge of the village, Martin and Beth had enjoyed a meal at Aynstoke Manor, their favourite restaurant. Martin had booked the table a few days earlier in anticipation of their need for a relaxing evening once the funeral was over, and he was congratulating himself on his foresight. Food and service at the Manor were excellent and the ambience was such that it was easy to unwind after a difficult day. Now was such a time. Martin's hunch his son's funeral would turn out to be a disaster had been spot on. They were sitting in the small lounge drinking brandy and coffee and had the room to themselves, apart from a pair of constantly-passing waitresses. But, having got his latest tirade against Jane off his chest and voiced his considerable worries about Nicky, Martin was ready at last to listen to his partner.

Beth said, "I share your anxiety about Nicky, of course I do. I've spent a lot of time with her this last week and I know how miserable she is. But I'm also very concerned about Adam. Do you realise how subdued he's been since Simon's death? I don't believe he's been out with those friends of his once since he heard about the accident. They've all been to visit him but he can't seem to be bothered with them. He's much too quiet. Goodness knows what's going on in his head right now."

Martin added more sugar to his coffee and stirred it vigorously. "He's not said much to me," he conceded. "He did admit he had no premonition of his brother's death. I think that made him feel very guilty. And he did tell me he thought a part of him died with Simon."

"That's awful!"

"I know. I didn't mention it before because it made me feel so helpless. But I still can't get over how Jane treated them both in the Priory earlier. I'm absolutely furious with her and I could....but what's the point? Do you know what's really sad, Beth? My ex has no idea how destructive she's been right from when the kids were toddlers."

"Oh, come on, Martin. It's time to concentrate on the here and now. There's no point in raking up the past again."

Martin was far from convinced. "What do you suggest, then?"

"Let's agree to keep an eye on Nicky *and* Adam. Adam worries me a lot, Martin."

Back in the saloon bar of The King's Arms, Johnny had consumed his six pints of beer, courtesy of Byron, and was already on pint number seven. The alcohol seemed to have little effect, other than to make his clear blue eyes glisten. Certainly his speech was not slurred: "Glad, you're an honourable friend, Byron, who doesn't renege on his promises. I must say you're generous to a fault. It's not everyone who admits so readily to being wrong."

Byron couldn't help laughing out loud. "You're something else, Johnny, but I bet this time tomorrow you'll be singing a very different tune. I'll tell you one more time so you can get it into that thick skull of yours. There's definitely something else troubling Nicky. I'd swear my life on it."

Johnny's new-found confidence took a dive. Suddenly uncertain, he plonked his glass down noisily. It was Tyler who tidied matters up: "Nothing's going to bring Simon back. It's very sad for Nicky and the rest of us but that's how it is. It's time we *all* moved on, you two included."

Martin and Beth, hand in hand and relaxed for the first time that day, had begun their walk home. The earlier storm had long since moved away and the setting sun was casting long shadows across the fields to their left. The local roads were deserted and the couple walked slowly, chatting about the day's events. Somewhere ahead a tractor started up, shattering the tranquillity of the evening.

After a couple of hundred yards, they faced the choice of following the road round to the right or heading straight ahead across the village cricket pitch. Martin chose the quicker route and ushered Beth towards the cricket pavilion some fifty yards in front of them. In normal circumstances it would have been a sound option because the grass, though still damp from the earlier downpour, was short and Beth's flat shoes made for easy walking. But no sooner had they covered the first dozen yards than they heard the unexpected roar of a wildly-revving vehicle behind them. Martin spun round to see a large, red tractor mounting the grass and accelerating straight towards them. His rapid glance noted an indistinct, hunched figure inside the cab. Sensing extreme danger, he reacted instantly by starting to run as fast as he could and propelling Beth to the open field to the left, still clutching her hand. This manoeuvre gained them a precious lead before the tractor altered course to pursue them.

Not many seconds later and Martin, already breathing heavily, took another swift look back. It was immediately apparent the tractor was intent on running them down and would catch up with them in a very short while. As the only shelter on the whole cricket field was the pavilion and they had just swerved away from it, Martin pulled Beth back to the right and headed as fast as possible towards the wooden building and possible safety. He had long prided himself on his fitness and regularly played badminton and squash in the Cartmel School gym, but this sudden exertion at the end of a long, trying day was playing havoc with his fifty year-old constitution. Almost ready to drop, he was saved by Beth. Ten years younger and noticeably fitter, she urged him forward and actually half-hauled him the final few feet to the pavilion.

This square timber construction had a narrow, covered balcony on all four sides, reached by three wide steps. Beth and Martin had barely negotiated these steps when the tractor slammed at speed into the structure right behind them. The force of the collision knocked Martin to his knees. Beth managed to remain upright, her involuntary scream lost in the tractor's engine roar. Stunned by the speed and violence of the attack and totally defenceless, they were sure they were about to be crushed to death. Fortunately the tractor had been travelling too fast to mount the pavilion steps and the driver had to reverse in order to make a second attempt. Martin and Beth took the opportunity to drag themselves five or six yards to the corner of the pavilion and were about to get to the safety of cover when utter mayhem broke out all round them.

The whole pavilion seemed to rise up in the air in slow motion before settling down again. Simultaneously they heard the harsh, discordant sounds of screaming engine and smashing timber. Martin felt himself propelled forward to the edge of the balcony before he tumbled head over heels onto cool, damp grass. Pieces of plank rained down on him as he attempted, ineffectively, to protect his head and upper body. All the while he could hear the wailing shriek of tractor engine as if the now-rampant vehicle was doing its best to demolish the whole of the pavilion. By rights, he should have leapt to his feet and fled the area but he'd taken a heavy blow to his head and could barely move. Anyway, his priority was to find Beth, from whom he'd become detached but, when he took a swift look round, she was nowhere to be seen. With desperately fumbling fingers, he reached in his jacket pocket for his phone and managed to push the button he used most often.

Back in the public bar of The King's Arms, Adam was downing his fourth pint of the evening. Having spoken only in monosyllables for a week or more and stonewalling Jack all evening, he now looked him squarely in the eye and, right out of the blue, asked, "Do you believe there really is a place called heaven? I ask because I need to know."

Jack brightened immediately. "You're speaking again. I was beginning to think....but that doesn't matter now." He leaned forward, delighted with this unforeseen progress. "Yes, I strongly believe in heaven. But it's true to say I believe in hell, too."

Adam frowned and some of his new-found assurance appeared to desert him. "I was afraid you might say that."

Jack was at a loss to understand the abrupt change of mood but was still pleased to have the opportunity to speak on a subject close to his heart. He was about to expand on his beliefs when his phone rang out piercingly, earning dirty looks from other drinkers in the bar. Impatiently snapping the phone open and raising it to his ear, he listened intently, turning white all the while. He then yelled out, "Hang on, we're on our way!" so powerfully that one of the drinkers at a nearby table dropped her glass in shock. Then, leaping to his feet and beckoning Adam to follow, Jack bounded towards the bar, from which position he caught Byron's eye in the adjoining saloon. He shouted lustily, "There's a madman on the cricket pitch trying to kill Martin. And Beth has gone missing. They need our help *now!*"

Within seconds, four men, a woman and a wildly-excited dog poured out of The King's Arms onto Market Square, leaving behind a group of bewildered customers and staff.

# 21

NICKY WAS ALONE. IT was mid morning and she was curled up on the leather sofa in the living room in Orchard Park with her iPod turned up high. It was how she liked to listen to her music.

She had an all-embracing musical appreciation, predominantly pop, but right now she'd chosen her 'Mellow' collection. This happened to be a classical selection because she was in the mood for calming, comforting sounds. Not that Mozart's 41st Symphony is especially soothing. Nicknamed the Jupiter, three of the four movements set a lively tempo. But she recalled hearing the claim, at a very impressionable age, that the symphony contains some of the greatest music ever written and Nicky loved it as much as her favourite contemporary songs. Usually she'd be on her feet waving her arms about conducting the performance but she'd a couple of matters on her mind vying for her attention.

Making herself comfortable, she ceased her humming and finger tapping and concentrated on these concerns. Initially she'd been relying on Simon to give advice on the first of them, but he'd made it abundantly clear he wasn't the least bit interested. Anyway she'd just helped bury him so he could no longer help her, ever, and she'd had to make up her own mind. This she'd done, and she actually reckoned it had been good for her to do so. She even believed she'd found a solution that matched her current needs. Content with her decision, she impulsively reached for her phone and typed in a message she'd been formulating overnight. Quickly checking the text, she stifled a grin, hit the send button and the message disappeared into the ether. She shrugged. It was to a young male acquaintance and it was too late to recall it now even if she wanted to which, she realised somewhat ruefully, she didn't.

Shostakovich replaced Mozart and the Andante movement from the Second Piano Concerto emptied her mind for six and a half relaxing minutes. Then, as Brahms' First Symphony filled the room, she turned her thoughts to the second, more urgent concern. Only the previous day she'd endured enough stress to unhinge her a dozen times over. If it hadn't been painful enough to bury her much-loved Simon, she'd learned later in the day she'd nearly lost her stepfather and Beth as well. Some unknown person, it appeared, had tried extremely hard to murder them both. It emerged that while she'd been quietly trolling through Richard Gere's old films and watching a DVD of 'Pretty Woman,' Martin and Beth had been out for a meal at Aynstoke Manor. Nicky was a great fan of Gere's and the DVD had seemed an appropriate way to round off her distressing day. And it might well have been had she been able to finish the film. Instead the lounge had suddenly filled with seven people, four family members plus Byron, Johnny and Tyler. It was immediately clear there'd been some sort of dire emergency and it had taken her the best part of an hour to get to the bottom of what had happened.

Nicky reviewed all she'd gleaned. Martin and Beth had taken a short cut across the Cartmel cricket pitch on their way home from Aynstoke Manor. A rampaging tractor had followed them and done its best to run them down. They'd sought the shelter of the cricket pavilion but the tractor had attacked and all but destroyed the wooden structure. Martin had been thrown clear onto the grass but Beth had been buried inside the building under piles of timber. By the time Jack and the others arrived on the scene, summoned by Martin's urgent call, the tractor driver had fled. As the young men frantically sifted through what remained of the pavillion, they discovered an abandoned, wildly-revving tractor crazily angled against a large stainless steel sink unit. Only a yard away they uncovered Beth, who'd been cowering under a pile of rubble in what remained of the ladies' toilet. Miraculously she was unharmed but Martin had suffered a nasty cut to his temple and Tyler had been called on to minister to his needs.

The whole episode raised a number of crucial questions for Nicky. Had someone attempted to kill *both* Martin and Beth? If so, who on earth could it be and what was the motive? Was it a random attack or had it anything to do with Simon's funeral? These and other queries would, of course, be tackled by the police but, unfortunately, by the time they'd arrived at the cricket field it was dark. Although they'd used their torches to scour the surrounding area, it was swiftly apparent that no meaningful enquiry could take place till the following morning.

Twelve hours later and Nicky was still thoroughly bewildered by the whole affair. She ventured to make sense of the totally unexpected attack on her loved ones but it was all too apparent she'd been desperately close to losing two more of her family. This was extremely frightening territory for her and she'd never felt so helpless. But, in this very turbulent period, it came to her how glad she was she'd sent her recent text. As if to underline the point, her phone rang out and she swiftly read the new message. It was good news. She'd arranged a special date with her male acquaintance, which actually made her smile, a remarkable achievement in the circumstances. But it did much more: it utterly changed her mood and gave her a quiver of sexual excitement, never felt before, which she felt right down to her toes. Checking her watch, she worked out she had only an hour to get ready. She intended to make use of every second. Her date, Ben Nicholson, might well be a lady-killer by reputation but she simply didn't care. She'd heard all the gossip about him but had dismissed it. Some friends and acquaintances had made scornful comments but she'd chosen to ignore them. Speak as you find was her motto. Besides, politeness was a quality she much admired and Ben had always been pleasant and respectful to her and, when all was said and done, that was what mattered. Added to that he was good-looking and she really fancied him.

She met Ben outside Mill House. He was already waiting for her, having changed out of his McAdams' work-gear into clean, fashionable clothing, making him even more attractive in her eyes. She'd had a rush to get ready but the admiring looks he gave her more than compensated for her efforts. Determined not to waste a second of their time together, she took charge of the situation. Guiding him round the back of the house, she retrieved the key from its hiding place and steered him into the library. But this time she had no intention of heading towards her secret room. Instead she used the Yale key Lee Bennett had shown her and unlocked the door into the main house before ushering Ben upstairs to the back bedroom, the very room her mother had used to entertain her lover. Here her instincts and her excitement took over. Aware of exactly what she wanted to do, she began ripping Ben's clothes off, and her own, before pulling him onto the bed.

A few minutes passed before another figure, swathed in voluminous outdoor gear, entered the library using a different key, one that had been recently cut on a market stall in Ulverston. This person ignored the Yale key and headed towards the back of the room. The large, dark knot was found and pushed to reveal the passageway beyond the sliding door. Once the earthen steps had been climbed to the secret room, the figure quickly opened the panel to expose the two-way mirror and the bedroom beyond.

The individual then became an absorbed voyeur, studying the passionate lovemaking in the bedroom.

Half an hour later and seething with barely-suppressed emotion, the figure finally moved, seizing an inconspicuous lever on the side of the two-way mirror and carefully prising it open. Sounds could immediately be heard from within the bedroom, but the individual was all too aware the slightest noise could carry the other way so remained motionless, listening attentively to the couples' animated love-talk.

Minutes later, as the lovers prepared to leave, they agreed the time of their next date, information carefully noted by the figure, who had already made a crucial decision. When the couple met again, they would pay a very high price indeed for their lovemaking. How dare they enjoy themselves so shamelessly! The individual fully intended they should both be harshly punished.

# 22

BYRON'S MORNING HAD NOT gone to plan. First Tyler had decided to cut short her visit and return to Manchester and then he'd been sidetracked by three important telephone calls, two from his agent and one from his Manchester United manager.

Even in the close season, the back pages of daily newspapers are full of football transfer rumours and for a few days Byron's name, not for the first time, had been linked with a move to Spain: 'Barcelona and Real Madrid move for Fullard' and 'Real offer United £12m. for Byron Fullard' were just two of the headlines. Only the previous morning, as he'd been getting ready for Simon's funeral, his dad had called him to the phone. He'd dashed down two flights of stairs to discover the caller was from the Daily Mirror attempting to get an angle on the current rumours. Barely concealing his impatience, Byron had given his stock answer: "Sorry, no comment."

He'd checked out the latest tittle-tattle on the internet and had shaken his head in disbelief. How did the papers get hold of these whispers? He wasn't sure but he certainly knew why they printed such rubbish. More than likely someone in Spain had dropped his name to the football writers who forever hang round the giant clubs searching for scoops. Their aim, of course, is to raise fans' curiosity, sell more newspapers and, perhaps, try to unsettle players like Byron. But if they were intent on getting him to contemplate a move to Spain they were wasting their time. A few Manchester United players, like David Beckham and Cristiano Ronaldo, had transferred to Real Madrid but Byron wasn't interested. Definitely not.

When United had signed him at the end of his university course, it was nothing short of a dream come true. After all, which youngster wouldn't be enthralled by playing for one of the greatest teams in the world? And over the last five years he'd worked very hard to establish himself as a first team regular, despite a few serious injuries, so much so he'd come to regard himself as a United player through and through. Real Madrid and Barcelona might also be first-rate teams and the Spanish League a very challenging environment but Byron was perfectly content to stay in England for the rest of his career, especially if it meant he could carry on playing for United. And that looked to be on the cards following his chat with the United boss, who'd assured him the club had no plans to sell him and were, in fact, about to begin negotiating a new four-year contract. That would take Byron to the age of thirty, still a prime age for a proven goalscorer.

His agent had felt the need to point out the advantages of going to Spain, the most obvious being the huge signing on fee, but the acquisition of money had never been high on Byron's list of ambitions. United already looked after him very well indeed, so much so he'd been heard to comment more than once about the obscene sums of money Premier League players are paid. And it came to something, he reckoned, when his earnings were on a par with the Prime Minister's. Anyway, his needs were modest enough. The Manchester flat and his BMW car were his main expenses and they barely dented his wages, the bulk of which were carefully invested by United's financial advisers. If he never played again he could, if need be, live off the interest from his investments for the rest of his life.

The phone rang out again but it was his mobile so he relaxed. It was Johnny. He was on his own in the office at McAdams and was eager to talk: "Martin and Beth are round at our house chatting to dad about last night," he confided. "Dad is keen to hear their accounts while they're still fresh in the mind and I'm sure he'll take them round to the cricket field so they can run through everything that happened there. I'm expecting Martin back here this afternoon, if he still feels up to it after that clout on his head. He has an appointment with one of our main suppliers at two o' clock. Jack's in charge again and turned up for work as usual but Nicky's having the day off. Ben Nicholson, that lad I was telling you about, was here earlier but he's breezed off somewhere, which is a bit of a surprise because he's usually a reliable worker."

Byron let his pal prattle on. Johnny would soon move on to what he really wanted to say. Sure enough, he rattled off a few more comments before asking, "How about meeting me for lunch in The King's Arms? There's a lot going on I need to talk to you about." No sooner had Byron agreed than Johnny was raising another question: "Was there anything controversial about Edward IV's life? I mean, did he have any questionable relationships during his reign? I have an important reason for asking."

Byron was certain he had but he couldn't for the life of him think what it might be. He said, "I can think of at least two contentious issues relating to Edward's reign. The first is to do with his birth, so I don't know whether that counts, but I'll tell you anyway and you can judge for yourself. Edward was born at Rouen, Normandy, in April, 1442. Richard, Duke of York, his father, had been away fighting nine months previously so it's been suggested that a lowly archer fathered Edward. But as his mother, Cecily Neville, was a most haughty lady, I think it most unlikely she'd allow a low-bred archer to bed her. Anyway, Richard recognised Edward as his son so there's no question of his rightful claim to the throne. The second matter concerns Edward's queen. He wedded Elizabeth Woodville secretly and most historians agree it was a glaring error of judgement. Elizabeth was desirable but very manipulative and the marriage created lasting hostility, especially with Edward's brother, the Duke of Gloucester, who later became Richard III." He ended lamely, "Don't know if that helps any."

Johnny considered briefly. "Could well do. How about I see you in the pub at midday and we can discuss it. I'm still really worried about Nicky."

"Nothing new there, then," thought Byron, as he went to help Tyler with her packing. Controversy and relationships and Nicky seemed to go hand in glove. Byron sighed. His best mate was clearly still hung-up on Nicky and it could well cause huge problems.

By the time he arrived at The King's Arms, Byron was more than ready for a drink. He'd driven Tyler to the nearby station at Cark, unsure when he'd see her again. Then, in the cause of keeping fit, he'd run at least five miles round the local lanes on one of the hottest days of the year. When Johnny joined him, they found a quiet corner and Byron could contain his curiosity no longer: "What's all this about questionable relationships, then?"

Johnny took a long swig of beer before replying: "I'm having trouble getting Nicky and some of her new acquaintances out of my mind. She used to be so straightforward. Not long ago I could read her like a book and our relationship felt really comfortable. Then she dropped me and I feel I don't know her at all. She's hard work, to put it mildly. It's made me wonder whether your King Edward ever met anyone like Nicky, or whether the world's great expert on relationships can explain to me why she's suddenly ditched me and started dating a bloke like Ben Nicholson."

Byron grinned and prodded his friend in the ribs. "I'll choose to ignore your sarcasm for the moment!" he said. "As for Edward, I doubt very much whether any lady ever kicked *him* into touch. Not only was he a king with a great deal of power, which the ladies find a real turn-on, or so I've been told, but he had both looks and charm. Not unlike you in that respect."

"Who's being sarcastic now?"

"Not me, I promise you. Edward was also renowned for getting on with people and treating everyone equally. You do that, too, but you're not the first bloke to get dumped so why don't you just accept it and get on with your life?"

Johnny picked up his beer then plonked it down again, all at once looking thoroughly miserable. "Because I love Nicky. And because I can't just abandon her. She needs her friends now and she needs me. *You* told me that."

"I did, didn't I."

"So does that mean I can still count on your support?"

Byron deliberated but not for long. "Our manager at United is extremely fond of two phrases: 'I'll get back to you on that one' and 'we'll keep the matter under constant review.' Maybe the second one is about right for Nicky at the moment, don't you think? You can't understand her and I'm certainly not finding her easy to work out either, though I'm doing my best to see what makes her tick. But, to give you a straight answer to your question, of course you can always count on me. Just one condition: no more bets, Johnny. You've had six pints of beer out of me and you're not getting any more!"

Johnny suddenly looked a whole lot happier and actually smiled. "I don't know what you're talking about," he said, "but I'll be grateful for your help because I don't seem to be getting anywhere on my own. I mean, did you see Nicky when we all got back to Orchard Park last night? She was so pale I thought she was going to faint, but she wouldn't even look in my direction. In fact, she did her best to shun me completely."

Byron nodded sympathetically. "I think you might be exaggerating. I gave her a mug of tea but she was shaking so much I was afraid she was going to spill it. And did you notice Jack and Adam were really upset, too?"

"You couldn't help noticing. But what did you make of Martin and Beth's account?"

"That their would-be murderer is a madman. Definitely. Who in their right mind would try to run over a lovely couple like them? He needs locking up really quickly before he does any more harm."

"But that's the point," Johnny stressed. "Martin didn't get a clear view of the tractor driver so we don't know for sure it *was* a man. It could have been a woman or even someone younger. After all, driving a tractor these days is kids' stuff. And here's another point. Whoever drove the tractor knew the key was always left in the cab, or else found it by luck."

Byron looked aghast. "Are you telling me the key was left inside the tractor?"

"Afraid so, probably because there's no regular driver. From what I heard this morning, members of the cricket club take it in turns to cut the grass or roll the pitch so they're in the habit of leaving the key where it can be easily found. But this is Cartmel, Byron, not Manchester. People trust each other round here. I bet most of the villagers still leave their front doors unlocked, until they go to bed, at any rate."

Byron shook his head incredulously. "I'm sure you're right but it's simply asking for trouble with a lunatic about. Do you have you any ideas what the nut-case was thinking of?"

"Beats me. I think my dad's got his work cut out getting to the bottom of this one."

Johnny was right. Ed didn't yet know what to make of the tractor attack. He'd asked himself the same questions as Johnny and Byron, plus others besides, but he was still a long way from enlightenment. He'd pored over Martin's and Beth's statements, and the Crime Team had scrutinised the scene of the attack and the tractor but no clear-cut clues had come to light. Police officers had carried out house-to-house enquiries but, while a number of villagers had heard the tractor, nobody had admitted seeing the driver. A thorough search of the tractor might well provide leads but it would be a slow process. The vehicle's interior was filthy and it would take days of dedicated work to sift through all the debris the searchers had found. The Crime Team had also found numerous sets of fingerprints both inside and outside the cab but, again, it would take time to eliminate all the legitimate users. And if the driver they were looking for had worn gloves, it might well prove a fruitless task.

Ed had been to the cricket field and studied the terrain, the tractor and what remained of the pavilion. A number of matters were crystal clear. First, all the evidence he'd observed strongly supported the statements he'd taken from Martin and Beth. Secondly, the tractor's massive impact on the pavilion steps was extremely worrying. Had Martin and Beth been in the way of the vehicle, they would have died instantly. It was as simple as that. Thirdly and most significantly, the driver had escaped and was still at large. This person continued to pose a real threat to Martin and Beth and, perhaps, to others. Ed had warned them both to be extra vigilant, especially as neither of them could come up with any reason for the attack or with any ideas concerning the identity of the driver.

But, when all was said and done, Ed was not too disappointed with the preliminary stages of the enquiry. It was still early days and he was a patient, tenacious detective who would never dream of abandoning a case until he he'd investigated it fully and achieved a satisfactory outcome. But one thought kept flashing into his mind and he couldn't subdue it. Was there a dangerous maniac loose in Cartmel and would that person strike again? It was an imponderable that didn't bear thinking about.

# 23

NICKY FELT PERFECTLY CALM. It was a real shock in the circumstances. After all, it wasn't long since she'd buried her beloved Simon, witnessed her mother making erotic love and come extremely close to losing her step-father and his partner.

The triple trauma of death, adultery and attempted murder could so easily have triggered an instant nervous breakdown and unhinged her completely. Instead Nicky was convinced the decision to go to bed with Ben Nicholson had saved her sanity. She'd dated him on a whim, made love to him with abandon and couldn't wait to repeat the experience. But it hadn't been all plain sailing and she had a number of regrets, especially where Johnny was concerned. This was because he'd always been her very good friend. Unfortunately their relationship had never quite hit the heights for her and this, she readily accepted, was mostly her fault. When he'd attempted to initiate a more physical rapport, it had momentarily upset her and she'd slapped him down and told him brusquely she wasn't ready for that sort of thing. He'd accepted the admonition but how was he to realise she'd changed her mind? How was he to know she wanted to break away from someone good and wholesome like him and have a naughty spell and go wild? After all, recent experiences had taught her that life can be so fragile she must cram everything in while she still had the chance.

Yes, Nicky had plenty of regrets and had been hiding her feelings of guilt by blatantly ignoring Johnny. What was really sad was the more she snubbed him, the more he seemed to come back for more. It was a vicious circle she needed to break because she really valued his friendship and didn't want to lose it. What had done much to destabilise her was observing her mother's lovemaking in Mill House, and the attempted murder of Martin and Beth had further upset her. But these were nothing compared to Simon's suicide which had totally devastated her. Simon had been her perfect soul mate so how could she ever recover from losing him? While she needed Johnny's friendship and relished the thought of more bedroom romps with Ben, nothing could ever compensate for losing Spud. Others, especially members of her family, had tried to help fill the awful void left by Simon's death. Adam, for example, had been exceptionally caring and sensitive but it wasn't the same and never could be. Nicky sighed deeply. Life was very cruel but she wasn't going to get far by feeling sorry for herself. An excellent way to take her mind off these matters would be to take Casper for a ride and then pamper herself with a long soak in the bath. It would have the added bonus of allowing her to anticipate her forthcoming assignation with Ben.

A few hours later, Nicky lay with Ben in the bedroom at Mill House. On the first occasion their lovemaking had been fast and frantic. This time it was tantalizingly slow, allowing her time to gaze round the room. Her mother's lover was an interior decorator but he'd not yet got round to working on this wing of the house. If the master bedroom was anything to go by, it was due for a painstaking makeover that would cost Ray a small fortune. The silly man had more money than sense! Nicky spared a moment to stare up at the mirror above the wash basin, behind which was her secret room, and allowed herself to relax and smile. She felt completely secure, and why not? The only other person alive who knew about her secret room was thousands of miles away in South Africa. Closing her eyes, she pulled Ben closer and allowed his tender lovemaking to carry her away to far distant places.

Only yards away inside the secret room a figure stood absolutely still in front of the two-way mirror, observing her every move and listening intently to each sigh and grunt. This individual had a two-pronged plan to implement. Judging the moment to be perfect for the first, more straightforward part, the figure swung into action and reached for a large camera that had been handily placed on the adjacent desk. This was a Nikon D300, a digital SLR, outdated now but still a photographer's dream and capable of taking superb photographs. Attached to the camera body was a long, quite heavy 70-200 millimetre Nikkor lens with a silent wave motor. Altogether this was an excellent piece of equipment, ideal for taking distant shots and equally good at zooming in for close-ups. The individual handled it lovingly before turning the camera on and carefully checking it was set to 'Programmed-auto.' This was to make absolutely certain the flash wouldn't fire, just in case any light was spotted in the room beyond.

The figure then raised the camera and held it steadily so the front of the lens was less than an inch from the two-way mirror. Painstakingly rotating the focusing ring, the individual brought the pair of lovers into sharp view before making a final, minor adjustment. Delighted with the composition of the shot, the figure pressed the shutter-release button smoothly down to record the photograph. There was a barely discernible click as the shutter opened and shut. The sound was certainly nothing to be concerned about and the individual repeated the process twice more before reviewing the three photographs taken in the monitor at the back of the camera. Pleased with the results, the figure packed up the equipment and prepared to leave the secret room. The first part of the assignment had been successfully accomplished. The second, more demanding task remained and the individual silently withdrew, intent on more success.

Half an hour later, Ben left Mill House on his own and walked back towards Cartmel with a swagger. He'd just been to bed for the second time with his boss' gorgeous daughter and life felt great. He'd had his eye on Nicky for a long time, never believing for a moment he'd get inside *her* knickers. After all, she was a very classy lass and way out of his league. He'd never dreamt someone as impressive as Nicky would give him a second look. Especially when she was dating that Hampson bloke who, Ben had to admit, was not only fairly loaded but a hunk as well. But he was to learn that women have minds of their own and are prepared to change them. And how! Almost overnight, Nicky had gone from barely being aware of him to smiling in his direction and actually chatting him up. It was a revelation to Ben, who'd always been the one to make the first move. He had to admit, though, it was a novel experience being pursued by a very sexy lady and he couldn't help enjoying himself, particularly when he received Nicky's saucy texts.

There was one problem. Nicky had warned him to keep quiet about their meetings. "Say nothing," she'd told him, explaining she didn't want all and sundry knowing her business. "I mean it, Ben," she'd insisted on their second trip to Mill House. *"Say nothing!"* But that wasn't Ben's way. He knew he should keep his mouth shut but he'd already blabbed to a couple of his mates simply because he couldn't keep his exciting news to himself. One of these so-called pals had immediately told his girlfriend, Daisy Leigh, who was well-known locally as a loud-mouthed gossip. Ben couldn't help wincing. He was under no illusions that if Daisy Leigh knew he'd slept with Nicky then all of Cartmel and beyond would very soon know. Very soon. It took a lot of the gloss off his elation and made him sweat. Nicky had some very powerful male supporters and he didn't want to upset any of them. Martin Reed, for example, was not only Nicky's dad but Ben's employer. Ben definitely didn't want to start looking for another job, especially as he enjoyed his work and had virtually no qualifications or skills to boast about. Her brother, Jack, almost as forceful, was already being groomed as the next boss. Jack might well be a practising Christian but he had a nasty temper. Ben had only witnessed it once but it was more than enough to scare him. One of his co-workers had grossly exaggerated the number of hours he'd worked and had then been stupid enough to insist he was telling the truth. In just sixty seconds of near-berserk action, Jack had felled then fired the brainless idiot. Adam, the other brother, didn't give the impression of being someone Ben should be cautious of, but looks can be deceiving. He'd been labouring at McAdams long enough to have developed a good set of muscles and he carried himself with quiet confidence. Then there was Hampson, Nicky's boyfriend, or should it be *former* boyfriend. How many times had Johnny won the All Weights World Wrestling Championship? He was huge and powerful and had legendary speed. He was incredibly quick. The bigger the opponents, the faster they fell. Ben had seen him in action a couple of times at county shows and he positively did *not* fancy the idea of standing up to Johnny and ending up as mincemeat. And finally there was Byron Fullard. Ben shuddered. Everyone really liked and admired Byron but men, even the big 'toughies,' were very wary of him. Ben couldn't put his finger on it but there was just something about Byron that shrieked BEWARE! With those ice-blue eyes that could look right through you, he was the very last of all of Nicky's champions that Ben would care to cross.

Damn Daisy Leigh anyway! Why couldn't she keep her gob shut? Ben promised to give her a piece of his mind when he met up with her. Doing his best to shake off all pessimistic ideas, he turned his thoughts back once more to Nicky. His love for her was certainly pure. Pure lust! He laughed out loud, all thoughts of Daisy Leigh forgotten. Nicky had turned out to be wonderfully wild and so eager to please. He began to fantasize about her in various stages of nudity and what he intended to do with her next time he got her into bed. Hearing a vehicle approaching, he turned casually to watch as it turned the bend behind him, instinctively stepping nearer the grass verge. He saw a plain white van bearing down on him at no great speed and noted the indistinct, muffled figure behind the wheel. As the van was about to draw level with Ben, it suddenly swerved and caught him totally unawares with its bull bar. He was swept up and lifted clear of the road before being flung with force into a four-foot high dry-stone wall at the side of the carriageway. The white van barely slowed and continued its journey towards the centre of Cartmel.

The human body is able to withstand dreadful injuries and medical books are full of accounts of human beings surviving the most horrific wounds. Ben wasn't killed outright, even though his body was mangled and disfigured beyond recognition. He actually survived for over two minutes after the impact, still with a huge erection, before he drowned in his own blood.

# 24

E D WAS VERY WORRIED. The DI read through Ben Nicholson's fatal
accident report once again, dropped it onto his desk and gazed into
space.

Just when he thought matters couldn't get any worse, they got a whole
lot worse. What was going on in his home village? First a near-deadly
attack on a couple who happened to be his friends and neighbours, and
now a traffic fatality involving a local man in his mid-twenties who'd
been left for dead on the roadside less than half a mile from the centre
of Cartmel. Ed shook his head in disbelief. He'd not long returned from
visiting Ben's family and updating them on the enquiry. It had been a most
unnerving experience and not just because he knew the family well. Both
parents, a pair of grandparents and an older sister with a snivelling toddler
had been present and had asked a series of awkward questions, only a few
of which Ed had been able to answer.

He took a swallow of coffee and thought hard about hit-and-run
accidents in general and Ben's death in particular. On the face of it, the
fatality was merely another statistic, one of many similar incidents Ed had
encountered during his career. But it was always going to be a lot more
complicated when the incident took place in your own village and no
witnesses rushed forward with relevant information, like the identity of
the driver or the offending vehicle's registration number. And what might,
perhaps, cloud the issue even more was that Ed had heard the whispers
about Ben sleeping with Nicky. The DI didn't care for such gossip but
neither could he ignore it. He'd called in to see Nicky, who was doing
her best to recover from yet more emotional shock. She'd confirmed the
rumours, albeit reluctantly, and given full details of her whereabouts at the

time of the accident. But what on earth was his son, Johnny, going to make of this development?

Ed pondered Ben's death and whether it had been accidental or deliberate but it was impossible at this stage to come to a definitive answer. He'd visited the scene of the incident with the dedicated accident team and studied the whole area. There were no tell-tale marks on the road or verges so it wasn't clear whether a cold-blooded killer had deliberately mown Ben down or if a careless driver had momentarily lost control of a vehicle and had then panicked and driven off. Ed hoped it was the latter but feared it was the former. Either way, the driver was in very serious trouble. At this point, Ed's biggest fear was that there was a clever and devious villain on the loose in the locality, one who was intent on a programme of mayhem. But he knew the importance of staying focused and patient. Experience reminded him it was vital the police follow best practice procedures and to remember that the smallest scrap of knowledge can lead to an arrest. To this end, his team were again conducting house-to-house enquiries and visiting south Cumbrian garages to check on damaged vehicles.

Ed's trusted sidekick, Detective Sergeant Steve Riley, was currently concentrating on the tractor attack and had been interviewing possible suspects. One of these was Gaz Morris, who'd recently returned to Cartmel to live with his mother. He'd been heard promising revenge on Martin for sacking him from his job at McAdams. But Morris had an alibi for the attack on the cricket field. He claimed he'd spent the whole evening watching television at home and his mother had backed up this statement. Steve had commented that Gaz's mother was very obviously frightened of her son, which must cast some doubt on the alibi. He'd also investigated Rob Bailey and his girlfriend, Kim. This was on the instigation of Johnny, who'd passed on Byron's comments that there was something odd about the couple who'd attended Simon's burial. Steve had discovered the pair working in a hotel in Grange-over-Sands. They, too, had an alibi. They claimed they'd been together the whole of the evening in question in their rented flat in the seaside resort. Steve had also mentioned, in passing, that Kim Holden was the most stunning-looking girl he'd ever seen. Ed couldn't help grinning. Only a week before, Steve's wife had given birth to twin girls. He was so totally besotted with his wife and daughters that if he thought Kim Holden was stunning then she must be very special indeed.

Ed reluctantly put his coffee aside. He had a mountain of paperwork demanding his attention and several outstanding cases in Barrow, though it was the two incidents in Cartmel that preoccupied him. A further thought caused his heart to thump erratically. Only minutes ago he'd been concerned he might have a cunning villain loose on his patch. But what if there were two evildoers in his home village, either working as a pair or independently? Common sense, of course, dictated that was most unlikely. And it was *extremely* unlikely, wasn't it?

# 25

NEWS OF THE TWO serious incidents had not filtered through to the tourists and Cartmel businesses were open as usual. Groups of shoppers drifted from one establishment to the next, committed to finding bargains, while drinkers sat outside the pubs and teashops in Market Square, basking in glorious sunshine.

Nicky had returned to work, ready to confront the world and to face Johnny. She'd thought her life couldn't get any worse but she'd been wrong. Details of her love tryst with Ben had spread all over the village. It was most embarrassing. She needed her friends as never before and she needed Johnny. She'd half expected her ex to cold shoulder her and it would have served her right had he done so, but Johnny had hugged her warmly, promised his continued support and told her how sorry he was to hear of Ben's death. It had made her squirm and realise how badly she'd treated him.

A couple of coffees later, they were back on good terms. But, after the initial hug, Johnny kept his distance and Nicky realised that, although they might be good friends again, there was going to be no easy return to the close relationship they'd once enjoyed. She could live with that, just so long as Johnny bore her no ill feelings. Yet his hug had been so warm and....but it was best she didn't go down that track at the moment, realising with a flash of self-awareness she sometimes didn't understand herself at all.

Not far away, the individual with the Nikon D300 digital camera was deciding which of the three photographs taken inside the secret room was going to be printed. A careful choice, one which displayed Nicky and her lover in a very compromising position, was made and the compact flash memory card removed from the camera. The card was placed in the relevant slot of a cheap, brand new inkjet printer and the required photo selected. The individual then methodically checked the settings before pressing the print button. The machine whirred into life, clutched the single sheet of A4 photographic paper from the tray beneath and began the printing process. Seconds later the finished print was spewed out and critically inspected. It had never been anticipated that Nicky would be caught in flagrante delicto, but it had happened and couldn't possibly be ignored. Now, satisfied with the final result, the individual switched off and unplugged the printer before inserting the photo into a large brown envelope, selected for its self-sealing properties.

Throughout the whole printing operation, meticulous care had been exercised as it was vital no link could ever be made between the photograph and the photographer. Strict precautions had been taken. Thin medical gloves had been worn throughout. The memory card would first be formatted and then buried where it would never be found. The printer, also, would be discreetly disposed of, making it virtually impossible to trace the print back to its source.

Later that day in the Hampson's large kitchen, Byron enjoyed an unexpected dinner. The meal had, in fact, been prepared for Ed but he'd phoned Johnny to say he wouldn't be home till late so Byron had volunteered to take his place. "Can't waste excellent steak like this," he said, with his mouth full. "Your dad's loss is my gain."

"He's missing too many meals lately," grumbled Johnny, adding unnecessarily, "It's because he's got so much on his plate at the moment."

"Who'd be a cop? Not me. Professional football is no bed of roses but I'd hate your dad's job."

"Don't think I'd fancy it either," agreed Johnny, "but it's not all bad news. Dad says he's never bored and the pay's not bad. And you get to retire pretty early on a decent pension."

"Even so, it'd not be my cup of tea. I know you meet people from all different backgrounds but I guess the bulk of your time is spent with petty criminals. How awful to keep on seeing what a mess they make of their lives. It would really get me down. And it must be difficult setting a good example and making sure you always keep within the laws. Just imagine, Johnny, having to keep below thirty miles an hour on your Kawasaki in built-up areas and never drinking more than a couple of pints of beer an evening. It wouldn't suit you."

"Probably not, when you put it like that, but it's not just cops who feel obliged to set a good example. You're a great role model for youngsters to follow. And what about someone like Jack?"

"I take my hat off to Jack," Byron said, with obvious admiration. "At least he tries to practise what he preaches, most of the time anyway. To tell you the truth, I'm sometimes a bit envious of people like him, people who have real faith and attempt to live decent, unselfish lives. After all, it can't be easy being a Christian these days."

"You never cease to amaze me, Byron! I happen to know lots of people are very envious of you but I'd never have guessed *you* were envious of anyone."

"I like to surprise people now and again, even my friends. And what about you, Johnny? Do you admire Jack and Christians like him?"

But Johnny seemed not to hear and reached for the bottle of red wine. "You've been right all along," he almost whispered, and filled his glass to the brim.

Byron was bemused by the sudden change of subject. "What are you talking about?"

"Nicky. You're right about her. It came to me this morning when she was being so nice to me. There *is* something on her mind, something else motivating her, something other than Simon's death. I feel it strongly but I've no idea what it is."

"So I've been right all along. Well, I won't crow about it. Don't forget, though, you told me Nicky was nice to you for a while not so long ago. It didn't last, though, did it?"

"You do cheer a fellow up."

Byron grinned. "Never mind that. What else do *you* think might be on her mind?"

Johnny took a long slurp of wine. "I've absolutely no idea. But you heard the rumours about her and Ben, which she didn't even attempt to deny. That's a Nicky I don't recognise at all. And do you know what I couldn't help noticing this morning? I might be wrong but she didn't seem terribly upset Ben had been killed, only that we all knew she'd been to bed with him. I thought it might make her a bit self-conscious, maybe ashamed, but she just seemed angry Ben had blabbed about it." He finished his wine, shook his head sadly and said, "This is *not* the Nicky I know and love. Definitely not. I'm worried about her, By, and I need your help."

Johnny's uneasiness was shared in the Reed household, so much so that Martin had insisted the family sit down together for a chat. He'd already discussed matters with Beth and had a number of concerns he was keen to raise with Nicky and Adam. There'd only be the four of them because Jack was spending the evening with a group of his Christian friends.

Martin spoke up as soon as they were seated in the lounge: "Before I forget, your mother phoned this morning. She'll be at Mill House for a few days to oversee the improvements there. She insists on seeing both of you."

Nicky and Adam exchanged agitated glances. Martin couldn't help feeling sympathy for them, especially after Jane's performance in the Priory. He said, "Don't worry, Nicky. I've not said anything to her about the rumours concerning you and Ben. I'll leave it to you to come clean, but I suggest you do it sooner rather than later before your mother hears them from someone else. But, one way or the other, she's *not* likely to be amused."

Nicky suppressed a shudder but managed a quick nod before she lowered her head. Martin turned his attention to Adam. "As for you, my boy, it's high time you resumed your normal routines. You've been hibernating in your flat long enough. Beth has pointed out all your friends have stopped calling here to see you, and who can blame them? You've virtually ignored them. My advice to you is to get your life back on track before it's too late."

"I suppose that's a fair point," Adam replied, somewhat grudgingly. "There's another Doctor Who convention coming up soon in Newcastle. I might ask one of my mates to go with me. But tell me, dad," he said, smiling disarmingly, "did your parents get on your back and dole out lots of advice when you were my age?"

Martin looked suddenly ill at ease and waved the question away. He said, more than a little frostily, "If you hadn't already noticed, Beth and I are really worried about the pair of you. We're…" He was clearly intent on saying more when the phone rang. He shook his head impatiently and took the call from his armchair. After listening intently for a few seconds, he suddenly shouted, "We'll be round right away," which made the others sit up and stare wide-eyed. Leaping to his feet, he yelled hoarsely, "That was the police. Our factory's on fire. The offices are ablaze!"

# 26

A S JANE DROVE TO Mill House, the last subject on her mind was its refurbishment. Her thoughts, not unlike Martin's, were on her two youngest children. Where she differed from her ex-husband was in the conclusions she'd reached.

Jane strongly believed her children were too pampered for their own good. As far as she was concerned, the molly-coddling had started immediately after her divorce from Martin and affected all areas of their lives. For example, she considered how easily all three of them had secured positions in the family business. None of them had had to face the stress of applying for jobs on the open market, and she knew none of them would ever be sacked from McAdams, however badly they might perform. It was a similar story with their home. They lived in an expensive house on an exclusive estate and were provided with all of life's luxuries. Adam, it was true, had moved to his own flat but, from all accounts, hadn't foregone any of his comforts. Jane hadn't visited the apartment but, apparently, he had a full Sky television package so he could watch all the sport he was interested in, plus a large high definition TV to watch it on. She wouldn't mind wagering his dad picked up the bills.

In her opinion, Martin cosseted and over-indulged the three of them. He'd bought Nicky a horse and almost certainly paid for its upkeep. Adam had been given a Harley Davidson, which was definitely not a cheap toy, and dad probably paid the bike's insurance and running costs. Jane couldn't recall what extravagances Jack enjoyed but she wouldn't mind betting he took full advantage of his father's generosity. None of this munificence had occurred when Jane had held the reins. She didn't approve of spoon-feeding children, especially her own. Her parents had never spoilt her and it had clearly done her no harm. So why should she pander to her own children's whims? She simply wouldn't have tolerated it.

Jane remembered the arguments with Martin: "What's the point of being well off if you can't give your kids all the extras we never had?" he'd regularly complained. She'd stuck to her guns but no sooner had she left the marital home than he was showering them with gifts like there was no tomorrow. No wonder they'd all wanted to stay with Martin rather than move in with her. He'd bought their affection. She couldn't help feeling bitter. Even Adam had chosen to stay with his father. And after everything she'd done for him.

She was not in a happy mood when she reached Mill House. There had been more rows with Ray and she'd encountered heavy traffic and endless stretches of road works on the long drive from London, all of which had given her a thumping headache. As she unpacked the car, she was really looking forward to a relaxing, stress-free evening. Opening the front door, she discovered a pile of post which she carried through to the kitchen, but it would have to wait until she'd made herself a cup of tea and taken some aspirin.

Later, in a somewhat better frame of mind, Jane turned her attention to the mail. The third item she came to was a large, manila envelope without name, address or any other writing. Opening it anyway, she extracted the contents: a single sheet of A4 picture paper. One look at the photograph and she instantly forgot her headache. She stared at the print for a full minute, her eyes wide and her nose wrinkling with distaste. It was a coloured photo of her naked daughter making love, captured in an advanced stage of orgasmic rapture. Jane made herself look at the print some more. It was a close-up so she was unable to come to any conclusions about where it had been taken. She also failed to recognise the bed and was completely unaware it was the very same bedroom where she, too, had experienced sexual bliss. But who had sent this photograph and what was she to do with it? And, just as important, what was she to say to Nicky? Jane didn't think for long. It wasn't her way. She made her decisions impulsively, always had, so why change the habit of a lifetime? She'd lock the photo in her private safe where no-one could ever set eyes on it. As for her daughter, she'd say nothing, absolutely nothing. It was all determined in an instant, which was how she lived her life.

So Nicky had a lover, Jane mused later. It surely had to be her boyfriend, Johnny, who plainly had more about him than Jane had ever guessed. The photo genuinely surprised her because she'd always assumed her daughter was somewhat prudish. Obviously not. But while she would never openly approve of Nicky's wild, uninhibited pose, she had to admit to a certain amount of admiration. Could it possibly be her daughter was more like her than she'd previously given her credit for? Perhaps, but that definitely would be a shock.

What Jane didn't realise was she'd made some important miscalculations. She'd never understood cameras, let alone those with telephoto zooms but, had she studied the print more closely before she locked it away, she might just conceivably have recognised her own bed. She might also have observed the tell-tale reflection in one corner of the photo, showing it must have been taken through glass. That, surely, would have set alarm bells ringing. Yet another misjudgement was to discard the manila envelope without inspecting it. Had she done so, she'd have detected it hadn't been folded and pushed through her letter box, which meant someone must have left it inside her front door.

And what did all this signify? It showed that not only Nicky but another unknown person had access to Mill House whenever they wished. Jane, renowned for having a volatile temper, would undoubtedly have erupted like a volcano had she known.

# 27

MARTIN HAD MANAGED TO grab only a few hours' sleep following the inferno at McAdams. Although extremely tired, the business was his pride and joy and he was determined to get it running smoothly again.

The fire had spread rapidly through the office section of the factory. Fortunately one of the locals had spotted the flames from half a mile away and summoned the fire brigade. Two fire engines from nearby Grange had answered the emergency call and quickly got the blaze under control, but not before serious damage had been done to the whole of the reception area. The general office where Nicky and Johnny worked was extensively damaged, while Martin's private office was now a smouldering ruin, not only destroyed by the flames but by the large quantities of water used to quell the blaze. Fortunately the inferno had not fanned out to the surrounding workshops which contained thousands of pounds' worth of equipment needed in the construction of driveways and conservatories. Martin dreaded to think how appalling it might have been had the tongues of flame spread further. As it was, he was just about able to survey the devastation with a wry shrug. It was bad, very bad, but it could have been a whole lot worse.

He'd spent nearly every daylight hour on his phone. The insurance company had been contacted and an assessor had already visited the site to make a preliminary report. All being well, brand new buildings would be erected in situ, but it would inevitably be a lengthy process taking months rather than weeks. Next he'd concentrated on hiring a group of temporary buildings to form a new reception area which, hopefully, would be delivered and erected at the side of the car park in the next forty eight hours. These, once they were complete with new telephone lines and other necessary paraphernalia, should allow the business to continue trading as before. Jack, meanwhile, was running McAdams from the Reeds' home in Orchard Park, helped greatly that backup copies of all important files had been stored safely away from the fire.

Ed joined Martin at the factory and contemplated the ruins. He followed Martin's gaze and shook his head gloomily, finding it hard to take in the destruction he observed. "And here was me hoping for a mug of McAdams' coffee to perk me up," he said, in an attempt to lighten the mood.

"Afraid not," Martin responded. "I could do with a jug of it myself, believe me. Trying to sort this lot out is a nightmare. I've had to cajole, bribe, threaten, beg, and all before breakfast! But I'm positive that not even a few sticks of dynamite would stir our telephone company. I've met a few lousy customer services departments in my time but theirs is the absolute pits. Without phones this business is in serious trouble but they don't seem to give a damn. I'll try them again later but I'm not optimistic. Jack's having to run the business from Orchard Park on one measly line. There's no way we can maintain McAdams like that." He put his hands in his pockets despondently but managed to rouse himself. Turning to face Ed, he added wearily, "But you didn't come all this way to listen to our tale of woe. Have you any good news to cheer me up?"

"Afraid not," Ed said, echoing Martin, "but that's not unusual in cases like this. It's still very early days."

"In cases like this? Do you mean to say you've come across other situations where people like me are nearly murdered and then get their properties set ablaze?"

"It might surprise you to learn that cases like this are not unique," Ed admitted. "Have you spoken to the Fire Officer yet?"

"No. He was rooting about the ruins of my office this morning but I didn't care to interrupt him. Has he spoken to you?"

"Briefly. He phoned me with a preliminary report. It's not good, Martin. There's strong evidence a fire accelerant was used but you probably expected news like that. The Fire Officer thinks it was petrol but we'll know for sure when the boffins complete their investigations. I was hoping to be able to identify the arsonist when we checked your CCTV surveillance camera. As you know, we removed the disk from the camera at the front of the factory for study. Fortunately it was undamaged but when we reviewed the film it showed nothing remotely suspicious. That would suggest the fire-raiser approached the factory across the field at the rear of the building and, presumably, returned the same way. This villain's either very lucky or exceedingly cunning. And, as the factory was empty at the time of the attack, it's going to be difficult to find a witness."

Martin did not look a happy man. "Par for the course, if you ask me," he said bitterly. "Looks like this villain's got it in for me. What about the incident at the cricket pitch? Any developments there?"

"Despite extensive enquiries and widespread coverage of the attack in the Evening Mail, we're still unable to identify the driver. We have received a couple of anonymous calls. One was malicious and the other a hoax call, both a complete waste of time. Fingerprinting of all those known to have driven the tractor is ongoing so it remains to be seen whether we'll be left with any unknown prints. I might add we've drawn a similar blank with the investigation into young Nicholson's death."

Martin's shoulders sagged dejectedly. "It's all doom and gloom. I must say I'm really glad we live in a gated community," he said. "Some of the locals have scoffed at our security and think it's way over the top for a village such as ours but I'm actually thinking of increasing it. With a lunatic on the loose, you can't be too careful, can you? One of the first phone calls I made this morning was to a security firm we use. The way I feel now I'll certainly implement all their recommendations. For a start, I'm seriously considering installing at least two more CCTV cameras to cover the house. After what we've suffered, I couldn't cope with our home being targeted."

Ed nodded. "You must do what you consider best but you will recall I did warn you to take extra care till we catch the person, or persons, responsible."

In the Fullard home, Byron was keen to spend some quality time with his parents. He actually felt guilty he'd been using the house like a hotel, not that his mum and dad would ever complain. They were simply happy he'd chosen to spend the summer with them.

They were in the kitchen, which was a large room like the Hampson's but appeared bigger because the units, worktops and walls were light-coloured. Everywhere was spick and span, the result of good teamwork. There were attractive views of conifers and heathers through the open French windows at the far end of the room with brief glimpses beyond of the twelve-foot wall that surrounded Orchard Park. Dennis had brought some of the garden into the house. He was potting some plants next to the sink unit and managing to drop small quantities of peat onto the tiled floor. Jilly was keeping a close eye on his antics, managing to smile indulgently at the same time. Almost absent-mindedly she swept forward and scooped a handful of peat back into the container her husband was using.

Byron found it difficult to believe that in three years' time his parents would be collecting their old age pensions. But the question he asked was addressed to his mum: "Your comment this morning as I was leaving for my run was a bit enigmatic. What was that all about, then?"

Jilly attempted to put her thoughts in order: "Your dad and I can't help worrying about all that's happening next door. The Reeds are a lovely family but so much seems to be going wrong for them. We can't understand it."

When Dennis merely nodded in agreement, Byron asked, "It is very tense over there but is there anything in particular that worries you?"

Jilly shook her head. "It's the totality of it all that's so disturbing. We were just starting to come to terms with Simon's death when we discovered Nicky didn't want to go out with Johnny any more. Then someone tried to run over Martin and Beth with a tractor. Someone actually *did* run over Nicky's new boyfriend, if we're to believe the rumours. Finally we learn McAdams was nearly burnt down. What on earth is going on?"

Byron couldn't help going across and giving her a hug. "It's a real tale of woe, isn't it? I'm upset, too, but it's knowing how to help that's the hard part."

Jilly seized on that: "I knew you'd understand. To me, the main problem is Simon's death. How can you ever get over that? You can't, of course!" Her long fingers played nervously with her wedding ring. "But it's the youngsters I'm worried about. We've known Jack, Nicky, the twins and Johnny all their lives. We've watched them growing up with you, Byron. How could we *not* be anxious about them? I feel somewhat differently about Martin because he's quite a bit older. He appeared out of nowhere to marry Jane and take over McAdams but, from all accounts, he'll be retiring one of these days and handing over to Jack. I certainly don't want any harm befalling him, or Beth, but it's the younger ones I'm really concerned about," she stressed.

"We don't believe a word of these awful rumours about Nicky and Ben Nicholson," said Dennis, spilling more peat on the floor and vainly hoping his wife wouldn't notice. "We know Nicky's not that kind of girl."

Byron briefly considered confirming those particular rumours were true but decided it would serve no useful purpose. Instead he said, "Johnny's still in love with Nicky and he's determined to support her through all this trouble."

Jilly smiled: "That's so like Johnny. I have such a soft spot for your best friend but the poor boy looks lost at the moment. He needs your support, Byron."

"Don't I know it. I've a few ideas on that score."

When he offered no further explanation, his mum said, "My thoughts keep going back to Simon's death. I know Martin still has no idea why the lad took his life because he told me so. I must confess I don't understand either. What could possibly make someone like Simon commit suicide when he had so much going for him? I just don't get it. I know there was a girl involved but he should have been able to cope, surely. And as for him not liking Salford, so what? Nobody was asking him to stay there forever. I can't make any sense of it."

Dennis turned the tap on noisily and gave one of his pot plants a good soaking. "I heard he was very taken with the Welsh lass," he said. "If it's true she played fast and loose with him then that's the kind of thing can affect any normal, hot-blooded male."

"It can," Byron agreed, "but I really can't imagine Spud having much trouble with girls. But what else was so awful with Salford and his life there? He loved the place when he first went there so what changed so drastically? It had to be something absolutely massive, whatever it was."

"The really sad part is we'll probably never know," said Jilly. "The Reeds should be allowed to mourn Simon in peace but it's impossible when all these other dreadful things keep happening. It might be easier to make sense of it all if we lived in a city but this is Cartmel, for goodness sake! Where will it end?"

Byron was pondering the same thought hours later. Having a quiet moment, he sought to take stock of everything that was affecting his friends and neighbours. He considered long and hard but came to no definite conclusions, other than there were a couple of people, both women, he wanted to have a chat with on Johnny's behalf. Before he abandoned his thinking, it came to him he would continue doing everything possible to assist his friends. But at the back of his mind he was aware that by doing so he might well be placing himself in very real danger.

# 28

B ETH STRODE OUT OF the main entrance of Cartmel School and spotted Byron. "It's good to see you," she said, smiling broadly. "Your phone call has made me very curious."

Byron walked forward to meet her and grinned back. "I wanted to have a word with you, if you don't mind. It's about Nicky. Johnny and I are worried about her."

Beth suddenly appeared flustered as she linked arms with Byron and guided him away from the school grounds. "I'm not often escorted home from work, especially by handsome, young men," she said, "and it saves Martin making a special journey to collect me. He's become incredibly paranoid about security these last few days."

"I can't say I blame him."

She squeezed his arm. "And we're concerned about Nicky, too. Losing Simon was such a devastating blow so please don't underestimate how traumatic it's been. She and Spud were *so* close. I guess she might have gone off the rails a bit recently and I have to admit I was shocked to learn she was dating the Nicholson lad because he's definitely not the sort of fellow Martin and I had in mind for her. I suppose it wasn't so surprising in the circumstances and might even have done her some good, but please don't tell Johnny I said so. In fact, I actually believe she's been coping well since the funeral. But what's your take on how she is?"

Byron felt it was time to be totally honest: "What bothers me is how much and how quickly Nicky has changed."

Beth stopped mid-stride and looked up anxiously at Byron. "You make it sound serious. Don't you think she's managing well, all things considered?"

"I agree she's coping with the mourning, from what I've observed," said Byron, trying to sound reassuring, "but I'm certain there's something else troubling her, something other than Spud's death." He explained what he'd previously spelled out to Johnny, stressing how odd it was that Nicky had chosen to finish with Johnny and particularly the strange timing of her decision. "And what makes it even more bizarre is how she then started dating Ben when she wouldn't even have *looked* at him a fortnight ago. It just goes to show how much she's changed and I don't know how to account for it," he ended lamely.

Beth was clearly nonplussed and stood stock-still. "You're starting to worry me. Does Johnny feel the same?" When Byron nodded emphatically, she added, "Your concern is very welcome, of course, and does both you and Johnny credit but what you say is a real shock to me and will be to Martin. I've not considered any other problems simply because I'm not aware of any. Simon's death has been so massive for all of us, but Nicky especially, that it's dwarfed everything and at the moment I can't see beyond it. But tell me, do you have any idea what else is troubling her? You'd better let me know if you do because she's suffered more than enough."

Byron shook his head as they continued their walk. "I honestly don't know. I've no idea and neither has Johnny. We're both hoping you have a handle on it."

Beth said, "I would tell you if I could, believe me, but I know of nothing else that might be affecting her, nothing at all. I'll discuss it with Martin, never fear, but I'm positive he's not aware of anything untoward either, otherwise he'd have said so. But you know Martin. At the moment all his thoughts and energies are spent getting McAdams up and running again. He's little time left for anyone else, me included." When Byron remained silent, she added, "I'm sorry I can't be of more help. I'd offer to approach Nicky directly but I don't think she'd take too kindly to it. You know how private she is."

"I don't but Johnny certainly does," Byron replied with a twinkle in his eye. "Never mind, we'll have to revert to Plan B, but I'm not optimistic that chatting to Jane will bring much progress."

"Rather you than me! But please tell me if you learn anything of significance. And let me know, also, if you have any views on our Adam. Martin and I have our concerns about him, too."

Had Nicky happened to listen in on this conversation she probably wouldn't have been too upset. She'd just arranged another date and there was the promise of some excitement in her life again. Josh Reynolds was another of her dad's employees but he had much more about him than

Ben. Josh was intelligent, came from a good family and was definitely fit. He was, perhaps, a bit on the shy side but Nicky was confident she could soon put that right. Most important, he wasn't a blabbermouth and could be relied on to be completely discreet. The only down side was they couldn't meet at Mill House for a few days because Jane was back in residence, personally supervising its refurbishment.

Forewarned by their father, Nicky and Adam had been summoned to a meeting with Jane at Mill House. It had not gone smoothly. Jane, as was her way, had attempted to lay down the law on certain matters, expecting both her children to toe her line. Normally they would have done so without question but on this occasion Nicky wasn't prepared to be dictated to. The one-sided conversation had gone agreeably enough until Jane tackled her daughter on the subject of propriety and boyfriends. Nicky remained silent during Jane's lecture but, when the word 'tart' was mentioned, she exploded. Adam watched in total astonishment as his half-sister confronted her mother for the first time in her life: "That's the second time you've used that word to describe me," Nicky shouted, "and I won't have it. I've not forgiven you for using it in the Priory and I won't accept it now." She paused for breath then spat out, "Isn't it a case of 'like mother, like…?' Oh, forget it, I can't be bothered!"

Jane, puce in the face, had been about to say something impulsively but had thought better of it. Instead she sought to reassert her authority after this totally unexpected confrontation, but her usually compliant daughter was in no mood to back down. Adam was amazed to observe mother and daughter standing eyeball to eyeball, something he personally would never dare even contemplate. Just for an instant he was afraid his mother was going to slap Nicky but, fortunately, she regained her composure and the moment passed. He was grateful soon after when Jane, complaining of a headache, retired to her bedroom and he and Nicky made their escape.

No sooner were they outside on the roadside than Nicky rounded on him: "Why don't you stand up for yourself?" she asked angrily. "Our mother made Simon's life an absolute misery. Show some backbone, Adam, for goodness sake, and don't let the same happen to you." They were so engrossed with each other they didn't notice the plain white van with the bull bar pass slowly by. Perhaps they should have been more observant because they might have recognised it was a McAdams vehicle and that the bull bar had an obvious dent to its nearside.

It wasn't the first time Jane had used a headache to escape from a tricky situation and it wouldn't be the last. She'd been extremely close to trying to knock her daughter's head off her shoulders, so it was as well she'd retreated to her bedroom. But she was far too angry to dwell on Nicky's behaviour. That would do later. Right now she needed a distraction. On a whim she used her phone to call Mark de Lacey, her interior designer and current lover, who was working downstairs on the new kitchen design.

An hour later they were naked in each other's arms in the small bedroom she'd earmarked for such occasions. Mark, she'd discovered, was an excellent lover. Not only was he sensitive to her needs but he was readily available when she needed him. In addition, he didn't sulk when she ignored his advances, unlike her present husband. Ray could sulk for England if he didn't get what he wanted, which was causing problems in their relationship because he wasn't getting his way very often at present. It served him right for being so critical and argumentative! But saying 'no' on a regular basis had brought Ray to heel as Jane had known it would, and each time she relented and took him to her bed again, he'd been so pathetically grateful he'd promised her everything she wanted. Just so long as he kept writing the cheques, especially for the refurbishment of Mill House.

Languorously, Jane rolled off Mark and lay beside him, shuddering with delight at his inventive lovemaking. She knelt above him, raising her left arm in the air, encouraging him to kiss her neck and caress her breasts. She was consequently able to gaze in the mirror over the washbasin and study her own reflection. The view greatly excited her.

In the secret room behind the mirror, the individual with the Nikon D300 SLR camera was determined to take advantage of the situation. Visiting the room only on a whim, the individual held the camera steadily and fired off three rapid shots. Taken at a wider angle than the one used to capture Nicky's photos, these shots included Jane *and* her lover. The individual had yet to formulate plans for these latest pictures but that was the beauty of the situation. They were an available option until a suitable use could be found for them.

An hour or so later found Jane thinking deeply. She had a lot on her mind, not least her daughter's recent outburst. She was therefore not best pleased when the doorbell rang and rudely interrupted her train of thought. Opening the front door of Mill House, she was more than a little surprised to discover her visitor was Byron.

"I wasn't expecting to see you," Jane said acidly. "What can I do for you?"

"Good afternoon, Jane," Byron said, inclining his head with punctilious politeness. "May I have a word with you. It's important."

Jane frowned but took only a moment to make up her mind: "You'd better come in, then." She led the way through a narrow hallway to the drawing room on the far side of the house. This was a large, square room with beams low enough to make Byron duck his head. It was dimly-lit, most of the light coming from two small windows and strategically-placed lamps either side of the huge fireplace. The period furniture looked expensive but uncomfortable, which was borne out when Byron was invited to sit in one of the antique armchairs.

Jane sat on an upright chair next to a valuable Georgian oak desk. Unusually for her, she was wearing trousers which were dark in colour and complemented her pale blue blouse and dark blue scarf. Crossing her legs, she regarded her visitor gravely for a few seconds before asking, somewhat irritably, "And what can I do for the famous Manchester United footballer?" She leaned forward, checked her wrist-watch ostentatiously and waited expectantly.

Byron hesitated. He'd not worked out in advance what he wanted to say, having learnt from experience it was best to try to judge Jane's mood first, though that was easier said than done. He decided not to jump straight in. "You have a lovely place here. I'm impressed," he said, waving his arm to encompass the whole property and hoping the flattery would relax Jane into a more receptive frame of mind.

Nodding only briefly and failing to smile, Jane said, "It's an ongoing project. We're working through the whole house room by room, from front to back. I'm fortunate to employ an interior designer with an eye for properties such as Mill House, one who knows how to treat them with the reverence and care they deserve."

It crossed Byron's mind that Jane and her designer knew next to nothing about how to restore seventeenth century houses and even less about reverence but he merely said, "It's fascinating, isn't it? Just to think the original owners here were probably alive at the time of the Great Plague of 1665 and the Fire of London the following year."

Jane managed a mocking smile. "I know nothing of history," she confessed, "but one of the family mentioned in passing that you actually *enjoy* studying English history." She added dismissively, "I must say it's a very odd pastime for a professional footballer."

Byron grinned. "You're well informed, but it's no secret. Some seem to find it amusing that a bloke like me should be interested in history but it doesn't bother me in the slightest. As it happens, I've just started a riveting book on the Plantagenet kings."

Jane looked thoroughly bored. "I never bother with books," she said scornfully. "Horrible, dusty things! I own a whole library at the back of the house but it's all locked up because I can't be bothered with it. But I'm sure you didn't come all this way to talk to me about your strange obsessions," she said, frowning and checking her watch again.

Byron realised it was time to get to the point. With more hope than expectation, he plunged ahead with as much confidence as he could muster: "I'd like to talk to you about Nicky. I know she's missing Simon badly but have you noticed any significant difference in her behaviour recently?"

Jane frowned and sat back in her chair. "What on earth has my daughter's behaviour got to do with you?" she asked, in a suddenly frosty tone.

Byron thought it was a pretty fair question and wondered if he could possibly come up with an answer that might just satisfy Jane. He doubted it but he was determined to have a go anyway: "I'm convinced something has happened to Nicky recently, other than Simon's death, because she's changed such a lot. You really can't help but notice how different she's become. I'm worried about her and so is Johnny. "

Jane stared back, unsmiling, but didn't take long considering her response. "You're taking a lot on yourself," she answered coldly. "I'm not at all sure of your motive. In fact I have absolutely no idea what you're talking about and, even if I did, I certainly wouldn't share it with a *professional footballer*." She spat the final words as if football was an occupation worthy of deepest contempt. Her eyes couldn't help straying over Byron's left shoulder to the landscape painting of Tarn Hows on the wall near the fireplace. This particular oil painting, of one of the Lake District's most famous beauty spots, concealed the built-in safe where she'd placed the revealing photograph of her naked daughter. But, very angry with herself for her momentary loss of control, Jane immediately looked away from the painting and the safe behind it. A swift look at Byron was enough to convince her that her secret was secure. Reassured and fully determined the photo should remain safely where it was, she rose from her chair and announced disdainfully, "Well, it was kind of you to visit and share your anxieties with me, Byron. Unfortunately, I cannot help you in any way so if you'll please excuse me, I have other matters to attend to."

Seconds after his dismissal, Byron found himself outside Mill House with Johnny, who'd been impatiently waiting on his Kawasaki. Johnny gunned the engine into life. "Any joy?" he asked as the engine idled.

Byron jumped on the bike behind his best mate. As he adjusted his helmet, he yelled in Johnny's ear, "Beth shares our concern for Nicky. She knows nothing but will share anything she finds out. Jane showed no anxiety for Nicky. None whatsoever. But I'm convinced she knows something although there's no way she'll co-operate. We're going to have to manage without her."

Johnny's choice retort was lost in sudden engine shriek as he accelerated the Kawasaki back towards the centre of the village.

# 29

J ACK PUSHED HIS DINNER plate to one side and continued his surreptitious study of his siblings, knowing Beth was watching them, too. It was fascinating! He couldn't get over how two people had changed so much in so short a time. But perhaps it wasn't so surprising when he remembered how swiftly he'd transformed himself when he'd become a Christian.

First Jack concentrated on Adam who'd withdrawn right into himself. It was as if his half-brother suddenly possessed an all-enveloping, hard shell, which he'd erected round himself after his twin's death. If he was hoping to repel all invaders he was surely succeeding. Despite family and friends doing their best to draw him out, he was unwilling to resume the social life he'd led prior to Simon's suicide. In only one way, Jack concluded, was he true to his old life: he still took more days off than he worked. There was a single ray of hope his dad and Beth were encouraging for all their worth and it had to do with his obsession with Doctor Who. Adam had finally booked two nights at the forthcoming convention in Newcastle for himself and one of his friends. This same friend was pressing him to rejoin The King's Arms' darts team where he'd been the leading light and there were heartening signs he would eventually resume his place at the oche. Jack recalled it was Adam who'd told him that oche was pronounced 'ockey' and was the darts' throwing line. And it was Adam who'd actually taught him how to throw the darts, only to beat him out of sight in game after game.

If Adam had withdrawn into his shell then Nicky had certainly emerged from hers. In some ways she'd altered more radically than her younger brother. From being a quiet, dutiful daughter following straightforward, family pursuits, it was as if she'd turned overnight into a siren, suddenly aware of her good looks and, more significantly, how to exploit them. Jack was mesmerized by the metamorphosis. If recent rumours were true, and he didn't doubt they were, his sister who'd previously been perfectly content to spend her spare time with her horse or at the gym now craved the attention of men and got her excitement, not from keeping fit, but from regular sex. Honest and reliable Johnny had been well and truly ditched!

Unlike his stepfather and Beth, Jack had no long-term worries about his siblings. While in no way approving of the changes he was witnessing, he believed they were only temporary. And there was always the added knowledge he was praying for them both regularly. In the meantime, it was really enthralling to observe the pair of them. Prior to their evening meal, he'd come upon Adam mooching about in the garage with an oily cloth in his hand, muttering something about his Harley needing an oil change. As he was standing only yards from his practice dartboard, Jack had impulsively handed him a set of well-used darts. Adam had accepted the three darts and had then dispatched them with clinical precision, showing he'd lost none of his old skills.

Jack found it equally absorbing keeping an eye on his sister and was particularly amused by her futile attempts to organise clandestine dates in a small community like Cartmel. She should realise it was well-nigh impossible to keep assignations secret, especially when the lads involved worked under his direct supervision. He had to admit he'd been shocked when she'd dated Ben Nicholson because Ben had been a well-known loudmouth with a penchant for boasting about his conquests. The rumours about the pair of them had been quick to surface and were exceedingly graphic, to put it mildly. If Jack had been a girl he'd have blushed! Josh Reynolds was a much better option because he was a dependable young man who'd definitely be much more circumspect. But Nicky had turned one lad down at least. Gaz Morris had been given short shrift, by all accounts. Jack was delighted by this turn of events as Gaz was a thoroughly nasty piece of work. It was he who'd been heard more than once to threaten Martin, yet still had the audacity to apply for his old job at McAdams. It had given Jack little pleasure in turning him down.

Had Nicky been aware of the interest her love life was inspiring, it's unlikely it would have made a scrap of difference to how she went about organising her dates. As it was, she was so embroiled in her own affairs she was unaware she and her men-friends were under the spotlight. But Beth and Johnny had been absolutely correct in one important respect. Had they attempted to influence or moderate her behaviour in any way, they'd have been told to go where it was very hot. Now that she'd finally stood up to her mother, her confidence was sky-high so she'd tolerate no opposition to her plans from anyone.

And there was another reason for the spring in Nicky's step: her mother had returned to London, which meant Mill House was once more available for use. Her first two meetings with Josh had been at a hotel in nearby Grange. Though not exactly a seedy rendezvous, it had proved far from ideal so she couldn't wait to introduce Josh to the privacy of the bedroom in the Templeton property where she really could relax and let herself go. Josh had been timid the first time she'd taken him to bed but he'd soon taken to lovemaking like a dog to his biscuits, as she'd known he would. Their next meeting was due to be at Mill House that very evening. She could hardly wait.

Jack was not the only one to be intrigued by Nicky and her affairs. The individual who'd witnessed Nicky's lovemaking and photographed it from the secret room was already making arrangements to view the planned evening appointment with Josh. This person found it difficult to believe Nicky had not heeded the very direct warning she'd already been given. So be it, but let it be very clear: the next punishment would be no less severe than the first.

# 30

I T WAS SATURDAY EVENING and Byron and Johnny were in The King's Arms' saloon bar. Johnny was out-drinking his pal by four or five pints to one and, as usual, the beer seemed to have little effect other than to loosen his tongue. Like the beer, he was in full flow: "Am I glad I chickened out of tackling Nicky about her men friends. Her dad tried to give her some advice yesterday morning when we were working together at the Reeds' place. She gave him what for, I'm telling you, and poor old Martin went off with a flea in his ear. He won't try that line again in a hurry."

Byron grinned. "Seems like Nicky's got her dander up," he commented.

"You're not kidding. She's fired up all right, but where's it all come from? I've never seen her talk to her dad that way before and I felt really sorry for him. As if he doesn't have enough to worry about with the fire and everything. We all know he's really worried and that it's perfectly normal to tackle her about these boyfriends of hers, but she's not prepared to accept criticism, none at all. She's going to get herself a reputation if she's not careful, but definitely not the sort you'd want to boast about. And I'll tell you something else. She's not making much effort to keep her love-life private. Josh Reynolds phoned her twice yesterday and she openly flirted with him and then carried on as if nothing had happened."

"What's it like at work now?"

Johnny sat forward. "Fraught. Very fraught. Martin and Jack are both running round like headless chickens trying to keep the business going. Jack is constantly complaining he only has one telephone. There should be more lines next week but it's definitely hard graft at the moment. Both bosses are keeping their cool pretty well but that's likely to alter if our telephone company doesn't come up with the goods like it's promised. At least the security angle is better because it's only Beth who **has** to leave the Park at the moment. I can't say much about Adam because he rarely turns in for work these days. His attendance has gone from poor to diabolical. As for me having to sit down in the Reed's lounge with Nicky every day, it's a strain, that's for sure. But it isn't for Nicky. Whenever the labourers come in the house, she drops what's she's doing and blatantly chats them up. It's hard to fathom how much she's changed. Even my dad remarked what a tease she's become. He's been in and out regularly to chat to Martin and the rest of the workforce and he notices things like that."

"He's trained to. But how's the investigation going?" Byron asked.

Johnny shrugged. "You know dad tells me nothing. Clam-like doesn't begin to describe him, but I heard him tell Martin they'd got to the end of the tractor fingerprinting. Apparently there were no prints they couldn't account for which probably means the villain wore gloves. But it's just possible the driver was a regular and, if that's the case, I sincerely hope it's not someone we know well. That would be awful. Dad also told Martin his team have abandoned trying to discover some vital clue in all the gunge they found inside the tractor. It would have taken a team of scientists to sift through it all. Shame, really, because the villain involved might just have shed a single, all-revealing hair that could have provided a decent DNA sample. But the cops claim it'll be better to spend time on those jobs with more chance of success and I'm sure they're right."

"I've said it before," said Byron with feeling: "I'm glad I'm not a policeman,"

"Dad **will** get this villain. It might not be today or tomorrow but he will catch him or her, and I'll tell you why. Villains make blunders. However clever they are, or think they are, they eventually mess up. Martin was telling us someone came forward who actually spotted the arsonist disappearing into the wood at the back of the factory. Unfortunately they didn't get a decent look so couldn't give a description. They only saw a figure melting into the trees. Dad's sergeant, Steve Riley, searched through the woods hoping to find some evidence the arsonist might have left behind, like an empty petrol can, but he had no joy. This villain is certainly playing his luck and seems to be on some sort of mission but he or she **will** make a mistake. It's as inevitable as Christmas. Or me wanting another pint." Johnny raised his glass, swallowed the last of his beer and made his way to the bar.

Byron stretched his long legs and looked round the saloon. It was busy as you'd expect for a Saturday night but there were more than a few present he didn't recognise, most likely visitors, though they clearly knew him from the smiles and telling glances in his direction. One face stood out from the crowd. Rob Bailey's girlfriend, Kim Holden, was sitting at the far side of the bar. She was in conversation with a woman of similar age and still appeared strikingly attractive, even at a distance. Byron pointed her out when Johnny returned with the drinks.

Johnny had a good stare. "What's she doing here, I wonder, and without her boyfriend? She's absolutely gorgeous. It's a pity she's spoken for."

Byron nudged his friend in the ribs. "What about your loyalty to Nicky? A few pints and you're anybody's."

Johnny smiled. "You only think you know me well. I'm still carrying a torch for Nicky, even though she couldn't care less about me at the moment. But I'm fed up discussing my non-existent love-life. Let's talk about yours for a change. How about you and Tyler? When are you going to make an honest woman of her and get married?"

"Tyler has set the date of our wedding for August next year and that's all right with me because there'll be no major football tournaments then," said Byron, very matter-of-factly. "You'd better put it in your diary, Johnny, because I want you to be my best man."

Johnny's jaw dropped. He carefully put his tankard down. "Are you joking? No, I can see you're not. When was all this arranged? Why didn't you tell me before? Of course I'll be your best man. It'll be an honour and I won't let you down." He reached over the table and seized Byron's hand and crushed it in his own.

Byron winced, pulled his hand away and rubbed it ruefully. "I'm glad I'm not a goalkeeper. You could just have ruined my prospects. I called Tyler last night; we chatted, as you do, and it was decided. I'm glad you approve because I'm a very, very happy man. I might add that you're the first to know."

Johnny was stunned and could only watch dumbstruck as his best mate got up and made his way to the washroom.

When Byron emerged a couple of minutes later he found Rob Bailey's girlfriend blocking his path. Up close, Kim was even more attractive than he'd realised. Though very slender, she was certainly well-endowed in the right places. But it was her face that captured his attention. She had a wide, generous mouth and beautiful, violet eyes that regarded him quizzically. As he waited for her to move out of his way, she stood studying him for a few seconds before taking a step closer. Then, standing on her toes, she placed her right hand gently under his chin and kissed him firmly on the mouth. Reluctantly, it seemed, she pulled away with the beginning of a smile animating her face. Still facing him, she waited expectantly for him to respond.

# 31

JOSH REYNOLDS WAS PRONOUNCED dead at 3.15 p.m. and was initially identified by personal items in his wallet. The medics who attended the emergency call didn't bother to check the young man's pulse or heart. When a heavy vehicle runs over a man, then reverses and runs over him again, there's no need for such niceties. In such cases, death is instantaneous.

Ed and Steve Riley were on the scene within thirty minutes, Ed driving through from Barrow and picking Steve up en route in Ulverston. Ed talked briefly to the middle-aged lady who'd found the body but she was in a state of deep shock and could tell them little. Both officers had developed strong stomachs over their years of service but the less experienced detective sergeant took only the briefest look at the victim's mangled body before vomiting his lunch over the grass verge at the side of the road. Ed, who'd instantly recognised Josh Reynolds, went very pale. Swiftly turning his attention to the medics, he tried hard to concentrate on their answers to his questions. He learned nothing he didn't already know so he sought out his young colleague. "There was doubt in our minds about Ben Nicholson's 'accident,'" he said carefully, "but this is clear-cut. This is murder, Steve, pure and simple."

Steve, still busy wiping his mouth with a tissue, merely nodded. Discarding the tissue in the hedgerow, he turned back to Ed. "Both Nicholson and Reynolds worked at McAdams and were the lovers of Nicky Reed, if we're to believe the rumours. In which case, one of us ought to visit the young lady."

Ed said, "I'll go but I'll have to stop off at the Reynolds' home first. You see what you can find out here. There are two properties about two hundred yards past Mill House and others towards the village centre. See if anyone saw or heard anything."

Nicky enjoyed her brisk walk home after the visit to Mill House with Josh. All in all, it had been a much more therapeutic way to spend an afternoon than working on the business accounts and was a splendid antidote to the growing tensions at home. If it wasn't Martin lecturing her and issuing dire warnings, it was Johnny trying too hard to be nice to her. The trouble was that ever since the fire at McAdams, her home had become her workplace and there was no escape from all the stress, especially as Martin had become so security-conscious. She understood his concerns to a point but there was no way she could lead her life stuck indoors. For a start, there was Casper to attend to and then there were her meetings with Josh. She was happily recalling what an accomplished lover he was becoming when Jess, the Labrador, barked and bounded towards the front door. The visitor was Ed and one look at his stern face was enough to cause Nicky's well-being to plummet.

Ed made sure Martin joined his stepdaughter in the lounge. When all three were seated, he wasted no time: "I'm afraid I've more awful news to share with you so I'll get right to it. Josh Reynolds has been run over and killed less than a hundred yards from where Ben Nicholson met his death." He paused to study the two Reeds on the sofa to gauge their reactions. Martin lowered his head but not quickly enough to hide the sudden tears that sparkled in his eyes and slid down his cheeks. Nicky responded equally spontaneously. A demented gaze appeared on her face and she let out a high-pitched wail and collapsed onto Martin, who put his arm around her and did his best to comfort her.

Ed stayed silent till the pair recovered a modicum of composure. He proceeded gently: "Young Reynolds was killed at about three o'clock. A woman out walking saw the body on the road near Mill House and called the emergency services. I arrived at the scene at 3.45 and I've just spent an hour at the Reynolds' home. You should both know that Josh was deliberately run over by a vehicle which did not remain at the scene and whose driver did not telephone for help. We're treating the death as murder."

Martin continued to console Nicky, his head rocking from side to side as if this information on top of all the other bad news was too much to bear. In a voice quivering with emotion, he asked, "Does this mean you'll be treating Ben's death as murder as well?"

"There are certainly similarities with the two deaths," Ed replied. "They occurred within a hundred yards of each other, both drivers fled the scene and the victims were known to the two of you. But we're keeping our options open at the moment as we can still only conjecture whether Ben's death was a hit-and-run case or deliberate murder."

Nicky sat up and dried her eyes but succeeded only in smearing her mascara. The mad look in her eyes returned momentarily but she shuddered and it went away again. Looking towards the detective inspector, she muttered, "They were killed because of me, because they were my lovers. They were both run over after I'd been to bed with them. I've been taking them to Mill House, my mother's home, and using a room there."

This information was clearly news to Martin, who was distinctly angry and about to comment when Johnny poked his head round the kitchen door. "Sorry to interrupt," he said, "but Steve Riley is on the phone. He needs to talk to you, dad. He says it's urgent."

Ed left the lounge for five minutes but when he returned it was clear father and daughter were in the middle of a huge row. They both shut up as soon as he re-entered the room but it didn't take a mastermind to deduce that Martin was very unhappy Nicky had been taking her lovers to Mill House and that Nicky was far from pleased she'd had to admit it. Ed, too, was shocked by Nicky's behaviour. It seemed really out of keeping with the girl his son favoured, but it wasn't his place to comment so he made the decision to change the subject: "I left my sergeant at the murder scene. Acting on information received, his investigations led him to your factory site, Martin, where he discovered an abandoned van, one of the McAdams' fleet, it would appear. The bonnet of the van was still warm, showing it has been used this afternoon. It is damaged so we'll have forensics take it in for testing but we believe it may have been the vehicle used to run over Josh Reynolds."

Martin reacted instantly, swaying in his seat as he attempted to come to terms with this information. "One of our vehicles?" he gasped, turning white. "I don't know what to say."

Ed understood the emotion but it was facts he needed right now. "I take it you operate a strict policy of checking everyone who uses your company vehicles. I'd certainly like to study all the paperwork, particularly for the last two weeks. Perhaps you can also explain your procedures to me."

Martin put his head in his hands as if he was trying to hide from some dreadful demons that had started to attack him. He began to stand up but thought better of it. Turning an ashen face to Ed, he said listlessly, "It's my turn to give *you* some bad news. All our vehicle paperwork, every scrap, got burnt in the fire. I've been meaning to initiate a new scheme but I haven't got round to it yet. There's been so much to do, I just haven't had the time."

It was a body blow but Ed had known worse. "So how have your workers gone about borrowing company vehicles since the fire broke out?" he asked evenly.

Martin scratched his head and gathered his thoughts: "We currently have eight vehicles and they're usually parked in the yard next to the main car park. There's a wooden box in the main storeroom and we've been keeping the van keys in there, just as a very temporary measure, you understand. Each key has a label with the vehicle registration number written on it and when workers need a van they choose their key from this box. They're then supposed to return the keys to the storeroom. I asked Sam Barber, who's in charge of our storeroom, to keep an eye on the vans and their keys. Two days ago he told me that when he checked the vehicles, one or two still had their keys inside. This happened, apparently, on three days recently. Yesterday I asked Johnny to go down to the factory to find out exactly what's going on but I've not yet had time to talk to him."

Ed sighed. It was even worse than he feared. "Let me get this straight," he said, maintaining his calm. "Are you telling me that any of your workers can simply collect a key from your storeroom, drive a van away and that later they may, or may not, return the key to its rightful place?"

Martin couldn't help feeling guilty because, however you analysed it, the current set-up was an absolute shambles and he, as Managing Director, was responsible. "Yes," he conceded reluctantly, "that is the system at present."

Ed nodded grimly. It was time for the sixty-four dollar question: "With this in mind, can you be absolutely certain that only McAdams' workers have access to your vehicles?"

Martin considered the question only briefly. "No," he said grudgingly, "I'm sorry to say I can't claim that. As matters stand, I have to admit anyone can sneak into our yard and 'borrow' one of our vans."

"It would seem that way," agreed Ed. "Do you think, as a matter of priority, you can institute a foolproof system for your vehicles, with appropriate paperwork, of course?"

Martin merely mumbled his agreement. It meant more work, more time, but he'd fit it in somehow.

Ed moved on: "We'll need to examine all your vehicles first thing tomorrow," he stressed, "so please keep the keys secure until my team has finished its work. The checks shouldn't take long and it's not our aim to disrupt your business. There is one final point I should make at this time.

It's a vital one, Martin. You, your business and your workers, it would seem, are being targeted by one or more persons who are prepared to go to any lengths to achieve their aims. In light of this very real danger, you will very probably want to meet as soon as possible with all your staff and update them on the current situation. If you feel it would be helpful to have me or DS Riley at this briefing, you only need to ask."

Nicky didn't hear her father's response. She was being washed by wave after wave of conflicting emotions that pulled her all ways and filled her whole being. It struck her with depressing certainty her dad would be nagging her to forgo any more dates until the maniac responsible for the attacks was safely behind bars. This would clearly make a great deal of sense. And yet Nicky was far from sure she could obey such a request. There was a growing part of her that now craved excitement and sexual satisfaction and she didn't think she could deny it. More to the point, perhaps, and irresponsible or not, she realised she didn't **want** to deny it.

# 32

BYRON HAD RELUCTANTLY PUT aside his book on the Middle Ages and spent the evening at Johnny's playing catch up with all the news. There was plenty of it.

Johnny, lounging comfortably on the sofa in the lounge, was keen to be updated, too. Bursting with curiosity, he asked, "So did you tell Tyler you've been snogging Kim Holden in our favourite pub, then? I bet you didn't."

From the depths of one of the armchairs, Byron pretended to be very disappointed. "You mustn't judge other people by your own deplorably low standards. Of course I told her. Tyler and I have no secrets."

"Honestly?" Johnny asked, his tone hinting his doubt. "And how did she react?"

"She laughed it off, of course, because she knows I was entirely innocent. Entirely."

Johnny snorted in disbelief. "Entirely innocent? You came back with lipstick all over your mouth and a silly grin all over your face. Wait till I see Tyler. I'll put her right."

"Your problem," said Byron, "is that you're jealous. You can't bear it that the delectable Kim chose to kiss me and not you."

"You really do live in cloud cuckoo land, don't you!" said Johnny, shaking his head in disbelief. "But why should she bother with you when she's already got a boyfriend? Or when she could have a really handsome bloke like me, who's *not* spoken for?"

Byron laughed out loud. "Handsome?" he said, with as much assumed derision as he could muster. "What mirror are you looking in? Everyone knows I have good looks plus charisma and charm in bucketloads. The only thing you have in bucketloads is all the beer you swill. I mean, take a look at that gut on you. Is the word 'exercise' in your dictionary? I don't think so. I invited you to join me for a run later tonight and you turned me down **again**. Now, I'm a supremely fit individual who girls naturally fancy, but you're….well, look in that mirror."

Spluttering with indignation, Johnny declared, "I spend at least an hour every day on my weights. I could beat you into a rice pudding if I chose."

Still grinning, Byron reached across and prodded his mate in the midriff. "In your dreams! You live in a weird fantasy world, my friend."

Johnny shook his head vigorously but couldn't help smiling. "You'll be telling me next I'm imagining all the havoc I've just told you about and that the murders and arson are another figment of my imagination."

"Not quite," said Byron. "In fact I think it's all getting really serious. No wonder Martin is so obsessed with security. If Ben's death turns out to be a deliberate hit-and-run, as we suspect, it'll make it a double murder. Is your dad having sleepless nights?"

"Not yet, but I can tell he's worried. He's hoping for the crucial breakthrough but it's not happened yet."

"What I don't get is this psychopath's motive. I can just about understand someone having a go at Martin and the business, though I've absolutely no idea why, but what about the attacks on Nicky's lovers? How do they fit in?"

Johnny reached for an unopened can of beer. "Search me," he shrugged. "Who loves or lusts after Nicky enough to murder her boyfriends?"

"Maybe I'm looking right at him," replied Byron, with a straight face.

Johnny's mouth dropped open. "You're joking, at least I hope you are. We're talking here about a cold-blooded maniac who runs over people deliberately. And that attack on Martin and Beth was so calculated. Do you remember how frightened they were when we got round to the cricket pitch? This madman's incredibly dangerous, and we don't know the next target. It could be Nicky for all we know."

Byron tossed a chair cushion in Johnny's direction. "Don't get your knickers in a twist," he said smoothly. "But it occurred to me this psycho might well have a pop at us if we show too much interest. It could get really dangerous. Are you sure you're ready for that?"

Johnny opened his beer with well-practised ease and sighed loudly. "I don't have a choice, do I. Nicky's still got me well and truly hooked. I'm in to the bitter end."

Martin had spent the day chasing new staff. He was desperate for two new labourers to take over from Ben and Josh. Their deaths had left him with a gaping hole in his workforce at a time when the company's order books were overflowing. Luckily there were always young men in south Cumbria looking for labouring jobs, especially as no great skills were required in paving driveways, which provided the bulk of McAdams' work. Anyway, training was given on site and it wasn't as if the tasks were demanding. Martin thought it ironic he'd made such a big deal of Simon getting his A-Level qualifications and then a university degree, when the lad could have managed at McAdams perfectly well without. After all, Martin was the first to admit he hadn't done particularly well at school and had never been anywhere near a university, and it certainly hadn't held him back.

He'd had mixed fortunes with his staff recruitment. One promising youngster had been appointed but two others he'd interviewed had turned out to be worse than useless. He was eager for more trainees but he wasn't that desperate. At least he'd cleared the air with Adam after a discussion involving a good deal of ranting on both sides. His son, it seemed, had seen some sense at last and had promised to pull his weight and turn up for work regularly and punctually. His contribution would certainly be useful but not immediately as he was driving over to Newcastle with his pal for the two-day Doctor Who Convention.

It suddenly occurred to Martin he hadn't sorted out the new vehicle scheme as he'd promised. His heart sank. Would his workload never moderate? There was nothing for it but to tackle the job at once and get it sorted ready for the morning shift. As all the paperwork was at the factory, he'd have to leave Orchard Park for an hour or so. His spirits rose. He'd been cooped up in the house for too long and could do with some fresh air. The only downside was that Beth had taken the car to attend a parents' evening at her school so he'd have to walk. That decided, he gathered together what he needed for the task, left a note on the kitchen table for Beth and the others and left the house. The Park was filled with warm evening sunshine and birdsong; it was a few minutes after eight.

Ed had been in Barrow all day dealing with yet another murder. A young wife had taken a carving knife to her cheating husband before turning herself over to the police and signing a full confession. It was an open-and-shut domestic incident but had still demanded all his attention, and he'd silently fumed he wasn't dealing with the more urgent crimes back in Cartmel. By the time he'd completed all the paperwork, Ed was more than ready for a steaming mug of coffee and the chance to put his feet up for five minutes.

Johnny's perceptive comment had been spot on. Ed **was** worried. He and Steve had assessed all that had happened in Cartmel to check if they'd missed any vital clues or could come up with any fresh strategies. Nothing of significance had emerged from their appraisal so Ed had resolved to adopt a more proactive role. Steve would take over some of his bread and butter work in Barrow as well as maintaining his supporting role in Cartmel, leaving the DI more time to concentrate on the murders. Ed had also begged his supervising officer for more officers to add to his team and his boss had been sympathetic to this request. The next major task was to re-evaluate the security position. As it was quickly apparent the Reeds were at the epicentre of all the recent attacks, it made sense to make safety a central issue for them, their home and their business. With that in mind, Ed had sat down with Martin and Jack and discussed ways of making their properties more secure. And he hadn't forgotten the safety of the individuals involved. All the Reeds were to be issued with personal alarms. He'd even faxed a colleague at the Northumbria Police Headquarters in Newcastle to keep an eye out for Adam, who'd be at the Metro Radio Arena for the next two days on his Doctor Who quest.

But thinking of Adam reminded Ed of other twins. Steve's newborn daughters, Amy and Zoë, were doing well and growing apace. He smiled. He'd already made the effort to visit them twice, despite being up to his neck in demanding cases. He reckoned it was easy at a time like this to get so deeply involved with your work that you forgot what was really important. Ed enjoyed being a detective but, when all was said and done, it was only a job. His priority had to be his family which, in his case, meant his son. And Johnny was going through such a rough patch that Ed was mightily glad Byron was at home for the summer to provide some stability and support.

Martin checked his watch and was shocked to discover it was nearly midnight. Once again he'd got carried away with his tasks, but at least the revised vehicle paperwork was finished. When his staff clocked on in the morning, they'd not only have an updated system for signing out the firm's vans but they'd also have a brand new reception area to use. The temporary buildings had been erected to the side of the car park as planned and were finally fitted out and complete. It was all-systems go and Martin could afford to relax a little. There were, perhaps, a few advantages of running a large company from the comfort of your own home, but not many. He'd not be the only one to heave a huge sigh of relief that the business could now return to something approaching normality. But it was time to lock up, go home and get to bed.

Town and city dwellers, used to well-lit roads, would have found the lack of street lights in Cartmel totally disconcerting, to put it mildly. There is nothing as black as country black. Martin would normally have thought nothing of walking home in the dark but, as he set off back to Orchard Park, he recalled the tractor incident and instantly realised he should be acting with more caution. With hindsight, it would have been sensible to call a taxi or ask Jack to collect him. He shrugged. He'd be home in fifteen minutes and it was too late now to be arranging a car ride home. Putting his best foot forward, he set off purposefully, but he couldn't help pivoting round nervously to see if anyone was following him.

Martin was wise to be wary; he and Beth had already had one close call. He therefore listened carefully for the tell-tale sound of approaching footsteps and kept spinning round to make sure nobody could get near him without being spotted. Unfortunately, he'd badly misjudged matters and was checking entirely the wrong direction. The watcher, who'd been looking out for him for a number of days and who'd observed him leaving the factory was, in fact, a hundred yards in *front* of his quarry and already deciding on a suitable ambush point.

The rest of the short journey was not good for Martin's health. The nearer home he got, the more nervous he became and the quicker his heart pumped. It was ridiculous, he scolded himself, but it made little difference. The slightest noise had him wheeling round, convinced he was about to be attacked. Thinking he'd be safe when he entered the walled area of Orchard Park, he was swiftly disillusioned. The blackness was more intense here than anywhere on his brief walk. Admittedly there were lights on in his own home but they were over a hundred yards away and he was still in deep shadow. While extra security lights had been installed on the side of the house, he was unsure how they were triggered. Security experts had recently advised on other improvements but Martin had yet to study their recommendations. He certainly had some constructive ideas *right now*, beginning with a halogen lamp atop the giant tree he was fast approaching. But he was so engrossed in his thoughts he nearly missed the sudden noise behind him. Swinging round instinctively, he anxiously sought the source of the sound. For a couple of seconds his straining eyesight caught nothing, but then a vague shape zoomed into view. Thoroughly unnerved, Martin moved quickly off the roadway onto the grass and automatically raised his arms to ward off any potential assault. The fast-approaching shape swiftly materialized into a car which Martin recognised as his neighbour's Audi. The car slowed to a stop and a voice boomed out, "You're out late, Martin. I thought a busy businessman like you would be abed by this time of night."

Martin dropped his arms and clutched his chest, afraid it might explode. He managed to murmur, "Howard, it's you! You'll be the death of me. I thought you were about to attack me."

Howard Tyson, retired barrister, guffawed. "Not me, Martin. I've never been into that sort of thing. I've been out to dinner with some of my old solicitor friends." With a cheery wave, he continued his journey, travelling only five further yards before inadvertently triggering the newly-installed lamps, which suddenly flooded the whole area with dazzling light.

The watcher, who'd been preparing to strike, immediately ducked into the shadow of the giant tree less than ten yards away and silently cursed the Audi and its occupant. Martin, totally unaware an assailant was so near, had been extremely fortunate on this occasion. The Watcher was disappointed but justice wasn't cancelled; it was merely postponed.

# 33

E D SAT DOWN IN his dining room, now a makeshift office, with a mug of freshly-brewed coffee, a very large, fresh doughnut and his Daily Mail. It was nine in the morning and he couldn't wait to get stuck into his snack.

The doughnut, oozing strawberry jam, contained a disgusting number of calories but that didn't deter the detective inspector. He'd actually parked on a double yellow line in order to buy it which, he reckoned, made eating it a double sin. He couldn't help smiling but it brought to mind the double murder of Ben and Josh, which was never far from his mind. It quickly removed the smile from his face. Recent forensic testing of the McAdams' vehicles had thrown up a second van, the one with a damaged bull bar. While the belated analysis of the bull bar had revealed insufficient microscopic residue to stand up in a court of law, there was now enough evidence to re-grade Ben Nicholson's 'accident' as murder. Ed had long been convinced the collision between Ben and machine had been deliberate so the re-classification was no real help to the investigation. But, like Byron, he was struggling to find a motive for the recent spate of offences. He simply didn't get it. Why would anyone try to kill Martin and Beth, set fire to the McAdams' premises *and* murder Ben and Josh? He'd studied the available information from all sides but was short of positive ideas. He was obviously missing something significant and the extra calories he'd consumed weren't helping his brain come up with ideas. What had he overlooked?

He went over the whole series of events one more time, beginning with Simon's death. The lad had certainly chosen a wild, inhospitable place to crash his car. It was just the kind of desolate spot one *would* choose to commit suicide, Ed concluded. The crash had also tied in handily with Simon's visit to his girlfriend's house in Wales. In their subsequent report, the north Wales police had clearly stated there was no evidence anybody else had been involved in the tragedy. And Simon's letter to his father, which family members agreed was a simple suicide note, backed up this supposition. The Salford police had then found Simon's mobile at his digs. Could anything of significance be read into this discovery? On balance, Ed thought not. Simon had obviously made up his mind to take his own life because he'd written and posted his suicide note *before* he left Salford. And Nicky had made it clear he'd turned his mobile off and was making no effort to return her increasingly despairing calls. It would, therefore, have made good sense for him to leave the phone behind. Taken in its entirety, the suicide evidence seemed straightforward enough, though one point still bugged Ed. Why had Simon made a point of visiting Charlotte Owen's home if he was already committed to taking his own life? What on earth was the point of making such a fuss at the house if he'd already decided to drive his car over a nearby precipice? Maybe he'd made up his mind to give the Welsh lass one final chance. Other than that, the DI had no answers to these questions.

He turned to events nearer home and considered the tractor attack on Martin and Beth. It had come right out of the blue, but was the ambush intended to kill both of his neighbours or just one of them? And what about the arson attack on the McAdams' site? As the factory was empty at the time, the inferno was clearly aimed at destroying the business, suggesting, perhaps, that Martin, not Beth, was the prime target. But Ed realised he was dealing here with probabilities, not certainties. His overriding priority must be to establish the villain's real motives, though it was disappointingly evident he was still a long way from understanding the basic reasons behind these attacks.

It was the two murders that truly bothered Ed. Both had been carried out so cold-bloodedly that even the DI, after all his years of experience, was taken aback by the killer's total ferocity and ruthlessness. But he was convinced Nicky was right. She claimed Ben and Josh had been murdered because she'd been to bed with them. Her contention was entirely plausible because they'd both been killed immediately after she'd made love to them at Mill House. The killer, Ed decided, must have kept a close watch on the property and followed both victims. Yet despite extensive enquiries, not a single witness had come forward who had observed either the murderer or the vehicles involved.

Ed had taken extra precautions to protect the Reed family and their property although he was all too aware that anyone determined enough could circumvent the best safety measures. At least he was now able to keep a closer eye on the investigation from his base in Cartmel. Although it might well be a case of locking stable doors, he and Martin had arranged for more surveillance cameras to cover the Reed's home and business. Even a squirrel would find it difficult getting by these defences undetected. The DI had also done his best to spread the available police resources as widely as possible and had preached the importance of personal security to the Reed family. But he was still dependent on the individuals concerned doing their bit. His colleague in Newcastle had certainly played his part. He'd reported that Adam had attended every session of the Doctor Who Convention and had been observed to enjoy himself thoroughly. The DI wished every aspect of the case could be so simple because, all in all, the investigation was proving a baffling experience. It was even more vital, then, to carry on as conscientiously as possible and trust the vital breakthrough would come. But he remained confident it *would* happen and he licked the last vestige of strawberry jam from his fingers with relish.

Ed might not have managed it but Nicky reckoned she'd worked it out. She'd thought long and hard about the murders of Ben and Josh. Their killer, she decided, had to be a local and someone she knew well. The murderer, also, had to be someone who fancied her and someone who knew all her movements. She could think of only one person who fitted these requirements: Johnny! But surely that couldn't be. Not dear, dependable Johnny, her long-time friend and the son of the detective inspector who was in charge of bringing the murderer to justice. It couldn't be, could it? Yet on one level it made perfect sense. After all, it was obvious Johnny thought the world of her, even though she'd treated him abominably. Yes, it was evident he still cared because of the many thoughtful things he did on her behalf, not forgetting the way he gazed at her with those limpid blue eyes of his. And who knew her movements better than him? Didn't he live right next door and didn't the pair of them work together all day long? Oh, yes, she certainly had very compelling reasons for making him her number one suspect. He was just like one of those obsessive stalkers she'd read about so from now on she'd be watching him very closely. Fingering the personal alarm the police had given her, she was positive she had Johnny figured to rights so just let him make one false move!

It remained to be seen whether she *was* right about Johnny but she'd certainly been spot on about all the nagging. It had gone on virtually non-stop since Ben had been run down. Martin had been the main culprit. He hadn't stooped to her mother's level by calling her a 'tart,' but his reaction to her using Mill House for her assignations was much more telling. He told her she'd 'disappointed' him. This simple accusation made her feel so low she couldn't look him in the eye. Yet, when all was said and done, she couldn't regret going to bed with Ben and Josh because they'd helped maintain her sanity at a time when her whole world had exploded round her.

Nicky had listened to the advice Martin and the others had given so freely but that didn't mean she was prepared to follow it. She would forego using Mill House, at least for a while, but only because her mother, it seemed, was still totally unaware she'd taken her lovers there. Nicky had recently broken the habit of a lifetime by standing up to Jane but just to think about that now made her tremble like a sapling in a gale. It was definitely *not* something she wished to repeat because if Jane ever discovered the truth, that her daughter had taken lovers to her very own bed, she'd be absolutely incandescent. No, now was the time to avoid further confrontation. But that didn't mean she intended to abandon her sex romps. On the contrary, she was determined to take another lover. After all, it was what she wanted and what she reckoned she needed. And she'd already cast her eye on a likely lad, her dad's latest employee, who'd only been working at McAdams for a couple of days.

Now the police had ordered the release of the two bodies, the funerals for Ben and Josh could go ahead. But Martin and Jack were the only Reeds to witness Ben's cremation in Barrow. Nicky did return to the Priory with the rest of her family for Josh's memorial service but it turned out to be a more traumatic experience than Simon's funeral, if that was possible. No sooner had the family taken their places, than she felt the need to settle her nerves. Turning to her step-brother, she said, "Perhaps I shouldn't say this, Simon, but I can't help being very relieved our mum has returned to London."

Adam actually smiled. "I know how you feel," he agreed, "but you just called me *Simon*."

Nicky blanched and wished a great hole would appear to swallow her up. She attempted to speak but no words came. Instead she started to shake as the tears rolled down her cheeks.

Still smiling, Adam grabbed her hand and squeezed it. "Don't worry, Nicky," he whispered. "Everything's going to be all right."

But Nicky's heart raced and she was not to be pacified. What on earth had she said? How could she make such an appalling mistake? How could she forget Simon was dead? Gulping air into her labouring lungs, she made herself bring back memories of her Spud. Poor Simon! He'd always been so sensitive, turning solely to her for help and advice time and time again. Adam had always needed a lot less support and his mother clearly approved of his independence. Could that possibly have been the beginning of Jane's alienation of Simon and the ensuing problems between her parents? Nicky had always loved Adam but she'd never attempted to create a special relationship with him, not that he appeared to mind. But had the twins really been so dissimilar? They'd definitely had their differences, of course, typified by their attitude to schoolwork. Martin had approved of Simon's effort and progress and showed his disappointment with Adam for not trying harder, while Jane had liked the way Adam spent time outdoors, engaged on practical activities, and disapproved of Simon's bookish habits. These views had become more divided, the arguments more intense until total acrimony and divorce were inevitable.

But ever since Simon's death, Nicky had started to see Adam in a new light. The pair of them had spent a lot of time together and she'd become aware of his many admirable qualities. After all, he could be extremely thoughtful and kind when he chose to be. Not long ago she'd convinced herself the twins were not at all similar, but now she was beginning to see they were truly identical. Of course they *looked* very different in adulthood but the differences were only superficial. It amazed Nicky she hadn't noticed this before. Suddenly, the loss of Simon didn't seem quite so daunting. She actually wondered if she could get closer to Adam, the thought crossing her mind that this was something to be encouraged. Looking down at her lap, her mind a whirlwind of conflicting thoughts and feelings, she observed Adam was still holding her shaking hand. She made no effort to remove it.

# 34

BYRON HAD BEEN WARNED about Jess' habit of chasing squirrels and rabbits. The Reeds' Labrador couldn't resist a chase through the woods. It was all very well but Byron took his dog-minding responsibilities seriously.

Wading through dense undergrowth half a mile from his original route, he tried to keep Jess in view as she chased after some creature or other. It was not easy. What helped were the dog's frantic yelps as she closed on her quarry, possibly a deer. His pursuit eventually led him out of the main wood to an area marked by large slabs of rock, interspersed with stunted trees and sparse ground cover. Byron wasn't sure where he was but he finally spotted Jess, thoroughly spent, getting her breath back on a flat piece of rock. As he approached the spot, it took him a moment or two to realise he was overlooking the back of the Templeton house. As for Jess, she was regarding him with soft, brown eyes and was panting far too heavily to resume her chase, but Byron took no chances and secured her with a lead before dropping down on the rock beside her.

He was on a level with the Mill House roof and casually studied the house below him. The room he could see on the ground floor, the one with the large double doors, had to be the library, the room devoted to dusty books that Jane had told him were of no interest to her. There was little else to involve him and he was about to turn away and resume his running when he spotted movement through the window to the right of the double doors. A dark, bulky figure hovered there momentarily before disappearing from view. Byron's curiosity was stirred. He was positive Jane was back in London so who was wandering about in her library? Instead of retreating to the woods, he looked for a way down to the small garden beneath him, meaning to investigate the library's mystery visitor. Determined to hang onto Jess, it took him a couple of minutes to get halfway down the tricky descent when, without warning, the dog growled. He looked towards the house. The silhouetted shape he'd observed through the window was now standing motionless outside the double doors less than fifty yards away.

Byron studied the figure in front of him. It was tall and chunky, covered in voluminous, shapeless clothing, which cunningly concealed every one of the individual's features. He attempted to see the face beyond the hood but it was pulled too far forward. As he scrutinised the still figure, he couldn't help noticing that he himself was being carefully observed, too. Very cool and confident, Byron thought. Brazen. Then Jess barked and the spell was broken. The figure moved instantly towards the side gate. Though not appearing to run, the individual covered the yards swiftly and had soon disappeared from view. It had to be a male, Byron decided. Definitely. Byron negotiated the rest of the steep slope as fast as possible, listening hard for engine noise that would give a clue to any vehicle the hooded stranger might be using. Unfortunately, the house was in the way and no noise permeated the building. By the time Byron had rushed round to the front of the house, the road was empty and silent. He was disappointed but he figured what he'd witnessed was significant enough to report to the police. First he wanted to check the house and see if anyone was at home.

His knock on the front door was answered by a man in spotless overalls who clearly didn't recognise the Manchester United footballer so Byron introduced himself.

"I'm Mark de Lacey," the overalls replied, with well-practised charm. "I'm working here as an interior designer for Mrs Templeton, the owner. Unfortunately she's not here at present. Is there any way I can be of help?"

"I hope so. I was at the back of the property just now and I spotted someone in the library. He was acting very strangely and made off before I could talk to him."

Mark de Lacey frowned. "That's odd. I've been working on the new kitchen, which is next door to the library. I heard nothing."

"I take it there's a door from the kitchen to the library. Is it locked?" asked Byron.

"Yes, I'm sure it is but I can't honestly say I've ever tried it."

"Do you mind if I check it out. I'd like to see what's of interest in this library." When Mark de Lacey hesitated, he added, "I'm a friend of the family and I intend to tell the police what I've seen. In light of the two recent murders, I'm sure they'll soon be swarming round this place."

"You'd better come in, then," said Mark, and he led Byron through the hallway, past the drawing room where Jane had entertained him and into the kitchen. "I've another full day's work here and then I'm returning to London," he said, the relief in his voice tangible, as if every hour spent away from the capital had been torture.

Byron looked round. The room was only half the size of his parents' kitchen but the hand-made units were most impressive. Mark was in the middle of tiling the wall and Byron approved of the complementary colours Jane had chosen. There were two other doors, one clearly a back door. Byron made his way to the other internal door and tested the handle. It was locked. Mark retrieved a key from under one of the units. "Try this," he suggested.

Moments later Byron was on his own in the library, leaving Mark to get on with his tiling. The first thing he did was to check the double doors that led into the garden. They, too, were locked. Interesting. The hooded stranger evidently had his own key, plus the presence of mind to lock the doors even when he was in a hurry and under pressure. A cool character indeed. Byron conducted a leisurely but thorough survey of the whole room. As Jane had signified, it was full of dusty books but little else, so what was there here to attract the Hoody? Byron looked all round extremely carefully and found nothing that might interest the mysterious stranger, absolutely nothing. But feeling he needed to tell the police what he'd witnessed, he used his mobile to dial Ed's home number.

Twenty minutes later Byron was joined at Mill House by the DI and four other police officers. He briefed Ed fully on all he'd observed and left him to carry out his own examination of the property, after which the two of them met up in the library.

"I don't get it," Byron said. "We know Nicky brought Ben and Josh through those double doors and into the main part of the house, but why would the Hoody come in here? We know he must have watched out for Nicky but he wouldn't have done so from this room."

The detective inspector merely nodded before changing the subject: "Was there anything else about this individual you can recall?" he asked.

Byron pondered. "It was difficult to judge his height. I'd say he was about six feet tall, give or take a couple of inches. He looked large and awkward but there was nothing ungainly about the way he moved. In fact, he was really quick. Thinking about it, I'm positive a lot of the bulk he carried was padding to help disguise him."

Ed nodded again, absorbing this extra information. "And how certain are you the individual was male?"

"Good question," conceded Byron. "Instinct tells me the person I watched has to be male. His whole stance was masculine. And I tell you something else, Ed. There was real aggression there, even when he stood watching me. *Especially* then. He was too cocky, too sure of himself to be female. I've met some butch girls in my time, but this one was a fellow, I'd bet my life on it."

Ed weighed the evidence. "Thanks for your help, Byron; it's much appreciated. And I'd listen to your instincts if I was you because I've never known you to be wrong. You imply this fellow is *very* dangerous so he will be. And don't forget he had a good look at you and knows who you are. Think on it."

It was excellent advice so it was a great pity Byron didn't take it more seriously.

# 35

"**B**LOW ME IF SHE hasn't started chatting up Tom Vincent. And he's only been working at McAdams about five minutes," Johnny said incredulously. It was lunch-time at The King's Arms and Johnny was bending Byron's ear about Nicky's latest indiscretions.

"I thought she was a reformed character."

"Don't know what gave you that idea. This Tom Vincent seems a decent bloke and he's a good worker, but Nicky seems determined to go to bed with every one of McAdams' workforce, everyone except yours truly."

Byron smiled and played an imaginary violin. "My heart weeps for you, Johnny. But I did think she'd be a bit more cautious, especially after losing two of her lovers so carelessly."

"You know she won't take even a hint of criticism from me so I'm the last person to give her any advice. I only raised my eyebrows fractionally when she was oozing her charm all over Tom this morning and she really whacked me. She said it was only a gentle prod but I'd hate to upset her seriously because my rib is still sore." Johnny grinned and rubbed his chest ruefully.

"Perhaps you should warn this Tom, or somebody ought to. Poor lad doesn't know what he's letting himself in for."

Johnny shook his head. "He's got no chance. When Nicky works her charms on you, you'd go to hell and back for her. I guess I'm sore, in more ways than one. She still refuses to go for a ride on my Kawasaki but I know for a fact she went out with Adam last night on his Harley, even though he didn't turn up for work all day. In fact, he and Jack haven't been in for the last two days. That's really unusual for Jack because he almost never misses a day, but I can't remember the last time Adam worked two consecutive days, despite his promises to Martin. When I made a joke about it, Nicky almost bit my head off. She told me in no uncertain terms to lay off Adam. I can't do right for doing wrong!" He took a long swig of beer but it did little to soothe him.

Byron picked up his own glass but put it down again. "I feel very sorry for your boss. All his kids are giving him aggro when he could do with their support."

"Kids. Who'd have them," agreed Johnny, and then a thought struck him. "How about your Edward IV? Did he have any children?"

"Only ten legitimate ones, plus several bastards."

"Wow! He didn't believe in sitting around twiddling his fingers, did he? But being legitimate was really important in those days, wasn't it."

"It was everything," agreed Byron. "Bastards got nowhere. It reminds me of a rhyme:

'Father dear, what is a bastard?' said a young and mischievous elf.

'A bastard, my boy, is a child of joy. In fact, you're a bastard yourself!'"

Johnny laughed. "That's not funny," he said. "So what happened to these kids of his?"

"His eldest son became Edward V but he had the shortest reign of any English king: two months and seventeen days. He and his brother, Richard, Duke of York, were imprisoned in the Tower of London. They both disappeared and have been known ever since as 'the princes in the Tower.' Nearly two centuries later, two skeletons, believed to be the princes, were discovered in the Tower and reburied in Westminster Abbey. The bones were tested in 1993 but, unfortunately, no proper identification was possible."

"Sad," said Johnny, taking another long slurp of beer. "So who did them in, then?"

"Good question. It was probably their uncle, Richard III, who was Edward IV's brother and who seized the throne in 1483. But Henry Tudor, who became king two years later, also had a lot to gain from their deaths so he was more than keen to blame Richard."

"As I said before," said Johnny, "who'd have kids?"

"You would, like a shot. And you'd *jump* at the chance if Nicky mothered them. Just imagine, Johnny: ten or more babies, with Nicky!"

A faraway look gleamed in Johnny's eyes. "You're very cruel and you hit a bloke where it really hurts. But you're probably right."

Byron prodded Johnny's midriff none too gently. "Of course, I'm right. It's a well-known fact."

Johnny couldn't help laughing. "I have to admit you know me well. Too well," he said grudgingly. "And you sure do know your history, but why is it always the males who get the mention? I bet Edward IV's daughters were soon forgotten."

Byron shook his head. "You'd be so wrong. His daughter, Elizabeth, could hardly have been more important. She married Henry Tudor and was the mother of Henry VIII."

"I see what you mean. Even I've heard of the infamous one, he of the six wives." Johnny finished his beer with obvious enjoyment before a thought struck him: "I wonder what Henry VIII would have made of our Nicky. I'm sure he'd have lusted after her and wanted to marry her, but would he later have divorced her or had her executed?"

Byron shrugged. "Who knows? More to the point, would Nicky have fancied *him?* But before you go into that, I need to return to Mill House. I want to find out more about the Hoody. We know he must have been watching Nicky when she dated Ben and Josh because they were both killed straight after they left the Templeton house. I'd like to find out *where* he did his watching."

"Dad would be grateful for any more help, you know that," Johnny said candidly. "But I'd better get back to work. We can't all take off time when we feel like it. Anyway, I want to be with Nicky so I can keep an eye on her."

When Byron began another virtuoso performance on his imaginary violin, Johnny threw an exaggerated punch at him.

After changing into his running gear, Byron made his way to Mill House, keen to discover more about the Hoody. All was quiet. The property looked deserted in the early afternoon sunshine, though Mark de Lacey's van was parked outside so he was probably working inside on the kitchen refurbishment. Byron strode round to the back of the house and made his way up the bank of rock he'd descended the previous day. It was very warm so he was soon perspiring freely and was relieved when he reached the top. Pausing to catch his breath, he looked all round wondering if the Hoody had chosen this very site to keep watch on Nicky and her lovers. It was an open area with lots of scattered rocks, small trees but few other signs of vegetation until one reached the tree line, about a hundred yards away. Byron wasn't certain what he was looking for but it was another of his senses which roused his attention and made him shiver. Something was wrong. The silence was too intense, which made him think back to the previous afternoon. He remembered Jess' desperate barking plus the clear sound of birds. There had been a lot of birdsong, he recalled, but now the woodland was eerily silent. There might, of course, be a bird of prey in the vicinity scaring other birds into silence or....in his peripheral vision, he caught the merest glimpse of black in front of the timber line. He swung half round and concentrated his eyes on that particular location.

The brief view of black suddenly magnified into a hooded figure wielding a bow as tall as the individual brandishing it. At that distance, approximately seventy yards, Byron's keen eyesight distinguished an arrow being pulled back by muscular arms, making him realise all too acutely he was in deadly danger and that he'd seriously underestimated the figure in the hood. While he was here searching for the Hoody, the Hoody was hunting for *him*. Byron was under no illusion he'd made a grave error of judgment, perhaps even a fatal one. He knew all too well about the power of the longbow and how, throughout history, too many had underrated the weapon to their cost. Only recently he'd read about the Battle Agincourt, 1415, and how a relatively few English archers had slain thousands of French knights in full battle armour, many of them at a distance of a hundred yards or more. And Byron was facing the archer dressed only in singlet and shorts. He also couldn't have chosen a more open, vulnerable situation. If the Hoody managed to get a clear shot at him he would die; it was as simple as that.

The only decent cover was back down the slope he'd just climbed, but that wasn't a viable proposition simply because it would take too long to descend the rock face. The Hoody could cover the seventy yards that separated them before Byron was a quarter of the way down. Jumping down was out of the question, too, unless he fancied broken limbs or more damage to his injury-prone knees. No, the only feasible option was to stay where he was and outmanoeuvre the Hoody. He was, after all, a highly-trained, professional sportsman and that should count for something in a situation like this one. But he'd better not stay where he was because an arrow was already thrumming its way towards him. If he didn't move really rapidly, he was going to be well and truly impaled. He therefore threw himself to his right, hit the ground, rolled and bounded to his feet. He never saw the arrow but he heard its deadly whoosh as it exploded close by him, hit rock a mere foot away and disintegrated. Byron wasted no time looking for the spent missile. He had eyes only for his antagonist, who was already running towards him and pulling back on his bow to release another arrow. The Hoody's attack suggested a level of violence and supreme self-assurance that Byron wanted no part of it. In that moment of very genuine peril, he made his choice: he ran. He chose to sprint at right angles to the approaching Hoody, making it as difficult as possible for his opponent to hit a fast-moving target. But the strategy placed him in an even more dangerous predicament because the distance between them was closing rapidly.

As he sped across the rocky terrain, trying to maintain his speed and avoid pitfalls, Byron heard the second arrow whistle by. It was so uncomfortably close he knew he must take immediate evasive action before a third one could be released. At once he veered away from the Hoody and made for the nearest trees only yards away. These would provide more cover but there was also the undergrowth to contend with, which would slow him down appreciably. Just as he crossed the tree-line, a third arrow zoomed past his chest and slammed into a tree to his right, missing him by inches. The deadly hiss of the projectile added urgency to his flight. Swerving again, he headed through waist-high bracken towards a patch of open ground, which it was imperative to cross before the Hoody could take aim again. Worryingly, the ground beyond was uneven and the undergrowth thicker, with patches of bramble predominating. He needed to find a path. Changing direction once more, he headed up a slight incline to a copse of silver birch trees that were interspersed with holly bushes. Here he paused momentarily and listened for any indication of pursuit. There was none but he knew better than to delay. The Hoody had shown he was more than ready to skewer Byron to the nearest tree, given half a chance, so he set off again, expecting the searing agony of an arrow in his back any second. Wading through more dense brush, which both slowed and tired him, he finally spied a track ahead. It was a great opportunity but it presented him with a dilemma. Which way should he take? The wrong choice might lead him straight to the Hoody, but now was not the moment for hesitation. Turning left, he belted along the path as fast as he could, grateful that all his recent running had left him in great shape. He hoped he'd left his opponent far enough behind to be safe but he wasn't prepared to take any chances. Although he covered the ground rapidly, his eyes devoured the terrain, searching for signs of danger. Maintaining a steady speed, he soon reached the end of the wood, which was adjacent to the Cartmel racetrack. Slowing to a trot, he made his way across the racetrack to the shops at the edge of the village and to safety, for the time being, at any rate.

After Byron had showered and changed, he met with Ed and Steve and told them all about his second sighting of the Hoody. They asked lots of questions but the DI made only one comment: "It's as I feared. We have an extremely violent psychopath on our patch. And I assure you, I *don't* use the term lightly."

Byron and Johnny chose not to go out that evening. Instead they spent a relaxing few hours at the Hampson place watching England play Russia at Wembley. It was England's final football match before the World Cup in South Africa and Byron, particularly, was keen to see his team do well. Although England won the match 2-1, their forwards looked far from convincing and there was a call from one of the commentators for Byron to be called into the squad, even at this late stage. Johnny voiced his agreement but Byron dismissed the idea out of hand. "No chance," he said decisively. "England might have to play six or more games if they do well in the tournament. There's no way I could manage that at the moment. I'll stick to my original plan, thank you, which is to get into shape for next season."

"That's a shame," Johnny responded, "but you know best."

"As it happens, I now have another reason for not going to South Africa. The Hoody did his best to kill me this afternoon so he's made it a *personal* matter as far as I'm concerned. I want to see the maniac caught before he murders anyone else."

No sooner had Byron spoken than Johnny's mobile rang out. Johnny listened carefully, at once alert and serious. "Who's there with you?" he asked the caller. Looking suddenly stern, he walked across the room before adding, "Listen to me, Nicky. Stay in the house and keep the doors locked. Don't go outside under any circumstances. Byron and I are on our way." Johnny switched his mobile off and said urgently, "Martin has spotted an intruder close to the house with his new surveillance equipment. He's at home with Beth and Nicky, just the three of them, so we need to get round their fast." He was already hurrying to the front door when Byron's shout stopped him in his tracks.

"Wait!" he yelled. "This could be a trap. It could be the Hoody expecting you to go rushing out of that front door so let's *not* do what he expects. Instead, open the front door just a bit but don't show yourself, do you hear me. I'll go out the back. If it's all clear, you can follow me over to Nicky's."

Johnny nodded grimly and made his way slowly to the front door. He opened it slightly, making sure he took the evasive action suggested. At the same time, Byron left the house by the back door. He'd been eager for a chance to meet the Hoody again but hadn't anticipated the opportunity would come quite so swiftly. Even so, the last thing he wanted was to rush headlong into more danger. An arrow can be just as lethal in the dark. Keeping in the shadows, he moved stealthily round the side of the house until he was in a position to check if the Hoody was watching the front door. All seemed quiet and in order so he retreated a few yards before sprinting across the grass towards the Reeds' property. Halfway there, Byron heard some muffled shouting coming from the far side of the house but could make no sense of it. He headed towards the source of the disturbance, hoping Johnny would be following behind. As he burst round the corner of the house between two large flowering shrubs, he saw Nicky illuminated outside the back door. She'd clearly disobeyed Johnny's instruction and was shouting angrily at someone who Byron couldn't see. Neither could he understand Nicky's garbled tirade nor why she'd put herself in such danger. And where were Martin and Beth? He had other unanswered questions but now wasn't the time to loiter. Dodging round more bushes, he headed away from Nicky and the light towards the high wall that surrounded Orchard Park, the direction she was shouting. Slowing to a stop, he made a systematic study of the garden in front of him. Though he recognised the Reeds were in extreme peril, he saw the necessity at this stage to proceed extremely warily. He'd had a series of close shaves earlier in the day and had developed a more than healthy respect for the Hoody, who he feared was lurking close by.

As his eyes became accustomed to the darkness, he looked hard for anything that stirred. He was rewarded with an almost imperceptible movement straight ahead and spotted a dark individual silhouetted against a large shrub. It had to be the Hoody. Had he chosen to stand ten yards further back, Byron would never have spotted him. Byron could see just enough of him to conclude he wasn't wearing the hooded garment and voluminous padding from their earlier encounter. There was also, fortunately, no sign of his longbow but Byron wasn't fooled. On a number of occasions recently, the Hoody had proved to be completely unpredictable and capable of sudden, extreme violence. It was more than likely he had a knife or some other deadly weapon so Byron needed to proceed with utmost caution. But something totally unforeseen developed. The Hoody suddenly turned and ran towards an old tree, which had branches spreading over the wall surrounding the Park, and began to climb purposefully. Byron knew he needed to intervene before the Hoody managed to escape over the wall. Rushing forward, he leapt at the figure and pulled him to the ground. Though jarred by the fall, he hung on and sought to establish a stranglehold on his writhing opponent. As they grappled together, the thought struck him the Hoody wasn't as big as he'd expected but he hung on doggedly anyway, hoping Johnny would turn up quickly.

As he fought to subdue the Hoody, Byron heard Johnny's laboured breathing some way off and couldn't help feeling encouraged. Good old Johnny! He might well be a world champion wrestler but he was definitely no long distance runner. "Over here," he yelled. "I need your help."

"Hang on," gasped his friend. "There's a squad car on its way and dad and Steve are driving over from Ulverston."

Long seconds later, Johnny blundered into the clearing, swiftly sized up the situation and flopped on top of the Hoody, totally thwarting any hopes the fellow had of making his escape. "You're nicked!" he announced with finality. "You're going nowhere, pal!"

Byron, able to relax a little, asked: "Are Martin and Beth OK?"

"They're fine," Johnny reassured him before nearly bursting his eardrums by shouting at the top of his voice, "Nicky, bring a torch, but keep your distance. This bloke is dangerous."

They followed the progress of the torch as it wound its way towards them through the blackness. Johnny then urged Nicky to hand over the torch and stand well back but she was having none of it: "You must be joking. You're not leaving me out of this," she said and all three of them edged closer as she directed the torch at the Hoody's head. He was seen to be wearing a black balaclava. It covered all of his face except his eyes, which stared back at them unblinking.

There was an expectant hush as Johnny reached forward. "Now, let's see who you are," he said and, with one fluid movement, he ripped the balaclava away from its owner's head.

# 36

I T WAS FORTY EIGHT hours since the dramatic arrest at the Reeds' place and both Ed and Steve had managed only a few hours' sleep during that time. They were both suffering from fatigue but it's amazing what a combination of adrenalin and caffeine can do.

Their latest shift had been a long one. At the end of it, they gathered in Ed's dining room to review the Cartmel case and discuss their priorities for the following day. Ed had drunk about a gallon of coffee while Steve had consumed a similar amount of sweetened tea. Ed put his empty mug aside and made himself comfortable on his chair. He said, "Let's not forget the man we have in custody told us one huge lie right at the beginning of his first interview yesterday morning. He gave us the wrong name, but since then I believe he's told us the truth. Put it this way, we've checked every part of his statement and it matches exactly with what we know. But let's listen to a section of the second interview to see if there's anything extra we need to check. Hopefully, the process will also help us decide what we tell the press. Even the nationals are now sitting up and taking an interest in this case. I'll have to give them a statement but I intend to sleep overnight on it."

Steve nodded. "I don't blame you but the sooner we get things sorted, the sooner I can get home to my family. My girls will be forgetting they've got a father."

Ed smiled. "I'll play the relevant part of the interview so have your notebook and pencil handy." He switched the recording on and adjusted the volume.

Ed: *"We checked the name you gave us yesterday and it doesn't exist. In other words, you told us a big, fat porky. Now, I'm going to ask for your name again and if we don't get the correct one I'm going to add the charge of wasting police time to the charges of arson, attempted murder and murder we've already discussed. I must remind you these are extremely serious charges so I strongly suggest you tell us the truth and give us your real name."*

Detainee: *"I told you yesterday I never murdered anybody. I swear to it!"*

Ed: *"We'll discuss that, never fear, but only when we're certain who we're talking to. Tell us your real name."*

Detainee: *"Robert Anthony Martins."*

Ed: *"Let's get this absolutely clear. You no longer claim to be Rob Bailey. You now say you're Robert Anthony Martins. Is that correct?"*

Detainee: *"Yes. But I don't just say I'm Rob Martins. I am Rob Martins."*

Ed: *"We'll check it out, never fear, like we'll check everything you tell us. Now tell us where you're from."*

Detainee: *"My home's in West Wycombe, Buckinghamshire. I was born there and went to school there and I worked not far away till a few weeks ago as a machinist in one of the furniture factories."*

Ed: *"So what bought you to south Cumbria?"*

Detainee: *"A photograph."*

Ed: *"Photograph? I think you'd better explain."*

Detainee: *"It was a photo in the Daily Mail. As soon as I saw it I decided to come up to Cartmel."*

Ed: *"Tell us about this photo."*

Detainee: *"It was the picture of a man called Martin Reed. One of my family recognised him."*

Ed: *"I remember the photo you're talking about. But why would you and your girlfriend, Kim, come all the way to Cumbria because you recognised Martin Reed from a photograph in the paper?"*

Detainee: *"Kim isn't my girlfriend; she's my sister. Her name is Kim Martins."*

Ed: *"We're learning a lot but we'll check that as well. Now, I'll repeat the question: why did you both come to Cartmel?"*

Detainee: *"We came to see Martin Reed. I wanted to meet and talk to him.*

Ed: *"We need to know why you were so keen to meet Martin Reed."*

Detainee: *"Because Martin Reed isn't Martin Reed. His real name is Alan Martins and he's our father."*

Ed: *"I hope you realise this is a statement which may well have far-reaching consequences. Martin Reed is a well-known and highly-respected figure in the local community. He's a business owner in Cartmel and has a family here. He also happens to be my neighbour and friend. Can you prove he's Alan Martins and your father?"*

Detainee: *"I certainly can. Alan Martins was born in High Wycombe in 1960. His future wife, our mother, Lucy, whose maiden name was Baldwin, was born in 1962, in Bourne End, Buckinghamshire. Alan Martins and Lucy Baldwin were married in High Wycombe Parish Church in 1980, on our father's twentieth birthday. I was born a year later and Kim two years after that, in 1983. All these facts can be verified and it should be easy enough to find the relevant birth and marriage certificates. There are also plenty of people in the Wycombe area who remember Alan Martins."*

Ed: *"These facts will be checked, along with the others. I ought to tell you that the man we know as Martin Reed married a local woman named Jane McAdams soon after he arrived in this area, but you probably already know this. If he was legally married to your mother, as you claim, then he's committed bigamy, which we will obviously need to investigate. But it's still not clear to us exactly why you travelled up to Cartmel."*

Detainee: *"That's easy. Our father left our home in West Wycombe at the beginning of 1985. He walked out on us all and simply disappeared. It would seem he made his way up to Cartmel. I was only three at the time but I can just about remember him, though the memories are very vague. Kim, my sister, was a year old so she recalls nothing of those times. We don't know why he left us. Still don't. But he totally wrecked our family. Our mum never recovered and it ruined her life and ours. She died last month, only a short while after we spotted Martin Reed's photograph in the Daily Mail. Her doctors told us she died of cancer but I'm convinced she'd lost the will to live. I think she died of a broken heart and I blame my father."*

Ed: *"If this is all true, I suggest you made the trip to Cumbria with revenge on your mind. I suggest you travelled here intent on injuring the man you believed had harmed your family. Would that be correct?"*

Detainee: *"Not exactly, no. I came to see him, to confront him, maybe, but I didn't plan him any harm."*

Ed: *"But you changed your mind, didn't you? You actually tried to murder him and his partner, Beth Alderton, didn't you? You came upon a tractor and did your best to run them both over. When that failed, you set his factory alight."*

Detainee: *"I was very angry with him, I admit that, but wouldn't you be if you were me? When I first got to Cartmel and saw for myself all he owns, I lost my temper. He has a factory, a big, posh house on a private estate and he and his children have piles of money. We had none of that. He left us in a council house living on benefits. Mum was always skimping and doing her best but there was never enough to support us all. I can't begin to tell you what it was like. We were always the poor relations and the other kids at school were forever making fun of us. So, when I saw my father was absolutely loaded while we'd gone without all those years, I was so angry. And then I found that tractor just sitting there with the key in the ignition and I couldn't resist the chance to get my own back. Kim told me not be so stupid but I couldn't help myself. When he and his fancy woman came waddling along the road after visiting their swanky restaurant, it was like a red rag. I started up the tractor and drove straight at them. But I'm glad I didn't kill them. Kim was really upset so I promised her I wouldn't do anything so idiotic again. I admit I set fire to the factory but I made sure it was empty so nobody would get hurt."*

Ed: *"And what about last night? Are you trying to tell us you disguised yourself in a balaclava just so you could have a friendly chat with the man you claim is your father?"*

Detainee: *"I swear I only wanted to talk to him. I wanted to ask him why he ran off and left us all. I reckon I've got the right to ask him that. When I got to the house, I didn't try to break in. I could have got past that girl, Nicky, easily enough if I'd wanted to but I didn't. You can say what you like but I never hurt my father, or his poxy daughter."*

Ed: *"If what you've told us is correct, that 'poxy daughter' is your stepsister. But before we move on to discuss your alibis for when Ben Nicholson and Josh Reynolds were murdered, is there anything else you wish to tell us."*

Detainee: *"I guess I should own up to trying to see my father last Wednesday night. I followed him home from his factory. It was very late and I was about to speak to him near his house when his neighbour drove up in a big, expensive car, an Audi, I think. This neighbour said he'd been out to dinner with some old friends, but then all the lights came on so I made myself scarce."*

Steve couldn't help yawning loudly as he watched his boss turn the recording off. "It's been a very long couple of days, Ed," he said, "but it's been very constructive overall. Listening again to this tape convinces me we've got half the case cracked."

Ed admitted, "It would seem so but there are a number of loose ends to tie up with Rob Bailey, or should I say, Rob Martins. At least his alibis for the two murders are watertight, which means Ben and Josh's murderer is still out there needing to be caught. Damn it all, Steve, this was the scenario I *didn't* want. I was afraid we might have a *pair* of villains to deal with and that fear's turned into reality."

Steve nodded gloomily. "But can we be positive this Rob Martins isn't in cahoots with the murderer?"

"There's not a shred of evidence to support it," Ed said. "Martins only came to this area very recently and there's nothing to suggest he knew anybody here before he arrived, including his father. We've checked every fact he gave us and we haven't discovered a single flaw in his statement. Did you notice he even volunteered information, like following Martin home the other night. I checked with my neighbour, Howard Tyson, and it was just as Martins explained. Basically, then, after that first lie I think Martins has told us the truth. Did you notice, for instance, how he reacted when I asked him about archery?"

"Mystified doesn't begin to describe it. So unless he's a superlative actor...."

"Exactly. We won't rule out the possibility of collusion completely at this stage. Let's just say it's highly unlikely. But this Rob Martins has certainly thrown a spanner in the works. When I told Martin Reed what he was claiming he went deathly white. He was so shocked he had to sit down, but not once did he deny the truth of it. I can see all too clearly now why he became so angry when I pointed out his photo in the Daily Mail. I've no idea how he's going to react but Rob Martins is right in one respect: he deserves to know why his father walked out on them all."

"I'd certainly want to know. Has Martin told Beth and his other children?" asked Steve.

Ed threw his hands in the air. "I don't know. And I've even less idea how they'll respond. I'm only pleased it's none of *my* responsibility, though the outcome might well impact on our investigation. I sincerely wish there *was* a way of knowing what Nicky and the others will say or do. But it's Martin's mess. He dug the hole and he'll have to climb out of it. Our job now is to focus on our murderer, who's still at large and highly dangerous."

Steve reached for his empty mug and examined its floral pattern. "At least Byron is absolutely certain Rob Martins isn't the Hoody he saw at Mill House. As soon as we arrived at the Reeds' house he told us that Rob was far too slight, and you have to say the Martins lad *is* slim, to put it mildly."

"The Hoody is altogether bigger, it would appear," agreed Ed, "but beyond that we know very little. Too little. His clothing covers him completely and he flits here and there without anyone seeming to notice. All the known sightings of him are in and around Mill House. But it's only Byron who's actually seen him. I've been doing some thinking about the first sighting, which was *inside* the library. I've looked all round that room and I still don't know what he was doing there. I can only imagine he was wanting to get into the main part of the house for some reason or other but heard Jane's interior designer working in the kitchen so decided not to bother. That leaves the question Byron was trying to answer: where was he waiting when he murdered Ben and Josh? The even bigger question is: *why* was he watching them? There's also the matter of the longbow he used. Members of our team have visited all the archery clubs in the vicinity and we've studied lists of members' names, without any success. The archery experts we consulted suggest our Hoody could well be a loner who makes his own bows and arrows and practises in private. That wouldn't surprise me! Apparently there's a great deal of information about longbows and how to use them on the internet. For instance, I discovered they're still made from yew and the best wood comes from Oregon, though English yew is still suitable."

Steve scratched his head. "There's a lot to take in. But I'm interested, like Byron, in where the Hoody did his watching. It only makes sense to me if he was waiting *outside* Mill House. I'll go and check the house and surrounds tomorrow and see if I can come up with any leads."

"Be careful. You'd better take a couple of the team with you. I'm getting paranoid about this Hoody and the danger he poses. I'm due in court for Rob Martins' first appearance and I intend to oppose any application for bail. I prefer young Martins in custody where we can keep an eye on him. I also want further words with his sister. I've a few more questions for that young lady. It would also be useful to chat with Martin and check on his state of mind. And I mustn't forget the press. They'll be baying for an update."

Steve grinned and checked his watch. "You can bet on it. Now, if you'll excuse me, I'm going to head off home and look in on my daughters and get to bed. If I'm to be any use later this morning, I need some beauty sleep."

# 37

"DON'T YOU DARE SAY 'I told you so,'" warned Johnny.
Byron laughed. "Well, I did mention Rob Bailey was shifty, now didn't I?"

Johnny waved that away. "Let's change the subject. Let's talk about Kim, Rob's sister. Seems like she was unattached when she gave you that snog in The King's Arms. She obviously fancies you, Byron, and she's available."

"I wish you wouldn't use that word. Girls like Kim don't snog. As for her being available, what's that to me? I told you before, I'm happily spoken for. Tyler has agreed to become Mrs Fullard. End of story. You, on the other hand, obviously find Kim Martins attractive so why don't you do something about it?"

"My heart is elsewhere, as you well know."

"Your very best friend," said Byron, "needs to point out that Nicky has moved on. It's difficult to accept, I know, but it's happened. Get used to it."

"I can't, not yet, at any rate. Anyway, we now know Kim is Nicky's stepsister so it would seem like incest."

Byron shook his head. "You're a really sad case. I suppose you're going to tell me next that Nicky still needs you."

"How did you guess? She didn't turn up for work this morning, which is hardly surprising, is it? It's not every day you learn your dad has another family you knew nothing about. She's invited me round later so I imagine she wants to talk. But whatever she wants is all right by me."

Byron put his arm round Johnny's shoulder. "You're absolutely hopeless! I should play my violin again but I know it won't do any good."

In fact, Johnny was nervous about meeting Nicky. Her moods had been so variable he wasn't sure what state of mind she'd be in. He actually had no idea why she'd asked to see him but it never crossed his mind to refuse. And when he turned up at the Reed's front door dressed in new jeans and with his hair freshly washed, it was Nicky who let him in. Looking cool in linen slacks, a cool white tee shirt and with her hair tied back from her face, she looked gorgeous. His heart flipped over but a voice in his head told him not to get his hopes up.

"Thanks for coming over," she said casually, and turned and led the way into the lounge. They'd met there often enough after the factory fire but always either side of the large dining table. This time she directed him to the leather settee and then sat next to him.

Johnny felt the need of a deep breath but, before he could speak, Nicky reached over and put her hand on his shoulder. It felt much lighter than Byron's arm and he was still ordering his thoughts when Nicky said, "I want to apologise for the other night, for disobeying you. I know you have my best interests at heart but when I saw that ridiculous figure in the balaclava I couldn't resist opening the door and giving him a piece of my mind. It was irresponsible but I couldn't help it."

Johnny decided he liked the feel of Nicky's hand on his shoulder. "It's fine," he said. In fact, it was anything but fine. Byron had painted him a vivid picture of the highly-volatile Hoody, who would have posed a very real threat to Nicky, but Johnny was reluctant to spoil the current mood by saying so.

Nicky gave his shoulder a gentle tweak before clasping her knees and fixing him with a level gaze. "What it is," she said, "is that I'm fed up with being bullied. It's happened all my life. My mum's *the* expert intimidator but she's not the only one. What happened in the Priory at Simon's funeral was absolutely typical and I made up my mind I wasn't going to put up with it any more. I actually stood up to my mum when she had another pop at me and I felt really good about myself. I also tried to persuade Adam to take a firmer line with her. He's been letting her dominate him, like she constantly made Simon's life a misery. Then I got the jitters about confronting her and nearly reverted to how I used to be. But not quite. When the Balaclava showed himself, the worm turned and I was out there yelling like a fishwife!"

"I missed that part," Johnny said, flattered that Nicky was so willing to explain herself, "but Byron mentioned it."

"I bet he did. I don't think Byron approves of me at the moment."

"He thinks the world of you," Johnny replied, determined to be loyal to his best mate. "And he held on to the bloke in the balaclava till I turned up, didn't he?"

"He did. I don't mean to disrespect him. It's just…oh, forgive me. He's been so supportive and here I am criticising him, but so much has happened to me these last few weeks that I don't know whether I'm coming or going. I simply know I *do* need my friends right now. You *and* Byron, especially after all that came out yesterday." Nicky carried on gazing into Johnny's eyes. This was the man she'd suspected of murdering her two lovers: dear, old Johnny, who'd always been there for her and who even now clearly fancied her. How could she have been so mean?

Johnny's heart did another flip but he managed to smile reassuringly and Nicky was encouraged to share the rest of her news: "We've all had such a shock," she confessed, "and it's been very emotional to put it mildly. I still don't know what to make of it. Dad called Jack, Adam and me together straight after breakfast. He looked awful. Well, you know what he had to tell us and he just came right out with it. He explained how he used to be known as Alan Martins and lived in High Wycombe. It was there he married a woman called Lucy when he was twenty years old. They went on to have two children, Robert and Kim. You also know what happened next. Alan Martins left his family and moved to Cumbria and became Martin Reed. He met our mother and married her. He settled here, had two more boys, made a success of the business and has been a part of our lives ever since. Now, it may seem very odd but I don't recall anyone ever asking him about his early life. You don't openly question your parents, do you? And he never once raised the subject with us. Now we learn it was one of his other children, the Balaclava, who tried to kill him. What a mess!"

Johnny wanted to reach out and hug this girl who was struggling to keep back the tears, but he merely asked, "How did the others react?"

Nicky composed herself. "Jack was all understanding and sympathy but Adam laughed out loud and I thought he'd really lost it until he said, 'Remember all those lectures, dad, about being responsible and making the right choices, and here you've been hiding another family all these years? What hypocrisy!' You could see that hit really hard. Our dad couldn't say a word in his defence, not then, at any rate."

"And what about you? What do you make of it?"

Nicky threw her arms in the air, abandoning all pretence of being relaxed. "That's a tough one," she answered, "and I wish I knew the answer. I also wish I could tell you why Simon took his own life and why someone would want to murder the men I get close to. But at the moment I haven't a single clue."

Johnny couldn't help noticing Nicky's suddenly reddening cheeks and wild eyes and hastily changed the subject: "What else did Martin have to say?"

Nicky dabbed her eyes with a large tissue. "He broke down and cried like a baby. It reminded me of what happened after Simon's death, which didn't do *me* any good. But he did attempt to explain what had gone wrong. He told us he'd got married far too young and then felt more and more trapped after Rob and Kim were born. His wife, apparently, had no ambition and was happy to live in the next street to her mum. Money was always tight and he was in a boring, dead end job. One day he just walked away from it all. Without planning his escape, or so he claims, he got on a train and then another and eventually got off at Grange-over-Sands because he happened to like the name. Soon after that he bumped into our mum and the rest, as they say, is history. I asked him if we had any other relatives and he told us his parents were dead but he had a younger sister called Helen, who he thought was still alive. Even Jack shook his head at that one, particularly when dad said he had no idea whether this sister had any children. Finally he apologised for letting us all down, which Jack and I accepted, but Adam told him he should go and see Rob and Kim and tell *them* he was sorry. I guess Adam had a point because our dad phoned your dad and arranged to see Rob at the police station in Barrow. Your dad's probably told you what happened there."

Johnny couldn't help wondering how on earth he could possibly help Nicky when he, too, was so woefully short of answers. "Dad tells me very little so I've no idea what took place in Barrow," he admitted, "but from what I've seen of Rob Martins, I doubt he'd give Martin much encouragement."

"It seems you're right. Dad felt so guilty when they met he broke down and wept, while Rob was really upset because he's certain he's going to jail. Dad says Rob is incredibly bitter and thinks he'll never forgive him. And Kim, apparently, is so angry about everything that's happened she refuses even to meet dad at the moment."

Johnny nodded. "I suppose it's to be expected. But what do you make of your new stepbrother and sister?"

"I don't think much of them at all. They've made no effort whatsoever to meet us and explain themselves so why should I bother? As far as I'm concerned, they're total strangers and they can stay that way."

Johnny looked concerned. "The police will have to release Rob on bail shortly. I hope he and his sister go straight back to Wycombe and keep out of trouble."

Nicky appeared not to hear. "There's a charge of bigamy hanging over our dad. He's afraid *he* might end up in jail."

"That's nothing to do with my dad," Johnny said. "His job is to hand over all the papers to the Crown Prosecution Service, who are responsible for prosecuting people in England and Wales. It's then up to the CPS to decide if he's to be charged or not."

Ed had, in fact, just finished the relevant paperwork for the CPS. He personally didn't think there was much point in bringing a prosecution against Martin for bigamy because Lucy Martins, his first wife, was now dead but, thankfully, it wasn't his decision. The recent spate of lawlessness in Cartmel had already put a huge strain on the relationship with his Reed neighbours and he didn't want more problems muddying the waters. But work he'd done earlier in the day with Steve had thrown up more potential complications. They'd been going through witness statements compiling a list of alibis for the murders of Ben and Josh and for the times Byron had seen the Hoody, which they'd needed to update following Rob Martins' arrest. This presumed, of course, that the Hoody *was* the murderer. Between them, they'd come up with some interesting developments. Of all the villagers the police had interviewed, a handful had been unable to provide adequate alibis for both murders, while another group couldn't account for their whereabouts for one of the murders. This latter cluster included four McAdams' employees, including Jack and Adam. Ed understood it was often very difficult to recall where you'd been at any given moment but it seemed inevitable he'd be knocking on the Reeds' door at least one more time to seek further information. He sighed. The Reeds were going through a very rough patch but the DI had two murders he intended to investigate fully, even if it meant ruffling more feathers.

Nicky paced up and down her bedroom reflecting on her exchange of views with Johnny. She'd been reminded yet again what a dependable friend he was. Before he'd left her, he'd described the Hoody's attack on Byron. Although he'd done his best to spare her feelings, it had been a graphic account reminding her of the very real danger the Hoody presented. On the credit side, it was reassuring to know Johnny and Byron were fighting her corner. She'd had her doubts recently about both of them but she reasoned that had been blatantly unfair. The wrestler and the professional footballer were, she recognised, an awesome combination and the Hoody had better watch out! She'd watched Johnny win one of his world titles at close quarters and he was simply invincible. And she'd seen for herself that Byron had an extra quality even the most macho of men treated with utmost respect. Yes, she reckoned she was extremely fortunate to have them both on her side.

Her attention turned to her brother, Adam. Ever since he'd held onto her hand in the Priory, Nicky had felt very confused. She still felt sheepish for calling him 'Simon' though it was clear Adam was actually delighted she'd done so. It had definitely brought them closer together, but how close was still to be established. Then, as she stopped her pacing, it hit her like a heavyweight punch to the jaw. She hadn't thought of Simon for *two whole days*. And suddenly she was shaking uncontrollably.

# 38

IT WAS SATURDAY MORNING in the Fullard household and Jilly was changing beds and washing the linen. She'd climbed the stairs to Byron's room at the top of the house, only to discover she was out of breath and needed a rest. Standing in the doorway, she cast a critical look at her son's room. She had to concede it was tidy but that had been his way right from the early days. As she got her breath back, she considered news she'd picked up only the previous day. It appeared that Byron had been attacked by a madman with a bow and arrows in the nearby wood. Jilly had heard this information from Johnny, who'd only let it slip because he'd presumed she already knew all about it. She didn't. Byron was *not* one to share such moments with his parents. In fact, her son had been extremely reticent about the whole episode, which was absolutely typical of him. If pushed, he'd have simply explained that what she didn't know couldn't worry her. It was all very well but he had no conception of the depth of a mother's love, of her concern for him. It made Jilly think of another event in her son's life, one she'd forced to the back of her mind all these years.

This had occurred when Byron, aged sixteen, had moved from Cartmel School to Barrow's Sixth Form College to continue his education. In his final year there and right out of the blue, one of his 'A' Level teachers, a maths specialist called Susan Fletcher, had accused him of rape. It had been an absolutely dreadful period, made worse for Jilly and her husband by Byron's response to the accusation. He'd merely shrugged it off and refused to discuss it with his parents. Even when taken in for questioning, he'd declined their help and kept his own counsel. There had been one particularly unpleasant scene when Sue Fletcher's husband had turned up at their front door demanding to see Byron and threatening all manner of retribution. Jilly, who'd been in the house on her own, had had the devil of a job getting rid of the man. But Byron had been unmoved. Nothing, it appeared, would induce him to discuss the matter with them. Just when it seemed the whole episode would be made public and Byron formally charged, Sue Fletcher had withdrawn the allegation. Hours later they learned she'd resigned from her teaching position and that her husband had left her. Rumours soon flourished she'd been having an affair with one of her students and the rape allegation had been her way of allaying her husband's suspicions. Despite Jilly's best efforts, she never got to the bottom of her son's involvement in this sorry business.

She collected Byron's bed linen and turned towards the stairs. Her son had excluded her from his decision-making then and he was still doing so now, leaving her none the wiser about his part in the Cartmel murder enquiry. She sighed. Her husband was very demonstrative and a good communicator, especially where his feelings were concerned. Jilly, who'd always found it difficult to show her emotions, let alone talk about them, had come to the conclusion Byron was more like her in this respect. But she was exceedingly proud of her son, especially his footballing achievements, and she was looking forward to seeing him settle down with Tyler Seddon who, she reckoned, would make him an excellent wife and might even provide her with the grandchild she craved.

In their large double garage, Dennis was sorting through piles of old family photographs, trying to decide which ones to scan onto his computer. He wasn't having much success with the task as he couldn't stop thinking about Martin's secret family. Dennis found it fascinating his neighbour had another wife and two grown-up children tucked away in Buckinghamshire, but what truly enthralled him was that Martin had walked out on them all. While everyone who heard the story seemed to revile Martin for his duplicitous behaviour, Dennis actually admired him. At least his neighbour had had the guts to leave when he was so unhappy. It made Dennis think of his own situation. He'd put up with what he considered a disappointing marriage for years but lacked the courage to do anything about it. Those who knew him reckoned his relationship with Jilly was really happy and secure. How little they knew! Their love-life had been virtually non-existent for years because his wife had such a low sex drive. It was something Dennis had never come to terms with, so much so that some years earlier he'd had an intense affair with his neighbour, Jane, who at the time was unhappily married to Martin. Dennis, some years older, had to acknowledge their relationship, though having its exciting moments, had been a sordid affair which filled him with shame whenever he thought about it. It had lasted six months before, somewhat reluctantly, he'd told Jane it was over. To this day, he was still unsure whether Jilly was aware of this liaison. What was clear was the pair of them continued a marriage that Dennis felt was warm and friendly but devoid of any passion. It did cross his mind he was, perhaps, being a little unfair on his wife, but he swiftly dismissed the thought. After all, it wasn't *his* fault Jilly was so reluctant to get involved in lovemaking.

Jilly, in fact, was wrong about her son. Byron was *very* affectionate, much more like his dad in that respect, and Tyler would have laughed uproariously at the idea he was unable to show or share his feelings. But he hated concerning his parents with his problems, something he'd learned when, aged eleven, he'd had a brutal fight with an older boy at school. He'd made the mistake of informing mum and dad, who were so alarmed their first response was to keep him indoors for a week and wrap him in cotton wool. It was then he swore he'd never involve them with his troubles again. As for the incident at the Sixth Form College, he felt more than a little guilty because it was he who'd been Sue Fletcher's young lover. Her accusation had provided a steep learning curve for him, making him realise how naively he'd behaved. But he wasn't the sort of person to make the same mistake twice, which brought him back to the present. He'd seriously underestimated the Hoody but he wouldn't do so again. From now on, the bow-brandishing Hoody had his total respect.

That Saturday morning, Byron had taken himself off to see Nicky. Very concerned about this young lady, he was keen to try to understand her recent, uncharacteristic behaviour. He probably wouldn't have bothered if Johnny hadn't been so emotionally involved with her but he wanted to save his friend from any more serious hurt. Nicky wasn't at home but he caught up with her at the field where she kept her horse. He was glad to be out and about because heavy overnight rain had made the air fresher and the grass greener. Spotting him standing by the gate, Nicky led Casper over, giving Byron time to study her. Slim and lithe, she looked attractive in bright yellow tee shirt, beige jodhpurs and long, black riding boots and it was all too easy to understand why Johnny was still smitten with her. Giving Byron a grin, she tucked a stray wisp of blonde hair behind her ear and said cheerfully, "It's good to see you, By, but what brings you to this neck of the woods?"

Byron smiled. "It's ages since you called me 'By.' Why, it must have been back in our early teens when I had a crush on you." He watched her closely to see how she'd respond.

Other girls might have blushed, but not Nicky. "What rubbish you speak!" she exclaimed, her eyes sparkling. "You never had a crush on me but I had one on *you*. All us girls did."

It was Byron's turn to grin. "That was then, Nicky. We've all moved on, you especially."

Nicky suddenly looked sad. "I've had to. My life's been torn apart these last few weeks. It's a wonder I've not been carted off by the men in white coats."

It was a casual comment but Byron quickly adjusted to the change of mood. "That's why I've come to see you. I'm worried about you. We all are."

Nicky looked away, her eyes glistening with sudden tears. "By 'all,' I suppose you mean Johnny," she said, her voice quivering with emotion. She shook her head helplessly. "He's been so good to me and I…" But she couldn't finish the sentence and turned away again.

This time Byron moved in, put his arms round her and hugged her gently. He said quietly, "We're worried because you've changed so much. I hardly recognise you, Nicky."

She pulled away. "Of course I've changed!" she declared heatedly. "What do you expect, for goodness sake?"

But Byron held her arms. "Don't get me wrong. I know enough's happened lately to send you absolutely crazy. In fact, I'm surprised you can still manage to do everyday jobs like looking after your horse. No, I'm talking about how you changed *before* Simon died."

Nicky released herself from Byron's grasp and turned her head away. "I don't know what you mean," she muttered.

"Oh, come on, Nicky! It's not hard to grasp. One moment you and Johnny were getting on really well, then the next you'd dumped him, just at a time when you needed *all* your friends, specially loyal ones like Johnny. I mentioned all this to you when I got home, if you recall. You didn't give me a straight answer then so how about telling me now what went wrong?"

Nicky suddenly looked troubled. She opened her mouth to say something but then thought better of it and turned instead to gaze towards the distant hills. Byron, staring at Nicky's back, realised his gamble had failed and he'd had a wasted journey. Not quite. He hadn't obtained the information he'd come for but he was more certain than ever there *was* something Nicky was withholding. It had to be significant but he had absolutely no idea what it could be. Shaking his head with barely-suppressed frustration, he said softly, "It's OK, Nicky. Just remember if you ever want to talk, Johnny and I are always here for you." He took one last look at Nicky's back, noting it was now heaving with emotion, and made his way back through the gateway.

In the Hampson household, Ed was doing his best to tidy up the dining room. His temporary office looked as if a large group of revellers had just decamped after a rowdy, all-night party. The long dining table was covered with empty food containers, interspersed with untidy piles of papers and dirty coffee and tea mugs of varying shapes and sizes. Ed wrinkled his nose and opened a couple of windows in an attempt to disperse the stale air. He had only himself to blame for the mess. Normally it would have been tidied before he went to bed but his meeting with Steve had lasted longer than expected. Plenty of food and liquid had been consumed at their lengthy confab but Ed could claim only modest progress in the pursuit of the murders of Ben Nicholson and Josh Reynolds and he was a worried man. Together they'd looked again at the alibis they'd accumulated and at the re-interviews, not only of all their suspects, but of every member of the McAdams workforce, from Martin, the managing director, to Tom Vincent, the newest recruit. A few of the suspects and a couple of the workers were still unable to provide satisfactory alibis for one of the murders. Adam was one of these but Ed figured, from past experience, that there was nothing particularly suspicious or unusual about this, especially for those individuals who lived on their own. But much of his unease happened to centre on Byron, who was turning out to be the key witness. After all, it was he who'd seen the Hoody on two separate occasions and given the police a description of what he'd observed. A team of police officers had subsequently scoured the area of woodland behind Mill House but no stray arrows or other Hoody evidence had been discovered. Unfortunately Byron was the *only* witness who claimed to have seen the Hoody. While Ed had no reason to doubt his version of events, he desperately needed corroboratory evidence. But despite multiple appeals to the public and a large police presence in the area, not one single person had come forward with any other information that confirmed Byron's sightings of the wild bowman. This left Ed with a real dilemma. Should he rely on Byron's testimony or should he pursue other lines of enquiry?

Satisfactory progress had been made in one direction. There was now much less need to guard members of the Reed family. This was because the man responsible for the attacks on Martin and his property had been caught and his threat nullified. Rob and Kim Martins had returned to Buckinghamshire, where Rob would be required to wait under very strict bail conditions until his trial date could be arranged. The pair of them were now the responsibility of the Thames Valley Police, though Ed's problems didn't end there. He was still concerned about Martin and the fallout following the discovery of his second family. If the DI wasn't careful, such a well-publicised family rift could upset his own investigation. His superiors were already breathing down his neck and demanding more headway with the case. It was therefore vital he and his team re-doubled their efforts to find the murderer. Dropping a pile of unpalatable food containers into a black plastic sack, Ed reasoned he needed all his skill and determination to catch a killer who, despite his team's best efforts, still remained as elusive as ever. It also came to him some good luck in the search wouldn't go amiss.

Ed's son was another looking for some good fortune. Johnny figured providence had *not* smiled on him these last few weeks. In fact, he felt Lady Luck had well and truly deserted him and he couldn't help dwelling on Byron's recent casual statement that he and Tyler were soon to be married. While Johnny was absolutely delighted with this news, it had taken a great chunk out his confidence. His best mate had everything going for him. He had a wonderful career, for which he received fabulous remuneration, and he was going to marry the love of his life. Johnny, on the other hand, had a very run-of-the-mill job with average pay and no clear-cut prospects, added to which, the girl of his dreams had ditched him. She'd then embarked on a number of affairs, further rubbing his nose in it. Even the delectable Kim had ignored him and chosen Byron for a kiss. Sometimes life sucked and Johnny couldn't help feeling his immediate future looked pretty bleak. There was only one thing for it. It was time to get astride his Kawasaki and blast his way round the lanes. That was usually a sure-fire way to cheer himself up and blow away his self-doubts.

Over at the Reeds' place, consternation reigned. Everyone there still felt raw about the discovery of Martin's secret life. Beth had confidently imagined she understood human nature and what made people tick. She'd particularly assumed she'd got Martin sized up. She'd been so wrong. Her partner had deceived her completely and she still hadn't recovered from the shock of it. He'd never been keen to tell her about his early life and had been even more reluctant to talk about his family. Now she knew why. She'd even learned Martin had a sister living somewhere in the south, so maybe there were nephews and nieces, too. Yet another family. Beth didn't know what to make of it, nor how to deal with the man who'd deceived her so thoroughly. She loved Martin deeply but needed time and space to think matters through. That Saturday morning she'd driven to the stores in Barrow in an attempt to forget her troubles for a few hours. Hopefully, some retail therapy would work wonders for her well-being.

Amid all the dire happenings in the Reed household, there was one significant constant in Jack's life: he was certain nothing could ever destroy his deeply-held religious faith. Until very recently there'd been another. Jack had revered his step-dad, but that trust had just taken a tremendous hammering. His real father had let him down badly on numerous occasions before disappearing without trace, but he'd been able to rely ever since on his new dad, who'd proved to be a real father in every way. Martin had not only introduced him into the family business and been responsible for his training, but was almost ready to install him as the new managing director. In fact, Martin had always been so totally dependable that Jack was stunned to learn of his double-dealing, so much so he urgently needed some counselling. Yet when the guidance came it wasn't at all what he expected. His church leaders told him unequivocally to forgive Martin, maintaining that inner peace could only be achieved by overlooking his step-father's mistakes. After giving full consideration to this advice, he realised it was in his own best interest to follow it. Anger and bitterness, when all is said and done, are extremely destructive emotions which play no part in the life of a practising Christian. Having made his decision, he knew he must share it with his siblings. With that in mind, he spoke to Nicky as she was making tea in the kitchen and then walked round to see Adam in his flat in the Square. The final piece in the jigsaw would be to talk to his stepfather when he returned from catching up with his paperwork at the factory.

Nicky took her pot of tea and sandwiches into the lounge and made herself comfortable in one of the leather armchairs. After riding Casper and spending the early afternoon at the health club, she had a raging appetite. She'd taken account of Jack's decision but, surprisingly enough, her step-dad and his new family weren't at the forefront of her thinking. Instead she was concentrating on her chat with Byron and on how she intended to spend the evening. As she was all too aware of Byron's concerns, she'd been expecting him to question her again so his approach hadn't surprised her. Anyway, she could hardly blame him for the interest he showed on his friend's behalf. But it certainly didn't mean she was going to blurt out what she knew about the secret room and her mother's lover. It was a pity she couldn't put Byron's mind at rest, if only for Johnny's sake, but some matters needed to be kept very private. As for her plans for the evening, she had a definite course of action in mind involving Tom Vincent, the new worker at McAdams. Quite simply, she intended to take him as her lover. There was risk involved for both of them but she was confident she could minimise the dangers. The truth was she missed the excitement of her love affairs and couldn't wait to start another. It helped that her mother, together with her interior decorator friend, Mark de Lacey, were both back in London, which meant she could use Mill House again with impunity. A few texts later and an evening date with Tom was all arranged. Life looked worth living again.

Adam wasn't nearly so analytical as his step-sister and was often oblivious of problems until they loomed so large they seemed insoluble. Currently he was experiencing an array of difficulties but the solutions he chose didn't always meet with approval, like his habit of missing work when it suited him. And while Jack might well forgive Martin for the mistakes he'd made, Adam had no intention of doing so. His dad's blunders clearly showed what a hypocrite he was so he could get on with his own mess and stew in it. It would serve his dad right because, while Adam was having to cope with startling changes in his life, his beloved father virtually ignored him, expending all his energy on his 'new' family and working even longer hours on the family business. To add to Adam's woes, he reckoned only Beth and, maybe, Jack, showed any real interest in his welfare but even their involvement was fitful at best. If he'd learned only one lesson in the period since Simon's death, it was that he had to rely totally on himself for solutions to his problems. But there was one silver lining: all his difficulties could be set aside for a while. That evening there was an important darts match in The King's Arms against arch rivals and he'd agreed to play. Not only that, he was the star player, an indispensable member of the local team. He smiled for the first time that day. The evening looked like being a memorable one and he couldn't wait for it to get underway.

# 39

THE SALOON BAR OF The King's Arms was packed, which was unusual even for a Saturday evening. Most of those assembled were supporters of the Kings, the pub darts team, but there was a small group who were noisily backing the Rose and Crown team from Ulverston. There was already plenty of tension in the air because this was a grudge match, a return contest which would decide the South Cumbria Darts League Championship. The two teams had met three months earlier in Ulverston in an ill-tempered encounter, won narrowly by the R and C's. Now, in this final match of the season, both teams were level on points so whoever won would become League Champions.

Jack stood at the bar ordering a round of drinks. He also attempted to give Adam some last-minute encouragement, but it was impossible to make himself heard above all the shouting and cheering. For those not in the know, it was extremely difficult to connect Jack and Adam as brothers. While Jack looked every bit the smart, well-groomed executive, Adam appeared as if he'd just got out of his bed which, more than likely, he had. Over six feet in height, he didn't look particularly tall because he was stocky with it. He'd exchanged his normal leather motorcycling gear for his dart-throwing attire: trainers, jeans and a bright red tee shirt embossed with The King's Arms logo. His newly-shaved head and plentiful ear studs shone in the bright pub lights but his jowls hadn't seen a razor blade for days. What was striking was the brand new tattoo on the back of his neck, the letters HD heavily embellished in Gothic script. This was not an advert for High Definition television but was all to do with Adam's love for his Harley Davidson motorbike. Smiling ruefully, Jack abandoned his attempt to converse with his brother and merely gave him a reassuring thumbs up before returning to his table with a tray of beer. Managing to unload the tray without spilling a drop, no mean feat in the heaving crowd, he passed tankards to Johnny and Byron before taking a satisfactory swallow from his own.

Murmuring his appreciation, Johnny took a quick look round the saloon bar, thankful the crescendo of noise was abating. "I didn't realise darts was such a big deal," he almost shouted. "We don't get excitement like this in wrestling, I'm telling you. I'm looking forward to the match tonight as much as one of your cup games at Old Trafford, Byron. It's a real edgy atmosphere so you should feel right at home."

Byron grinned. "I do. It's nothing like the tension of a European Champions' League tie against the likes of Real Madrid or AC Milan, but I must confess I've never experienced anything like it in Cartmel. And Adam looks extremely cool."

"He is," Jack confirmed. "He didn't throw well at Ulverston three months ago. In fact he's the first to admit he was poor that night, probably because their supporters managed to goad him into mistakes, but he's up to the challenge tonight. I'm really looking forward to his tussle with the R and C's number one, Theo Chambers. I happen to know there are issues to resolve between those two but, if Adam gets in the groove, Chambers had better watch out."

Johnny took a long draught of his beer and said, rather too casually, "I thought Nicky would be here this evening."

"She intended to be," Jack said, "but when I looked in on her earlier I could see she has other plans. I think she's arranged a date."

Johnny tried, not very successfully, to hide his feelings: "It's probably with Tom Vincent. She's been chatting him up for days."

There was a moment of strained silence before Byron changed the subject: "How's Beth? I haven't seen her for a while."

Jack pursed his lips. "Dad's recent troubles have hit her hard. Finding out he had another family came right out of the blue for all of us but it's been especially tough on Beth. She's still adjusting to it so she's taken herself off for the day. Let's hope a bit of space does the trick and she can start trusting dad again. I happen to ...." But Byron and Johnny didn't hear the rest of Jack's pronouncement because a booming loudspeaker announced the beginning of the darts match. It was exactly eight o'clock and the league title would be decided within the next two hours.

But, by the time Adam stepped up to the oche for his first round encounter, some twenty minutes later, the Kings were down a point and Johnny was already on his third pint of the evening. Playing the traditional Five-Oh-One, Adam threw steadily and beat his opponent with a tidy finish of seven and double twenty to level the score. The lead then see-sawed back and forth and both Adam and Theo Chambers remained unbeaten, the crowd growing even more on edge as the confrontation between them approached. In a brief lull in the proceedings, Johnny downed the last of his pint and shuffled off to the bar for a replacement.

Jack watched him go and shook his head. "He still fancies my sister," he stated unnecessarily, "but I wish he wouldn't drink so much."

Byron nodded rather absent-mindedly. "He does; she's a lucky girl." Then, seeing a chance and keen not to miss it, he added, "As we're talking about Nicky, there's something I'd like to ask you. I couldn't help noticing how she seemed to change suddenly just before Simon died. Have you any idea why?"

"Did she?" Jack put his tankard down and stroked his forehead. "I can't say I recall anything like that. Have you talked to Nicky about it?"

"A couple of times. She's reluctant to speak about it."

Johnny's return terminated the conversation. Byron had tried to understand Nicky's strange behaviour but, despite his best efforts, he was still in the dark. Thwarted yet again, he turned his concentration back to the darts. Jack, meanwhile, looked away and put his brain into gear. So Byron had noticed the difference in his sister and he, too, was clueless about the cause. What were they both missing? A sudden roar from the crowd caused him to look towards the dartboard. Theo Chambers was stepping up to the oche. Six feet six inches tall and gangly with it, he was hard to miss. It was time for his much-anticipated encounter with Adam and there was nothing, not even his sister's enigmatic behaviour, that was going to make Jack miss **this** confrontation. It was a decision he was later to regret.

Chambers was coolness personified. Running a huge hand through his shock of red hair, he selected one of his three arrows. He then waited calmly for the cacophony of cheering to die away, which showed a great deal about his temperament and experience. It seemed he was so tall he'd only have to lean forward to place his dart into the heart of the bull's-eye. But that wasn't his way. He chose the classic, erect style and his first dart showed the wisdom of his choice: a treble twenty. By the time it was Adam's turn to throw his three arrows, he was already facing an uphill battle. Although he acquitted himself well, he was always trailing Chambers, who was not the sort of player to let a good lead slip. The R and C's number one threw relentlessly and, within no time at all, he'd put his team a game ahead in the best of three and within striking distance of the Championship.

Adam still had a chance of defeating Chambers if only he could win the next two games but his rival already had the advantage. Adam made certain he didn't forget the basics. Before he began the second game, he carefully cleaned all three of his darts with an alcohol-based wipe. Grease and dirt can cause even the most minute deviations, which are to be avoided, if at all possible. By the time he'd selected his first arrow and was ready to throw, there was an expectant hush. He, also, was not to be rushed and he composed himself by taking a leisurely look round the saloon, hoping to spot Nicky. But his half-sister was nowhere to be seen and he turned back to the dartboard disappointed. He'd been wanting to impress her with his skills but she hadn't bothered to put in an appearance. He'd show her anyway! Freeing his mind of all distractions, he fixed his eyes on the board and threw his first dart.

Johnny's attention was well and truly wavering. So Nicky was almost certainly meeting up with Tom, the lad she'd set her sights on soon after he arrived at McAdams. It was nothing short of calamity. Johnny had been counting on her getting bored with these love affairs but it clearly wasn't happening, not yet at any rate. Gazing absent-mindedly round the saloon and completely oblivious of all the sudden cheering, he noticed a lanky figure with spiky hair skulking by the door. It took him a couple of seconds to realise he was staring at Gaz Morris, Nicky's old boyfriend and the one who'd been fired from McAdams for bad timekeeping. Rumour had it Gaz had disappeared down south again after a brief stay at his mum's place but Johnny was convinced he'd been doing his best to chat Nicky up once more. Plainly he didn't want to be spotted because he quickly lowered his head and sidled out of the door. But what was Gaz doing in Cartmel and how long had he been back? More to the point, why was he so reluctant to be seen? Johnny made a mental note to mention the sighting to his dad. By the time he turned his attention back to the darts, it was to discover Adam had duly won the second game and, with the match now tied, there was still all to play for.

Moments later and with Johnny now fully attentive, Chambers strode forward to start the third and final game, the one which would decide the League Championship. Exuding supreme confidence, he looked towards his group of supporters and raised a massive fist aloft. As their cheers filled the bar, he grinned and turned to the dartboard, obviously fired up and determined to do well. His first arrow was a triple twenty, which elicited more raucous support from his fans and groans from the followers of the Kings. It was swiftly followed by yet another triple twenty plus a triple nineteen, a total of 177. With these three darts, Chambers was already over a third of the way to his target and in danger of running away with the match *and* the Championship. Swaggering back to his knot of admirers, he couldn't help looking smug as he milked their applause. He was replaced at the oche by Adam, who threw well enough but was so far behind he knew he'd have to throw like a world champion to stand any chance of winning.

By the time he came forward again for his third series of throws, Adam was 161 short of his 501 target while Chambers was only fourteen shy, a very simple finish for such an accomplished thrower. It was a mammoth deficit at this stage. But there was still hope. It was possible to score the 161 with his next three darts but the odds were stacked against him achieving it. Some of the spectators were quick to work out the arithmetic and the room was full of tension once again. Adam took a deep breath to release some of the stress. When he was finally settled, he launched his first dart and emulated his opponent by scoring a treble twenty. Normally there would have been spontaneous applause for his skill but the atmosphere was so strained hardly anyone so much as blinked. A brief moment later the second dart winged its way into the treble seventeen, another excellent score, leaving a mere fifty to win both match and Championship. A bull's-eye with his third dart would clinch it. Now there was total silence inside the room. Everyone, including the R and C's rowdy followers, seemed mesmerised by the significance of Adam's final dart. Even the bar staff caught the mood and stopped serving so they, too, could watch the drama unfold. Theo Chambers, all truculence melted away, couldn't bear to watch and turned his gaze away. He was the only person present that night who failed to witness Adam's final throw into the centre of the bull's-eye. In the ensuing pandemonium, when it dawned on all those assembled that the Kings had actually won the championship, Adam was lifted aloft by at least a dozen of his delirious fans and paraded round the saloon.

Johnny was one of the few present that night who was not in the mood to join in the jubilation. He couldn't help wondering just what he had to do to win Nicky back. He sank the last of his pint and beckoned to Byron that it was time to leave.

# 40

BETH ARRIVED HOME LATE. She'd spent the morning shopping, the afternoon watching a film at the multiplex cinema and the evening catching up with a retired teaching colleague. Emotionally spent, she was ready for a good night's sleep, but there was a snag. There were matters she needed to sort out with Martin and he still hadn't returned from the factory.

Jack was in the kitchen snacking and he wasted no time telling her about Adam's triumph in The King's Arms. Beth was delighted with the news but her priority had to be to talk to Martin. "I needed to get away today for a bit because I've a lot on my mind," she confided. "Now I have a few issues to discuss with your dad."

Jack nodded and checked his watch. "It's nearly eleven o'clock so I'm surprised he's not home. What on earth does he find to do at the factory? I hope he doesn't expect *me* to spend all my time there if and when I take over."

"He's probably avoiding me. Things are a bit shaky between us at the moment."

"Hardly surprising in the circumstances. Shall I give him a ring and tell him to get a move on?"

"Please, Jack. The sooner we talk the better."

Jack disappeared into the hallway, leaving Beth to sink onto the nearest chair, heave a huge sigh and contemplate her bitten nails. She'd been less than frank with Jack. The situation with Martin was more than 'a bit shaky.' It was pretty precarious. Unless they quickly mended some fences, their relationship was as good as dead. Beth had been deeply hurt to discover her partner had another family and, quite simply, she'd felt there was no way she could accept this state of affairs. Until now, that is. The time she'd spent in Barrow had given her the opportunity to do some serious thinking. While it would have been so easy for her to walk out on Martin, what would that do right now to Jack, Nicky and Adam? Jack was strong and would cope but the younger two would really struggle. Indeed, another setback could well spell disaster and Beth couldn't bear to inflict more pain on either of them. And what about herself? Did she really want to abandon an otherwise happy relationship and try to survive on her own again? Martin had been incredibly weak and deceitful but she now knew she could live with the situation and with him. The sooner they sorted it out, the better it would be for all concerned.

Jack returned to the lounge looking a bit perplexed. "I can't raise him," he said. "I've tried both phones but he's not picking up either. He can be a stubborn so-and-so when he chooses."

Beth got tiredly to her feet. "You'd better drive me round there but make yourself scarce for a while, please. What I have to say to your father is for his ears alone."

Ten minutes later when Jack braked his car right outside the McAdams' main entrance it looked far from promising. The factory was in total darkness. Jack attempted to lighten the gloom: "At least the old sod's still here," he announced, pointing to a Mercedes illuminated by the car lights. "I bet he's having a nap in his office."

But Beth was in no mood for facetious remarks. "Show some respect!" she snapped and hurried out of the car. She arrived at the front door a split second before Jack and tried the handle, which opened smoothly enough. It was not immediately followed by the banshee wail of the alarm.

"So much for our new safety measures," said Jack, his voice strained. He felt tentatively for the row of light switches just inside the door. Fluorescent light instantly flooded the reception area. He peered all round nervously, preventing Beth from moving forward with an outstretched arm. "You stay here for a moment," he ordered. "I'll go and find him."

But Beth pushed his arm away. "I don't want to stay here on my own, thank you. We'll search together."

Jack hesitated only briefly. "OK. Come on, then." He lead the way down the corridor to Martin's office. The door was wide open and there was enough light from the corridor to show it was empty.

Jack stood still, uncertain what to do next, but Beth walked resolutely on down the corridor. "Let's check the storeroom," she said, almost whispering. "His car's still outside so he's got to be somewhere nearby."

"Don't you...." Jack began, but never finished the sentence.

Beth saw the first traces of blood when she opened the storeroom door and switched on the light. There were bright smears of red on the rubberised floor at her feet. Just for a second she hoped the liquid might be paint but, as her eyes followed a clear trail of the crimson, she saw an inert body on the floor some ten yards in front of her. She could tell it was wearing Martin's clothes but it certainly didn't look like Martin. That was because the head had been beaten almost to a pulp. A bloody hand, wearing the gold watch she'd given Martin on his fiftieth birthday, had tried unsuccessfully to ward off the killing blows. As she stared with growing horror, she couldn't help noticing a widening red pool to one side of the body.

Jack, peering over her shoulder, quickly shielded her from further view and this time she didn't protest. When he ordered her to return to the office area and call the police, Beth obeyed without hesitation and walked back along the corridor zombie-like, only to slump to the floor in total despair after a few yards. Managing to rouse herself, she leant against an adjacent window ledge and succeeded in making the call before vomiting her dinner down the wall. She'd set off to the factory determined to make matters right with Martin and now she faced the dreadful job of telling Nicky and Adam that they'd lost their dad as well as their brother. How on earth would she find the strength to do that?

# 41

E D PUT DOWN THE phone and stared into space. He'd just taken a call from the Assistant Chief Constable of Cumbria and he was *not* best pleased. The ACC, initially all sweetness and light, had promised his continued support for Ed and his team, but later in the one-sided conversation he'd informed the DI, very brusquely in Ed's opinion, that Detective Chief Inspector Andy Lancaster would be arriving hotfoot from Carlisle to "oversee the investigation." It was a real blow. It wasn't that Ed had anything against Andy Lancaster. They'd worked together on a number of occasions and he respected Andy's way of tackling cases. But their methods were very different and Ed was far from convinced Andy's old school ways would work in Cartmel. But, hey, the ACC had spoken so Ed had better get used to the idea. Anyway, he told himself, it was common knowledge Andy's son was dating the Chief Constable's daughter so there was definitely no point in making a fuss. He should have guessed such a move was on the cards but it still chewed him up. And there was more. The ACC was also calling up an offender profiler, whose task would be to identify the Cartmel killer by analysing the murders and the manner in which they'd been committed. Ed grimaced. The Assistant Chief Constable had certainly asserted his authority but it remained to be seen whether the introduction of two new faces would succeed where Ed and his team had so far failed. One vital point the ACC hadn't spelled out was exactly what "oversee" meant. Did it mean Andy would merely supervise the enquiry or would he be taking total control? Whichever it was, Ed felt an urgent need to crack on with the investigation. If he could only establish who the killer was, any fresh input would be superfluous.

Not surprisingly, his first reaction to Martin's murder had been to wonder whether Rob Martins had been up to his old tricks. He'd been quickly in touch with the Buckinghamshire Police, who were able to confirm they were closely monitoring Rob's whereabouts and that he and his sister, Kim, hadn't left the Wycombe area.

Ed and Steve studied the McAdams' security film one more time, searching for any clues that might reveal the identity of the murderer. The film, taken from the CCTV at the front of the factory, had recorded someone entering the premises at a little before ten thirty that Saturday night and what appeared to be the same person leaving twenty three minutes later. The detectives were positive this individual was masculine and was the killer they were seeking. The camera had then captured the arrival of Jack and Beth after another interval of twenty minutes.

Unfortunately, Ed and Steve were unable to obtain any useful leads from the film, basically because the lone male was so swathed in voluminous garments as to be completely unrecognisable. In fact, the film appeared to show someone dressed very like the person Byron had described and nicknamed the Hoody. This individual had clearly gained immediate access to the premises but it was unclear whether it was because he was expected or whether it was simply because Martin had failed to lock the front door. But twenty three minutes was a long time for the Hoody to be in the building with Martin. What on earth was he doing all that time? Subsequent checks of all Martin's phones, his diary and his appointment book failed to show up any appointments for this part of Saturday evening, which hadn't helped to clarify matters.

To add to Ed's woes, there was little good news from the forensic team. There was no sign of the murder weapon and no tell-tale bloody footprints on the rubberised storeroom floor. He was assured there was bound to be a lot of blood on the killer and his clothing but the murderer had exited the building as calmly as he'd entered before disappearing into the night. It was significant the killer had shown absolutely no sign of panic on his way out, even though he was seen to be carrying a parcel which, Ed presumed, contained the murder weapon. This once again suggested the individual they were pursuing was extremely cool, calculating and cunning. The DI rapidly came to the conclusion he was not going to be able to identify the murderer before the arrival of Detective Chief Inspector Andy Lancaster. It was certainly disappointing, meaning his team would have to try even harder to find the vital clue.

Beth was another one staring into space. She'd endured the most distressing night of her life, worse than the hours she'd spent with Nicky when Simon went missing. There was no peace to be found at their home in

Orchard Park. Instead of it being a much-needed sanctuary, the house had suddenly become the focus of the police enquiry. Teams of policemen and women descended on it and searched the place from top to bottom before fanning out to other Cartmel properties, including Adam's flat in Market Square. They didn't explain what they were looking for but they were very thorough, taking away numerous articles for further examination.

Beth, Jack, Nicky and Adam congregated in the lounge but conversation between them was monosyllabic. Jack found Martin's whisky and doled out generous measures but the situation was all too much for Nicky, who collapsed into Adam's arms suffering such convulsions that Beth immediately summoned the family doctor. Strong sleeping pills were prescribed, and not just for Nicky.

At the Hampsons,' Johnny and Byron were coming to terms with the news. They'd gathered to watch the opening match of the World Cup between the host nation, South Africa, and Argentina. But the report of Martin's death had totally ruined any interest in the football they might have had. So great was the impact Johnny had even pushed his untasted beer to one side. "I'm utterly gob-smacked," he said. "I don't know what to say any more. I can't begin to understand how Nicky will cope with having her stepdad hacked to death, on top of everything else that's happened to her."

"She's handled it all so far. We'll just have to hope she can handle this, too."

"Hope!" scoffed Johnny. "I can't imagine she'll have any of *that* left."

Byron didn't attempt to answer. His best friend was angry and bitter but it was not surprising in the circumstances. His mind turned instead to the information Ed had passed on to them both. The visitor to McAdams, the purported murderer of Martin Reed, was a Hoody lookalike. This was pleasing news. Byron was no fool. He was well aware the police had some misgivings about his description of the bow-wielding Hoody. Of course they did. He knew they didn't disbelieve his story but they didn't totally believe it either. It was their job to treat *all* evidence with caution until such a time as it could be proven beyond doubt. After all, he was the only person actually to have seen the Hoody. Now there was tangible proof, if only on security film, that the Hoody existed. Even so, the cops were taking nothing for granted and he'd had to rely on Johnny providing him with an alibi for Martin's murder. But Byron had another compelling reason for finding Ed's news interesting. He had very personal motives for pursuing the Hoody, as he'd attempted to explain to Johnny. The Hoody had tried hard to kill him. Very hard. Byron would never forget the deadly hiss of the arrows fired at him. And what would be the best way to get his own back and help Johnny help Nicky? That was easy. He reckoned he owed it to himself and to his friends to make sure the Hoody ended up where he deserved: behind bars for the rest of his life.

# 42

E D'S HEAD WAS BURSTING. On top of all the tasks involved in leading a major murder enquiry, he'd just had a lengthy meeting with DCI Andy Lancaster. Physically the pair were poles apart. Ed was big and bulky like his world champion wrestler son, while Andy was tall and thin. Ed always attempted to look smart for work, but the DCI was less bothered and tended to wear suits that were so ill-fitting they looked as if they might slide off their owner at any moment.

On the whole, their meeting had been useful and had cleared up a few grey areas. Andy, for instance, had made it clear right from the outset he had no intention of moving in and taking charge. "It's your patch," he'd conceded. "You and your team have all the know-how at your fingertips. I need to do a lot of checking and reading up of the case notes before I can make a worthwhile contribution. And the same will apply to Malcolm Glover, the profiler, who'll join us tomorrow." With that, he'd loaded up his car with the relevant files, which contained forensic reports, scene-of-crime photographs, witness statements, bagged evidence and the court transcripts of Rob Martin's brief County Court appearance. He'd then transported the whole lot to his temporary lodgings in Ulverston.

Ed was relieved. Some senior officers love to assert their authority and make it absolutely clear *they* are the ones pulling the strings. Andy, thankfully, was not one of them which gave Ed some leeway. He'd utilised the breathing space by taking in a handful of suspects for questioning. Gaz Morris was one of those questioned but, after providing the police with a satisfactory alibi, he'd been released without charge. Ed had also quizzed Jack, Adam and other McAdams' employees but they, too, had been released, together with articles of clothing and other items taken from their homes. His next job was to finish his own notes and add details to his own offender profile.

As for Beth, it wasn't just her head that was bursting; her heart felt like it was about to explode. The only thing keeping her going was her deep concern for Martin's children. Jack, as the new managing director of McAdams, now had the responsibility of the business to contend with and he'd immediately immersed himself in meetings with the firm's accountant and bank manager. Even so, he looked haggard, as if he suddenly had the weight of the whole family on his shoulders. But it was Nicky and Adam who really worried Beth. Both had retired to their beds, reluctant to talk to anyone, though the house phones were ringing constantly as friends and acquaintances called to convey their sympathy. Beth was at her wits' end. Time, perhaps, would be the main healer and she could only pray it worked miracles for all of them, herself included. There'd be the added burden of another funeral to organise once the police released Martin's body. She hoped she'd be allowed to get on with her plans without interference, including from Jane.

Over at the Fullards' house, Byron and Johnny sat through England's first match in the World Cup with a minimum of concentration. Johnny was so preoccupied he ignored his beer once again. Even a last-minute winning goal failed to spark much enthusiasm. Byron, pleased with the victory, quickly turned his thoughts back to the Reeds. "What sort of boss will Jack make?" he asked.

Johnny shrugged. "All right, I think. He knows the business inside out and gets on well with people, but he won't live and breathe the job like Martin did. He has other priorities. Anyway, he knows how to delegate. I fully expect him to push more jobs my way."

"And how will you feel about that?"

Johnny shrugged again. "That'll be fine, but I think there might be problems with Adam. I can't see Jack showing the same patience his dad did."

Byron nodded. "Jack has a fiery nature when he gets going but I reckon he'll have his work cut out with Adam. The lad has a mind of his own these days."

"If they *do* fall out, Nicky will side with Adam. Definitely. Those two have got really close recently."

This was news to Byron, who filed the information away before changing the subject: "I admire you for your continued support of Nicky,

I really do. By all means carry on helping her, but isn't it time you moved on?"

Johnny reached for his unopened beer. "Well, I've some news for you on that score. Nicky keeps making it clear she's not interested in me, except as a friend, so there's a lass I've got my eye on. I'm thinking of asking her out. But I know you, Byron. Let me work this out on my own, please."

Byron grinned and prodded his friend in the chest. He was surprised *and* pleased. "I've no idea what you mean," he said innocently. But it was excellent news. Matters hadn't gone his best mate's way for long enough and Johnny could do with a boost to his morale.

Nicky continued to ignore the phone whenever it rang but she did check her texts. Only two attracted her attention. The first was from her mum, who informed her she'd be travelling to Cartmel in a couple of days' time and would stay till after Martin's funeral. She'd be on her own as Ray was bogged down with business demands. The second text was from Tom Vincent and was a positive reaction to Nicky's recent friendliness. His message made no mention of Martin's death but it did suggest they get together as soon as possible. This really pleased Nicky as she was in desperate need of a diversion: anything to stop her thinking of violence and death. But she'd better act swiftly and take Tom to Mill House before Jane returned home and quashed the opportunity. She sent him a text at once before returning to her bed and waiting impatiently for his response.

Adam took no notice of any calls. Back once more in his flat, he found it impossible to concentrate on anything for more than a few seconds. He'd set his Skybox to record the England match but, even though he'd been looking forward to the World Cup, he couldn't bring himself to watch the game. He also couldn't be bothered to tidy his flat. Looking round with lacklustre eyes, he overlooked all the mess, some of which the cops had made when they'd invaded his space and demanded to see all the clothes he'd worn on Saturday. His triumph at The King's Arms was now a distant memory. One thought kept recurring: he must pull himself together.

It was late in the day and Ed's work was still not finished. Anyway, he had far too much on his mind to attempt sleeping. Despite a huge police search of various local properties and numerous wheelie bins, there was still no sign of the murder weapon or of any bloodied clothing that might have been worn by the killer. Earlier in the evening he'd tried to reassess his case notes but hadn't got very far. He tried again to think about the

Cartmel murderer and what he thought he knew about him. It wasn't a great deal. He studied his scribbled summary and tried to make sense of it.

> *Offender: Male. Almost certainly white & aged between 18 and 35; more likely to be in 20s. Tall (between 5 ft 10 and 6 ft 4 inches) Fit and agile; able to move quickly. Good skill with a bow (suggests keen eyesight & excellent co-ordination). All 3 victims from well-known Cartmel families/worked at McAdams. Ben from working class background; other 2 middle class. Ben and Josh in 20s; Martin 50. Both younger men Nicky Reed's lovers/Martin her stepfather. 2 younger men hit-and-run victims on road near Mill House (which both had left after assignations with Nicky). Does this suggest they were murdered because they were Nicky's lovers? Both hit-and run victims run down with McAdams' vehicles. Martin battered to death late on Saturday evening in his factory. Not clear if he knew his murderer or let him into the factory. Killer's motive also unclear. All 3 murders brutally/ruthlessly carried out & killer made certain all 3 were dead. 1st 2 murders suggest killer was hiding in/near Mill House. Does this suggest he is close to/in love with Nicky?*

All in all, Ed concluded his knowledge of the murderer left a lot to be desired. He could just as easily have added a long list of all those things he *didn't* know. No wonder the Assistant Chief Constable had brought in more help. Three murders had been committed in Ed's village right under his nose and he still hadn't brought the killer to justice. Searching for inspiration, his thoughts went back to one of the courses he'd attended. He'd learned about the "Homicidal Triad," which suggested murderers follow a clearly-defined pattern which involves bedwetting, animal cruelty and starting fires. Did this theory offer any help in the Cartmel case? Ed remembered Rob Martins had started a fire but that didn't help because Rob had watertight alibis for all three murders. He also recalled Adam had once had a spell of bedwetting but that it was his brother, Simon, who'd reacted most violently to Jack's bullying. But that hardly helped because Simon was now dead!

Ed shrugged away his disappointment and decided it was time for bed but, as he put his notes away, random worries swirled round his mind. One of the most notorious mass murderers of all time, the Yorkshire Ripper, had been interviewed a number of times before he was finally caught. How awful it would be if that was the case in Cartmel. But there was one overriding concern haunting Ed and keeping him awake at night. Right from the outset of the investigation he'd realised it was inevitable he would know the murderer and probably know him very well. The knowledge made him *extremely* uneasy.

# 43

I T WAS AUGUST BANK Holiday Monday and the second day of the Cartmel race meeting. Visitors poured into the village from all points of the compass. By mid morning the car parks were packed solid, with the swarms of race-goers committed to having a good time and making the most of the warm weather.

The Racecourse and its environs might have been overflowing but the village streets and shops were strangely quiet. It was especially peaceful in Orchard Park because the residents made a point of staying in their homes until the crowds departed. But Ed was one who wished he could break the habit of a lifetime and attend the races. That was because anything would have been better than spending his day explaining to DCI Andy Lancaster the many complexities of the Cartmel murder investigation. It was hard work going over the evidence again with a fine tooth comb under the watchful eye of his superior officer, but then he could hardly complain when Andy had gone out of his way to be so accommodating. It had to be grin-and-bear-it time for Ed, at least for the time being, while Andy got himself up to speed with the enquiry. At least Malcolm Glover, the profiler, had made himself scarce, preferring to study the case notes on his own so he could come to them with totally fresh eyes.

Johnny was using the Bank Holiday to give his Kawasaki a service but he'd be taking great care with the motor bike's oil change. He'd managed to get a dollop of oil from his last bike onto the concrete apron at the front of the house and his dad had *not* been amused. The service was a useful task for Johnny to undertake as it helped to take his mind off other troublesome matters. It even made him forget his forthcoming date with a lass who, though five years his junior, was very keen to go out with him.

Long may it continue, he thought, as he cheerfully worked away on his bike but still managed to sing along to a noisy rendition of 'Sylvia's Mother,' a track by Dr Hook from his favourite country and western collection.

Byron would have preferred to have gone running as part of his keep-fit regime but every road into the village was used by the crowds attending the races. It was therefore best to give all local roads a wide berth at such a time. Instead he'd erected a deckchair on the lawn underneath the lounge window. He'd made himself comfortable and was making inroads into his book on the Plantagenets. There was no sound to be heard from Johnny's iPod but his friend's tuneless attempt at singing had him wincing more than once. "Even worse than me," muttered Byron, "and that's saying something." Johnny had promised to pop over for a beer once his Kawasaki was running sweetly. Byron covered his ears and hoped the service wouldn't take long.

In the Reed household, Beth was spring-cleaning. She'd decided to tackle neglected tasks as an antidote to feeling so downcast. The idea was that the harder she worked, the less time she'd have to think about Martin. Except it didn't pan out that way. Whatever jobs she undertook, her partner remained in her thoughts. Most of the time he monopolized her thinking; other times he was just on the periphery. She sighed as she eyed a huge basketful of ironing with a distinct lack of relish. Would she ever get over Martin's death and the manner of his dying? And what about the children? Would they be able to move on once the grieving process had taken its course? There was one possible blessing. Her initial fears about the younger two appeared to be unfounded. So far, at any rate. Both Adam and Nicky had come out of their shells and promised to help organise their dad's funeral, the sort of involvement Beth fully intended to encourage. And Adam had agreed to come round to Orchard Park every day for his evening meal, which would kill two birds with one stone. It would ensure he ate at least one square meal a day, as well as giving Beth a regular opportunity to keep a watchful eye on him. In fact, the arrangement was bound to be beneficial. Adam was not the greatest cook in the world and, left to his own devices, would undoubtedly have relied on a steady diet of takeaways. Beth could now be certain he'd not only be eating more healthily but that she'd also be able to advise him on more personal matters, like changing his socks. She was slightly less concerned about Nicky, mainly because that young lady suddenly had other distractions. If Beth was correct, Nicky had another man in her sights. She was mindful that Nicky's somewhat lurid love life was worthy of some rigorous examination, but now was hardly the time. "Let's get the funeral over and then we'll see," she told herself, a decision she was later to regret.

Jack was spending his day attempting to make sense of all the business files he'd discovered on Martin's laptop. He wasn't getting very far. Martin had used his own shorthand system which was complete gobbledegook as far as Jack was concerned. But it didn't matter. Jack had made up his mind to run McAdams *his* way. He had many ideas formulated over the last few months that he was keen to initiate. "Be yourself," he'd been advised. Well, he had every intention of being so and he planned to carry the business into the twenty-first century at the same time. Part of his new strategy would involve the re-training of the entire firm's workforce. This would almost certainly cause some dissension but he couldn't help that. Omelettes can't be made without breaking a few eggs. It did just cross Jack's mind that such a policy was bound to cause friction with a few of the workers, like Adam, to name but one, but he was determined to stamp his own personality on the business. Adam would have to take his chances like the rest of them.

Nicky was using her day off to meet Tom Vincent and take him to her love nest at Mill House. She'd been looking forward to the date for two days and there was no way she was going to be deterred by the race meeting, or anything else for that matter. Besides, she'd had another text from her mum who was driving up from London that very evening so she was determined to go to bed with Tom in private, comfortable surroundings while she had the chance. As Mill House was on the outskirts of the village, she and Tom wouldn't be bothered with hordes of race-goers passing the property. She anticipated the roads would be empty by midday and would remain so until late afternoon, by which time she'd be back home.

By mid afternoon, Ed had finished his appraisal of the Cartmel investigation to an appreciative Andy Lancaster, who had departed to his digs in Ulverston with even more paperwork to study. Ed waved him off before returning to the lounge and heading towards the framed photograph on the mantelpiece that had yet again caught his attention. It was a favourite of his, showing his wife, Laura, holding a four year-old Johnny. The photo had been taken on a family holiday to Paphos, Cyprus. Ed loved it because Laura looked so happy. He studied the snapshot for a minute or so before replacing it. Moments later he slumped into an armchair in front of his TV with only his memories and a glass of whisky for company. It transpired that 'Ali Baba and the Forty Thieves' was showing but Ed couldn't be bothered to change channels. He just needed to chill out for an hour or so and give his brain a complete rest.

Beth's brain most definitely hadn't settled into rest mode. She had her own position to weigh up and there were important choices to be made now her partner was dead. But she was reluctant to ponder her options and vaguely questioned why. Instead, she made up her mind to wait and see what was in Martin's will and discover how the family settled without him. After the funeral would, perhaps, be the ideal time to consider her future. Turning her attention to the kitchen floor, she wondered whether she had the energy to give it a much-needed scrub but decided on a cup of tea instead. With a heartfelt sigh, she got up wearily to turn the kettle on.

As Byron continued his study of the Plantagenets, a shadow fell across him; it was Johnny. His best mate had changed from his overalls into light shorts and a vivid purple tee shirt. He sported a huge pair of sunglasses and was still listening to his iPod and intoning strange, unmusical sounds.

"Give me strength!" said Byron, with as much patience as he could muster, which wasn't a great deal.

Johnny looked totally blank. "What?" he asked loudly.

Byron looked away, shaking his head.

Johnny mouthed a few more discordant tones before disengaging his iPod and popping it into his pocket. "Wonderful piece of equipment," he said brightly, tapping his pocket lightly. "See what your friend, Edward IV, never had the chance to listen to. That's deprivation, Byron, of the very worst kind."

"Give me strength, *please*! And let me tell you that you are to singing what I am to wrestling. And no, Edward never had an iPod and he never owned a Kawasaki either. But the greatest joy in his life was not having to put up with your excruciating attempts at singing."

Johnny grinned. "Haven't you heard that sarcasm is the lowest form of wit? Your Edward not only missed out on two of *the* iconic inventions but he also never got to hear country and western music. Now that really *is* deprivation. But don't look at me like that, Byron. I only came over for the beer."


Jack had long since given up trying to make sense of Martin's business files. Instead he imported his own onto the laptop and spent a couple of hours updating addresses, telephone numbers and other essential details. Satisfied with the results, he checked the computer's memory. It was nearly full, which would never do. Without a second thought, he highlighted all of his stepdad's incomprehensible files, now redundant, and deleted every single one. With a few clicks he'd totally eliminated Martin from the business. Sitting back at his desk, Jack allowed himself to smile. For the first time he felt totally in charge of McAdams; it was a good feeling and made him feel special. Of course it was very sad about Martin, but too many people depended on the firm for their livelihood so it was necessary he act decisively and move the business forward. He did have one significant concern for his stepdad that he continued to pray about. He sincerely hoped Martin had died a Christian.

Nicky was also feeling decidedly better than she might have expected. This was purely the result of her love tryst with Tom at Mill House, which had succeeded in taking her mind off all other depressing matters, as she'd known it would. Reality would kick in soon enough so it had been vital to get out and about and enjoy herself while the opportunity presented. And she'd certainly done that! As she parted from Tom and began to walk home, she was able to wash her mind of everything that had made her miserable and concentrate solely on her new lover and their lovemaking. The road was as quiet as she'd anticipated and she was so deep in contemplation she neither saw nor heard the vehicle coming up behind. It was only when there was a sudden squeal of brakes she became aware it had stopped right by her. Frowning at the interruption to her daydreaming, she noticed the van was part of the McAdams' fleet but she had no idea of the identity of the driver. As she attempted to stare through the glass and establish who was behind the wheel, the driver wound down the window. Looking straight into the cab, Nicky's frown changed into a warm smile and, when the driver beckoned her, she almost ran round the vehicle and clambered into the front. The van set off at once, heading towards the village.

# 44

J ANE WAS IN A foul mood by the time she reached Mill House. She'd left
London early, anticipating more roadworks and delays on the journey
home, forgetting it was a bank holiday weekend and that the motorways
would be quieter than usual. It had also slipped her mind there was a race
meeting in Cartmel and that her arrival in the village would coincide with
the hordes of race-goers leaving. The last mile of her journey had taken
sixty-five morale-sapping minutes and left her fuming.

As she lugged her man-sized suitcase up to the front door, she barely
noticed that Mark de Lacey had painted it, as per her instructions. But
she couldn't help noting the date over the door, 1641, had been carefully
picked out in new, glossy-black paint. Her anger boiled over. "What the
hell's he playing at?" she hissed aloud. "What do I care about the frigging
date on the house?" She dropped her heavy case and aimed a kick at it.
"My name's not Byron Fullard. I don't give a damn about history. There's
no future in it." Opening the door, she manhandled the suitcase into the
house, scooping up an armful of mail on the way.

Later, after a long soak in the bath and a quick snack, she sat in the
lounge with a large wineglass full of red wine and tackled her mail. Amid
the usual advertising circulars, her memory was jogged when she came
to a large, plain brown envelope. Frowning, she studied it for a moment
before tearing it open and extracting the contents. Once again it was a
single coloured photograph on A4 paper. This one was not of her naked
daughter; rather, it was one of herself in the arms of Mark de Lacey, her
interior decorator and lover. But it was just as compromising and, she
had to acknowledge, was an excellent likeness of them both caught in
the throes of sexual passion. Jane's nose wrinkled with distaste as she sat

staring at the photo. Her bad mood had returned with a vengeance and even a long draught of wine did nothing to ease her disquiet.

Minutes later, having recovered Nicky's photo from the safe where it had been locked away for the last fortnight, she climbed the stairs and headed for the back bedroom carrying both pictures. It took only a swift scrutiny of the room to conclude that both photos depicted this room and this bed. But why hadn't she recognised before that Nicky had been using Mill House to entertain her lover? Why hadn't she even identified her own bed and why…but it was too late to consider these questions now. Instead she laid the photos side by side on the bed and studied them more thoroughly. Then, turning towards the wash basin, she raised her gaze to the mirror above it. Her eyes narrowed as she tried to peer through the glass and see what lay beyond. Jane stood indecisively for a long moment. For perhaps the very first time in her life, she had absolutely no idea what to do or how to proceed.

# 45

NICKY WAS MISSING. THERE was no sign of her anywhere. Normally if she couldn't make it home, for whatever reason, she'd phone and explain; she'd always been thoughtful like that. But there'd been no word from her for nearly five hours. Beth, already panicking, made herself sit down with a cup of tea and think hard, although it didn't help in the slightest. It merely raised more questions, more worries. Where on earth could Nicky be? She hadn't come home or phoned so there had to be something seriously wrong. Had to be.

Ignoring her tea, which had gone cold anyway, Beth got up abruptly from her chair and walked round the room, feeling she had to keep on the move because anything was better than sitting around imagining all that could have gone wrong. The most dreadful scenarios had already raced round her mind, giving her palpitations and the most dreadful sinking sensation in the pit of her stomach. All this on top of everything else was too much to bear. She'd already checked right round the house and phoned all the family and friends she could think of but nobody had seen Nicky since early afternoon. The only person she couldn't contact, simply because she didn't have the number, was Nicky's new boyfriend, but that was already in hand. Jack, Adam and Johnny had all promised to track Tom Vincent down to see if he could account for Nicky's whereabouts. If that didn't turn up trumps, Beth would have only one viable option left. Her spirits, already at low ebb, plummeted.

When the phone rang, she raced to answer it. Jack's tone was soothing but his call brought further despair. He'd visited Tom's home and closely questioned the lad, who insisted he had no idea where Nicky was. Tom claimed he and Nicky had parted on friendly terms at Mill House soon after three o' clock and that he'd then trotted home across the fields, choosing that particular route because he was all too aware of what had happened to Ben and Josh. He'd presumed Nicky had gone straight home and was unable to throw any light on her disappearance. Jack had left Adam and Johnny outside the Vincent home but all three would be returning to Orchard Park at once.

Beth checked her watch. It was nearly six o'clock and there was still no word from Nicky. It was all unrelenting gloom and positive action was urgently needed.

Resolved to waste no more precious seconds, Beth picked up the phone and dialled Ed's home number. It was necessary to report Nicky's disappearance and make it official.

# 46

A NDY LANCASTER HAD BEEN extremely busy. Realising Ed's home in Orchard Park was no longer an appropriate location for the swiftly-expanding triple-murder enquiry, the DCI had been quick to move the headquarters back to Barrow. While it might have been handy in the early stages of the murder hunt to have a meeting place close to the scene of the crimes, there were very definite advantages in establishing operations at the large, secure police station that was available in nearby Barrow.

Ed didn't mind the change of location one little bit. In fact, he was greatly relieved to have his living room cleared of all the accumulated clutter and to be able to call his house his own again. And the journey to Barrow certainly didn't faze him. This was because he'd grown accustomed to the regular travelling during his long service in the south Cumbrian force. He was even relieved, after the initial disappointment, that he no longer had total control of the enquiry. Let the DCI take all the plaudits for solving the Cartmel case, if there were ever to be any. Sometimes it was a whole lot easier to be a member of the team, rather than its leader. And Ed was all too aware the murder enquiry was rapidly growing into something of a monster.

This was certainly a view shared by the DCI. As well as organising a suitable base for the enquiry, Andy had spent many of his weekend hours studying the case notes and formulating a number of new strategies he wished to see pursued, only for Nicky's disappearance to put them on the back burner. The meeting he'd called for nine o' clock that Tuesday morning suddenly had a whole new agenda. The Cartmel investigation had now been elevated to Major Incident status and had been awarded the random code name 'Operation Mandarin.' Studying the meticulous notes he'd made earlier, Andy looked critically at the white board in the operations room. Under the heading of Operation Mandarin, he'd written important sub-headings followed by further notes. It was his attempt to summarise the enquiry to date. Some of the details caught his attention and had him nodding with approval: scene forensics; crime scene enquiries; possible motives; post-mortems; significant witness interviews. He'd tried to simplify the series of complex events and, all in all, he was happy with his notes, but there was one heading that caused him to ponder long and hard. There was little to report under the heading of 'Media,' a deficiency that needed to be rectified immediately, if only to make the population at large fully aware of Nicky's disappearance. There was going to be a media scrum very soon and mayhem was going to break out in and around Cartmel, if it hadn't started already, and he liked to keep on top of such matters. Anyway, saturated press and television coverage at this stage could only be welcomed, particularly if it led to Nicky Reed being found.

Andy liked to use his daily briefings to involve the whole team in any investigations under his control and was not unlike Ed in this respect. He also liked to keep all of the case under constant review. By the time he'd reached the end of his team briefing covering the three murders, he turned to Nicky's disappearance: "As far as the missing woman is concerned," he announced, "I see the alternative scenarios as follows: One. Nicola Reed has been incarcerated in some unknown place and cannot escape. Two. Nicola Reed is dead, either as a direct result of her incarceration or because she has been unlawfully killed. Three. Nicola Reed has deliberately disappeared. We've already flooded Cartmel with extra officers in our search for Nicola and that high level of deployment will be maintained for the rest of the day, when we'll review matters again." He then led a full discussion on further tactics he intended to arrange in the search before asking his team if they had any questions or points they wished to raise. When these had been fully dealt with, he dismissed the team but asked Ed to stay behind. "I need you to re-check four of the suspects' alibis," he told the DI, handing Ed a file of papers. "These four alibis were actually provided by either Ben Nicholson or Josh Reynolds, who are now both dead. It's very clear these alibis are no longer acceptable so all four suspects will need to be re-interviewed. The alibi provided by Adam Reed is not quite so pressing as a Mrs Lord of Priory Close, Cartmel, has also accounted for his whereabouts at the time of Ben's murder. But please check it nevertheless."

Ed nodded agreeably, coming to the conclusion it was sometimes much simpler taking orders than giving them. He already had a full workload and the extra task shouldn't inconvenience him too much. But before he set off back to Cartmel, he made sure he popped into the canteen and grabbed a coffee to help him on his way.

Johnny had arranged to meet Byron in The King's Arms at lunch-time. He had a lot on his mind. "It's been really odd at work this morning, I'm telling you," he said, sipping his beer half-heartedly. "No Martin popping in and out and no Nicky. It's strange running the office on my own, and hard work, too. Jack's promised me some help if Nicky doesn't show up soon, but I sincerely hope we don't have to go down that route."

"How's Jack been?"

Johnny attempted to smile but didn't quite make it. "He's rushing round like a demented fly. And trying very hard to keep the company ticking over. Too hard, probably. If he keeps that pace up he'll rush himself into an early grave. And Nicky going missing on top of everything else has really raised his stress levels. I was ready for all sorts of trouble when Adam didn't show first thing and Jack phoned him up. But everything was sweetness and light when Adam promised he was on his way."

"Interesting. I thought Adam might have insisted on having time off to search for his sister."

"Me, too," agreed Johnny, "except he claims he's already checked all the places he can think of. He told Jack he doesn't know where else to look. But he's not the only one. Half our workforce were out all night scouring the neighbourhood. I should know because I was one of them. But there's absolutely no sign of Nicky. She's just disappeared off the face of the earth." He sank his beer despondently. "Any ideas?"

Byron nodded. "I have actually. I'm still convinced Jane knows more than she's letting on so I intend to pay her another visit this afternoon." He grinned. "I must like poking my nose into hornets' nests!"

Beth was on indefinite compassionate leave from her teaching post because she simply couldn't bear the thought of going to work when so many dreadful happenings had blighted their lives and Nicky was still missing. There was also Martin's funeral to plan. But being at home brought no relief from her pain because the house suddenly seemed cold and empty, like a mausoleum. Normally there'd be cheerful music playing but it only aggravated her already-raw emotions so she'd turned it off. In fact, nothing she attempted seemed to soothe the deep-seated distress she felt. She sat doing nothing and she tackled a multitude of jobs but neither stopped her mind racing with morbid thoughts. What really upset her was how the police had conducted their search for Nicky. They'd virtually ransacked every square inch of the house and had then removed numerous items for further investigation, including Nicky's computer and other personal belongings. Beth could probably have lived with this but it was their questions that really upset. The cops appeared to believe Nicky might actually have **wanted** to run away, that she had, perhaps, chosen to vanish deliberately. The suggestion was, of course, absolutely ridiculous. Beth had done her best to assure them that Nicky would **never** willingly leave her home and family, but they'd insisted on continuing their probing. She'd finished up screaming at them to leave. Where would it all end? The Reed family was disintegrating in front of her and there appeared to be nothing she could do about it.

Byron arrived at Mill House soon after two o'clock. While he'd sounded supremely confident when he'd told Johnny about seeing Jane again, actually confronting her face to face was another matter altogether. As he rang the front door bell he, too, noticed the newly-painted 1641 above the lintel. But he had no time to dwell on the date because the door opened to reveal a frowning Jane, casually dressed in navy trousers and aquamarine blouse. "Not you again," she said regarding him distastefully and making no effort to invite him inside. "This is becoming a habit I could well do without."

Byron fought to stay cool and find a way to mollify Nicky's mother. "Well, it's always a pleasure to see you, Jane," he countered, with as much sincerity as he could muster. "I need to talk to you about Nicky. It's extremely important."

Jane scowled. "We've already been there, Byron. I had nothing to say to you before and I have nothing to say now. I have more pressing matters to...."

"It's a matter of life and death, Jane. Nicky's life. You know I'm not a policeman but I am a close friend and I care very deeply what happens to your daughter."

Still glaring angrily, Jane gave the impression she'd made her mind up. "I don't take kindly to pestering, Byron. It appears Nicky vanished about the time I arrived here late yesterday afternoon, yet the police still saw fit to turn this house upside down and subject me to a barrage of questions. I'm in no mood for more harassment."

Byron sought to soften his tone but it was very difficult in the face of such hostility. "I understand how you feel but the fact remains your daughter has vanished and her life may be in very real danger. There's an exceedingly dangerous maniac on the loose in this area. He's already killed three times so if you know anything that may help to account for Nicky's disappearance, anything at all, you need to mention it **now**."

Jane stared at him indecisively for a couple of heartbeats before coming to a decision. "Get out!" she snarled forcefully, and then more stridently: *"Get out!"*

Byron turned away. He'd lost again, big time, and the defeat felt much worse than last time, on a par with missing an open Cup Final goal. He was trudging dejectedly back to his car when her voice stopped him in his tracks: "Wait right there," she ordered. "I'll be one minute."

# 47

IT WAS MID-AFTERNOON BEFORE Jack found the opportunity to grab a lunch-break. It was his first day in charge and he was already beginning to understand how his stepfather had become so engrossed with running the business. The thought both amused and exasperated him.

Chomping on one of his favourite beef and horseradish sandwiches, he turned on the TV in his office and flicked through the main channels, only to discover his missing sister was the main news on every one of them. Even an injury to England's football captain, which threatened to rule him out of the final World Cup qualifying match, hadn't managed to push Nicky's disappearance off the top of the news. Jack instantly forgot about his many tasks as he watched Andy Lancaster's urgent appeal to the general public to find his sister. He settled on the detailed report on BBC1, which included a recent and very flattering photo of Nicky on her horse, together with a few random shots of Cartmel village. It was an excellent piece of journalism and he had nothing but praise for the DCI's part in it. The investigation was suddenly a national story and Jack was delighted, especially in light of his earlier misunderstanding with Beth.

That morning at breakfast he'd somewhat thoughtlessly expressed the view that if Nicky had run away she was bound to think better of it and swiftly return home. Beth had been appalled by this comment: "I can't believe you actually think your sister would intentionally leave home," she'd said, unable to contain her displeasure. "Don't you recall how upset she was that Martin walked out on his Buckinghamshire family? The very *last* thing she'd do is run away. You should be ashamed of yourself for even considering it!" And Jack was ashamed. He could only think it was the pressure of his new position as managing director. That and his intense worry. But if he'd only known it, his fears were very similar to Beth's. He, too, was witnessing the breakdown of his family with growing helplessness. And none of his ceaseless prayers seemed to have been answered, not yet at any rate.

Andy was thrilled with the TV coverage. A single phone call was all it had taken for the Assistant Chief Constable to set the process in motion. The ACC had even arranged for the interview to be held outside the impressive Magistrates' Court in Abbey Road, Barrow, which was only a short walk from the Operation Mandarin headquarters. Andy was equally confident Nicky's disappearance would be front page news in all the national dailies. In his experience, such widespread coverage would inevitably lead to numerous 'sightings' of Nicky. As a consequence, he'd already organised additional telephone lines together with extra telephonists to cope with them. All being well, the lass would be found very quickly and unharmed. That was Plan A. Plan B would necessarily involve poring over the case notes yet again.

The DCI was particularly keen, come what may, to revisit the 'possible motives' file. Ed's team had brainstormed a diverse list but these had either already been shot down in flames or no longer appeared to fit the growing catalogue of crimes. Andy itemised all the Common Possible Motives that had become ingrained on his brain ever since he'd become a detective constable: *Sex; Jealousy; Racism; Robbery; Anger/fright; Power control; Gain; Payment; Hate; Revenge; Homophobia; Psychosis.* During his long career, he'd come upon plentiful examples of every single one of them, so much so he was rarely shocked these days by any murder. But, like most of his colleagues, he found it exceedingly difficult having to come to terms with psychotic killers. One of the main reasons was that psychotics often have the ability to hide their condition so that they seem completely normal most of the time. He recalled the definition of Psychosis: *any form of severe mental disorder in which the individual's contact with reality becomes highly distorted.* The wording gave more than a suggestion why experienced police officers felt such disquiet having to deal with this condition. It is because the psychotic's mental disorder is *severe* and his or her contact with reality becomes *highly* distorted. And why was Andy considering psychosis? It had to be that a part of him, and a growing part after his examination of the case notes, was convinced he was dealing with a psychotic in the Cartmel case. He fervently hoped he was way off the mark.

# 48

BYRON DID AS HE was told and stood where he was. Jane was renowned for blowing hot and cold and he was intrigued to find out if she'd had a change of heart.

He didn't have long to wait. Jane beckoned him into Mill House and led him into the lounge. Despite his curiosity, he couldn't help noticing the original oak plank door again. And the fireplace was from the sixteen hundreds, too. There weren't too many seventeenth century houses that were still lived in so he was impressed. Jane didn't invite him to sit. Instead she held up a pair of large, matching, plain brown envelopes before replacing them carefully on the coffee table in front of her. Without any hint of a smile or apology, she began: "By rights, I should have shown these to the police last night but I was so upset with their bullying attitude I just couldn't be bothered. With hindsight, it was a mistake." She shrugged. "There was another reason I didn't show them. You'd understand perfectly if I allowed you to study what's inside them right now, but I have absolutely no intention of letting you see either of them, *ever.* I suspect the police will need to inspect them but that's as maybe."

For the life of him, Byron couldn't work out what was going on here but he waited patiently while Jane controlled her emotions. "Whatever else you think of me, Byron," she said, gazing towards the fireplace, "please believe I love all my children very deeply and will do whatever I consider necessary for their well-being." Then, looking him in the eye, she continued, "With that in mind, I intend to tell you about these envelopes. I received the first one at the time of that awful fire at McAdams. It was here waiting for me after I'd driven up from London. It contains a large coloured photograph of Nicky in what I can only describe as a very compromising pose. I should have studied it more carefully at the time but I confess I put it immediately into a secure location. It's been there ever since and I've thought little more about it until now. The second envelope was with the rest of my mail when I arrived home late yesterday afternoon. This one contains a large photo of me and my...but that doesn't matter right now. It, also, is very revealing and extremely disturbing, which is why I made myself study *both* photos and envelopes. I came to some interesting conclusions. First, the envelopes were blank and so were not posted as ordinary mail. Second, this old house has a small letterbox and neither of the photos was bent, which means someone with access to the property placed the envelopes on the inside mat. I find that extremely alarming but it's a mere trifle to what else I worked out." Collecting the envelopes, she made for the door into the hallway. "Please follow me," she ordered.

Again Byron did as he was told and soon they were in an upstairs bedroom on the corner of the house. The room contained a large divan bed and a small hand-basin with a mirror over it. His curiosity well and truly aroused, he waited to discover what else Jane had to tell him. He didn't have long to wait. Placing the envelopes on the bed, she pointed dramatically at the small mirror over the basin. "There is no doubt, none whatsoever," she stated, "that both photographs were taken from the other side of that glass."

Byron's eyes widened. "Wow, that's quite a statement!" he said. Striding over to the mirror, he inspected it carefully then tapped the wall on either side of the glass. "The police have photography experts who will be able to tell whether your photos have been tampered with or manipulated. But apart from taking this mirror out or knocking a hole in your wall, I can see no easy way of proving your claim. If you're right and there is a space behind the glass, there must be access to it. Do I take it you've searched for a possible way in?"

"Oh, yes. I haven't yet taken to measuring all the rooms to check if there is an area that's not accounted for, but I have searched upstairs and downstairs thoroughly. I found nothing."

Byron walked across to the windows. "A secret room would make very good sense. I've wondered a time or two where Ben and Josh's murderer hid prior to his attacks. I used to think he watched from the top of the rocks at the back of your house. I had to discount that theory because it takes too long to climb up or down the rock face. But perhaps the killer was behind that mirror all the time, watching and waiting."

"That's too awful to contemplate," said Jane, shuddering. "But it's increasingly clear to me that I'm going to have to call the police back here."

"Afraid so," nodded Byron, "but before you do, I've had an idea. Did you search the library?"

"Yes, but there's nothing there apart from lots of old, dusty books."

"Maybe, maybe not. Your decorator fellow probably told you I spotted someone there while you were away. This bloke was a very cool customer and even had his own key. But what was he doing there in the first place? He made no effort to go into the rest of the house, which is pretty strange if you ask me."

"Mark is my interior designer," Jane said tartly, " and he did mention your visit. He also told me you called the police."

"I gave Ed a call," Byron admitted, "and we checked out the library. Same result as you but I'd like to give it another search before you call the cops. How about it?"

Jane shrugged indifferently. "I can't think there's anything worthwhile there but it's up to you. You can go through the kitchen."

"Thanks," said Byron, and made to move off when another thought struck him. "I couldn't help noticing the date of the house over the front door: 1641. Do you happen to know any of the history of Mill House?"

Looking thoroughly bored, Jane managed a dismissive shake of the head. "Not my scene at all, Byron, and I doubt if my husband knows anything, either. Ray's as totally uninterested in history as I am."

Byron was still smiling at Jane's response when he began his second examination of the library. The prospects looked far from promising. There were rows and rows of books but little else. If there was a hidden entrance in the room, it was very well concealed. And yet the Hoody had spent time here. For what possible purpose?

After half an hour of fruitless searching, Byron realised he needed a more radical approach. He therefore began to take the books off the shelves and pile them on the floor. In no time at all he was coughing and spluttering as he breathed in the disturbed dust. It was a thankless task as the cleared shelves appeared to be very ordinary indeed but he carried on until every shelf was emptied. It all looked so normal and he surveyed his handiwork unenthusiastically, deciding every single book would have to be replaced and the library returned to its original state. It was then that he spotted the dark knot on the light, cross-grained wooden panel. It was the only object in the whole room that attracted his attention and he was curious enough to investigate it. He felt the knot and tugged at it but it was only when he pushed it hard that he got a result. There was a sudden low whoosh of air and a whole section of shelving swung back, revealing a large, black hole in the wall. Byron could only stand and stare, totally astounded. "Wow!" he said for the second time that afternoon.

# 49

DCI Andy Lancaster and DI Ed Hampson were in broad agreement. As far as the Cartmel enquiry was concerned there was, at long last, a chink of light at the end of the tunnel. Not much, perhaps, but certainly a glimmer.

And it was all to do with Byron's phone call to Ed. The call had been brief: "Come round to Mill House and come at once." The DI had dropped everything and made for his car. Organising searches and re-checking alibis was important work but both would have to wait. Police tasks are often about prioritising and he'd sensed both urgency and excitement in Byron's voice.

Byron was waiting at the front of the house and quickly ushered Ed through to the library. The pair of them donned white coveralls and cotton gloves that the DI insisted they wear before entering the passageway. For the next twenty minutes they explored everything the secret room had to offer. When Ed exposed the two-way mirror, Byron could only stand and gape. Who had installed this mirror and for what possible reason? How did it tie in with the Cartmel case? He could stay quiet no longer: "From what little I've seen, I'm convinced the passageway, the steps and this room are as old as the original house, which means they've been here over 360 years. Fascinating! The entrance from the library and the two-way mirror are much more recent additions, of course. A house such as this was bound to have had somewhere for the carthorses so the library was probably built on when the old stables were pulled down. But the two-way mirror is something else!"

Ed managed a grin. "There are some funny people about. I mean funny peculiar. I can only ever remember the Bennetts owning this house before

Ray Templeton bought it. Old man Bennett was well-known for his wild parties. It wouldn't surprise me if he was a voyeur and had the mirror put in for his own kinky pleasures. But how the Hoody came to be using the facilities is anybody's guess. I'll get forensics to check for fingerprints and we might discover who else has been here."

Byron said, "I need to do some research on 1641, which is the date over Jane's front door. There was an Irish rebellion that year but I don't think it has any relevance for us. What's of far greater interest is that 1641 was the year before the English Civil War started."

Ed looked blank. "The Civil War? Why could that be important?"

"The Civil War, as I'm sure you know, was an out-and-out struggle between King Charles I and Parliament. This whole area was a hotbed of unrest. What might be significant for us is that there were battles fought near here between the King's followers, the Cavaliers, and Parliament's supporters, the Roundheads. For instance, I recall visiting the museum in Barrow and spotting a cannonball that had been fired during one of the local skirmishes. But there was a much more important battle fought at Lindal Close and that's only a few miles away."

"I still don't get it," said Ed.

"Don't you remember priest holes?" asked Byron, warming to his subject. "They were built in Elizabeth I's reign to hide Roman Catholics when it was high treason for them to be in England. What if supporters of Charles I developed this idea for their own safety at a time when the monarchy was very unpopular? Most priest holes in the sixteenth century were pretty inconsequential hiding places but this spot we've uncovered is something very different. If you had a supply of water and food you could survive here safely for days if not weeks."

"It's an intriguing theory but I'm more concerned about who's been using it in the last month or so."

Byron grinned. "Oh, well, I'll do the research anyway, if only for my own benefit."

Ed directed his torch from side to side one final time. He was clearly keen to head back to Barrow and report the discovery of the secret room and organise a much more thorough search. Byron was in no rush and offered to replace all the books on their shelves and leave the library just as he'd found it. In light of what was to happen later, it was an inspired decision.

# 50

TWO WHOLE DAYS HAD passed since Nicky had disappeared. Despite a large police presence in and around Cartmel, together with nationwide coverage on television and in the papers, she was still missing. Johnny was very down.

He'd tried to stay upbeat and tell himself she'd soon be found but it hadn't happened. It was all very depressing, so much so he'd cancelled the date he'd been looking forward to. "How can I possibly go out and enjoy myself with another lass when Nicky hasn't come home?" he told Byron plaintively.

Byron shook his head to that. "As long as you don't just sit around and mope. I know you, Johnny. You need to keep body and mind active or you'll go into a decline. I came round here reasonably cheerful, despite Nicky, and I find you right down in the dumps. You're like a big, black, soggy cloud spreading gloom and dismay everywhere."

Johnny forced a feeble smile. "Thanks very much! You love to exaggerate, don't you. Anyway, what have you got to be happy about?"

"Who said anything about happiness? I simply refuse to be thoroughly miserable like you. That's not going to help Nicky, is it?"

"I suppose not," Johnny conceded, and then in a louder voice: "All right, tell me something that will cheer me up. What was the news dad mentioned about Nicky? Remind me."

Byron took a rapid look round the public bar of The King's Arms. It was late afternoon and the only other customers were four senior citizens sitting in a group at the far side of the room. Even so, he nudged Johnny forcefully in the chest. "Keep your voice down," he stressed. "What your dad told us earlier was for our ears alone. He's not told us any major secrets, you can be sure of that, but he certainly doesn't want what he did tell us in the public domain."

Johnny rubbed his chest ruefully. "I understand that but I can't say I got the gist of what he told us," he admitted.

"Nicky's fingerprints were all over the secret room at Mill House," Byron spelled out. "There were very few others, none of which have so far been identified. A couple of Nicky's personal belongings, which Beth identified, were also found there. I'm certain our friend, the Hoody, knows all about this room and has visited it at least a few times but I'm equally sure he was careful enough to leave no fingerprints. Now, think about it, Johnny. How did Nicky get to know about the secret room? And how did the Hoody find out about it? Believe me, they definitely didn't find the entrance by luck. No way! Someone showed them or told them about it. One possible clue came from something Beth said. She told your dad that Lee Bennett had taken Nicky to Mill house just before he left for South Africa. Apparently it's common knowledge the lad fancied her so there's a good chance *he* showed her. But how did the Hoody find out? That's another matter. Anyway, Ed's in touch with the South African police. They're going to interview Lee and see what he has to say for himself. They'll probably press for his fingerprints, and his father's and his grandfather's, if the old bloke's still alive. Merely for elimination purposes, of course."

Johnny nodded absent-mindedly. "And what's all this about the Civil War? What's *that* got to do with anything?"

"Probably nothing," said Byron, and explained about the 1641 date over Jane's front door and its possible relevance.

"I know you're keen on history, By, but I'm with dad on this one. I think you're way off the mark. Surely it's how the secret room has been used recently that matters, not what happened there hundreds of years ago."

"Maybe," Byron conceded, but he was reluctant to agree wholeheartedly until he'd done further research on the matter. He was all too aware that history often has a way of making itself felt when least expected.

Over in Barrow at the Operation Mandarin headquarters, Ed was co-ordinating the hunt for Nicky. It's widely acknowledged that the first forty eight hours of any such search is the most significant. Unfortunately that window of opportunity had passed and she'd still not been found. Ed was disappointed but not demoralised. He'd come to the conclusion Nicky had been taken by force. While he could, perhaps, accept she might have decided to go off without telling anyone for a few hours, even a whole day, she was not the type of girl who would simply drift away and forget her loved ones. He was convinced that, had she been able, Nicky would have contacted her family the very same day she vanished.

Managing the search for her was such a demanding task that Ed had found there weren't enough hours in each day and he'd had to put all his other tasks on hold. He was now concentrating on the next phase of the operation, which was to instigate thorough checks of all the local farms and their adjacent land. It was another huge, manpower-intensive undertaking requiring considerable organisation. At least the widespread media coverage had caught the public attention and many had come forward with possible sightings and other information. Most callers were well-intentioned but there were the usual publicity-seekers and time-wasters. Some of Ed's time had to be spent assessing each sighting and assigning officers to investigate the more promising ones. With so many potential leads, it meant having to prioritise, sometimes on the flimsiest of evidence, which meant there was already a sizeable queue of new leads stacking up waiting to be tackled. But Ed knew the trick was to work systematically through the list and not to panic.

In contrast to Nicky's disappearance, there had been a total blackout of news on the discovery of the secret room. This embargo had been ordered by Andy Lancaster, in consultation with Ed. The two senior cops didn't want to draw any attention to Mill House and, as an added precaution, had ordered covert observation of the property just in case the Hoody decided to return. They'd also invited Professor Tim Harrold, a well-known Civil War expert, to take a look at the secret room to see if anything vital had been missed. He was driving up immediately from Cambridge, where he worked in the history faculty at the university. Privately, Ed was *not* confident the professor would bring anything of consequence to the investigation but it was a step that needed to be taken and, at the very least, it would keep Byron happy.

After her initial rant at the police, Jane had suddenly decided to offer her total co-operation. It was so like Jane. She'd come to the conclusion that, though she didn't much like the police or their methods, it was still better to work with them than against them. And, when all was said and done, it was her daughter who'd disappeared. She'd therefore promised to say nothing about the secret room, which totally bored her anyway, and had handed over the pair of envelopes and photos she'd discussed with Byron, with provisos Ed had been happy to agree to. These pictures were certainly repugnant but the DI had seen far more damaging ones during his career. Anyway, he'd never been one to judge other's lives. But he still couldn't help studying Nicky's photo with a high degree of sadness. Until very recently, she'd been his son's girlfriend and who knows how their relationship might have developed had matters been different. None of that was important now. What mattered was neither photo nor envelope, as Ed had suspected, gave the slightest clue to the identity of the photographer, though each had undergone every test known to forensics.

There was another, belated consequence of all that had happened to the Reed family. Beth had suffered a breakdown and had been taken to stay with her sister in Carlisle. Ed was not at all surprised when he heard the news but he was really saddened as he'd developed a soft spot for Beth. At first she'd refused to leave but, following doctor's advice, she'd eventually done so but only on the understanding that when Nicky was found she would return at once. Jack would now have to run his home as well as the business but Ed had no worries on that score. If the worst came to the worst and he couldn't cope with all the extra pressure, he could always hire a housekeeper. It wasn't as if he couldn't afford it. Ed reserved his concerns for Adam, who was clearly much more vulnerable. The lad had come to rely on Beth, so much so that Ed determined to seek out Jack and suggest he keep a close eye on his brother.

Just when Ed was wondering when the next piece of good news would arrive, he heard from his colleagues in South Africa. They'd traced the Bennett family easily enough in Cape Town, where they'd set up home. Lee Bennett had confirmed it was he who'd introduced Nicky to the secret room. After further prodding, it was also established Lee had learnt about the room from his grandfather before the old man died. His father, apparently, knew nothing of the secret. It remained to be seen whether this knowledge would be useful or not but it was encouraging there was now a steady drip, drip of information. Ed could only hope it would soon turn into a flood.

He was thinking it was time to go home when his desk phone rang. It was Steve Riley. The DS had only returned to duties that morning. One of the twins had suffered a lengthy bout of sickness and diarrhoea that had been so serious she'd been kept in hospital for a week. Fortunately she'd recovered fully and been allowed to return home. The two detectives chatted about this and other matters for a minute or so before Steve said, "I'd better explain why I've phoned you. I've been attempting to get back to speed with the enquiry so I was checking through some of the documents I'd missed in my absence. I happened to be reading the pathologist's final report on Martin Reed's death when Martin's DNA results came through. Prepare yourself for a shock. According to the DNA information we now have, there is absolutely no way that Martin can have fathered Simon Reed."

# 51

ED WAS BACK IN Barrow early the following morning for the 8:15 team briefing. Andy Lancaster read a progress report prepared by two of the team and then spent a few minutes reviewing the search for Nicky. At the appropriate moment, he asked Ed for his input.

The DI made his way quickly to the front. "The farm and farmland search is well underway," he said. "I've also brought in the Cumbria Police Underwater Search Unit, who are in the process of dragging all the local rivers, lakes and reservoirs. Following yesterday's briefing and the suggestions that came from it, Andy and I have agreed to request a helicopter sweep of the Cartmel valley and its environs. We're waiting for the Assistant Chief Constable to say yea or nay to this one but we're confident it will get the go-ahead."

Ed returned to his seat and attempted to concentrate on the rest of the briefing. It was very difficult. His mind was still reeling from the news Steve had passed on the previous evening. Martin's DNA was so unlike the sample Adam had provided after Simon's suicide that the pair couldn't possibly be related. Martin was therefore *not* the twins' biological father. It was as simple as that. Years earlier, Ed had heard the claim that one in ten men could be victims of paternity fraud. As a simple statistic it meant very little, but it was very different when you knew the individuals involved. Many families have their complications but the Reed family relationships had suddenly become highly complex. Unravelling these complexities could well be like trying to cross an extensive, unmarked minefield, with snipers taking pot-shots at you from all angles. But Ed had been quick to realise the DNA information might be the vital clue they'd been waiting for. After all, it is exactly this type of paternity fraud that can provide a motive for murder and, right from the very beginning of the case, the police had struggled to find a suitable motive for all the Cartmel mayhem. Questions needed to be asked but there was one that overshadowed the rest: who knew the truth?

As a consequence, Ed had drawn the short straw to interview Jane. Andy was in no doubt the DI was best-equipped to tackle the twin's mother and get the most out of her and he'd sent him back to Cartmel with encouraging words and a knowing smile: "You've known her a lot of years. You'll know what to say to her. But make sure you take Steve Riley with you to cover your back."

Ed had been about to argue but what was the point? Andy's first statement was true enough but his second was way off the mark. Ed doubted whether anyone knew the best way to treat Jane Templeton. He certainly didn't. In all the years he'd known her, he'd *never* been sure what to say to her or how to cope with her many, changeable moods. But he'd been chosen for the job so he might as well make the best of it. Before he and Steve set off, he made sure he got himself a large coffee. He reckoned he was going to need it.

There were two cars already parked outside Mill House. Ed remembered the Cambridge professor had arrived to study the secret room so one of the cars was probably his. Ed had met the historian briefly and doubted he would find anything of further use to the investigation, but let him dabble in the past. The DI reckoned there were far more pressing matters to pursue.

When Jane opened the door, Ed introduced his detective sergeant and informed Jane that Steve would be taking notes of the meeting. She invited the pair of them into the lounge and pointed to where they could sit but Ed was too on edge to appreciate either the seventeenth century features that had so impressed Byron or Jane's very expensive antiques. As they made themselves as comfortable as they could on their wooden chairs, Jane broke the ice: "One of your colleagues phoned to tell me you were on your way but stressed there's still no news on Nicky's whereabouts." She pursed her lips and was about to say more then changed her mind and looked away towards the window.

Ed sought to fill the sudden, awkward silence: "We'll tell you, of course, if there is...."

"Oh, don't be so pompous, Ed!" Jane blurted out. "How long have we known each other? Just tell me what you came for, for goodness sake!"

Ed tensed then relaxed. It was usually his policy in such circumstances to get straight to the point but he'd be blowed if he'd do so right now with Jane. He intended to try a different route and if she didn't like his line of questioning, she'd have to lump it. He asked, "What did you think of Martin when you learned he had another family in Buckinghamshire?"

Frowning, Jane gave every impression of being thrown by the question. "What did I think of Martin? I'm not sure what you mean."

"It's simple enough. Martin was your husband but he married you bigamously because he already had a wife and two children in the south. What did you think of him when you found out?"

Jane shrugged. "It merely confirmed what I already thought."

"Which was?"

She looked Ed in the eye. "That he was weak. Very weak!" she spat out.

"Weak? Yet he took your father's ailing business and transformed it into a successful company. That doesn't strike me as weak."

She shrugged again. "He had his uses, I suppose, but you didn't have to live with him. I stick with my description."

Ed changed tack. "Did you ever have any idea there was another family? Another woman?"

"Never, especially another woman," Jane sneered. "He couldn't satisfy one woman, never mind two!"

"What about your children? Is it possible any of them could have known about the other family?"

To her credit, Jane didn't rush to answer. "No," she said, "I'm positive they didn't have a clue. It was Martin's secret and he kept it to himself."

Ed nodded. "And what about the secret room upstairs? Did you have any idea it existed *before* you checked your pair of photographs?"

Shaking her head vigorously as if to suggest the idea was absolutely preposterous, she looked at Steve and rolled her eyes in disbelief. Turning again to Ed, she said stingingly, "Do you actually believe I might have posed naked had I known? What do you take me for? It came right out of the blue, I assure you."

"And did you have any idea Nicky was using the upstairs bedroom to entertain her lovers?"

Jane's eyes narrowed. "No, I didn't," she said quietly, "but take care, Ed, you're stepping on delicate ground."

"I have a need to ask," Ed said, equally quietly. "Two of those lovers have been murdered very brutally and your daughter has vanished without trace. The secret room is somehow connected to these events and we need to find that connexion. Urgently." He fidgeted on his chair in an attempt to get comfortable before asking, "Can you think of anyone who might have wanted your ex-husband murdered?"

Again Jane didn't hurry to reply. "I can think of no-one unless you count me," she said, trying hard not to smirk. "I've wanted to murder the stupid man often enough. Fortunately for me I was in London when he met his death."

"And have you considered that *you* might be targeted by the murderer?"

The hint of a smile disappeared instantly to be replaced by a worried frown. "No, I haven't," she said hesitantly. "Why, do you think I'm in danger?"

"I have no specific information, Jane, but if you take a look at the list of victims, it stands to reason you might consider exercising some caution."

The warning clearly hit home and it was Jane's turn to shift uncomfortably. While she was temporarily disconcerted, Ed decided it was time to ask his key question: "Last night we received a report on Martin's DNA. Are you aware he is not the father of your twins?" He watched her carefully, eager to gauge her response to his question.

This time there was only a brief delay. "Certainly I knew. But I swear to you my husband had no idea the twins weren't his. I always made him wear a condom. He reckoned later that one of them must have leaked and I did nothing whatsoever to dissuade him from that view."

Ed carried on studying Jane. Her eyes were unusually bright and there was more red in her cheeks than make-up could account for, but there was no hint of remorse in the gaze she returned. He said calmly, "In other words, you let him believe a lie."

"I let him believe what he wanted to believe. Martin was *desperate* to be a father so I merely let him assume the boys were his. To have done otherwise would quite simply have ruined him and I wasn't prepared to let that happen."

Ed couldn't help himself. "How noble of you!" He regretted the sarcasm immediately. It wasn't like him to judge other's actions and the last thing he needed right now was to alienate Jane Templeton.

Suddenly the red spots on Jane's cheeks were much brighter. "How dare you come into my house and pronounce judgement on me," she snapped. "You know nothing of what happened, of what it was like for us. I made a decision I felt was right for all concerned. For *everyone*: the twins, Martin, the biological father and, yes, I have to admit it, for me, too. And do you know what? If I had my time all over again, I'd make *exactly* the same choice. The same, do you hear me?"

Ed gave her a little time to recover while he pondered all he'd heard. "Forgive my outburst," he said. "It was unforgivable. But there is one matter that puzzles me. How did you know for certain that Martin was not the twins' father?"

Jane twisted in her chair, all at once appearing ill-at-ease, and took her time before replying. "It was a difficult period but, because of what's happened to Nicky, I know I need to tell you the truth. For the nine months I carried the twins, I had absolutely no idea who their father was. To be honest, it could have been any one of four men." She shook her head, looking positively haunted. "But I needed only one look at my newborn babies to know for sure who'd fathered them."

Ed waited but when it was clear nothing more was forthcoming, he asked: "Apart from you, who else knew who the father was?"

"Nobody, I swear. Martin was over the moon. He just accepted the boys as his and never, ever doubted it for a single second. The real dad had disappeared off the scene by then. He was a total ne'er-do-well, I'm sorry to say, and he'd have run a mile if he'd even **suspected** the truth. I haven't set eyes on him since the night of the conception. It was a one night stand and that's all it ever was." And then, with a great deal more conviction, she added: "I'm a completely different person these days."

Ed nodded reassuringly, wondering just how much Jane **had** changed in the intervening years. But he didn't dwell on the thought. It was time to ask the other key question: "You claim you were the only one who knew the truth. How certain can you be?"

"I can't for the life of me think anyone else could possibly have known."

"Think very hard, Jane," Ed pressed. "This is vitally important. Could anyone else have found out?"

"I can't see how. The twins' birth certificates record Martin as the father. I certainly never told anyone and I hope it goes without saying I never wrote anything down."

"You told me you knew as soon as you saw your babies," said Ed. "Was there anyone else who could have worked it out?"

Jane thought hard but not for long. "No," she replied. "Martin was too elated to query anything and the real father was no longer around. There was no-one else."

"What about the other two men you considered **might** have been the father. What about them? Is it possible one of them figured it out?"

Looking thoroughly tormented, Jane threw her arms in the air and sobbed, "I don't think so but I can't be certain. *I just don't know!*"

Ed's chair was very uncomfortable and he needed to stretch his legs. He got up and walked past Steve to the window. In the small side garden, he spotted Professor Tim Harrold pacing up and down looking agitated about something or other. Ed ignored him and returned unhurriedly to his chair. Jane was busy blowing her nose with a tiny handkerchief and trying to compose herself. She said wearily, "I'm sorry. I'm not much help, am I?"

Ed waved that away. "We need to be as certain as possible that nobody else knew. I don't wish to intrude into your private life, Jane, but it is vital we rule out these other two men. Is there an easy way we can accomplish that?"

Jane looked thoroughly miserable. "No, there isn't. It would be very easy to lie to you at this point but I know I've got to come clean."

Ed nodded sympathetically. "It has to be your decision, of course, but I can promise we will be discreet."

"These secrets have a way of coming out," Jane said sadly. "This is such a difficult situation but I'll have to trust you. One of the two men died at least ten years ago. A massive heart attack. The other was Dennis Fullard. We had a fling all those years ago."

Five minutes later, following more reassurances but no more revelations, Ed and Steve found themselves outside Mill House and walking towards their car. Both said nothing. For his part, Ed was overjoyed to be out in the fresh air, even though the wind had got up strongly. Jane Templeton made him very twitchy. She'd given them plenty to mull over, especially her startling confession. But they were going to have to be patient because, just as they reached the car, the professor called out and came running towards them. Tim Harrold was not your typical professor. Short, balding and considerably overweight, he was dressed more like a tradesman than a historian but he could still move fast when he needed to. As he caught up to them, he called out breathlessly: "Am I glad to see you both! You must come with me and let me show you what I've discovered. It's so exciting, I can't get over it. The ingenuity takes my breath away. They've used a pulley system that's so simple it's absolutely brilliant. And there are some costumes dating back to the sixteen hundreds that are in magnificent condition. Wait till you see it all!"

The historian turned back, almost pulling the DI round the side of the house. They went willingly enough. Ed had made up his mind some time ago that the secret room had little more to offer the investigation but it appeared he might have miscalculated.

# 52

BYRON HAD A LOT on his mind but was still keen to do the run he'd planned, even though there'd been heavy overnight rain. He'd checked his local map and was ready to explore some new territory. It would mean re-tracing his route through the woods where the Hoody had attacked him and then heading by Headless Cross and Boarbank Hall to Flookburgh and on to Cark. From there he could follow the winding road back to Cartmel. It would involve a round trip of about eight miles, including some serious hill work. As full training for the new football season was fast approaching, the run would be a good test of his fitness.

Filling his haversack with his map, phone, a spare T-shirt and socks, some lunch and a large bottle of water, he recalled the message he'd received late the previous afternoon. It was from Ed and reminded him of the call he'd made to the DI when he'd first discovered the secret room. Ed's voice had the same level of awe and excitement.

Byron had rushed over to Mill House and met up with Ed, Steve Riley and Professor Tim Harrold. It was over two hours since the professor had made his find of a second secret room but he was still rushing round like a ten year-old. He knew of Byron's interest in history and insisted on giving him a personal tour of his discovery, chatting non-stop throughout. Byron didn't share Tim's passion for the Royalist clothing but he was totally enthralled with the second room. The professor claimed the entrance was nothing short of ingenious but that was a definite understatement. The way in from the original secret room was so brilliantly concealed that Byron would never have found it if he'd searched for it all year. The new room was smaller than the original but, whether by luck or judgment, it was perfectly airtight, which had greatly helped to preserve the costumes found there. Tim was quick to suggest there'd probably been a second entrance to this room, accessed from the main upstairs bedroom, but that it had been blocked off during an earlier renovation of the property.

The professor had prattled on about the wonderful pair of Royalist costumes which would grace any museum in the country. One point, particularly, caught Byron's attention: the clothing, it seemed, was full of ancient flea dirt. Tim had then caught up with the two cops, giving them and Byron his considered opinion on the secrets of Mill House: "It has all to do with the fierce struggle between King and Parliament in the middle of the seventeenth century," he explained enthusiastically, as if to one of his classes of Cambridge undergraduates. "It must have been clear to Charles I's supporters there was serious trouble brewing. As there were a number of influential Royalists living in the Cartmel area who needed to protect themselves, I can virtually guarantee Mill House was built a year before the outbreak of the Civil War with security in mind. The secret rooms would have been used only as a last resort to hide some of these Royalist dignitaries. But I doubt the need ever arose. That was because there was a decisive battle fought at Lindal Close, which is only a few miles from here, on the first of October, 1643. It was between Furness Royalists and a force of Parliamentarians. Although the Royalists vastly outnumbered their opponents, they were attacked with such resolution and courage that they ran before a shot was fired. The battle was all over in fifteen minutes. 1600 Royalists on horses, together with 200 foot soldiers, fled westwards, many of them drowning as they tried to cross Duddon Sands. A further 400, including their leader, Colonel Sir William Huddleston, were taken prisoner. There were only two Parliamentarian casualties, and one of those hurt himself with his own pistol! Altogether, it was a disaster for the Furness Royalists, made worse the following year when the whole of northern England was lost to the King after the Battle of Marston Moor. The Civil War eventually ended on 30th January, 1649 when Charles I was beheaded in the Palace of Whitehall. The country was then ruled by Oliver Cromwell as Lord Protector until the monarchy was restored in 1660."

Byron had double-checked all this information for himself and it still totally fascinated him, especially as much of it was very much *local* history. But Ed, after his initial excitement, was not in the least bit interested. He summed up the police response very coolly and concisely: "There's only one point that concerns us right now. Only one," he stressed. "Can we make use of these secret rooms to catch our murderer?" Then, fixing the professor with a stern gaze, he added, "Those costumes stay here until further notice. Even more important, *say nothing* about the secret rooms. *Nothing to anyone until further notice.*"

It was mid-morning before Byron set off on his run. In truth, he was pleased to get out of the house for a while. His parents were at loggerheads over some matter or other. His dad could be a bit insensitive at times and his mum responded by not speaking to him, sometimes for days. Byron knew better than to intervene. He left Orchard Park moments before his dad drove off for a round of golf, both hoping the dust would settle before their return.

Byron had no qualms about retracing his steps in the woods where the Hoody had opened fire on him. He didn't believe the Hoody would be lurking there on the off chance he might pass by. Nor was he concerned about his parents' marital problems. They'd been together through thick and thin for long enough and couldn't live without each other. But he was extremely worried about Nicky. What had happened to her? He'd never been one of those who believed she'd skipped the area. Even with all her many troubles, she was not the sort of girl to cut and run. No, he was certain she'd been abducted but, as the days passed with no news of her, it was increasingly difficult to stay positive. And what about Johnny? Outwardly unscathed, Byron knew his best mate would never settle until he knew Nicky's fate. And it was as if Johnny had gone into hibernation, simply hiding himself away from the world. The same could be said of Adam and Jack. All three were doing their jobs and then retiring to their respective homes. He'd seen little of Johnny these last few days, which was most unusual, and even less of Nicky's brothers.

When he was in the mood, Byron loved running. And so it was now. The overnight rain had freshened everything and he fairly zipped along the first part of his course, which was mostly the grass of Cartmel Racecourse. Neither did he dally in the woods, maintaining such a steady pace he hardly had time to recognise where the Hoody had shot arrows at him. In no time at all he was out of the woodland and heading towards the hills. This was the start of the steep climb that took him by Headless Cross to Boarbank Hall, a nursing home run as a Catholic religious community by Augustinian sisters. Byron skirted the grounds and headed in the direction of Flookburgh, a once-busy fishing village on the shores of Morecambe Bay. Here the country was wilder and uninhabited, the hills slashed with deep ravines that were choked with rocks, brambles and other vegetation. This was the new country he'd checked on his map but he took care to watch his footing, aware a slip could send him hurtling into one of the deep, narrow gorges. According to local tradition, the last wolf in England had been killed in this very area in 1834, though Byron knew that information to be total poppycock. The reality was there had been no wolves in England since the end of the fifteenth century. But try telling that to the good folk of Flookburgh!

Hardly pausing, he rummaged in his haversack for his bottle of water and took a long swig from it. He'd already worked up a good appetite but it was too early for lunch. If possible, he wanted to get to Holker Hall in Cark before he munched the cheese and tomato sandwiches he'd prepared earlier. There was some wonderful parkland there and, if he was lucky, he might get a sight of the large herd of roe deer that lived on the estate.

Earlier there'd been a stiff breeze in the Cartmel Valley and plenty of cloud cover but about noon the sun made its first appearance of the day and the wind died down. Looking up, Byron saw only blue sky towards the west, which was where the bulk of the Furness weather came from. He grinned. It was going to be another warm August afternoon and he celebrated by taking off his T-shirt and consigning it to his haversack. Had there been any passers-by, they would have been struck by the bronzed, supremely-fit athlete wending his way resolutely to the top of the hill. Here the views were superb. Flookburgh and the whole of Morecambe Bay stretched away to the horizon but Byron barely paused. It wasn't that he didn't admire the beauty; it was simply that he had a tight schedule and was keen to keep moving. Besides, he was fancying his sandwiches and there was still a fair way to go to Holker Hall.

It was then he saw a middle-aged woman about a hundred yards ahead, peering down into the nearest ravine. He suspected at once that someone had fallen over the edge but, as he got closer, he saw the top of a bald head which, he guessed, belonged to the woman's partner. Both were talking volubly, the man standing on a narrow ledge about six feet from the surface. As Byron reached the scene, it was apparent the man was inspecting a large bundle at his feet. At first glance, it looked to be a shapeless package of indeterminate matter but, whatever it was, it was definitely agitating the couple. The woman knelt down issuing instructions while the man below tried to manoeuvre the bundle. He was very gentle. As Byron stood and watched, the man carefully turned the shapeless mass about ninety degrees. All at once Byron felt his hair stand on end. What he was staring at was not inanimate; it was human. It was at this point he made his second mistake. He was certain the couple had discovered a dead body but the bald-headed man suddenly called out, his voice filled with wonder, "She's alive! She's very, very weak but she's alive!"

The middle-aged woman stepped a little to one side, allowing Byron a closer look. He saw what he now took to be a woman who had clearly gone through such a desperate struggle that it had nearly killed her. Her clothing was so torn and bespattered with mud that she must have crawled for hours up the steep, rock-strewn ravine through brambles and driving rain in order to reach the ledge where she'd been spotted by the couple. Wet hair was plastered across her face which, where it wasn't ingrained with grime, was covered with matted blood from a long gash which ran from her lower cheek into her hairline. But what on earth was she doing on her own in this inhospitable place and in such a desperate state?

Byron was just about to ask the couple if they'd called the emergency services when he spotted the young woman's hands. Like her lower legs, they were badly-scratched and so caked with filth they made him shudder. But then, with growing horror, he noticed the ring on her index finger. He'd seen that band of gold many times and would have recognised it anywhere. Switching his attention back to the woman's face, he studied the bloodied profile with growing intuition. The woman was Nicky Reed. There was no doubt about it; none whatsoever.

# 53

I T WAS ANOTHER EARLY briefing for Operation Mandarin. Ed nursed his first coffee of the day and listened attentively to Andy Lancaster who, after reading his prepared introduction, was in full flow: "Nicky Reed was discovered in a ravine near Flookburgh and flown by air ambulance to Furness General Hospital early yesterday afternoon. She was taken immediately to the Intensive Care Unit, where she stayed overnight. She is suffering from hypothermia, two broken bones in her left foot, three cracked ribs, a deep gash on her face, a black eye, severe bruising and sundry other ailments. All the injuries, her doctors inform me, are consistent with her falling, jumping or being pushed into the ravine a number of days ago. Just how many days is a matter of conjecture. She was found five minutes after midday by a couple of Flookburgh residents. Byron Fullard, the Manchester United footballer, was also present. Beth Alderton, the partner of Martin Reed, and Nicky's two brothers were allowed to see her last night but she remained unconscious and unable to recognise them. This morning she was still classed as critically ill but the staff in the Intensive Care Unit report some slight progress in her overall condition. But I must stress the word 'slight' and remind you all that Nicky is still seriously ill and will remain so, I'm informed, for some time. Although the ICU is already a secure area, we have activated a round-the-clock guard on Nicky as we regard her as a very important witness. After consultation with her family, the decision has been made to ban all visitors until further notice. There are to be *no* exceptions to this rule." Andy took a good look round the room and consulted his notes before continuing, "The ravine where Miss Reed was found is being treated as a crime scene. Ed and a forensics team spent most of yesterday afternoon there and he will continue the briefing."

Clutching the remains of his coffee, Ed made his way to the front of the room. "I can't tell you at this stage whether Nicky Reed fell, jumped or was pushed into the ravine," he said. "This means, of course, we can't be sure whether we're dealing with an actual crime scene or not. Personally, I believe she *was* pushed deliberately by a person or persons unknown but, at present, I have no proofs to back up this belief. And our efforts are being hampered by the effects of the heavy storm two nights ago, which has washed away much of the evidence, if it ever existed. But I can tell you this. You've heard the appalling list of injuries Nicky suffered, yet she still had such will to live she managed to fight her way almost to the top of this ravine." He pointed to a series of photographs taken at the scene on a nearby blackboard. "Had it not been for the heavy rain, I believe she'd have made it."

Ed downed the rest of his coffee. It was lukewarm but still tasted good. "There are two important points Andy and I want to bring to your attention. The first concerns *how* Nicky Reed came to be in this deep ravine in the first place. If she didn't jump or fall into it, then somebody must have pushed her. That somebody must have had relatively easy access to the ravine, because it's a long climb up that hillside as I can personally testify. It happens there is a track quite close by running up the hill from Flookburgh, which is used by local farmers. It doesn't have a good surface but, because we've had such a dry summer, it was certainly an option for four-wheel drive vehicles. I say 'was' advisedly. The rain the other night has not only made it into a quagmire, it's wiped out any tracks we might have been able to find. But the search for clues goes on. The forensics team will return to Flookburgh immediately after this briefing and will report to you here tomorrow."

Ed, ready for another caffeine rush, looked at his empty mug with some disappointment. He put it down and went on, "There's a second point we need you all to think hard about. Nicky was found on a narrow ledge only six feet from the top of the ravine. Some lettering was found scratched into the hillside above where we found her, just two feet from the top. At this stage we can't be positive, but we believe this lettering is Nicky's handiwork. Had she been able to stand on that ledge, the four letters we found there would have been at her chest height. Here's where you can help. We're pretty certain the four letters are 'pnds' but interpretation is difficult because there's a clear horizontal line through the letters. There's a photograph of the letters at the front of the room for you to study, along with the other pictures. We're left with a number of questions. Did Nicky write these letters on the hillside? If so, what do they mean? For instance, are they an acronym, like BBC or NATO? Did she later change her mind and cross out what she'd written? Why would she do that? If she *was* leaving us a message, it's imperative we understand what it was so get your thinking caps on and, if you have any brainwaves, let us know at once, please."

Ed returned to his place and Andy resumed: "There's one final item I wish to bring to your attention this morning. Malcolm Glover, the profiler, has been going over the case-notes and has given us his initial report. Ed and I are still studying it but there are some points he's made we wish to share with you right now. According to Malcolm, we're looking for a white male in his late teens to mid twenties who knows the Reed family very well. He almost certainly lives in or near Cartmel as he is extremely familiar with the village and its surroundings. This male is strong, agile and well-co-ordinated, possibly a sportsman. He has murdered three men to date, yet has managed to remain undiscovered among a relatively small population, which requires exceptional qualities such as ingenuity, nerve and downright cunning. Above all, he is *exceedingly* dangerous, and not merely because of the nature of his murders. And get this: Malcolm stresses it's highly likely he'll try to kill again."

As Andy sat down, there was a brief disturbance among the group of detective constables gathered together at the back of the room. One of them muttered audibly, "Sportsman? How about that Fullard fellow? He *always* seems to be where the action is, doesn't he." Everyone present knew of Ed's friendship with Byron and turned to look in his direction but he merely shrugged and chose to overlook the remark.

Had Byron heard the comment, it's likely he'd have ignored it, too. He had more pressing matters to consider. Johnny had met him for lunch at The King's Arms, totally transformed by the news of Nicky's helicopter ride to the hospital in Barrow. That was the good part. The bad was his best mate was downing his beer like there was no tomorrow.

"Hey, hang on," said Byron, as Johnny drained his third pint and lined up his fourth. "You're due back at work in twenty minutes. I don't want you drunk in charge of your computer."

Johnny waved that away. "It's OK," he grinned. "Jack's taking the afternoon off to settle Beth back into Orchard Park. It seems there's no way she's going back to Carlisle now. He's left me to file all the latest invoices and I can do that in my sleep."

Byron was hardly convinced but he knew Johnny's huge capacity for beer better than anyone. Anyway, it was great to see his friend looking and acting like his old self. "What's this about Martin's funeral, then?" he asked, changing the subject.

"Beth's letting everyone know it's to be Saturday week at the Priory. All the arrangements are in place, apparently. She's even agreed that Rob and Kim Martins can attend, so long as they're monitored by the cops."

"That's very commendable in the circumstances," said Byron, "but doesn't Beth realise how ill Nicky is? I'd have thought she'd have wanted to postpone the funeral till Nicky is better or...."

Johnny plonked his glass down, spilling some of the contents, but he appeared not to notice. "Don't say that; don't even think it!" he ordered, going red in the face. "Nicky's going to make it. She's got to."

Byron knew just how critically ill Nicky was but realised his friend was nowhere near ready for such a brutal truth. Instead he leaned forward and prodded Johnny's chest. "Let's hope she makes the funeral, then, even if it's in a wheelchair," he said lightly.

Pacified, Johnny nodded and drank more of his beer thirstily. "I've missed coming in here these last few days," he said, with a glint in his eye. "But only for the beer, you understand."

"Of course. What else?" Byron gave his friend another quick dig in the chest.

Johnny moved smartly out of the way. "Give over and show some respect," he ordered with a sudden smile. "Do you realise you're talking to the new McAdams' accounts manager *and* IT supremo *and* transport supervisor. Jack's been delegating jobs in my direction like there's no tomorrow. I'm going up in the world! I bet your mate, Edward IV, would be well impressed with my array of titles."

"You might be right but he had a few of his own. He was Earl of March, Duke of York, Earl of Ulster, Earl of Cambridge, King of England, King of France and Lord of Ireland."

"Well, thanks for that, Byron. Are you sure you haven't missed a few out? You sure do know how to make me feel good about myself."

Byron laughed. "You did ask. But, seriously, you're doing really well. If your mum was still around, she'd be very proud of you."

Johnny's eyes instantly filled with tears and he quickly grabbed his glass. "I need another drink," he mumbled thickly, and almost ran to the bar.

Byron watched him go and shook his head. Johnny was a supreme world champion wrestler. He was incredibly brave, prepared to face any man and not give an inch. He'd been tested time after time against a series of formidable opponents, yet always seemed to find ways of winning his bouts. But at this moment he was *so* emotional. Byron could only hope Nicky made a full and speedy recovery. As far as Johnny was concerned, any other scenario was not worth contemplating.

# 54

E D WAS HAVING A nightmare. He was at the bottom of a deep gulley filled with mud and all sorts of foul rubbish. A few yards away an attractive woman was staring blank-eyed towards him. Feeling he ought to recognise her, he watched her carefully, certain she wasn't breathing. But, hard as he tried to reach out to her, he couldn't move a single muscle. At first he thought the woman must be Laura, his wife, but he soon realised it was Nicky Reed, his neighbour.

And then Ed was awake and taking long seconds to work out where he was. It was pitch-black in his bedroom but there was a strip of light showing under the door. Johnny must be having a disturbed night, too. Feeling suddenly hot and sweaty, he clambered out of bed and opened the window, something he'd forgotten to do earlier. Then, having checked his phone to make sure he'd not missed any calls, he decided to call on his son.

Johnny was sitting up in bed reading the latest Jack Reacher paperback. He looked up when Ed poked his head round the door and managed something resembling a smile.

"You OK?" asked his dad.

Johnny nodded.

"Thinking about Nicky?"

His son nodded again, tried to smile a second time but couldn't manage it.

"I've checked my phone and there's no news," Ed said cheerfully. "The longer we hear nothing, the better it is for Nicky. And remember, Johnny, Nicky's a *real* fighter. She won't ever give up, you can count on it. And there's one more thing I'd like you to know." Ed quickly explained about the four letters they'd found near the top of the ravine where Nicky had been found. "We're pretty certain Nicky scratched these letters and then put a line through them. But we still have no idea what she was trying to tell us. You and Byron know Nicky well. See if the two of you can come up with an answer and get back to me immediately if you do."

Johnny mumbled his agreement and went back to his book. But he wasn't reading a word of it.

Ed returned to bed and had just made himself comfortable when his phone rang. As he reached for it, he checked the digital alarm clock. It was 6:12, which meant he was due to get up in less than twenty minutes.

Andy got straight to the point: "I couldn't sleep so I popped over to the hospital to check the guard roster in the ICU. There's some really encouraging news. Nicky Reed regained consciousness for a few minutes about an hour ago. Unfortunately she became so agitated the doctor thought it best to put her back into a deep sleep, but not before she'd spoken a few words."

It was typical of the DCI to be up and about in the middle of the night checking what was going on. Most people need their eight hours of sleep but Andy Lancaster wasn't one of them. "Did you manage to hear what she said?" Ed asked.

"I didn't but the doctor and one of the nurses did. This is where it gets interesting, Ed. They both swear she mentioned something about a secret room."

Ed did some very quick thinking. "I've had an idea," he said, dredging up a brainwave he'd had a day or so earlier. "Maybe, just maybe, we can use this talk about the secret room to flush our murderer out into the open. But any such plan will depend on tight security so stay where you are and persuade the doc and nurse to keep quiet for the moment. I'll be round shortly."

Before he did anything else, Ed popped back into Johnny's room. "Wonderful news! Nicky has regained consciousness. It was only for a short while but I'm positive she *will* get better, son. I feel it in my bones."

This time Johnny had no trouble flashing a broad smile.

# 55

"**W**HERE'S THE SECRET ROOM?**"** screamed the front page headline of the local Evening Mail. Ed had been busy and his plan to unmask the Cartmel murderer was rapidly taking shape. Andy studied the story with growing satisfaction. It was only two p.m. and the news was already being delivered to tens of thousands of Furness homes. If that wasn't pleasing enough, the story had also been reported on the local TV at lunchtime and would be repeated on later bulletins.

Andy read the Mail's report from beginning to end. Written by Jamie Draper, the Mail's chief reporter, it covered all the items Ed had fed to the paper's editorial team that morning. "*Nicky Reed, aged 26, who was rescued from a ravine near Flookburgh and flown to Furness General Hospital early yesterday afternoon, has made a dramatic recovery. Although critically injured, she regained consciousness in the early hours of this morning and was able to speak briefly to staff in the Intensive Care Unit. She was clearly heard to talk about a secret room. Detective Inspector Ed Hampson, who is investigating Miss Reed's abduction, is excited about this latest development and is very keen to track down the room. At a hastily-convened meeting at Barrow Police Station earlier today, he said: 'Nicky Reed is very concerned about a secret room that we are certain is somewhere in or near Cartmel, her home village. We believe this room holds the key to finding the person or persons who kidnapped her. We are led to believe the room holds vital clues which, when recovered, will lead to the arrest of the person or persons responsible for a number of serious crimes in the Cartmel area this summer. These crimes include three murders and two attempted murders.' DI Hampson went on to make an appeal to the general public: 'It is imperative we find this secret room as soon as possible. I therefore urgently appeal to*

*anyone who has any information that may help us to get in touch with the*
*police immediately. Telephone Barrow Police on 01229 824532.' "*

Nicky had now featured on the front page of the Evening Mail on consecutive days. Yesterday's headline, *"Nicky Reed is alive!"* had definitely caught the public imagination. The Furness General Hospital switchboard had been inundated with calls from well-wishers, the majority of whom didn't know Nicky personally. Andy could only hope today's story turned out to be just as successful. And it would if the Cartmel murderer, who was becoming better known as the Hoody, could be brought to justice. This, when all was said and done, was the one and only aim of Ed's plan.

The DCI considered the plan. He reckoned it was well-conceived and hoped it contained enough truth to capture the Hoody's attention and draw him into the trap. It was based on the simple assumption the murderer was unaware the police had found the secret room. There were some clever touches. Andy particularly approved of Ed's *'we are led to believe the room holds vital clues.'* If that didn't make the Hoody sit up and think then nothing would! All being well, the killer would decide he had no other option than to return to the room to remove these *'vital clues'* and then the police would grab him.

And arresting the Hoody was *exactly* what Ed had in mind. But it was never going to be easy. Precise planning, close attention to detail and lots of luck might just result in a good outcome, though there were too many imponderables for Ed's liking. For instance, did the Hoody actually believe the secret room was still a secret? Would he go along with the *'vital clues'* deception? Did he accept Nicky had made a 'dramatic recovery' and had spoken about the secret room? The Hoody was nobody's fool. So far, he had shown exceptional abilities but if he suspected any danger, any whatsoever, he was unlikely to go anywhere near the secret room. Time, of course, would tell but, if the Hoody *was* coming, it would be in the next few hours.

And Ed was as ready as he could be. Knowing the Evening Mails were distributed from about two o'clock, he'd concealed himself in the secret room an hour earlier. Steve Riley and two armed police officers were waiting in the adjacent secret room. It would need only a signal from Ed for them to activate the pulley system and come rushing to his aid. The DI had considered employing a watcher or two outside Mill House to warn of the Hoody's approach but he'd abandoned the plan. The Hoody had shown himself to be extremely canny and Ed didn't want to scare him off. Let him approach Mill House and see absolutely nothing that would deter him from entering.

While formulating his plan, Ed had remembered the second secret room was airtight. That would never do so he'd driven out from Barrow meaning to drill some holes in the back wall of the room, enabling Steve and his two armed colleagues to breathe freely while they waited there. But when Ed arrived at Mill House it was unoccupied and one of the accompanying officers had had to utilise his housebreaking skills to enable them to gain entry. Ed couldn't account for Jane's absence and it really worried him. Only recently he'd suggested she should be mindful of her own security and now she was nowhere to be found. But, as he didn't want to compromise his plan at this sensitive time, the DI chose not to raise the alarm. It was a decision he hoped he wouldn't live to regret.

Inside the secret room, Ed sat on his chair in the pitch-black, checked his watch and made himself comfortable. He had a large bottle of water, plenty of chocolate to nibble and a few other essential supplies. Having nothing better to do, he began to go over every aspect of the Cartmel murders in chronological order, using his excellent memory to recall the salient details. With little to distract him, he was pleasantly surprised how clearly he could recollect all that had happened. Time was definitely on his side and he was able to sit and concentrate as never before. The Hoody might well put in an appearance in the next eighteen hours, or he might not turn up at all. In the meantime, Ed could mull over all the Cartmel crimes and it was in doing so another exciting thought struck him. It was just possible he might work out the Hoody's identity *before* the killer put in an appearance. Now that really would be something!

# 56

BYRON WAS SPENDING THE evening at the Hampson place. Ed, he'd been told, was working a late shift so Johnny had been left in charge of the cooking. Not for the first time, the normally-immaculate kitchen was untidily cluttered with pans, jars, spilt food and innumerable other odds and ends.

Byron surveyed the mess but diplomatically chose not to comment. Instead he asked, "So have you called the hospital today to check on Nicky?"

"Twice. They're reluctant to tell you anything unless you're family but I managed to prise out of them that 'she's doing as well as can be expected' and that 'she's holding her own.'"

Byron grinned. "Great news! It means you can cheer up and enjoy your meal. When I heard you were cooking steak tonight, I looked out a bottle of Merlot. I fancy a glass with our meal and it might help you relax a bit as well." He added meaningfully, "And you *need* to relax, Johnny."

There was a sudden sizzling as Johnny wielded a large spatula over his frying pan. "Open your wine, then. The steak's nearly ready."

Later, when the meal was all but finished and Byron had enthused about his best friend's improving culinary skills and thanked him for the meal, he pulled a piece of paper out of his pocket and placed it in front of Johnny. "Is this what Nicky scrawled on the side of the cliff?" he asked.

Johnny took a quick look. "Not quite," he said. "The '*PNDS*' should be in lower case."

"Right, I'll remember that, but I wonder if it makes any difference." Byron shrugged. "Upper or lower case, I just don't get it at the moment. Have you had any bright ideas?"

Johnny shook his head gloomily. "It rings no bells at all, I'm afraid. Dad told me to think about acronyms but none of the letters suggest much at all. And taken together they mean a big fat zero."

"I was afraid you might say that. But we'll have to stick at it, Johnny. Nicky left that message for a reason and we've got to find out what it is. When I saw her in that ravine she was more than half-dead. She'd spent hours, if not days, struggling up that steep slope in the most appalling conditions. Then, when she was near the top, she went out of her way to scratch those letters in the hillside. I reckon it's *got* to be something really crucial."

"You're right, I know that, but what was she doing in the ravine in the first place?"

Byron took a slurp of wine. "That's a very good question and I wish I knew the answer. If our friend the Hoody had it in mind to get rid of Nicky, why didn't he kill her *before* he shoved her over the edge? Why didn't he make *certain* she was dead? You and I both know Nicky is very strong, physically and mentally. Why did he take such a risk with her? He showed total ruthlessness when he murdered Ben, Josh and Martin. All three murders were nothing more than callous executions, yet he gave Nicky a real chance to survive."

"Thank goodness he did and she took it," said Johnny, pouring himself more Merlot and downing it in one go.

Byron nodded vigorously. "But why did he do it, Johnny? Why?"

Johnny couldn't come up with an answer but it might have surprised him that over in the secret room his dad had just asked himself the very same question. And Ed had actually come up with an answer. The trouble was that if his thinking was correct the consequences were potentially devastating. He even seriously wondered if his own career could survive the fall out.

# 57

IT MIGHT HAVE BEEN thought that a community the size of Cartmel would have only a handful of its residents wide awake at three a.m. But the supposition would have been quite wrong.

Johnny and Byron were two of the locals who were not asleep. After their meal, Byron had helped clear up the chaos in the Hampson's kitchen. The work seemed to take the pair of them for ever but eventually the room looked shipshape again, so much so they felt they were entitled to retire to the living room and watch England's latest World Cup match, which Johnny had recorded earlier. The tournament had now reached the knockout stage. England had gone on to win the game in extra time but Byron, especially, was not impressed. The team had not played well and the indifferent form didn't bode well for their future progress. It was therefore a somewhat disconsolate Byron who returned to his own home soon after one o'clock. He went quickly to bed and straight to sleep but he was soon awake, unsettled by the letters '*PNDS*,' or should he only consider the letters in lower case? He was convinced these letters were significant but, for the life of him, he couldn't get a handle on their meaning. Even when he tried to shut them out of his consciousness, sleep eluded him.

Back at the Hampson place, Johnny was very aware his dad had not returned home. Such night-time absences occurred infrequently and only when the DI had something important on the go but, until now, he hadn't been out so late during the current investigation. Johnny lay in bed wondering where his dad was and what he was doing. It was an intriguing example of role reversal, the son worrying about the father and unable to sleep till Ed put his key in the front door and Johnny knew he was safe.

At the Reeds' home, Beth tried hard to drop off to sleep but her brain was far too alert. While she couldn't bear to stay at her sister's in Carlisle, she was unable to relax now she was back in Orchard Park. So much had happened and she simply hadn't come to terms with it all. And while she understood the hospital's decision to ban all visitors from seeing Nicky, she'd been reduced to having to phone regularly for medical updates. The doctors and nurses in the ICU had done their best to answer her concerns but mere words were a poor substitute for seeing Nicky in the flesh. Besides, Beth didn't understand a lot of the medical jargon used by the health professionals. They talked about draining the patient's blood, warming it up then pumping it round the body again to counteract the hypothermia; they described various levels of consciousness that meant very little to a lay person like Beth. The term 'comatose,' for example, was likely to result in her having a panic attack or worse. She did her best to understand it all in but it was more than difficult. At the very heart of her concerns, she felt a deep-seated dread but was unable to put her finger on its cause. By three o'clock that night, Beth was fully awake and convinced she was heading for a nervous breakdown.

Over in the row of terraced cottages between Cartmel School and the doctors' surgery, Ben Nicholson's grandparents were also awake. Ever since Ben had been mown down on the road near Mill House, grandma Nicholson had suffered from insomnia. Barely a night went by when she didn't rise from her bed in the early hours. More often than not she made herself a pot of tea and was joined by her husband. They tended to watch nature programmes on the Discovery Channel which helped to relax them. It was all very well, except that when it was time for them to get up each morning, they felt like zombies. But this state of affairs was infinitely better than the one endured by Poppy Reynolds, Josh's mum. So great had been the trauma she'd endured, her whole life had been turned upside down. An idyllic marriage had disintegrated in a matter of weeks and she was in the process of losing her home, the one where her beloved Josh had been born and raised, in the ensuing divorce. She'd become so bitter that many of her friends and acquaintances had deserted her.

In the secret room, Ed was still wide awake. He had very different troubles which made him question his whole approach to the Cartmel case and his part in the investigation. Was it only hours ago he'd been blissfully unaware of the identity of the Hoody? Well, he could hardly claim that ignorance any longer. His solitary time in the darkness had given him the opportunity to review every aspect of the case. With the aid of some lateral thinking, he'd been spectacularly successful. Right now he was ninety-nine percent certain he'd worked out who the Hoody was. But instead of feeling elation, the knowledge filled him with a profound sense of foreboding.

Now he was sure he knew the identity of the Hoody, everything had changed. Everything. The reason was simple. He felt he should have worked out who the Cartmel killer was much sooner. The clues had all been there but he'd either missed them or evaluated them wrongly. As a result, a number of Cartmel residents had been unnecessarily murdered, or nearly murdered. In the last few hours he'd come to believe that if he'd done his job properly, Nicky would not have been kidnapped then thrown into a ravine and left fighting for her life; and Martin would not have been bludgeoned to death. Perhaps even Josh Reynolds might have been spared his dreadful killing. Unfortunately there was more. The DI was aware he'd still not completed some of the tasks Andy had assigned him days ago. In some quarters this might be seen as a serious dereliction of duty, even though Ed could claim a very full workload. And what about Jane? If she was still missing as Ed feared, he'd have a great deal of explaining to do. One thing was for sure: whether the Hoody was about to be arrested or not, there would soon be a day of reckoning when the DI's performance would be closely scrutinised. If he was found to have mishandled matters or behaved unprofessionally, there would be consequences, and facing a disciplinary hearing might not be the worst of them.

Ed twisted in his chair and checked his watch for the umpteenth time before covering it carefully with his coat sleeve. It was five minutes past three in the morning, which meant he'd been incarcerated in the secret room for a little over fourteen hours. No wonder he was desperately uncomfortable and more then ready for a shower and his bed. But his deliverance wasn't to be for some time yet, for just when he was about to give the Hoody up as a lost cause, he spotted a flicker of light. It was very faint but he knew he hadn't imagined it. Someone was coming! With his heart pumping wildly, he took hold of his keypad and tapped twice to warn Steve and the two armed policemen in the adjacent room that their quarry was approaching. Normally, Ed would have been absolutely delighted to have the opportunity to arrest the Hoody. But not now. All at once there was a whole lot more at stake than the simple capture of the Cartmel killer. Right now he had to put all these thoughts aside because the Hoody was definitely on his way.

Holding the keypad in one shaking hand and a powerful torch in the other, Ed couldn't help being very afraid. But there was no way out now. In a few moments there was going to be a confrontation, probably a very violent one. He sat and waited for the flickering light to move closer towards him, certain all hell was about to break loose. There was one consolation, but only one: it would take but a single tap on the keypad to summon Steve and the other two officers to his aid.

# 58

THE HOODY WAS COMING. Ed's carefully-planned trap was working a treat but the DI felt more fear than satisfaction. Had he really worked out who the Hoody was? And how was he going to cope when he met the killer face to face? He tried, unsuccessfully, to stay calm as the flickering light got ever closer.

Taking a deep breath, he concluded he was as prepared as he could be. He was wearing a police assault vest and he had his keypad. The vest offered full front, back, side, neck and shoulder protection against bullets, all sharp-edged weapons and even hypodermic needles. It had eighteen layers of super-strong fibres, backed by a four millimetre layer of foam, and was generally acknowledged to be the last word in personal security. Even so, the DI had already anticipated problems. What about his head and the rest of his frame not covered by the vest? And what about the Hoody's renowned aggressiveness and unpredictability? Ed could only hope his three colleagues reacted rapidly when he pressed the keypad and that the killer submitted to arrest.

The wavering torchlight continued its steady approach to the threshold of the secret room but, without warning, it went out and the resulting darkness thoroughly unnerved the DI. After a brief pause, during which he saw and heard absolutely nothing, Ed panicked and snapped his torch on. He was lucky. The powerful beam caught the Hoody advancing stealthily in his direction. The killer stopped dead in his tracks only a dozen yards away and stared directly into the dazzling light, like a rabbit caught in headlights. He looked just as Byron had described him: tall and burly and wearing a massive, billowing garment with a hood pulled right forward that totally disguised his individuality.

The Hoody hesitated, clearly in two minds, and Ed knew he must take immediate advantage. At the top of his voice, he yelled, "I'm Detective Inspector Ed Hampson of the Cumbria Police Force but you already know that, don't you. And, make no mistake, I know exactly who you are and all that you've done. You're under arrest!"

Ed had feared there was likely to be utter mayhem when he confronted the Cartmel killer so he was hardly surprised when, without warning, the Hoody exploded into action and bounded towards him. Still seated, he just had time to press his keypad before the powerful young man was almost upon him. The Hoody had no obvious weapon but his rubber-gloved fists looked absolutely massive. Ed barely had time to blink before he was rescued from the violent attack. The pulley system that Professor Tim Harrold had boasted about worked as if it had been installed only that morning, rather than over three hundred and fifty years ago. The Hoody suddenly found himself facing three more cops who had materialised right behind the DI. Even more bewildering, two of them were armed with Taser stun guns. So unforeseen was this intervention, that the Hoody once again hesitated. The pause was to prove his undoing. Steve Riley took full advantage of the situation and cried out, "Armed police! Down on the ground! *Down on the ground!*"

The Taser is used by the police to subdue fleeing, belligerent or potentially dangerous subjects and might well have been specifically designed for the Hoody and for this very situation. It is an electroshock weapon which uses electrical current to disrupt normal muscle control, resulting in strong involuntary contractions which are excruciatingly painful. But the Hoody was having none of it. He had no intention of being arrested without putting up a determined fight and he made a desperate lunge at Ed, who was still nearest to him. One of the two armed cops, a southerner who'd recently made his home in Barrow, fired his Taser. He was eight yards from his target when the jolt of electricity, carried by a pair of wires and propelled by compressed air, hit the Hoody in the chest. As each strike carries an average delivery of 1,500 volts, the Hoody was immobilised immediately and fell to the ground in obvious agony.

Steve and the other two cops moved forward to secure the arrest. Although the Hoody was virtually motionless and unable to react, it was no easy task to fit handcuffs on him. But Ed, knowing all about the Hoody's destructive nature and his ability to run, ordered leg shackles as extra security. Only when he was fully satisfied the Hoody was no longer a threat, did he order the others to take him back down to the library. "Let's get him into the light," he said forcefully. "I've a mind to remove his hood and find out who he is, though I'm certain I know already."

They made their way down the stairs, Ed lighting the way. It seemed all the fight had gone out of their prisoner because he offered no resistance whatsoever. But when Ed turned on the lights in the library and moved towards him, it was a very different matter. The Hoody started to arc and twist his body so frenziedly, it took the combined strength of all four cops to restrain him. When he was reasonably still, Ed tried again and this time managed to grab the hood and draw it back so he could get a good luck at their prisoner. But what he saw shocked him to the core. Although he had correctly worked out the killer's identity, he barely recognised the person glaring back at him. That was because the Hoody's face was distorted almost beyond recognition with anger and hate. Drops of spittle formed on his lips and Ed had to withdraw rapidly before he became a target.

For a minute or so, the DI was made to wait until the prisoner's facial expression returned to a semblance of normality. He used the time to phone for another team to come and transport the Hoody to Barrow police station, where he would be held and questioned. As for Ed, he suddenly felt exceptionally tired and more than ready for his bed but first he needed to charge his prisoner. In a clear, ringing voice, he said, "Simon Reed, you are charged with the murders of Adam Reed, Ben Nicholson, Josh Reynolds and Martin Reed. You are also charged with the attempted murders of Byron Fullard and Nicola Reed." But Simon's malignant stare was so full of undisguised animosity that Ed felt the need to turn away. He glanced instead towards his detective sergeant and noted a very different reaction. Steve's mouth was hanging wide open; he was clearly having great trouble coming to terms with the Hoody's identity. And he certainly wouldn't be the only one. Ed gave him a quick nod as if to say, yes, you did hear what I just said and, no, I haven't made a dreadful mistake.

Ed completed the charge by reciting the caution. Like the majority of cops, he rattled through the words and, when Simon didn't bother to reply, he turned to Steve. "Well, that's it for now. Bit of a shock, isn't it. Now, I need you to wait here till you're relieved by the other team and then you can go straight home to that family of yours. I don't expect to see you again till tomorrow. As for me, I'll be back here in a few hours to clear up the mess we made upstairs. In the meantime, I'm going to look for Jane Templeton." He made one final check on the prisoner's security before personally thanking all three officers and heading for the door that lead into the kitchen of the main house.

Ed was fervently hoping Jane had returned home but a swift search of Mill House came up blank. Still shaking badly from his ordeal upstairs, he made his way through to the front hall and gazed out of the window into the darkness to check if her car was parked in its usual spot. It wasn't and

Ed let out a heartfelt sigh. Her absence took the gloss right off the Hoody's arrest. Jane had disappeared and there was no hiding from the fact. There was a very real chance she'd been kidnapped or even murdered and Ed had failed to report the matter. Whichever way it was, he reckoned he was in deep, deep trouble.

# 59

THE MEDIA SOON GOT wind of the Hoody's arrest and the morning newspapers were full of it. It didn't seem to matter the facts of the case were a bit thin on the ground, but then when did the absence of solid information hold back a good story? A young man had actually murdered his twin brother. It was unheard of!

What really stirred the imagination of journalists and public alike was that the surviving twin had then gone on to take his murdered twin's identity and had, apparently, even shaved his head and had his ears pierced numerous times in the process. The early morning radio and TV bulletins all picked up on the story and there was a great deal of speculation about how such a crime could have occurred. Although it is reasonably commonplace for family members to kill other family members, nobody seemed to be able to recall a twin killing a twin. The general consensus seemed to be that while it is thoroughly reprehensible to murder another member of your family, it is totally beyond the pale to murder your own twin. After all, twins, especially identical pairs, are supposed to have such a close affinity that nothing should *ever* threaten that bond. Yet Simon Reed, it appeared, had murdered Adam Reed and then stolen his identity. The whole country was fascinated by the story and hungry for more information.

Detective Chief Inspector Andy Lancaster first appeared on the main news channels at eight o'clock that morning. Wearing a new suit that managed to make him look even thinner than usual he explained that Simon Reed had been arrested overnight and charged with four murders, including that of his twin brother, Adam, and was being detained at Barrow-in-Furness Police Station. The DCI confirmed the Cumbrian police were no longer looking for the man they'd come to call the Hoody. He also stated the arrest had been carried out by his colleague, Detective Inspector Ed Hampson, together with three other police officers, two of whom had been armed with Taser stun guns. He refused to add any more details or to answer any questions.

By nine a.m. some of the TV bulletins were already carrying film taken inside Orchard Park. Showing only the Reed property, the pictures could only have been taken on hand-held cameras. At this stage, it wasn't clear whether the absence of film of the adjacent Hampson and Fullard houses was due to tactfulness or ignorance of their location. But so great was the interest in the case that BBC Radio 5 immediately announced its regular morning phone-in would be exploring the story in detail. Other stations duly called in experts on crime and family matters to put forward their own theories and explanations for the Hoody's heinous crimes. In only a few hours, Simon Reed had spectacularly achieved national notoriety.

Simon's arrest stunned the inhabitants of Cartmel when they woke up to the news that morning. It was all very well for the rest of the country to take a detached, impersonal approach to all that had happened in south Cumbria, but the Reed twins were so well known in the village that its residents were left completely bewildered. How was it possible to come to terms with a local lad who had not only murdered his twin brother but had also murdered his father and very nearly murdered his sister? Villagers were numb, unable to talk or think about any other subject. For members of the family and their close friends, here was yet another mammoth headache to cope with. Ed had been so tired after his marathon shift he'd overlooked a very important procedure. He'd forgotten to ask a colleague to inform the family of Simon's arrest. It wouldn't matter to Nicky, who was still unconscious in hospital, but Beth and Jack were about to get an overwhelming shock.

Beth, who'd gone to bed convinced she was heading for a nervous breakdown, heard the news on her bedside radio as soon as she woke but not once did she doubt the truth of it. Ed was not only her neighbour but an excellent cop and a good friend, so if he'd charged Simon with murder then it must be right. For a while she thought the news was going to tear her in two. Strangely enough, perhaps, all her immediate sympathy went out to Simon. She couldn't help that. What must the lad have gone through, be going through? If anything, the arrest helped put her mind at ease. For a while at least, she was able to put to one side the fact that Simon had murdered the man she'd loved, together with his other crimes, and concentrate on one simple fact: it was all over now. There would be no more murders in Cartmel, no more destruction. She could start to build her life again. She knew it would be very difficult but, for the first time for many days, she could actually see she might have a future. She would make a start by finalising plans for Martin's funeral. Adam and Nicky had both promised to help but that was no longer possible. So be it. She'd manage on her own.

Jack heard about the arrest as he got ready for work and suffered such a severe panic attack he had to sit down before he collapsed in a heap on the floor. Totally staggered by the news, he couldn't move from in front of his television. He just hadn't seen it coming and felt anger and guilt in equal measure. His own brother, Simon, a quadruple murderer! One thing was for sure: he wouldn't be going to his office as usual, but what he'd be doing instead was anybody's guess. As he sat glued to his chair listening to an assortment of facts and a multitude of contrasting opinions concerning his twin brothers, he realized he was going to need his faith as never before. When the phone rang out the first time, he chose to ignore it. It was probably a friend offering sympathy and support but what on earth could he say? First he had to absorb everything that had happened and try to come to terms with it and that was going to take time. Heaps of it.

Over at the Fullards' house, Byron and his parents saw the story unfold on the BBC news channel as they sat together for breakfast. Apart from an occasional brief comment, the three of them stared at the TV screen as if mesmerised. Jilly held both hands to her mouth, shaking her head repeatedly. Dennis, always the sensitive one, surreptitiously dabbed his eyes with a handkerchief. Byron was simply confused. Knowing now why Ed had been away from home last night, he began to consider some of the consequences of Simon's arrest. He didn't get very far. Time and again his thoughts returned to the Hoody's ruthless attack in the wood near Mill House and how he'd very nearly become another murder victim. So that was Simon's handiwork! With difficulty, he could just about manage to accept Simon had killed Adam and had also fired the arrows in the wood. But it was impossible to understand why he'd killed Martin and nearly killed Nicky. Byron could only hope these matters were resolved extremely quickly but he was certain it was not going to be easy.

Johnny had still been awake when his dad returned home in the early hours and he'd then slept fitfully until his alarm woke him. Despite feeling really listless, he was soon up and about. There was a note for him on the kitchen table. It read: *I could have done with your help last night.* He had no idea what his dad's message meant until he turned the TV on and it quickly became very clear. Simon Reed was alive. He hadn't committed suicide after all. Johnny found it hard to believe that Simon, who'd been the bane of his life while he was dating Nicky, was still around and once again causing all kinds of havoc. Astounded by the story that was enthralling television presenters and their guests, he decided how thoroughly cheesed off he was with Nicky's half-brother, yet how proud he was of his dad. He couldn't help getting caught up in a lively review of the Cartmel murders until one viewer demanded the return of capital punishment for killers like Simon Reed. That was too much for Johnny and he switched the TV off and turned his thoughts to Nicky. She remained gravely ill though the medics were now confident she was going to recover. It would take time but they were convinced she was going to make it. And that very morning she was to be moved from the ICU to the High Dependency Unit. Right now it was as much as Johnny could hope for and he grabbed his bag and left the house with a spring in his step.

Upstairs Ed slept blissfully on, totally oblivious of the very different kind of mayhem his arrest of Simon had set in motion.

# 60

E D WOKE A FEW minutes after ten o'clock with sunshine streaming into his room. He lay for a while enjoying the peace and quiet until it came to him his house phone was unaccountably silent. It was only when he checked it he discovered Johnny had unplugged it. He appreciated the gesture but when he dialled 1571 he found so many messages there was no room for new ones. His phone had never been so busy!

It was a similar story when he turned his mobile on; there were a further twenty messages in his inbox. It was all very strange but he needed some breakfast before he investigated further. As the coffee was brewing, he saw some scribbling under the note he'd left Johnny. It read: *Well done, you're famous. Turn the TV on*. Doing as he was bidden, he soon learned why so many were keen to speak to him. If anything, interest in Simon Reed and the Cartmel case had intensified since the news had first been broadcast. There was no fresh information but that didn't deter the broadcasters from milking the story to its limits. Ed endured it for ten minutes, during which he heard his own name mentioned at least four times. By then he could hardly wait to turn his television off. If that was fame, he wanted no part of it. Ignoring all the messages, he made one call to Andy Lancaster informing him he intended to stop off at Mill House and then drive straight through to Barrow. He listened to Andy's brief update before breaking the connexion.

After all the overnight drama, Mill House looked very tranquil when Ed drove up. There was still no sign of Jane or her car, which did nothing whatsoever to reduce his raised stress levels. Taking out a key he'd 'borrowed' on his previous visit, he made his way into the house and up to the secret room. After clearing away the mess that had accumulated there, he took one final look through the two-way mirror. This was where the Hoody had taken pictures of Jane and Nicky as they made love. Or, to put it another way, it was where Simon Reed had filmed his mother and his half-sister in highly-intimate acts of sexual intercourse. It was thoroughly distasteful whichever way you looked at it. In fact, the more Ed thought about some aspects of the Cartmel case, the more disturbing they appeared. But it was time to close the mirror and return to the Operation Mandarin headquarters in Barrow. Simon, hopefully, was rested and checked by his doctors and should be ready for questioning.

As Ed made his way to the front door, it suddenly swung towards him and he had to backtrack rapidly. Jane entered carrying a large holdall, stopping abruptly when she confronted the DI. She looked thoroughly exhausted but still managed to blurt out irritably, "I don't remember giving you a key to my house."

Ed almost gave her a hug. He couldn't believe how relieved he was to see her. "I thought you'd....but never mind that. No, you didn't give me a key," he said sheepishly. "I borrowed one I found in your kitchen because I needed to clear up the secret room." He paused to look closely at Jane, noting all her usual fizz was missing. "I take it you've heard about the arrest?"

Jane dropped her holdall, pushed the front door shut and leaned tiredly against it. "Heard about it? You must be joking! I couldn't help hearing about it. I think everyone in the English-speaking world must have heard about it. Even my husband has remarked on it, which is something of a miracle bearing in mind Ray's total commitment to making money. It seems everyone has become obsessed with my sons." She shook her head gloomily, looking as if she'd aged twenty years in the last few days. "I need to talk to you and I need to sit down. Please come through to the lounge."

Ed followed her to the room where they'd talked before, but this time he made sure he found himself a more comfortable chair.

Jane slumped into an armchair. "Have you really arrested Simon?" she asked.

Ed found it intriguing and odd she didn't seem at all shocked that it was Simon who'd been charged. He said, "We arrested him last night in the secret room."

"And you're sure it's Simon?"

"All the evidence points that way and he didn't kick off when I called him Simon. But we'll have a clearer idea when we question him."

Jane made no comment and seemed to shrink into her chair. "I've not had a good couple of days," she almost whispered, shaking her head dejectedly.

When it was obvious she wasn't going to clarify this statement, Ed said, "You went off without telling anyone where you were going. I've been worried about you."

Jane tried to suppress a yawn. "I decided to kill two birds with one stone," she said. "Well, three actually. I drove up to Carlisle to do some shopping and to get away from this place after you warned me I might be in danger. And I had a more important reason for choosing to visit Carlisle, which I need to come clean about." She tried half-heartedly to sit up straight before continuing, "It's time to tell you about the twin's father, the bloke I told you disappeared off the scene before my boys were born and who I haven't laid eyes on since. His name is Don Spedding and I think I might have uncovered a real problem. Or, to put it more accurately, I think *he* may be a problem."

Ed frowned. He wasn't sure what Jane was getting at but he certainly didn't want any more problems. "You'd better explain," he said.

Jane nodded listlessly. "It won't be easy. I've discovered a great deal these last two days and unravelling it has been difficult, believe me. It's really freaked me out!" She paused but only to collect her thoughts. "First I need to tell you something that happened when the twins were in their early teens because I believe it's relevant to the case you're investigating. But please understand I've never mentioned what I'm going to tell you to anyone before, not even to Martin." She took a deep breath and went on, "When Simon was fourteen years old he told me he sometimes heard voices in his head. As I recall, he wasn't very specific. He told me he heard the voices only occasionally but he would never tell me what they said, though I pressed him hard enough. I'm positive they frightened him, Ed, which is why he told me. I said he should see our doctor but he was adamant he didn't want to talk to anyone else. I didn't push it, especially as the voices petered out after a while, or so he claimed. I wish now I'd insisted, especially in light of what I've just found out in Carlisle."

Ed was not liking what he was hearing one little bit. "Go on," he said.

Jane shifted in her armchair. "I've been concerned about Adam, or should I say Simon, for some time now. He's changed so much, Ed, and I've found much of his recent behaviour deeply worrying."

Ed felt the need to interrupt: "Why didn't you mention this before? It might have saved us all a great deal of grief."

"I'm his mother," Jane murmured, as if that explained everything, "and I didn't know what I know now."

Frustrated, Ed could only nod and ask her to continue.

She said, "I found out a few years ago that Don Spedding had moved to Carlisle with Daisy Leigh's aunt, Rosie. But it was the recent rumours I heard that made me take the trip to Carlisle. I got Rosie Tattersall's address from Daisy and spent an evening with her. She told me all she knew about Don. It seems they lived together in Carlisle for two years but when he got very violent and started having extremely odd fantasies she threw him out. He had a number of relationships after that but matters went from bad to worse and, more recently, the police got involved. What I'm about to tell you is bad, Ed, really bad. For the last six months, Don has been held in Rampton, which is, as I'm sure you know, a high-security psychiatric hospital."

Jane was spot on. It *was* bad news and he *did* know all about Rampton. It's a state-run hospital in Nottinghamshire holding roughly 400 patients who are looked after by about 1,700 staff. The majority of the patients are transferred from prison but about a quarter of them are detained under the Mental Health Act and considered to need treatment in conditions of high security owing to their "dangerous, violent or criminal propensities." Some of the country's most dangerous criminals are held there, including Ian Huntley, the Soham murderer of Holly Wells and Jessica Chapman, both aged ten, and Beverley Allitt, known as "the Angel of Death," who murdered four children and injured five others. Yes, Ed knew all about Rampton!

Now Jane had started, she was eager to get it all off her chest: "I phoned Rampton and tried to get information about Don and his condition but they wouldn't tell me anything other than I had to go through the 'right channels,' whatever that means. I'd already been to see our family doctor because I'd become so worried about Simon and because he's known the twins ever since they were born. To cut a long story short, I told Dr Bennett all my fears about Simon, after which he gave me a diagnosis. It was one of the last things I wanted to hear, I can tell you. He reckons Simon is suffering from schizophrenia."

It definitely wasn't what Ed wished to hear either and his brain started the process of calculating some of the consequences.

Jane, meanwhile, had taken a quick breather while she pulled out a folded sheet of A4 paper from her handbag. "I hope you have some idea of how shocked I was," she said, "but this is where I need to refer to my notes because it gets a bit complicated. I learned, and I'll try to keep it really simple, that most schizophrenics have hallucinations or really odd delusions, that their symptoms usually begin in young adulthood, that there are no laboratory tests to help their diagnosis and that the main treatment is antipsychotic medication together with psychotherapy and social rehabilitation."

She looked up from her notes to make sure the DI was following. He was. "And now let me tell you how all this connects to Simon. He has never been to see a doctor about the voices in his head, so he's never been diagnosed with schizophrenia. But he has now and only because of what I told our doctor."

"So what did you tell him?" asked Ed, suddenly very curious.

"I told him how much Adam, but I suppose I now mean Simon, has changed this summer. Among other things I said he doesn't go to work very often, which isn't like him at all, and he's virtually stopped visiting his friends and socialising with other people like he used to. In fact, as far as I can see, he doesn't make new friends or keep his old ones, or even seem to bother with friends at all. Instead he sits around far more than usual and spends most days alone or only with his close family."

"That does sound like Simon," agreed Ed. "What did the doc say?"

"He told me these are all well-known symptoms of schizophrenia. Every single one! He also made it clear that Simon's early environment almost certainly had a part to play in why he became a schizophrenic, and that genetics plays a major part, too. In other words, there's a very good chance the illness is hereditary and was passed on from Don Spedding. So you can see why I've been doing my best to find out about the boys' father and his illness."

It was extremely bad news all round and there was much Ed needed to weigh up, but one matter bugged him. He said, "It was Adam you were worried about but it was Simon who heard the voices and Simon who's been arrested, even though you were convinced, it seems, that it was Simon who committed suicide. How do you account for that?"

Jane looked down and shook her head. "I can't. They were identical twins so perhaps they had identical problems. Perhaps they both inherited schizophrenia from Don or maybe just one of them did. I just don't know."

Ed didn't know either but he was going to have to try to find out. And very quickly.

# 61

"YOU WORRY TOO MUCH," said Andy Lancaster. He was sitting at a desk in his Operation Mandarin office clutching a mug of tea. He'd taken off his new jacket, revealing bright red braces that perfectly matched his tie. "You need to chill out!"

Ed, sitting opposite, conceded the DCI was probably right. He often got wound up over difficult cases. It was one of the reasons he was still only a detective inspector. But it was all very well for Andy to hand out the advice. He wasn't the one at the sharp end confronting life and death situations with violent murderers like Simon Reed. All Andy had done last night was sleep in his safe, warm bed while his subordinates had faced the danger.

But Andy was keen to press his point: "Don't you realise this arrest has made you a hero? The papers and television can't make enough of you. In just a few hours, the Cartmel case has gone from a local story to an international one. Don't you get it? You're famous! I've even been told you're big in Australia and America. And the Assistant Chief Constable phoned earlier to pass on his congratulations so you can be sure you're also flavour of the month with all the Cumbrian bigwigs." He slammed his mug onto the desk, which made Ed sit up and blink. "So do us all a favour, Ed. Stop beating yourself up!"

Ed's spirits lifted a fraction. Could all his doubts and fears have been for nothing? He decided it was time to change the subject and told Andy all about his meeting with Jane. The DCI heard him out and was thoughtful for a few moments. "It doesn't surprise me about the Reed lad," he said. "After all, we'd already come to the conclusion the Hoody was psychotic and, when all is said and done, schizophrenia is a *kind* of psychosis. I'd better have a word with this Doctor Bennett. As for Don Spedding, I'll check out whether he actually has been diagnosed with schizophrenia and why he's been moved to Rampton."

"Jane's response to the arrest was bizarre, to put it mildly," said Ed, harping back to his meeting at Mill House. "She didn't seem at all shocked that Simon had murdered Adam and taken over his life."

"Do you see anything sinister in her reaction?"

Ed shrugged. "I suppose not, but all this talk of schizophrenia leaves us in a real mess," he said gloomily.

Andy shook his head in disgust. "Why are you so determined to look on the black side? It's not our responsibility to decide whether Spedding and his son are schizophrenics. Neither should we be concerned *why* our killer did what he did. That's way beyond our remit. We did our job. You came up with a cracking plan. We implemented it and arrested our murderer. We're all convinced we caught the right man and I'm very happy with how matters stand. So just what is your problem?"

Ed didn't or couldn't answer so the DCI went on, "Anyway, you ought to know the doctors have examined Simon but insist he's not ready to be questioned. They want to spend more time with him and do more tests. Perhaps that's as well in the circumstances because ever since he arrived here he's refused to say a word. Jack Reed rolled up half an hour ago and asked to see him. In the circumstances, I gave permission and it was clearly a very emotional meeting for both of them. They had a long hug but Simon still hasn't said a dicky bird. I wonder if he understands the irony of us watching him through a two-way mirror!"

When Ed remained silent, Andy added. "Jack also asked permission to visit his sister. According to the latest bulletin, Nicky is making steady progress. She's no longer being sedated and the doctor in charge reckons she'll regain consciousness any time soon."

Ed visibly brightened. "That's great news. Johnny will be over the moon."

Andy smiled. "Thought that might please you. And as I can see no reason to prolong the prohibition of visitors, Jack is rushing back to Cartmel to collect Beth so they can see Nicky together."

Ed was pleased with the news and couldn't wait for the opportunity to interview Nicky. There were lots of questions he wanted to put to that young lady, but he had no time to dwell on what he might ask because Andy was inviting him to explain why he was so certain it was Simon he'd arrested.

Feeling on much safer ground, Ed launched right into it: "It finally came to me in the secret room. I worked it out back to front. I began with the Hoody's last violent act, which was to dump Nicky in the ravine. It made no sense. Why would the Hoody, who'd already proved he was a totally ruthless killer, take pity on Nicky? Why didn't he murder her like he killed his other three victims? He had plenty of opportunity. The only possible reason was that he loved her too much. And when I asked myself who cared for her so deeply, there was only one name I came up with. Simon Reed. Right from when he was a toddler, he and Nicky have been incredibly close. They've always looked out for one another and shared all their secrets. And that gave me another vital clue. We know Lee Bennett told Nicky about the secret room but the Hoody knew about it, too. *He could only know because Nicky told him.* And he's the only one she *would* have told. Once I had Simon as a suspect, I carefully examined his supposed 'suicide' and I now believe he deliberately drove his hire car, with Adam inside it, into the gorge near Betwys-y-Coed.

"That's a strong statement!" said Andy. "You'd better spell out your reasons."

Ed didn't hold back: "I'm absolutely positive Simon intentionally set out to kill his twin brother and take his place. He planned Adam's murder meticulously and I blame myself for not seeing it at the time. I think it happened like this: Simon made a point of returning home just before his supposed suicide with two aims in mind. One was to maintain the pretence he was very unhappy at university; the other was to visit Adam, find out all about his brother's lifestyle and the layout of his flat so he could move in later. Equally critical was the timing of the suicide. Simon had to wait till Adam visited the Doctor Who Convention in Manchester because he knew his brother would be there on his own. I'm sure we'll discover his plan was to catch Adam off-guard, take him prisoner and transport him to Wales in the back of his hire car before launching him into the gorge and returning to Cartmel as Adam. It will be extremely interesting to see if we can find where Simon had his ears pierced in Manchester and, perhaps, where he had his head shaved."

Andy jumped to his feet. "I think that's a great idea," he said. "If we can show Simon *did* have his ears pierced in Manchester and, perhaps, his head shaved, it will be strong proof he *did* murder Adam and take his place. I'll fax photos of the twins to the Manchester police and ask them to check the whole area where the Convention was held." He sat down again, his face animated.

"Yes, it would certainly be useful additional proof," said Ed, "but I believe I've already got the clincher. If you recall, Simon visited Charlotte Owen's home in North Wales just before his 'suicide'. He made sure he was seen and heard so we'd all think he was giving the Welsh lass one final chance. *But he'd already written his suicide note to Martin and posted it.* He didn't leave it in his Salford flat where he could retrieve it if he managed to talk Charlotte round. *He'd already posted it!* So why on earth did he try to see Charlotte when we he was about to take his own life? It doesn't make sense, does it? I think he knew she wouldn't be at home and the real reason he called there was to place himself near the crash scene. After all, he couldn't be sure when the wrecked car would be discovered or if the body inside would be recognised, and he needed the Welsh police to associate him with the body at the bottom of the gorge."

Andy rubbed his hands together before thumping his desk. "This is all very satisfactory. We're getting a formidable case together. Can you think of anything else?"

Feeling suddenly weary after his exertions, Ed said, "There's plenty more but I'll just mention two points now. The first was when Jane Templeton yelled at Simon in Cartmel Priory immediately before his funeral. When you get your ears pierced, they tend to bleed before the holes heal and Jane was observant enough to spot some blood on Simon's collar. That definitely points to Simon and she helped us by announcing it to everyone in the Priory. The second was when she told me today about Simon's schizophrenic symptoms. She made it clear he hardly ever goes to work or sees his friends; he just sits around all day on his own or occasionally with one of the family. But these are also the very ways that have helped him palm himself off as Adam."

Andy wrote a few hasty notes and was almost ready to call a halt to their meeting. "Before I forget," he said, "we now know Simon engineered one of his alibis but we're confident there was no intent to deceive on the part of the witness involved, a Mrs Lord of Priory Close, Cartmel, so we won't be pressing charges. But it just goes to show how manipulative and tricky Simon can be." Then, after thanking the DI for all his hard work, he said, "I'll carry on with my tasks here but you can get yourself straight home. There's nothing more to do at the moment and you need to catch up with your sleep."

Ed was not about to complain because he was mentally and physically exhausted. He tried to feel pleased about the arrest and Nicky's encouraging progress and failed miserably. At the back of his mind there was a vague feeling that something didn't quite add up but he had absolutely no idea what it was. He'd have to come back to it some other time because he was going to need all his concentration to drive safely back to Cartmel.

# 62

BYRON AND JOHNNY WERE spending the evening in The King's Arms. Jack had told them all about visiting Nicky in hospital and Johnny was over the moon. "She hasn't regained consciousness yet," he said excitedly, "but it shouldn't be too long now. She's still very ill but her doctors are convinced she'll eventually recover from all her injuries. She's going to pull through!" He was so beside himself he could hardly sit still, let alone stay quiet. A family group in the corner of the bar were curious enough to stop their own conversation to watch him.

Not wanting to rein in his best mate's enthusiasm, Byron was more than happy to let him prattle on. He'd been subdued for long enough and Byron was happy to see him more like his old self. His only concern was that Johnny was ignoring his beer. For a couple of weeks he'd been too depressed to sup his favourite tipple; now, it seemed, he was too elated. But Byron was confident normal beer-drinking would be resumed very soon. He was less convinced about *which* Nicky Reed would wake up in her hospital bed. Would it be the old Nicky, the one who'd dated Johnny and got on so well with him? Or would it be the new Nicky, the one who seemed to have time for all men *except* him?

It was as if Johnny had read his thoughts: "I hope she's happy to see me when she finally comes round. I'd be a lot more confident if Adam had been the one arrested. She never seems to look at me when Simon's on the scene."

It was a comment Byron had heard more than once. He said, "I remember telling you that a lass who loves like Nicky is really worth fighting for. She's going to need her friends when she wakes up."

Johnny made a move for his beer but changed his mind and pushed it away. "You keep giving me the same advice and look where it's got me. I keep offering my support and she keeps throwing it back in my face."

Byron reached out and gave his friend a prod in the chest. "I know. You're a real glutton for punishment. You can't help yourself, can you?"

"You're right there, By. I think I must need my head examining!" He pulled his glass of beer towards him and took a long, satisfying swallow from it. He then turned to the other matter that was taxing their thoughts. "I'm still trying to get my head round Simon murdering Adam and taking over his life. Dad is totally convinced it's what happened, so that's more than enough for me. And if the cops find Simon had his ears pierced in Manchester it'll be the all-important clue that proves his guilt once and for all. But I still can't begin to understand why he nearly killed Nicky. It makes no sense to me. Never has."

"Nor me."

"And there's something else that's hard to believe," Johnny added. "Simon fooled everybody. Big time. We all accepted he was Adam; even his family were taken in. Nobody ever questioned him. He came back from Manchester after the Doctor Who Convention, moved into Adam's flat and took over his life. Maybe he was quieter than usual and didn't turn up for work very often, but he hoodwinked the lot of us. The lad deserves an Oscar for his deception!"

"I guess he does," said Byron.

But how do you account for it?"

Byron shook his head. "I can't."

"It must be to do with him being an identical twin and always knowing what Adam was thinking. Anyway, that's the general view if you read the papers or watch TV, which are full of Simon and his antics, as I'm sure you've noticed. He's become a major celebrity overnight. Why, he's even more famous than you, By! And did you know that tens of thousands of people have been watching clips of Cartmel on YouTube? There are just as many speculating about Adam's life and why it was so wonderful Simon was determined to kill for it. There are also plenty asking how he got away with it for so long. The only thing everyone seems to agree on is that identical twins have a very special relationship. But if the Reed twins were so close, how come Simon actually murdered Adam?" Before Byron could come up with an answer, Johnny added, "I bet your Edward IV didn't kill off any of *his* brothers."

Byron couldn't help laughing. "How much do you want to bet?"

Johnny's mouth fell open and he nearly toppled off his chair. "Oh, no! You've got to be kidding," he spluttered.

"Not me. You should know I take such matters very seriously. If you'd put any money on that bet you'd have lost it. Edward had two brothers. Richard, later Richard III, was always loyal to Edward but George, Duke of Clarence, was a very different proposition. He made the mistake of plotting against Edward and was imprisoned in the Tower of London and put on trial for treason."

Johnny managed to close his mouth. "So what happened to Clarence?" he asked.

"He was convicted and executed in the Tower in 1478, no doubt on Edward's orders. Tradition has it he was drowned in a butt of Malmsey wine. A body believed to be that of Clarence was exhumed later. What's interesting is it showed no sign of beheading, which was the normal method of execution for those of noble birth at the time."

"Wow, what a way to go! But I won't let it put me off my alcohol." Johnny downed the rest of his beer, winked at his friend and made his way to the bar for a refill.

Byron's thoughts turned to Nicky and when she might regain consciousness. There were so many questions he wanted to ask her but he knew he'd have to wait his turn in the queue. He worked out what his first question would be. It was very simple. He'd ask her what 'pnds' meant. Nobody had yet worked out what the letters she'd scratched on the hillside stood for. As she'd been in really desperate straits when she made them, they must have been extremely important to her. But what did they mean? And why, after taking the trouble to make the marks, had she then carefully put a line through them? Byron decided the matter needed a lot more thought.

# 63

ETECTIVE CHIEF INSPECTOR ANDY Lancaster was in bullish mood. "This case is well and truly wrapped up," he announced to his team at the morning briefing of Operation Mandarin. "Our Manchester colleagues have come up trumps and it didn't take them long. They've found the establishment where Simon Reed had his ears pierced. The shop owner and the assistant who performed the piercings recognised Simon from the photographs we faxed through. They remember him clearly and that he was on edge. Both agree he hadn't shaved his head."

Beaming broadly, the DCI paused to study his team. They were all present looking relaxed and pleased with themselves, as well they might. "This is the final proof," Andy emphasised, "the icing on the cake. It is now abundantly clear Simon Reed kidnapped his twin brother, disguised himself as Adam, murdered him and then returned to Cartmel intent on taking his place and living his life. We're extremely confident we now have all the proofs we need to convict Simon Reed of murder, but there are a few other issues I'll ask Ed to tell you about."

Clutching a mug of coffee, Ed moved forward and faced the team. "Simon is still not talking and is being uncooperative in other ways," he told them, "but it's not significant right now. His doctors are still running tests and, until these are finished, all interviews with him are forbidden." Taking a quick slurp of his coffee, Ed took up a file and said, "We have a report here on Don Spedding. We were informed only recently that he, not Martin Reed, is the twin's biological father and that he's currently being held in Rampton Hospital. We are now in a position to report on both these matters. After comparing Spedding's DNA with the sample supplied by Simon Reed, we can confirm Spedding is indeed the twin's father.

Andy has also been talking to the Rampton authorities. Spedding has been diagnosed with paranoid schizophrenia and has been hospitalised at Rampton for his own protection and for the safety of others. He has not been classified in the most dangerous category but it has been deemed necessary to keep him locked up. We've been told he is responding to his antipsychotic medicine but that he will need to be held in Rampton for the foreseeable future. I have the full report here if you want any more information on him."

Ed dropped the file and picked up another before swallowing more of his coffee: "I can also update you on an interview Andy had yesterday with Dr Bennett, the Reeds' family doctor. It would seem Jane Templeton discussed her son's mental health with the doctor, but it's not clear at this stage *which* twin she was referring to. Mrs Templeton definitely told me it was Simon who'd heard voices in his head but, when this was mentioned to Dr Bennett, he was adamant she'd used the phrase "one of the twins" throughout the consultation. It's therefore clear we need further clarification on this matter, which I will seek, initially with Jane Templeton. I'll therefore have to get back to you on this one."

There was a short discussion on a few other matters before Andy, prior to closing the meeting, asked if there were any questions. A young WPC at the back of the room raised her hand and asked nervously, "Has anyone come up yet with an explanation for 'pnds'?"

From the silence that followed, it was clear nobody had. Andy stepped forward. Before declaring the meeting closed, he said, "We are expecting Nicky Reed to regain consciousness fairly soon. I have a number of points to raise with her and an explanation of those letters will certainly be one of them."

The timid WPC was not the only one grappling with the meaning of 'pnds.' Byron couldn't get the four letters out of his mind. He'd been trying to read his book on the Plantagenets all morning but the letters kept flashing into his head. Reluctantly he put his book to one side and tried to concentrate on Nicky and the message she'd scratched on the hillside above Flookburgh. He recalled the location where she'd been discovered. Somehow or other she'd managed to make her way from the very bottom of the ravine to a few feet from the top. She'd been caught in a heavy storm and was so badly injured and bedraggled he'd assumed she was dead. Attempting to visualise the scene, he closed his eyes and thought hard about all he'd witnessed.

And then, right out of the blue, it came to him. It was so simple he could kick himself for not seeing it before. Why hadn't he, or anybody else, for that matter, worked it out? It had been there staring at them all for ages. He now knew exactly what Nicky had written and, just as important, why she'd crossed it out. But he was under no illusion her message would be well received in some quarters. In fact, one way and another, her short message was nothing short of dynamite!

# 64

BYRON WAS DRIVING TO Barrow for a meeting he'd hastily arranged with Andy and Ed. It was over a year since he'd last visited the town but he knew his way round well enough and was looking forward to his first trip to the central police station.

Barrow is a coastal town at the end of the Furness peninsula and known the world over for its shipbuilding. The shipyard is particularly renowned for its nuclear submarines, surely the most sophisticated machines ever built, and certainly the most dangerous. Barrow's Vanguard nuclear subs all have four torpedo tubes, which fire the deadly Spearfish torpedo. More significantly they carry up to sixteen Trident II ballistic missiles, capable of wiping out entire cities. As each Trident missile has a range in excess of 4,000 miles and an accuracy which can be measured in yards, the Vanguard submarine is truly an awesome weapon system.

But Byron was not thinking of such matters as he drove his BMW towards the centre of town. All his thoughts were on the message Nicky had scratched near the top of the ravine and what he intended to say to the two senior cops he was soon to meet. He was very aware that what he was about to tell them would inevitably cause huge ructions, so he certainly wasn't anticipating an easy time of it. Finding an empty space in the multi-storey car park, he made his way to the police station where he asked to see DI Ed Hampson.

Two minutes later, Ed collected him from the enquiry desk and, after a warm greeting, escorted him upstairs to the Operation Mandarin Headquarters, pointing out matters of interest on the way. Byron saw only a handful of cops on duty as he was taken to Andy's large office. There, the doors were closed and Byron was invited to sit down opposite the two officers. After a brief interchange of pleasantries, Andy said, "Your request to meet us sounded urgent and we're both very intrigued. How can we help you?"

Byron smiled. "I think it's more a matter of how I can help you. I've worked out what the letters 'pnds' mean, the ones Nicky Reed scratched on the hillside."

The two detectives glanced quickly at each other but it was Andy who reacted first: "Then you'd better tell us."

Byron nodded. "If you recall, I was present when Nicky was rescued. She was on a narrow ledge about six feet from the top of the ravine and I thought she was dead. Luckily I was wrong. But we *all* got it wrong! The mistake we made was to assume she didn't make it to the top of that ravine. But I think she *did* get there. If you remember, she got caught in a storm that was pretty severe even by Cumbrian standards. As there was no shelter for her, I believe she fell the six feet onto the ledge, either accidentally or on purpose. Whichever way it was, I reckon the fall saved her life because a few more hours in the open would have definitely killed her. Now here's where it gets interesting. I believe she wrote her message *before* she fell."

Andy frowned. "That's a fascinating theory but how does it help us?" he asked.

"Nicky was very badly injured yet she still managed to climb all the way out of the ravine, only to be buffeted by the wind and rain," Byron replied. "Imagine how disoriented she must have been, but she had a message she was determined to share with us. Even though she was half-dead, she reached out and scratched those four letters in the only place available to her, which was on the side of that hillside. All along we've presumed she stood up on the ledge to make her marks. She didn't. They were only a couple of feet from the top of the ravine and she reached *down* to make them."

Byron took a piece of paper from his pocket on which he'd written 'pnds.' He passed it across the table. "Now turn it upside down," he told them.

Ed did so, saw the message and lowered his head. "Oh, my God!" he muttered.

Andy looked and was momentarily struck dumb. He studied it for a long moment. "This changes just about everything," he eventually groaned.

"It does," agreed Byron. "Nicky wrote Spud's name and then crossed it out. You know what that means. She's telling us loudly and clearly it wasn't Simon who dumped her in that ravine. It was Adam. It was therefore

Adam who returned from Manchester and it was Adam who murdered Simon, not the other way round."

"But we have clear-cut information it was Simon who planned the murder," argued Andy. "Are you trying to tell us all that evidence is wrong?"

"No. Simon *did* intend to murder Adam and take his place. I'm sure you'll find he did everything you thought he did. *Everything but one thing.* I'm sure he did kidnap Adam, have his ears pierced and his head shaved and make a fuss outside his Welsh girl-friend's house. But although his plan was to murder Adam, he didn't succeed in doing so. It was Simon who ended up dead at the bottom of that gorge."

"It might help explain some of the doubts I've had recently," said Ed, "especially after my last interview with Jane. She was too knowing, too casual when we talked about Simon's arrest. It's common knowledge Adam is her favourite. I bet she knew it was him all the time!"

Byron said, "It wouldn't surprise me. But now you know why no-one ever questioned Simon, not even his family. *It's because it was Adam all along. All this time, Adam was being Adam.* Last night Johnny told me Simon should get an Oscar for fooling us all. But Adam was simply being himself!"

Andy shook his head, trying to take it all in. "But why didn't Nicky scratch 'Simon?' Why did she have to write 'Spud?' he asked, still confused.

"She was nearly dead," answered Byron, "and the simple answer is that four letters were easier to scratch than five. Yet when you think about it she was very unlucky. Spud is one of the very few names where the letters still look correct when you read them upside down. Our three names, for instance, would all fail on their very first letter. But here's something really freakish." He reclaimed his piece of paper, scribbled down more letters and placed it on the table.

"NOWIS," read Andy. "What's it supposed to mean?"

Byron grinned. "It's 'Simon' upside down. So we'd have had a problem whichever name she chose."

Andy looked distinctly unhappy. "What you've told us is all very well but what we need right now is clear, unambiguous proof. We're going to look really stupid if we suddenly admit we arrested the wrong man, especially as the media has made such a big issue of Simon and how he took over Adam's life." He shook his head in despair. "This could easily turn into a nightmare! From now on we have to be absolutely certain *all* our evidence can be substantiated." He scratched his head, as if unsure which way to turn. "As for Simon not being the Hoody, I'm yet to· be fully convinced. One of the main reasons we were certain we were dealing with Simon was because he knew about the secret room. We were positive Nicky would only ever tell Simon. If that's the case, how did Adam know the secret?"

"Good question," conceded Byron, "and I honestly don't know the answer. If Nicky didn't tell him, and I don't think she did, I guess Simon must have done."

"And what about Jane and the ear incident in Cartmel Priory?" asked Andy. "That still points very strongly to it being Simon."

"That's a tricky one, too," Byron had to acknowledge.

But Andy wasn't finished. "And then we have to consider Nicky's relationship with Simon. Ed has just reminded us that Adam has always been Jane's favourite. What about Nicky's love for Simon? Wouldn't she do *anything* to protect him, like lying about his identity?"

Byron had realised his visit wouldn't be straightforward. Andy's questions had shown just how challenging the Hoody's identification was going to prove, but he still had a few ideas up his sleeve: "I realise it's difficult at this stage to accept Adam, not Simon, is the Cartmel murderer. But I've had time to think this through and I'll give you two good reasons why I'm absolutely positive it's Adam you arrested. The first is that Simon could **never** have hurt Nicky and pushed her into the ravine. He loved her far too much. The second, and the clincher, is to do with the championship darts match at The King's Arms a couple of weeks ago. Adam is the acknowledged expert at darts. Only he could have beaten a top-notch player like Theo Chambers. Expecting Simon to excel at darts is like imagining me beating Johnny at wrestling, or Johnny scoring a hat-trick for Manchester United. It's just never going to happen!"

Ed nodded vigorously. "Byron's got a good point there, Andy. Simon was always the bookish, stay-at-home twin. It's Adam who's the outdoor, sporty type. And what about the Hoody's attack on Byron? When I think about it, that level of skill could only have come from Adam. So maybe this confusion is all my fault. Perhaps I was too hasty in my judgement."

Andy waved that away and pondered only briefly: "We clearly need to resolve this uncertainty as swiftly as possible. We'll begin by speaking to those who know the twins best. Until we're able to talk to Nicky, we'll tackle their mother. But this time, Ed, I'll come with you. I've heard a great deal about Jane Templeton and I can't wait to meet her and see what she has to say for herself."

# 65

ANDY AND ED WERE on their way to Mill House to see Jane. It wasn't long since Ed had convinced himself Simon was the Hoody but Nicky's four scratched letters on the hillside had put that notion in serious doubt. He was now feeling the strain once more and told Andy uncertainly, "Byron did well, didn't he."

"He certainly put the cat among the pigeons!" Andy admitted. "But we can't afford any more slip-ups, Ed. From now on, we need to be totally certain of our facts. Let's make a start with the Templeton woman. She knows you're bringing me and I'm looking forward to what she has to tell us. I'll let you conduct the interview so I can observe. But don't pussyfoot around. It's absolutely vital we get to the truth."

The instruction did nothing to lessen Ed's stress and when Jane, clearly in a foul mood, opened her front door, he felt even more tense. After strained introductions, the detectives followed her through to the lounge but, when Andy beat him to the more comfortable chair, Ed got the feeling it wasn't going to be his day.

Jane settled in her armchair and looked across at Andy. "So you're the detective in charge of this case," she said frostily. "I've just returned from Carlisle. It's common knowledge there your son is dating the Chief Constable's daughter. I only met the woman once. She's got a face like a horse."

Most men would have been taken aback by such blatant rudeness but Andy ignored the comment. Instead he gave Ed a quick nod to begin the interview and kept his gaze fixed on Jane, more keen than ever to hear what she had to say.

The meeting could hardly have got off to a worse start. With as much

272

confidence as he could muster, Ed said, "We now know the man we arrested in the secret room upstairs was *not* Simon Reed. But that's no surprise to you, Jane, because you knew all along it was Adam. I'm right, aren't I?"

Jane tossed her head. "Of course you are!" she spat contemptuously. "What do you take me for? A complete idiot?"

"I should arrest you for wasting police time," Ed said angrily. "You could have saved everyone a great deal of trouble if you'd told me the truth."

Jane sneered. "The truth? Have you forgotten it was you who told me it was Simon you'd arrested? When I questioned it, you even confirmed it. What did you expect me to say, for goodness sake?"

She was right, of course. He *had* been certain it was Simon. He tried another tack: "You say you knew it was Adam. How can you be so sure?"

Jane shook her head and gave him another withering look. "You sometimes ask the most stupid questions, Ed," she said scornfully. "How can I be sure? Because I *know* my boys. I may live in London now and see my family infrequently but I only need to spend a few moments with them to recognise one from the other. Can you tell the difference between your son, Johnny, and his friend, Byron? Of course you can. Well, it's like that with the twins. Do you remember how I always dressed them the same when they were growing up? I was roundly criticised at the time for trying to confuse people who couldn't tell them apart. But that's not why I did it. *I wanted to be able to recognise them as individuals.* And it worked. I was able to tell who was who instinctively, and it's been that way ever since."

"Are you telling us they're noticeably different even though they're identical?" Ed asked, and he sensed Andy sit forward and stare even more intently at Jane.

She didn't falter. "Put it this way. I could always tell them apart though I acknowledge nearly everyone else had difficulties. Jack, for instance, was easily fooled and they used to take advantage of it."

"What about Nicky?" Ed asked. "Could she always identify them?"

Jane actually smiled. "Oh, yes! She and Simon were like two peas in a pod. I think she'd have recognised Simon if she'd been blind and deaf."

Ed nodded. "But how about if Simon went out of his way to look exactly like Adam and copied all his mannerisms? Would he be able to fool you then?"

Jane hesitated. "Jack and Beth, perhaps, might have been taken in, but not Nicky and definitely not me."

"You're very sure of yourself."

"As I told you before, Ed, I'm their mother. I've seen them grow up. I just *know* them."

Ed tried a different approach. "According to what you've just told us, the twins are identical but clearly different, so how are they different?"

She shrugged. "I don't think I can answer that question. You need to be extremely familiar with my sons to understand the subtle differences between them."

Ed said, "Let me try to make it easier for you. Would it be accurate, for instance, if I described Adam as a more sporty type than Simon?"

Jane screwed her face up in concentration. "Adam is more interested in sports and the outdoors, perhaps, but that's not to suggest Simon didn't bother with sport or didn't like being outdoors. As I said, the differences are really subtle. Simon liked reading more than Adam, but that's not to imply Adam doesn't read much."

"So could Simon have beaten the top darts player in the area, do you think, or could he have acquired enough skill as a bowman to become an expert?" Ed asked.

Throwing her arms in the air, Jane's bad mood returned. "How the hell should I know? Haven't you been listening? We're talking minor discrepancies here. I'll concede Adam would be more likely to take up darts and archery but I can't, in all honesty, tell you that Simon couldn't have been very good at those sports, if he'd so chosen."

Sensing he was getting bogged down, Ed changed direction: "At our last meeting, you told me that when he was about fourteen, Simon heard voices inside his head. Are you sure it was Simon who heard the voices?"

"Simon?" said Jane dismissively. "I'm positive I never told you any such thing. For most of his teenage years Simon wouldn't even have told me the time of day! You must have made a mistake."

"No mistake, Jane. You definitely told me it was Simon."

She shrugged expansively. "Well, you didn't have that nice detective sergeant with you taking notes, did you?" she said smoothly.

Ed's simmering resentment nearly surfaced but he subdued it. "Are we to take it, then, it was Adam who heard the voices?"

Looking suddenly unhappy, Jane simply nodded.

"And when you discussed these voices with Dr Bennett recently, are we to understand you were referring to Adam, not Simon?"

"I actually told him it was 'one of the twins.' But, yes, it was Adam I was talking about."

"Well, I'm pleased we've got *that* established. Now, let's talk about Simon and his suicide letter, which I take it you've read."

She nodded again. "Martin sent me a copy."

"Good, so let's consider Simon's mental health for a moment. Did you have any idea, any whatsoever, that Simon was so unhappy?"

"None," answered Jane. "The letter was a real shock to me. I had no idea his life had become thoroughly miserable. Later, of course, I realised it was a tactic to murder Adam and take over his life."

Ed said, "Yes, Simon certainly had a very devious plan to take control of his brother's life and it's clear his subsequent behaviour was extremely abnormal. But are you absolutely certain you had no inkling of Simon's abnormality *before* he wrote his suicide note?"

"None," repeated Jane, "or I'd have tried to do something about it."

Ed couldn't help himself: "It's strange, isn't it. You *claim* to know your boys well but you obviously don't know them as well as you think."

Jane's cheeks reddened, an ominous sign as Ed knew to his cost, but she said nothing and Ed turned to another topic: "We checked Don Spedding out. The Rampton authorities confirm he has been diagnosed with paranoid schizophrenia. They also faxed us his DNA details which we then compared with Adam's sample. You were right: Spedding is the twin's father."

She flashed him an 'I-told-you-so' look and was about to comment when the phone rang. While she answered it at her desk, Andy gave Ed the signal to finish the interview.

After listening briefly to her caller, Jane replaced the receiver. Suddenly radiant, she turned to the two detectives. "That was the hospital in Barrow," she announced. "They say Nicky has regained consciousness and is ready to receive visitors."

# 66

"**I**T'S GLARINGLY OBVIOUS WE made a serious error naming Simon Reed on the charge sheet. I'm now completely certain Adam is our murderer," Andy Lancaster told Ed as he sat with both feet up on his desk in the Operation Mandarin HQ. "It's easy to see why you thought Simon was the Hoody, though the real clincher in the case turned out to be Adam's outstanding skill at darts. But we should have realised it's far from easy to imitate someone and take over their life, even when you're an identical twin. Having said that, I have grave doubts Adam will ever see the inside of a court. Nicky, on the other hand, will make a wonderful witness *if* the case gets that far. She was clear, concise and convincing on the three separate occasions we visited her. Very convincing when you consider she's still in her hospital bed. She gave us a great deal of detail and I actually found myself believing every word she told us, which is a lot more than I can say about that mother of hers. I don't think the Templeton woman knows what the truth is, especially where her children are concerned." He aimed a rolled-up ball of paper in the direction of the waste bin. "Let's listen again to the summaries I made and check we've missed nothing but, one way or another, we're going to have to come clean and admit we arrested the wrong twin. Goodness knows what the media will make of it, let alone our bosses!" Shaking his head resignedly, he reached over and switched the recording on.

Operation Mandarin: Summary of interviews with Nicola Reed at Furness General Hospital, Barrow-in-Furness, Cumbria: 17-18 August, 2010. Attended by DCI Andy Lancaster and DI Ed Hampson. Summarised by DCI Andy Lancaster:

"Before Nicky Reed was prepared to say anything about what happened to her, she wanted to give Johnny Hampson the following message: 'I wish to apologise to Johnny for behaving so badly and to assure him he didn't deserve the way I treated him. He's always been very loyal to me and I know I can always count on his support. When I was at the bottom of the ravine, it was thinking of him that made me determined to get out alive.'

"When asked what happened to her after she'd been to Mill House with Tom Vincent, Nicky said she was walking home deep in thought when a McAdams' van stopped right by her. It was her half-brother, Adam Reed, offering her a lift so she got in the van with him. How did she know it was Adam? She thought that was a very odd question! She just knew it was him. They drove back towards the village but didn't stop there. Adam said he had a collection to make. It was unusual but she went along with it. He was strangely quiet which she didn't mind because it gave her time to think about the date she'd just had. They drove on for about ten minutes and when they got to Flookburgh he turned off and headed uphill. She had no idea where they were going and he didn't tell her. The road soon turned into an uneven track but when they hit a bad bump she stopped daydreaming and asked him where they were heading. He mumbled something she didn't catch. Soon after, they drove over a cattle grid and turned across a grassy field towards a barn at the far side. He told her there was something in the barn to collect and would she give him a hand. It never entered her head not to trust him so she went with him. It was there he tied her up and gagged and blindfolded her. The barn became her prison but she had no idea how many days she was kept there. She only knew Adam came regularly to feed her and talk to her.

"After that the shocks came thick and fast, particularly when Adam told her all about the murders he'd committed. The biggest shock was hearing Simon Reed had devised a plan to kill Adam, his twin brother, and take his place and that he didn't commit suicide. Adam murdered him instead and he told Nicky how it happened. He was at the Doctor Who Convention in Manchester when, out of the blue, Simon turned up and invited him out for a drink. Adam said his beer must have been spiked because the next thing he remembered was being trussed up in the back of Simon's car. Simon then drove him to Wales, talking non-stop the whole way. He said he'd heard

*voices in his head telling him to kill Adam and take over his life.
He told Adam he was envious of him, which Nicky found hard to
believe, though it certainly explained his actions. If that wasn't
enough, he also told Adam about the secret room and how to get
into it. Nicky said it would have saved her a great deal of pain if
she'd known this secret had been disclosed. Simon stopped once on
the way but Adam didn't know why and had no chance to escape.
Not long after, they arrived at the spot where Simon was going to
push the car over the cliff, with Adam inside. This time Adam did
get free. He knew Simon had already sent his suicide note and he
managed to overpower him and send him over the edge instead. He
then hitched a lift back to Manchester and carried on as if nothing
had happened."*

Andy paused the tape. "Here we have it, short and sweet. Simon **did**
set out to kill Adam but it was Simon who ended up at the bottom of
the gorge, and it was Adam who murdered him and it was Adam who
came back and committed the other murders. But if we're to believe this
account, we have to accept Simon was as candid with Adam in the hire
car as Adam was with Nicky in the barn. Above all, it means we have to
believe Nicky Reed and that she's telling us the **whole** truth. How do you
feel about that?"

"You said it yourself: the lass is very persuasive, though believing her
means accepting **both** twins heard voices inside their heads. But then they
are identical twins and Don Spedding's sons. I found it harder accepting
Simon was envious of Adam, though not, perhaps, when you consider
their lifestyles had become radically different. What we can't doubt is that
Nicky was really shocked to learn her beloved Simon had set out to kill his
twin brother, but it's equally clear she believes Adam's account totally. And
while there's no evidence Simon showed any abnormal behaviour before
his suicide letter, his plan to oust Adam proves he did become extremely
unbalanced, to put it mildly. Perhaps, then, we should believe Simon
heard the voices as well as Adam." When Andy nodded in agreement, he
turned the recording back on.

*"After returning from Manchester, Adam claimed his life, at least
to begin with, hardly changed. He carried on staying away from
work whenever he wanted to, which was frequently; he drove over
to Newcastle for another Doctor Who Convention; and he resumed
his darts career. He told Nicky he felt no guilt about killing his
twin. His actual words were, 'Why should I? I only did to him what*

*he was going to do to me.' But he went on to admit his life altered drastically when he started murdering other people. He told Nicky she was partly to blame. He'd already told her Simon was jealous of him and now he explained he was jealous of Simon because he and Nicky were so close. This was another of the shocks she mentioned. It never dawned on her that her close relationship with Simon might upset Adam but apparently it did. He claimed it drove him wild with jealousy and she promised to explain more of that later. What appeared to further destabilise Adam was visiting the secret room at Mill House and witnessing Nicky making love to Ben Nicholson. It upset him so much he made up his mind to punish them both. He told her he had no time at all for Nicholson so he determined to teach him a harsh lesson. He then said how easy it was to run him over and drive off afterwards. Maybe he got the taste for it because he did the same with Josh Reynolds. Adam actually liked Josh but he saw him making love to Nicky and that, it seems, was enough to seal Josh's fate."*

Pausing the tape, Andy said, "What a casual attitude to murder! No wonder Adam is still being assessed by the medics. But these twins really are identical, aren't they? They both heard voices and they were both jealous of each other. Can you go along with that?"

"It has the ring of truth," Ed admitted. "I happen to think anyone would be envious of the relationship Simon and Nicky had. They were true soul mates so I don't find it hard to understand Adam's jealousy. But where did all that murderous intent suddenly come from? Both twins had it in spades and neither Jane nor Nicky noticed it, which I find very worrying. But then we didn't spot it either."

"True. And nowhere was it more evident than when Adam killed his dad. I have to confess Martin's murder is the one I had most trouble with. Until I heard Nicky's explanation, that is! Let's hear more of her account."

*"Adam reckoned he had a fairly straightforward time of it until Byron Fullard spotted him coming out of the library at Mill House. Even then he was well-disguised and made his escape before Byron could confront him. But Byron went back next day to investigate and Adam was waiting for him, armed with a bow and arrows. Adam told Nicky nobody taught him how to use the bow, that he was totally self-taught. He also maintained he only tried to shoot Byron because he'd become 'a busybody who might be able to recognise him.' The attempted murder failed but Adam's visit to the*

*factory not long after had a very different outcome. Adam stated he didn't set out to see his father that evening but was passing the factory and saw his dad's office light on. It was straight after he'd helped The King's Arms team win the South Cumbria Darts League Championship and he wanted to tell his dad about his success. The door was unlocked and he went straight in. To begin with, his dad was pleased to see him but Adam was most disappointed when Martin didn't make more of his achievement. And he totally lost it when Martin spotted the tattoo on the back of his neck and voiced his disgust. It was the last straw as far as Adam was concerned and he seized a handy car wrench and bashed his dad's head with it. By the time his anger had subsided, Martin was well and truly dead. Liberally covered in blood, Adam then dressed himself in a spare boiler suit and made his escape, carrying the car wrench with him."*

Andy couldn't help shaking his head in disbelief. "Nicky told us Adam was very honest with her while she was tied up. He certainly was! It's the detail she's given us I find so unnerving. It seems both twins had been storing up all manner of grudges for a decade or more so Jane and Martin definitely have a lot to answer for. If Nicky's right, and I don't doubt she is, there was a great deal of animosity brewing in that family with each parent supporting one twin and criticising the other. It's not surprising their favouritism led to such discord, but who could have predicted it would end in mass murder?"

Ed said, "Johnny saw much more of the one-sided approach than I did and he was often appalled. He blames Jane more than Martin. Now why doesn't that surprise me? Thank goodness I only had one child, that's all I can say."

Andy smiled and checked his watch. He said, "It will soon be time to bite the bullet and tell everyone we messed up. With that in mind, I've already prepared a statement for the press and worked out what I intend to tell the Chief Constable. But first, let's listen to the rest of Nicky's account. There's not much more of it but it's a very important section, and not just because it's entirely in her own words."

*"While I was tied up in the barn, I learned more about Simon's jealousy. He told Adam he became thoroughly demoralised because so much was demanded of him, including the expectation he would obtain a university degree and take on a managerial role in the family business. There was no such pressure on Adam, who was*

*allowed to become a labourer and turn up for work when he felt like it. No-one made a fuss when he didn't bother, which Simon felt was so one-sided it really got him down. Hearing this upset me because Simon didn't tell me how he felt. I sensed something was seriously wrong with him but I had no idea what it was. As for the jealousy, I had little time to dwell on it because Adam was making it clear he wanted to become my new soul mate. That was another shock for me. He's my brother and I love him dearly but how could he ever believe such a relationship was possible so soon after he'd confessed to murdering my Simon? When he realised a closer bond was not an option and because he'd already told me all about the murders, he told me he'd have to kill me, too. I tried to talk him out of it but he wouldn't be swayed. Soon afterwards, he led me to the ravine and pushed me over the edge.*

*"I'm not sure how I managed to crawl out of that deep hole. I only know I kept thinking of Johnny and that he was my inspiration. After I'd made it to the top and before the storm came, I remember carving Spud's name on the hillside. Why did I write his name? It was to show everyone, me most of all, that I'd come to terms with his death. But putting a line through his name was just for Johnny. Recently I've been aware that Simon and his problems were never far from my mind and I'm determined to show Johnny I won't let that happen again. I simply want him to know that from now on he comes first in my life, if he still wants me, that is."*

Andy switched off the recording, rose to his feet and stretched. "Well, there you have it. Byron worked out what 'pnds' stood for, sure enough, but he got the meaning wrong. Nicky knew Adam was Adam all the time. When she wrote Spud's name she was totally unaware we believed he was the Cartmel murderer. As far as she was concerned, Simon was dead and buried and she never doubted it for a single second."

Ed sighed. "It took us a while to get to the truth but we got there in the end. I should take the blame for the trouble we're in because I was the one who named Simon on the charge sheet."

Andy waved that away. "We were both responsible for that decision," he countered. "Like we're both going to have to confess the truth to the media, as well as to our superiors, and take our medicine."

Ed ruefully rubbed the seven o'clock shadow on his jaw. "Perhaps it's time I thought about retirement."

"Rubbish! Your trouble, Ed, is you're a born pessimist. Try looking on the bright side for a change."

Ed managed his first smile of the day. "There is some good news. I phoned Johnny and told him what Nicky had to say about him. It made his day, as you can imagine, and now he can't wait to visit her this evening. Maybe some good might come out of this mess after all."

# 67

I T WAS SATURDAY, THE day of Martin's funeral, and crowds had begun to gather outside Cartmel Priory. Although it was a dull, overcast morning, there were noticeably more mourners than for Simon's funeral. This, surely, had much to do with all the publicity surrounding the Cartmel murders, though it was generally acknowledged that Martin was well-liked and respected.

Byron, resplendent in a dark, new suit, moved purposefully away from the Priory towards the adjacent grass. "Don't encourage him," he shouted back at Tyler, who made no effort to follow him. "Please! I can't bear to hear it all again." Once on the grass, he pretended to shield his ears with his hands.

Johnny shook his head. "Don't listen to the old misery," he told Tyler disgustedly. "He's got no soul, that's his problem." And then more loudly: "She held onto my hand. She wouldn't let go. They won't let her out of hospital yet but she promised to watch me wrestle at the Grasmere Show at the end of the month. She even said I could take her on my Kawasaki." He was so excited with his news he even forgot to grapple with the tie that constricted his huge neck.

Putting her arm round his waist, Tyler said, "I don't think Byron has a romantic bone in his whole body. I'm on your side, Johnny, and I'm absolutely delighted you two are together again."

Trying to hide a wide grin, Byron strolled back towards them. "Holding your hand? Nicky is making a superb recovery but she definitely needs her head examining! I intend to offer her some friendly advice before I return to training on Monday."

But nothing could prick Johnny's confidence. "Offer all you like, By, but Nicky and I are an item again. Get used to it!"

Jilly Fullard, observing her son from twenty yards away, smiled indulgently at this interplay. She was going to miss him when he went back to Manchester. Dennis attended most of United's home games and saw Byron on a regular basis, while she visited Old Trafford irregularly. But she had every reason not to be too upset. He'd recently confided he was going to marry Tyler so she had a great deal of planning to look forward to.

It was Tyler who spotted Rob and Kim Martins standing on their own by the far gate. She was surprised to see them, not having heard they'd been given permission to travel up from Buckinghamshire for their father's funeral. She studied the pair critically and had to concede they were a handsome couple. Kim, especially, had looks that attracted plenty of eyes but she was clearly aware of it and knew how to use it to her advantage. She gazed back but it was quickly evident she had eyes only for the two young men by Tyler's side.

There was a sudden commotion by the west door. Raised voices could be heard and Byron frowned. This was neither the time nor the place for any unpleasantness and he and Johnny prepared to intervene. But the disturbance was rapidly quelled by their neighbour, Howard Tyson. The much-respected retired barrister spoke briefly to two of Ben Nicholson's uncles, who'd arrived at the funeral intent on making trouble, but it was enough to soothe the situation. When Byron turned back to his companions, he was in time to see the waif-like figure of Kim Martins glide past him and whisper in Johnny's ear. His best mate was swift to respond: "Sorry," he told her, loudly and clearly, "but I'm spoken for. I plan to marry your stepsister, Nicky, in the not-too-distant future." Byron couldn't help noting the pride in Johnny's voice and he nodded his approval to Tyler but she was still watching Kim as she hurried back to her brother's side.

It was at that moment the cortege appeared at the gate but this time there were only two Reed family members to accompany the coffin. Beth and Jack both looked tense as they slowly advanced into the churchyard, though they relaxed somewhat as they became aware of the many well-wishers who'd made the effort to attend and support them. Beth was absolutely delighted the Cartmel case was all but closed and didn't hold it against Ed he'd arrested the wrong twin. But she couldn't help dwelling on a visit she'd received only the previous day. The mother of one of Adam's girlfriends had called round to claim her daughter was pregnant and that Adam was the father. Beth wondered if this meant the schizophrenia might continue into the next generation and cause even more havoc. Despite all the murder and mayhem, Jack's faith was as strong as ever. His family had been nearly decimated and his life turned upside down but it wasn't all doom and gloom because Nicky was definitely on the mend. It came to him as never before that God moves in mysterious ways.

Ed and Steve Riley turned up just in time to see the cortege make its way through the churchyard. They were in good humour and attempting to make the most of their time away from the pressures of their job. Ed, particularly, was feeling much calmer following the frantic arrest of the Hoody and even admitted as much to his younger colleague. "But I was none too pleased," he confided, "when Andy Lancaster was brought into oversee the case. I probably got it wrong because he's a decent bloke who did a good job overall. I really thought I was in serious trouble when I named Simon on the charge sheet instead of Adam, but the DCI was right. The Chief Constable barely mentioned it and the media hardly commented. They'd already moved onto the next story. All that worry for nothing!"

Steve smiled. "You can keep the responsibility of leadership as far as I'm concerned," he said. "I've enough on my plate looking after the twins. I only hope they don't grow up like Simon and Adam."

"No chance of that. But let's go and support Beth and Jack and give poor old Martin a decent send-off."

They followed the coffin as it made slow progress towards the west door. Byron, who'd been observing Rob and Kim Martins, waved at them as they passed before turning to Johnny. "Rob reminds me very much of Richard III," he said. "Richard was loyal to his brother, Edward, like Rob shows a lot of loyalty to his sister, but that's about as far as it goes."

Unable to resist loosening his tie and feeling better for it, Johnny said, "I take it, then, Richard didn't have Edward's charm and charisma."

"Definitely not. Many of Edward's supporters deserted Richard when he claimed the throne, which is why he ended up losing his life, his crown and his dynasty."

"Wow, he missed out big time!" said Johnny. With a huge grin on his face, he added, "Not like me, then."

Byron smiled. "No, my friend, not like you at all." Then, putting his arms round both Johnny and Tyler, he guided them into the beautiful Priory Church of St. Mary and St. Michael for Martin's funeral service.